The Goat Bridge

ALSO BY T. M. McNally

Quick

Almost Home

Until Your Heart Stops

Low Flying Aircraft

The Goat Bridge

a novel

by T. M. McNally

The University of Michigan Press
Ann Arbor

2008   2007   2006   2005   4   3   2   1

A CIP catalog record for this book is available from the British Library.

Library of Congress Cataloging-in-Publication Data

McNally, T. M.
The goat bridge : a novel / by T. M. McNally.
p. cm. — (Sweetwater fiction. Originals)
ISBN-13: 978-0-472-11511-2 (cloth : acid-free paper)
ISBN-10: 0-472-11511-1 (cloth : acid-free paper)
I. Title.   II. Series.
PS3563.C38816G63   2005
813'.54—dc22   2005008513

ACKNOWLEDGMENTS

Portions of this novel received the
William Faulkner—William Wisdom Gold Medal for the Novella

Other portions of this novel appeared in *Fourteen Hills.*

Photograph on page ix courtesy of Nenad Veličković

To—
Theodore Harrison
Celia Louise
Oscar Elias

Be faithful Go
—Zbigniew Herbert

The Goat Bridge

The Return

The wind was cold, as if from nowhere. On the flight, Zurich to
O'Hare, he had catnapped fitfully. The sky was full of winter storm-
clouds, and somewhere over western Pennsylvania, a mile or so still
into the sky, he had stepped into the lavatory to change the bandage
on his recently cut hand. It was a deep cut which traveled across the
entire palm. He stood at the sink, blinking, and rinsed his face. There
was the sound of a chime.

In customs he passed through quickly. The agent, a man with a
refreshingly rich Chicago accent, had asked him if he had anything to
declare.

A carton of French cigarettes, he said. But that's not what you have
in mind.

The agent glimpsed the rucksack lying on the counter, the bag of
gear with the tripod strapped to its side, and said, Journalist?

More or less.

The agent nodded with the authority of one who makes the disad-
vantaged often tremble—the keepers of the gate, they were the same
everywhere—and then the agent relaxed, almost smiling, and
returned the passport.

Welcome home, Mr. Brings.

Home, he thought. Chicago. The Windy City. He felt his heart lift.
Even if you want to leave it, there's still no place like home. He stood
alone now on the curb of the international terminal, facing a bank of
flags, as if this were a subsidiary of the UN, which caught him off
guard. Chicago, the city in which he had been raised. The city in
which the wind was often cold as the grave. He lit a cigarette, a
Gauloise Blonde, and inhaled the foreign nicotine.

His wife, R, would be at work now, even though it was a Sunday.
The day of proverbial rest. His wife would be in the office making up
for lost time. Long ago she would have delivered their son to daycare,
though not today. Not on a Sunday. Today he would have to call his

wife at her office to apologize for having arrived a day early. On the phone she would be cool but enthusiastic, her voice pitched and slightly nervous. It would be awkward, full of stumbles, that initial kiss.

He understood he hadn't spoken with his wife in over two weeks. And before that? An eternity.

The gash in his bandaged hand throbbed in the cold. He looked now over the sea of dirty taxis, and as he did so, he saw his life go by: not the entire life but rather the last moment of his awareness of it, thus indicating its entirety, and this startled him because of its fundamental lack of pain. There was no pain, only clarity, and having understood this startling fact, he became intensely curious about its origins and consequence—like a young man, having observed his beloved naked for the first time, uncertain if he is permitted to look at length. Mostly he wanted to raise and hold his gaze. And, as in a dream at the very moment of nakedness, the view disappeared. The body evolved into a tree or brook, into the very thin ice forming against the ledges of a freezing lake.

Daphne, he recalled, turned into a laurel tree, and Apollo wept.

He would have to call Elise soon, too. He ended up taking the El and sat in an empty car which filled up along the way. Thirty-five minutes later, deep into the city, he disembarked at Damon and Milwaukee. His legs were weak, his knees threatening to buckle. On North Avenue, he passed the junkyard with the psychotic dogs inside, now charging the dented and corrugated fence; he recognized a few of the panhandlers in front of the currency exchange, as if this were a tourist office. There was a new prostitute—a white girl with dirty-blond hair—and now he headed into the neighborhood blocks, each prospering and gentrifying—million-dollar houses going up, despite the weather. On Honore he turned left and recognized his wife's Jeep. The rust on the tailgate had continued to spread. The Garcia kids still lived across the street. The house was there, the Garcias', its roof sagging like a hammock: soon they would be property-taxed into oblivion. In the back, there would be a dog tied up, its hips held together with metal staples after having been hit several years ago by an ice cream truck. A mean dog, and consequently vicious—had it belonged to him, he would have put the dog down years ago. *Big dogs and little dogs.* The family loved that dog. He turned into the alley which led to his three-flat.

At the door he had to dig through his luggage for the key; the mechanism to the lock worked sloppily, as always, and he began to ascend the narrow steps. The carpet in the hall smelled like mildew and cold and smoke. On the second floor, he opened the door easily enough. He crossed the carpet, past the heavily burdened coat tree threatening to topple, and stopped to check the fridge. He discovered a beer and opened it. The cap fell from his fingers, numb with cold, to the floor, tinkling loudly, and then he heard a man's voice descending, saying, *What's that?*—not angrily, just a little fearful and faintly curious, as if the man might be smiling into a mirror admiring his teeth. Stephen recognized the voice, its particular Waukegan accent, and he stepped over the carpet which smelled of the dust of spent vanilla candles and vases of desiccated eucalyptus. He stepped toward the stairs, his rucksack still over his shoulder: light poured into the stairway through the skylight, and he saw himself, an eighteen-year-old boy, admiring across a wide lawn the figure of a nineteen-year-old girl with waist-length hair—lots of spring grass, and tall oak trees, a library in the distance filled with books. The girl, R—she would grow up to be his wife, though not without a lot of typical complications; then she would become the mother of his child. And now her voice fell pleasantly down the sky-lit stairwell.

Shhh, the voice was saying. Stephen won't be back until tomorrow.

He heard her say, her voice flushed, I want you to go down on me.

He heard the man laugh, good-naturedly, the way a man will to impress upon his lover that he is kind and sensitive and unselfish, and he felt the man's weight shift overhead on the joists. A big man who could shake a house. They would be on the futon in the room which had now become a room for guests—also an office, a storage room for common files. They would be, when the couple paused long enough to look up from their handiwork, admiring the city view: the snow beginning to fall through the early city light descending across the glass of the rooftop window. It was the window which had sold Stephen on the apartment, and the man, an acquaintance of Stephen's from college, the man who continually got away from R and then came back for more . . . How to make these decisions? Who to marry? Who to love? And how does one's affinity for love limit itself to the monogamous parameters which describe the typically civil union? It was dizzying, these simplest of complications, of equations, and standing below them, his head racing, Stephen listened to R's voice and the pitch of her rising breath. Having been here before, he knew where this was heading.

He kept the beer, left the apartment the way he had entered it: sadly, and overtired. The muscles in the backs of his knees were twitching with exhaustion. He walked to the Club Lucky where Jimmy or Nick dawdled inside, arranging furniture, and then he crossed the street, briskly, the way he might have had he been any-body else.

Nineteen ninety-three, he said to himself. This is your life. This is where the wind blows.

He hailed a cab at North Avenue.

Hyatt, he would remember saying to the driver. Downtown.

The air would be cold, filled with the city's brittle lights.

And then he leaned his head against the brittle glass. The window. He nursed the cold beer between his hands. He felt the cold, and the heat from the cab ascending from beneath the seats. Somewhere, anywhere, it was still possible to be warm. Having been away so long, he'd forgotten that, too. He saw his wife, rolling over the sea of sheets on top of their futon—blue, blue sheets—and then he saw his wife kiss her lover on the mouth.

That was sweet, she was saying, still flushed. Sweet.

2

Two years earlier—

The Adriatic Sea, the former Yugoslavia's fine pail of water, was full to the brim. From the rocky shore the blue water stretched out across the horizon, out and across to the island of Vis and, to the west, across the curve of the sky and into the land of Italy.

There was a sloop in the distance on the deep, blue water, beyond the bay of the island. He was sitting naked on the rocky ledge of Biševo—home of the Blue Grotto and a half-dozen goats. The sun felt warm on the ribs of his chest. He opened up a liter-sized bottle of water and considered going in for a final dip, and he could smell the sweat—the salt from his pores—languishing on the surface of his skin. Swimming in the coves, through the shallow translucent blue-green channels amid the rocky shoals and reefs, he had lingered for hours in the sun. His body over the past several days had become bronzed, his hair tangled and full of salt. To the right, a football field away, a local family picnicked: a mom, a dad, two boys of their own making beside a pitched tent to provide shade for the children. Earlier the dad, waving him over, had cracked open two iced beers, and they made a toast to the sea while the woman scolded her husband lovingly and took the children into the sea. Later, the man presented his camera and set it on a rock and hit the self-timer, and they watched the red light counting out the seconds as the camera prepared to photograph the two of them together drinking beer. Souvenirs, they'd always been a way of life—the gathering of a stone, or leaf.

The nature of the photograph: that which is stolen from the light cannot be forever lost. To Stephen's left, closer by, a group of tourists had recently arrived on the last boat and made their camp. They sat around a wicker table on an elevated ledge built up with white stones from the island. European, by the looks of it, except one—a large red-headed man with a wild thatch of balding, curly hair. From a duffel bag at the man's side a pair of black cowboy boots with fine stitching lifted its toes into the air.

The group had taken its place, spreading out towels upon the chairs—one tall, dark-haired woman nodding to Stephen while unbuttoning her hiking shorts. He had nodded back to the handsome woman, who stood off in the distance, unbuttoning her shorts, and now her shirt, and returned to his book. He was reading an account of Heinrich Böll's return to his destroyed home after the war; he was waiting for the light.

A few minutes later a woman stood, shrieking, kicking back her chair. Topless, she scooped down to remove her bottoms, and then she ran laughing down the makeshift pier to the sea. At the ledge, she had to slow herself, in order not to cut her feet. He watched her slip into the water, another gleeful shriek of recognition—why does one always forget what that feels like, that moment of slipping in?—and he watched her negotiate her footing beneath the water, her hands spread out against the surface, the fine azure plane of water, and now she paused, having selected her moment, and dove in. He watched her swim out a hundred yards, then another; he watched her curve into one of the shallow channels shimmering in the light. She looked like a pale fish, her hips flashing in the light, swimming through the blue sea.

When she climbed up from the water, onto the ledge of the pier some two hundred feet distant, he broke his rule and took her photograph—three frames. First she stepped up from the sea to the ledge, the water to her mid-thighs; she raised her hands to pull her yellow, tangled hair from her face and eyes, pulling it back to fall upon her neck; then she lifted herself by the strength of her arms, vaulting onto the cement pier—this, the moment of the Cartier-Bresson leap, as she lifted herself from the Adriatic Sea. Now she stood alone in the sun, and Stephen took a fourth frame while her friends called to her, laughing, waving her in. It was a good photograph, he knew, this final shot: the exclamation point to that preceding triptych.

The cistern contains: the fountain overflows.

He stood and draped a bandanna over the camera to protect it from the salt air, which was hopeless. He watched the woman calculate her steps along the rocky shore, returning to her companions, gingerly but also lazily. Several times she paused to pick up a rock, study it, squatting on her heels, and then rising to skip it into the calm water. Now he walked to the sea, towel in hand, and then he dropped the towel onto the flat of a warm rock and slid into the deliciously brisk sea. He tasted the salt in his mouth. He felt the tender waves drawing him in—water, it parts as easily for the body as it will a stone—as if by design, past the nearby islands and on to Rome. The Appian Way. Even when flooded, all roads lead to Rome. He floated deeply on his back, the salt creating more buoyancy; he drifted on his back, his ears lowered into the seawater, and lying so he listened to the still quiet so that when he finally raised his head into the air he felt as if he had become reborn into the sun and sky.

What the hell, he thought. I'm lonely.

He thought, swimming in to the shore, Right is right.

When he returned to the beach, he lifted himself up at the same spot the woman had. He rubbed his arms and shoulders, not quite chilled in the swift breeze, drying him fast, and retrieved his towel, which he cinched about his waist. Now he walked toward the group, briskly so as not to give himself time to change his mind. Assuming the woman knew he had taken her photograph, he wanted to give her the opportunity to ask him to destroy it. If she did, then he'd simply give her the film. Free to choose—yours to print, or not. As he approached he made out two of the party speaking German. And the big man, the man with the beard, and the boots in the bag, he was talking a blue streak. The pitch and the cadence: the American was definitely from the South.

The South, he thought. Yugoslavia. Land of the Southern Slavic States. One nation, under Tito. Then Tito died, and then the iron curtain fell off its rod. And now, the world knew, lightning was soon to strike.

A man waved to him, and then a second, tentatively, and now they waved together, as if deciding at the same moment. They waved him into their circle.

Hello, called a man.

That's him? asked the American.

Brings, said a man, his accent French. You are Stephen Brings?

Yes, Stephen said. Hello.

They offered him a chair. They offered him a cup of wine.

We're at the Palace, too, said the American. The concierge fellow, he told us you were already here.

The concierge?

He told us an American was here, that's all. It's not as if there's a lot of business right now, he said, laughing. Like Martinique after a hurricane. Bad for business. I'm David Summerville, he said. Galveston, Texas. They said an American photographer and Michel here recognized you is all. Nobody's giving away any state secrets.

Two others introduced themselves—the Frenchman, Michel; and the dark-haired woman who'd nodded to him earlier—Anna Castile, from Madrid. They were journalists and had been covering the war in Slovenia. The two Germans—a muscular man with a once-broken nose, early fifties, and the blond woman he had photographed rising from the sea—they kept to themselves, studying him as if from a distance. The blond woman sat beneath a thick, white cotton towel the breadth of a cape.

The man from Texas said, So how's the water?

Stunning, Stephen said. Blue and welcoming.

We're staying at the Palace for another week, Summerville said. R & R. I'm just stringing along. The others here are from *Focus*. La dee da. Except Michel, who's doing something for *Match*. Me, he said. I'm the oddball out. Have some more vino. It's good for you, 'specially when you aren't wearing any pants. The only thing worse than wearing short pants in this life is having no pants at all. He said, taking a generous hit from his wine, When in Rome.

Stephen said to the others, Have you heard anything about Dubrovnik?

No, Anna said. Nothing new, that is.

Are the buses still running?

So far that we know.

Clearly she was the serious one—dusky eyes, open wide, as if to provide a mask, and then to provoke. The cautious one, that would be the German, the man with the once-broken nose staking him out. Measure twice, cut once. Michel, the Frenchman, seemed more timid than probably he was, given the evident intelligence in his eyes. And the Texan was merely living up to the reputation of his state—all brass and sass and feigned simplicity. Soon, Stephen observed, soon the Texan was going to burn bitterly in the sun.

Vukovar, Michel said, appears to be next. That's the word this morning.

Three of them nodded, their mirth dampened. They all talked seriously a few minutes more. Stephen looked into the sky, observing the clouds, the sun which was beginning now to dip its way into the horizon, and said he ought to be getting back. His boat would be soon returning, and so he rose, lest he seem a gate-crasher, one of the dreaded sticky and lonely Americans abroad, and explained while checking the towel around his waist that he needed to be going. He brushed a trail of sand off the back of his calf with his foot.

Say hey, said the Texan. What's this FKK movement?

Excuse me?

There, said the Texan, pointing to what looked like a small pillbox, and on which somebody had graffitied in red paint the letters *FKK*. He said, That some kind of party? Some kind of Political Action Committee?

The woman spoke now, the blond. She laughed. She said, Oh David, you do not know about the FKK?

Nope.

The Free Communism from the Communist Liberation Party?

Stephen smiled, along with the German. So, she liked to tease. Not meaning to notice, Stephen noticed, not for the first time, that the German had a hefty dick. Thick-waisted, like a horse.

Stephen said, feeling patriotic, It means you go naked. If you like.

Ah ha, said the Texan. Well, by God, at least nobody here's breaking any laws of the state. Thank God for that. At least it's not the PLO or IRA.

It was then, for the first time, that Stephen caught the blond woman's eye. He told himself twice not to stare: the white towel covered her shoulders, not unlike a flag, revealing her chest. For a moment she held his gaze, then let her eyes descend along the flight and scale of his body. She lifted her eyes again, and smiled gently so as not to hurt his feelings, despite the fact of his towel, and turned to Anna. She said, speaking in German to Anna, I want a cigarette. She said in English, turning back to him, Michel explains you are widely known?

Not quite.

I don't know your work. But maybe I will look for it.

She smiled now, collecting her towel, which had slipped about her shoulders, and lit a cigarette. She caught his eye again, momentarily, and turned away, dismissing him. She was, as they say, on holiday.

Well then, Stephen said, turning. Thank you for the wine.

He turned and walked away, following the path to the pier and across the rocks, cutting up to where he had made his camp. Along the way he removed the towel from his waist and draped it over his shoulder. The family in the distance had apparently gathered on the other side of their tent where somebody was playing a guitar very well—a simple melody, marked by the repeated interval of a perfect fifth. He dressed in a pair of khakis and his canvas sneakers. He took the photograph he had not necessarily been waiting for: another picture of the sky, a sloop in the background, a well-dressed woman on deck.

As on a battlefield, most shots miss.

—

All effort was effort well spent, wasn't it? And he did have the photograph of the woman, not to mention the rolls he had shot in the Blue Grotto, often from the water. In the water, the world had become liquid; in the cave, the water and the sky had been transformed into a blue cathedral of light. His guide, wearing headgear like a sheik's, had stood on a shelf and passed him his cameras. That night, back on the island of Hvar, his last night at the Palace hotel, he had showered and washed the salt from his hair. He dressed and went to the patio where he stood behind a stone railing overlooking the town square. Passing below him, the same blond woman skipped by, and he knew she'd seen him standing there. A hitch in her step, a decision on her part not to notice.

Dressed, she seemed younger than he had first thought. Twenty-eight? Still a girl, broaching the cusp. He watched her skip by, wearing a pale blue summer dress, her shoulders newly bronzed, and as he watched her going by, he admired her stride—the muscles in her calves, flickering; the light glancing off her knees—and drank from his beer. He stood at the railing and listened to the music rising off the white-stone surface of the square beneath him. He watched the air filled with lavender now fill with the half-light of the rising moon.

He felt this late-summer breeze in his hair. He heard footsteps behind him, and then came a voice, saying hello.

He turned to face the German—the muscular man with the once-broken nose, the man with the thick-waisted penis. He was dressed now, wearing black jeans and a white shirt open at the collar. He was offering his hand in greeting.

Stephen switched his beer to his left, awkwardly, and shook the man's hand.

I am Peter Messinger, the man was saying, almost patiently.

Stephen Brings, Stephen said.

Yes, I know.

I almost didn't recognize you, Stephen said. Having all your clothes on.

The German nodded, again patiently. May I join you?

Please, Stephen said, turning back to the railing. He took a drink from his beer. The German was drinking a cognac, its bouquet filling the air, mixing with the smells of the sea and the lavender.

I know your work, Stephen said. I admire it very much.

The man nodded. You are on assignment? You are with Gamma?

No. To both. I'm just following my nose.

Excuse me?

Wandering.

Ahh. To wander. To wander is to Follow One's Nose. I see. My nose, it keeps running. All the lavender plants.

It's pretty, that lavender.

Yes, Messinger said. My wife loves the lavender.

They took in the night and sea air. The moon had risen even more. A fact about the island of Hvar: there is no pollution. Not in the water, not in the air.

The man said, I am sorry. About your child. He removed a packet of cigarettes, tapped them out, and offered one to Stephen. He said, I read about it. In *PHOTO,* I think. Please accept my sympathies and deepest feelings.

He produced a lighter and lit Stephen's cigarette first.

Thank you, Stephen said.

They smoked for a while. The few tourists and several locals were gathering below. Even if a war was coming there was also late summer. Peter Messinger said, I've been in Africa. Have you seen it?

Just Morocco.

I see. Messinger said, exhaling smoke, You are going to cover the war?

Which one?

The war of course that is coming. The *real* war. That is why you are here?

No, Stephen said. I'm just taking pictures. Pretty things, you know. The deep blue sea. Mostly I'm just looking for a subject.

You like the pretty, Peter Messinger said. Even when it is ugly. When it is hard. Yes, I know. You always depict things pretty. He said, Prettily, yes? I enjoyed the cowboys very much. And of course your little book of essays. Reading them in English, I am afraid I did not understand everything so well.

I was younger then, Stephen said. He worked at his beer politely. He said, I watched what was going on in Africa from Italy.

Africa is a toilet, the German said. It is a deep reach into the toilet. But Slovenia? An embarrassing feint. When confronted with several snakes, the hunter takes the plumpest first. Like in football, a head-fake.

I wouldn't know, Stephen said.

Venice was still sinking, Stephen did know that. Below him a group of people was dancing now to Latin music. He saw the girl, wearing that pale blue summer dress, dancing with the woman from Spain. He saw the bartender mixing drinks with a blender and he saw the handsome waiters hustling.

Peter Messinger said, nodding to the women, The Serbians, they have the army. The JNA. And Milošević, to stay in power he must make Serbia to be a Great Power. One of the Great Powers. That is why you hear all this about the Great Blah Blah Battle of Kosovo. It is like your Alamo, you know.

Messinger spoke like a German. One of zee great powers. At the Battle of Kosovo, circa 1400, the Turks had risen north, and having cracked Serbia's spine, or neck, had then settled in to live for the next few hundred years—spreading, among other things, the gospel of Islam, though often with the blade of a knife.

Messinger said, passing his hand over the square, The fight will be for here. Serbia requires a coast leading to the West to be a Great Power, like all Great Powers. The people are too stupid to understand there is no longer a place for Great Powers. They think being a Great Power will bring better shopping. But never mind. Croatia possesses the coast. The tourist economy, quite rich. No matter how you gaze at it, Croatia and Serbia will go to war. It is inevitable, I think. But it will be a *pretend* war.

Bosnia, Stephen said, studying the light on the white stones of the square.

Bosnia, Messinger said. The war will be about the land, not the coast. The Ustashas. The Chetniks. Jasenovac? There is still so much hatred because of Hitler. Now Germany has recognized Croatia, but we will not stop the war. Germany only *starts* wars. The French, being French, will pretend to do something but won't. Saigon. Algiers. The French and their failed military policies.

Not to mention Paris, Stephen said.

Yes, Messinger said, laughing. There is that, too. But of course there is always that. Germany will be afraid to act because Germany is Guilty and the British will do only what the United States permits. So between Croatia and Serbia, Bosnia will be crushed. Like a vise. Like a fruit or a child's head in a vise.

That's why you are here? To cover it?

For now. But you know, Stephen Brings, the world is so much smaller. Eventually we all meet. We should talk about more cheerful matters.

Stephen nodded. The art, like the collapsing Yugoslavia, had become fragmented by the sensibilities it provoked. He supposed he should feel flattered, standing here at the rail with Peter Magnum Messinger. Unlike Peter Messinger, Stephen had no understanding of the future of the world. He watched the women below him dance in the night air. There was a theology of being, right there, available to all if only you chose to bring it to your heart: those women, dancing in the sea air beneath the half-light of the waning moon.

Stephen said, finally deciding, Do you know somebody named Bianchi?

Messinger thought for a moment, then crushed out his cigarette. He shook his head, No. He said, He is a photographer?

Antonio Bianchi, Stephen said. He worked out of Rome. Usually had a boy or two for a bodyguard. He called himself the Paparazzo of the Empire.

Paparazzi, Messinger said. The shits.

He started out working for Fellini. A set photographer.

No, Stephen. I have not heard of him. He is a friend?

He's dead.

Ahh.

When he wasn't in Rome, he'd spend most of his time hanging out at resorts. Like this. Or Cannes. Hoping to get a nudie shot of Sigourney Weaver.

Fergie, Messinger said, nodding. There is money in that now. Big Bucks.

I thought you might have come across his name. I've been looking for a friend of his. One of the bodyguards.

Why?

Why what?

Why do you look for one of the bodyguards?

He's also a pornographer.

Messinger said, *Kinder*?

He's connected, I know that. Like you said, it's a smaller world—

You are looking for your son, then. That's why you are here?

No, Stephen said. He's gone.

Having said it, not for the first time, Stephen felt it likely to be true, and this panicked him, also not for the first time. What's lost is lost, like a coin, or a good cause. A year and a half ago his son had disappeared in the Piazza Navona, into the very thin air and light of day. It was important, he'd decided, to maintain one's faith, which at the time had been the kind of understanding followed by a great deal of bitterness. The amputation, now having been layered with scar tissue, still never felt complete—like a missing hand, and a man who, forgetting for a moment, will use its ghost to reach for another glass of wine, or his wife.

Of course, Messinger said, filling in the quiet. I am very sorry.

Stephen said, You'll go to Vukovar?

I think so, *ja*.

Godspeed.

They shook hands warmly. Messinger said, If you want me to make introductions with people I would feel honored. Not that you require such. But I could perhaps save you time? While you are looking for your next subject?

I don't know many people, Stephen said. But thank you. That's kind.

Stephen set down his glass and returned his eye to the women. Anna, she was close to his own age, but still she danced like a girl, all pent-up steam and vigor. She danced seriously. The German girl— Elise Kohlhaus, he would later learn—danced with her eyes open wide, her arms lifting into the air. Dancing, she had removed her impervious gaze. Unlike most who danced, she danced to feel the music, as opposed to being seen feeling it. The Texan, lobster-boiled and wearing his fine boots, stepped out from a bar, half-drunk, and made his way to the women.

Messinger said now, gesturing with his empty snifter to David Summerville, He is, as you say, a spoke.

A spoke?

Yes. Like your black people from the American South. The segregations?

I think you mean spook.

Ah yes. Spook. As spirit.

We don't say that much anymore.

You don't say spook? You don't say CIA?

Stephen laughed. Well, not all of us. Certainly not on the phone.

You Americans, Messinger said. You are so sensitive and you do nothing about these things. You do nothing about Haiti. You do nothing about Africa or Cuba. Have you seen the Kurds in Northern Iraq your president has liberated? You are the last Great Power. What is the good of shopping if you still think it? The offense, I am speaking about.

I wouldn't know, Stephen said. But I take your point.

Messinger said, pointing to Summerville, who was spilling his beer, He's not a *spook* then. He's a spy. A Secret Agent? I can say that? He will tell you he is a journalist but I will tell you he most certainly cannot be that.

Okay, Stephen said, turning. He wanted another beer. He wanted to watch the women dance.

Messinger said, pointing, Proper or not, he dances like a fat man from Texas. He said, touching Stephen's shoulder, We have our own problems, you know? Our own history of disasters. I did not mean to be argumentative. The Holocaust word?

No, Stephen said. I understand. I'm glad we were able to meet.

Messinger said, pointing to Anna and Elise, The dancing. It's soon to end. Now Messinger turned away, leaving, and then he stopped, turned again, and said, Stephen, it's going to end before you know it.

—

Later that night Stephen wrote a letter to his lost son, which he often did, and addressed it to his apartment in Chicago. Then he cleaned the salt from his lenses and packed up. In the morning, before sunrise, he took a fast boat to Split. Anna had been mistaken; the buses were no longer running. Instead he stood in the rain until he caught a ride to the Adriatic Highway. While still in the rain—that which was never supposed to happen, this rain in high season—beside the highway overlooking the sea, a truck carrying a load of sheep pulled over to the side and offered him a lift down the long and winding coast.

Second star to the right, he told himself.

Dubrovnik, said the driver, offering him a cigarette. No good.

3

Now, years later in a Chicago hotel, he slept like the dead. He saw a woman, her body cut in half, on a burlap stretcher in Koševo Hospital, where somebody had mistakenly bothered to place her legs alongside her ribs. He saw the corpses of half a dozen men, face down in the mud of the Sarajevo suburb of Ilidža. He saw a boy decapitated midstep by a piece of lamppost which had been set loose by an exploding mortar, and he saw a man, in flames, and a woman on a street and her teeth, scattered like seeds—small, white stones.

He saw, he saw; he slept like the dead.

It is sleep which builds a fortune, his father would say. Make sure you can always sleep at night, and you will be blessed. And while he slept he saw his father, dressed in his blue suit, worn at the elbows—this would have been the suit he had been married in—with his arms crossed over his chest, as if he had been caught engaged in the act of prayer. These are my hands, he might have said. This is my heart. In general his father had been a hopeful man, eager to see the good in everyone. Then his father and his father's suit of clothes had been incinerated in a vault and turned to ash.

His father had left him an eight-year-old European black sedan, a twenty-year-old stainless steel watch, a dozen acres and a farmhouse in Vermont and a solid hunk of cash. His furniture, which Stephen was to use after establishing his own permanent household, had been placed in storage, and the remainder of his father's estate had been liquidated in order to build a library. The library was to replace the one in which his father had studied as a boy—as had his son, Stephen, years later. The library would belong to a small and modestly endowed prep school in western Massachusetts. It would belong, his father had explained, to the future. The library was to be named after Stephen's mother, Arscilla Brings, who had died when he was a small boy—long before he could begin to remember her properly. A suicide, politely hushed up in keeping with the times: Stephen knew his father had loved her deeply; he knew she had been a tall, pale woman with raven hair and dark green eyes. She had green eyes, his father would say, like the Atlantic at dusk.

He must have meant they were deep as well. And having lost his mother at so young an age, and having no physical memory of her—only the few stories and the photographs—Stephen had been raised to think it commonplace: a boy, growing up in northern Illinois, beside his sad and lonely father. Summers at the lake, his father the architect had taught him to sail; winters, to skate. His father, having done his work, had left him to this world.

Where am I, he thought, waking.

The light was rising in the east. Any moment, any day.

Naked, he thought, we all look the same. Wasn't that the point? He stood before the all-purpose dresser-desk, upon which he had emptied his pockets the night before, and checked his wallet (very few dollars), which he placed atop the two money pouches, one for each ankle, each of which held three thousand marks. He collected the mess consisting of his address book—loose sheets, everywhere; he put away his passport and looked for his good pen. Finally he dialed Elise's number in New York, and then a half-trillion other digits making up his calling card, a process which he twice screwed up, blurry-eyed and unfamiliar with the details. In America it was always later in the East, he knew that. The hotel machine picked up, and he said,

—*Hey, El. It's me. I'm in Chicago. I'm not back yet but I'm going today. Actually I'm in a hotel. Later, it's not interesting I'm going to be here, I don't know . . . I'd like to I need a few days, okay?*

—*Ado says to say hello and to tell you he's met a girl just like you so it's too late for you, he's very sorry to say. Too Late for You.*

—*Hey I learned something I want to explain and it won't surprise you but not like this. Give me a week, I'll call. Okay? I'll call in a week. Be safe.* —*Love. Me.*

He placed the phone on the receiver. He changed the bandage on his hand and called down for coffee and for clementines. He inspected the bruise above his eye and uncapped his pen and, instead of writing a letter to his son, made a list of things to do:

—*Call Trib.*
—*Change money?*
—*Try for Elise in person?*
—*Do not change money.*

And later, just before finishing off his coffee, weak but typically American, he felt a rising wave of nostalgia—home, that was the pith of nostalgia. That was its etymological root. To be rootless was to lack a home. Rootless and fancy-free. *Root* was also the root of *radical,* that which would first revolutionize the status quo in order then to kill it. Cambodia, Technology, Alternative Rock. He drank the coffee and felt a longing to be back home and, nodding, just before he fell back into the oblivion of a jet-lagged and narcotic sleep, he wrote, shaking his head,

—*Go home.*

4

She welcomed him with open arms, his wife, though technically they had never married. The act of marriage, she considered, was an intrusive instrument of the federal government; so they said they were married, to avoid awkward explanation, but the real fact was that they were not. That he had never pressed the issue he had always taken as a sign of his misgivings; certainly, if it all broke apart, it would be far more simple to walk away. A marriage cast in the legal flesh is not the same as a marriage dressed in the current political fashion. To wit, there was so much less to lose, if only to the lawyers. And she loved him, he knew this, and he certainly knew he did love her, and so she welcomed him as was her way—standing on the stairs leading to the front and rarely used door of their building. She stood shivering on the cold steps in a blue wool sweater and black skirt. He exited the cab and looked up at his wife, her thick auburn hair all a-tumble—R, who spread her arms into the cold, brisk wind.

Stephen, she called breathlessly.

Stephen, she said, kissing him. She wrapped her arms around him, and squeezed him tightly, and he could feel the familiar cushion of her body against his chest. He could feel his heart beating against her body.

She stepped back, and laughed. Home from the wars, she said, wiping away a strand of tears. Touching the bruise above his eye, she said, It's the cold.

He hoisted his gear, which bit into his cut hand, and entered the dark wooden steps—the hall leading to their flat never having been finished. The staircase had been lined with six-inch-deep fiberglass to ensure warmth, good economy and sawdust. The lumber, still untreated, reminded him of an empty barn. Years ago, a job for his college summers, he had run a stable of forty horses for an all-girl camp. It had been a sweet job full of tender labor and care for all those horses and the kids who loved them. The currying, and the feeding. The singing of songs while bringing in the hay.

R had visited him twice that final summer from her hometown in Wisconsin. Even then R knew she wanted to grow up to be an activist. Active active active: field hockey and soccer, always running laps around the campus, around her parents' neighborhood, which sat off Lake Michigan in Milwaukee. She had been raised in an academic household, a three-story wooden house large enough to embrace comfortably her large Milwaukee family, the entryway always full of sneakers and balls and bats. That summer she was cheating with her other boyfriend, the same boy who would linger in perpetuity as Stephen's rival; that summer she had visited Stephen on one of his rare days off, and he had borrowed a car, and they had driven to a lake. She had recently shaved one side of her head, to be radical, and pierced one of her ears several times—shocking, then, and sexy. He remembered her taking off her sweatshirt, hooded and emblazoned with the crimson initials of their alma mater. She had a new bra, she said. Do you like it?

Now home at last he ascended the flight of stairs and entered the center of his living room. It was small, cozy, and recently picked-up.

I took the day off, R said, closing the door behind her, latching the dead bolts. It's all neat and—

It's fine, he said, shifting his weight.

R said, You got in yesterday?

Late. I didn't want to bother you. I couldn't remember what day—

It's your apartment, too, R said.

It was late. I was tired. I just went to a hotel.

That guy from *Aperture* called, she said, changing the subject. And Jack says you should call the minute you get in. There's a list by the fridge. Apparently you have a new dean. He wants to know if you're ever coming back.

Okay, Stephen said. Okay.

She put her finger to the bruise above his eye, and said, What's this?

A bump. Just a little turbulence.

She said, turning away, You want a beer? I think I'm going to have a beer. I thought we'd eat at Club Lucky tonight. For, you know—

Old times' sake.

There, she said, handing him a beer. What does that mean, anyway? Old times' sake. Beats me.

The beer, the glass of the bottle, felt cold in his hand.

Cheers, she said, clinking his bottle. Jesus, you sure look different.

I've lost a lot of weight, he said. He could feel his heart beating unnecessarily fast. He said, running his fingers through his hair, I need a haircut. It was a gesture of his father's, a gesture Stephen now undertook when he was nervous, running his fingers through his hair. He said, I get a haircut, I feel better.

I like it that way, she said, tousling his hair. You look like you just stepped out of the seventies.

He said, Do you have any Xanax? I kind of think I'm slightly freaking out. Not bad. Just anxious. A little manic. I don't want to get drunk.

Yeah, sure, she said. Upstairs. In the cabinet. You remember the way?

He let it go. It was, after all, just a jab to measure how they'd spar.

Silence: it wrecks, and then it ruins.

I remember, he said, heading up the stairs. I thought I might take a bath.

Okay, she said. Should I come? Keep you company?

In a minute, he said, calling down the stairs. Yeah. That'd be nice.

—

At the restaurant Jimmy came over to their table. And Nick. Nick and Jimmy just wanted to say hello. Nick presented them with a bottle of merlot, compliments of Jimmy. Stephen could never keep them straight.

For your return, either Jimmy or Nick said. Welcome home.

Thanks, Stephen said.

Mostly they were good customers because neither R nor Stephen could cook. For dessert they split a tiramisu. They ordered coffee, decaf, and R propped her foot up on Stephen's side of the booth. She was wearing fine leather boots she had bought in Rome. The laces must have taken twenty minutes each day to figure out. They looked good, though, those thin-soled brown boots; they looked good on R's feet.

She said, I thought a party might be in order. Nothing fancy. Just a few friends. Evans, maybe. Sheila wants to see you. And Susan.

Susan with the nose thing?

Yep. That's the one.

She was getting loose, he could tell, which made him happy. R, feeling loose—a hurricane of cynical sensibility seasoned by experience.

He said, I was thinking about Minnesota. That summer you came to visit.

I remember, she said. I thought you were sleeping with all the camp counselors.

I was wearing boots then. Tony Lamas. I was faithful and true.

Such a cowboy. Giddyap.

You were thinking about breaking up with me, Stephen said. We went to that lake.

She drank from her coffee. Champagne, she said. Yeah?

They called for a bottle, modestly priced. Jimmy or Nick brought it over with a pail of ice.

R said, lifting her glass, It will be easier. After we make love. She placed cautiously her booted foot between his legs.

She raised her eyebrow. He grasped the boot and massaged her ankle.

We're just nervous, she said.

How long have we known each other? Fifteen, sixteen years?

She said, Kids under the same roof. We were babies.

You still are.

Am not.

Are too.

I am. I am. She said, making an old joke, I am Bic Pentameter.

She said, finishing her glass, I'm glad you're back. Even if it's difficult.

He poured her a second glass and refilled his own.

She said, I had an AIDS test. Last summer. I was thinking, just to be safe. It's all people talk about—

I can imagine.

She said, Do you need an AIDS test?

I don't think so.

Think?

Yes. I don't think so. I can get one if you like.

No. It's not as if I don't trust you. I mean, I've only seen one guy.

— 21 —

Adam. And I know *he's* safe. She said, This isn't about morality, you know.

Adam, Stephen said. So how's he doing?

Jesus, she said. This is ridiculous.

What do you want me to say?

She reached for his water, her own being empty. I don't want to fight.

Do you want to break up? Like in college? Do you want to leave me?

You're the guy who keeps going away. Off to foreign wars. You say, Okay? Only one guy? Gee, R, I'm so glad to hear it's only one guy—

He said, I'm not going to talk about this. I don't think I need a test.

But you're not certain, are you?

I'm as certain I think as anybody should be. I don't have sex with hookers. I try to avoid spilt blood. Like you, I'm careful.

He put out his credit card. Soon he'd have to clean off its balance. Make a withdrawal. He said, locating the image from his past, In Minnesota you brought a new bra. You could see right through it.

I don't remember, she said. If you say so.

How long?

We were nineteen, she said, looking up.

I'm thirty-five.

Thirty-six, she said. Do the math.

He signed the check and slid the credit slip to the edge of the table; he put his water glass on top of it. Now he reached across the table and took her hand.

She said, I have a hard week coming up. There's a rally. People from Washington are coming in to observe. Lynn and the Girls, the regular NOW gang. We're expecting a lot of signs.

Signs?

For the rally. They're on the way.

Okay.

Hey, she said. We'll get through this.

Maybe we won't. Maybe we're not supposed to.

We get through everything. When we want.

He said, We should go home.

I want to laugh more, she said, rising. I'm not laughing enough. It makes me sad. She said, putting on her red scarf, and then kissing him, Stephen, I'm just really glad you're back.

The fact of memory—the way it screens off your past only to project bits of it unexpectedly onto the fabric of the present—what frightens Stephen is the fact of memory and his inability to recall his life at will. I want it back, he might say. Give it to me, please. Sometimes he can't remember the most simple facts of his own life. And if he cannot remember them, then who will? All of which begs the question: is any life worth remembering at all?

And if so, then whose? His son, Gulliver, was four. Stephen remembered Gulliver climbing onto his back. Teaching his son to skate. He remembered feeding Gulliver his first morsel of solid food—applesauce, from a jar the size of a tangerine. He remembered Gulliver taking his hand and saying, This way.

This way, Dad.

Loss never disappears; it merely transforms the space it fills—a body placed into a body of water, or fire.

My dad, he heard Gulliver once say. My dad is a photographer.

Yeah, Gulliver explained, nodding. He takes pictures. Not draws pictures. He *takes* pictures. Like that.

And then, if they are any good, he gives them back. In bed, together for the first time in months, R inspected Stephen's body gently. She had lit a candle, and she had removed her fine boots, and her blue wool sweater, beneath which she did not wear a bra. They are children of the North American Seventies; she with her wardrobe, he with his tangled hair. Like that guy from Styx, she said, putting her hand into it. The Bee Gees? She placed his hand on the oblique curve of her breast, just above her ribs, knowing this was his favorite part of her body. The body, and that which it holds, water and blood, and heat, sometimes malice, at other times tenderness or regret . . . the body amazed him still. The human form, and the way it's possible to gaze at it. Gulliver had emerged from that body, as had R's inexpressible grief at his disappearance. Eventually, having finally registered it, she had screamed into the very fact of it. A wail so piercing it had made him dizzy, though he had since heard similar expressions of that cry. A woman, cradling her assassinated little girl in Sarajevo; a man, after learning his family had disappeared into the smoke and ash and bloody woods of Visegrád. Stephen had become familiar with the language of suffering, of self-recrimination and grief.

If only, began the chorus. *If only* . . .

He could recall it all with perfect pitch. People said, Why don't you talk about it? Afterward, after the paperwork had all been filed, and more paperwork, and questioning, always the Italian questioning, and the aloof and meticulous carabinieri shaking their uniformed heads . . . *And why do you bring this boy to Italy?* . . . afterward R had disappeared inside herself as if she were retreating to the very center of her life, or the origins of the cosmos. She had slid inside herself, as if she were a pond, and waited for it to freeze over. Months later, she came back, chilled to the bone. She looked around, took a breath, and began seeing a shrink twice a week. They had by now returned to their home in Chicago. They had to figure out where to put all the toys. Stephen met briefly with a shrink of his own—a big, woolly man who reminded Stephen that pain often heals on its own terms. Life follows its own schedule, said his shrink, sadly, apparently burdened by his own passages of inexpressible grief. His shrink said, getting at the nub of things, *Pain is pain.* Then Stephen started taking more and more trips. He took a leave of absence. He helped R pack the toys and books and boots into a closet, in case Gulliver be returned to them, as if by airborne express, and thus they had gotten on with the silence which had become the making of their lives while waiting for the mail.

The disappeared, that's what you called people who had been silenced, never to be heard from again. When Stephen's father had died, Stephen had been struck by the finality and the stillness of that moment, but at least he had been permitted to see his father go. Dust to dust, there on the frozen ground. When Stephen's son was kidnapped, there had been no possible brace sufficient to protect his heart. He recalled, instead, the sound of his son, crying, not wanting to be put down for his nap. Not wanting to go home from the park. He recalled the echo of that wail, that torment, deriving from inside his son's small and perfect body. On Gulliver's thigh, there was a splash of birthmark, as if the water had been just a tad too hot. When R's water broke, they had been standing in a crowded El car, the height of summer. She was standing in a big flowered sundress, and then her water broke, and crashed to the floor, and a kid wearing a Bulls cap said *Gross!* and then other people started clapping and cheering, and a man had run ahead to fetch a cab, and the driver of the cab had said *No baby No baby Stay inside Please stay* and three hours later Gulliver had been born, and eventually circumcised, because he was to grow up and become a man. And then the boy disappeared, not having had an opportunity to become a man, and for months Stephen had slept with the voice of his son wailing.

No. No no no.

The disappeared, they can't go their way if you don't let them. The gash across the palm of his hand ached deeply. That Stephen had been becoming more relaxed in his grip served only to convince him he was letting go too swiftly. *Your wake-up call, please,* a voice had recently said to him. Meaning also *pay attention.* He had his life, and he had this life's work. He had his wife, in spirit if not in law, and this lost child they shared like an empty house, and now there was Elise, in Manhattan, telling him she hoped he'd come soon.

I hope you come find me, Stephen. You should not give this up.

Which way, once you heard the call, did you turn?

In their bedroom, R had lit a candle and placed his hand against the side of her body. She put her finger to the recent bruise over his eye, to the bandage covering the deep cut across the palm of his hand. She asked him about the beefy scar on his arm, just over the bicep, sewed up crookedly on the spot—*Does it hurt. Here?*—and she placed her finger against his ribs, counting them each. She said, Well, you're all in one piece, at least. She said, examining a thumbnailed and crimson scar on his penis, across the glans, What's this?

Nothing, he said. The shrapnel.

Jesus, R said, inspecting him. Jesus!

It's fine. It looks worse than it was, really.

I thought you wore stuff for that. Like for hockey. A jock strap or something. A flak dingy and helmet. That stuff!

It was a freak thing. I'm fine, he said. Really.

They would talk about it later, maybe. Actually he was pretty certain he did not want to do that. He said, Look, I told you, there was a little shrapnel once. I was scratched up. Like that. But that's nothing. Do you understand? Really. That is really nothing.

If you say so, she said. She said, looking closely, It looks like a scimitar. Like a sliver from the moon.

Yeah. I guess.

She said, letting him go, Okay then. Tell me a picture, Mister. Like you used to. She placed her head on his hip, facing his feet. She said, stroking his raised knee, Tell me a picture like you used to.

He reached for his bourbon, three fingers' worth, and said, What kind?

A sweet one, she said, kissing his leg. No metal objects. No blood. No fucking terrorists.

He thought of the picture of his wife when she was still a girl, beside a summer lake, showing off her new bra and unshaved arms and funky haircut. He said, instead, You'll like this one.

I'm waiting, she said, pulling back her hair. Go.

He ran his fingers across her ribs. He said, beginning, I was in Split. On the coast. The Adriatic Sea. The home of Diocletian's Palace. It's full of refugees now. Thousands. Tens of thousands.

Refugees, she said. I got it.

But this is before—

Always before. You always do that. You always go back to before—

Before the war really got going. Split, it's not a fishing town, but compared to Chicago, or Newark, it feels that way. In summer it's a carnival. Coca-Cola and beer and wine and mussels, delicious mussels and plump white fish and everybody dancing. It's a horseshoe, the harbor. You walk past the fishing boats, the nets smelling like fish. After a while, you like that smell. You love it. Past all Tito's luxe hotels, you come to the beach. In summer the water's blue. Deep, deep blue. Azure.

In the guest room, across the hall, the wind howled through the frame of the skylight. When their son had slept in the guest room, it had been *his* room. The candle flickered in the draft.

Okay, R said, listening. Azure. The fancy blue. Go on. Details.

So, he said. So I'm walking along this paved causeway, which bends beside the water. It's full of old people: fifty, sixty years old. Weathered, tan like a saddle. They're poor. They've come here for the sun because they're unemployed and the sun is free and warms up their old bodies.

The sun, R said, kissing his hip.

And then, past the avenue of the aged and infirm, you reach this area of boulders and rocks. The harbor, off to your left, is full of ships and fishing boats and ferries. But on, over the boulders, this is where the beautiful people go.

The pretty people, R said. The people who are not old.

Sunbathing on the warm rocks. There's a topless girl, with a bright green and red dragon tattooed across her shoulder blade, smoking a cigarette. One claw, it's going over her collarbone. She's insouciant.

Insouciant, R said. So that's the picture? *Insouciant?*

No. No. That's the foreground. That's the context.

Okay, she said, kissing him again. Go on.

I'm walking over the rocky trail like something out of an Errol Flynn movie. Then I see this couple, beneath me. They're young. They're dark-eyed and stunning.

Here we go, she said, teasing him, running her tongue lightly across the glans—over the scar, which tingled sharply.

No, it's not like that. The boy, he's rail-thin, twenty-four maybe. Obviously from a prosperous family. He's wearing a black suit. A Speedo thing, the swelling of the bulge. He's sitting up, cross-legged, facing me.

Okay, R said.

He's facing his girlfriend. She's like a sister, exact same body. She's sitting straight up. Topless. I can see the bumps in her spine.

Her spine, R said, her hand now lifting his penis. She held the growing weight of it in her hand, measuring.

Her spine, Stephen said. She's perfectly tan. She's wearing a black G-string. The uniform. They are like this perfect, identical pair, you see. Identical. Slight, lean, hungry on account of being so inexpressibly alive. She's facing her lover, or her brother, who's about a foot below her on account of the slope—

And?

That's the context, Stephen said. We've framed it in. You see this dark-eyed pair, naked on the cliff above the blue sea. There's a pine tree with ample boughs. But this—this is the shutter snapping. They're playing chess.

Chess?

Chess. The girl, she's studying the board, which is between her spread legs, facing the boy. And the boy is raising his hand preparing to move a knight.

Go on.

The word, Stephen said. The word I thought of?

Yes.

Mate. I went, I saw, I named it. *Mate.*

Oh God, R said, letting go of him, rolling onto her back, her hand to her heart. Oh God, that's perfect.

Yeah, Stephen said, nodding. It was pretty.

And then R rolled over and took him in her mouth, and they made love far more tenderly than the way they had last. Welcome home, she said, once. The candle flickered. The wind continued to howl. They maneuvered themselves about the bed to gain a better purchase and then, while he was inside of her, R came, and he was struck by the sound of it. The very sound of R coming, which took him by surprise. He'd forgotten, he understood, what it sounded like.

Later, tugging on the sheets, she said, For life, right?

What.

The mating. Like wolves. And geese. Like us.

He said, We're not wolves. Aren't wolves monogamous?

She said, not ignoring him, brushing back her thick hair, It would be a shame, you know. Otherwise. I used to *know* so. I love you, Stephen.

He kissed her forehead.

She said, I want you to take me there. To Split. To the emperor guy's palace. I'll go to the beach and take my shirt off and play chess with you in public.

He said, teasing her, You always take off your shirt in public.

Because I can, she said. Because I want to. It was easier then.

She was falling asleep now.

You're the way you always are.

But I'm not the beautiful people, she said. The beautiful people do not have stretch marks.

Sure they do.

Crow's feet, she said. No no no. She said, falling asleep, Because the sun is on the water. Mmmmm. I like it when the sun is on the water.

He reached for his bourbon, and she said, grabbing his arm, *Don't go, Mister,* and he said, *I'm here. Go to sleep.*

He stood into the chill air of his apartment. He felt the wind funneling through the ill-framed skylight. Before at times like this he'd check in on his son: watch him breathe, rearrange the bunnies and the bears. Now he stood naked and alone before the skylight, looking out across the rooftops of the city, and admired the lights. Snow was falling. Soon the wind would slow, and then stop altogether, and then the snow would fall more deeply, silencing the city it fell upon. The great unfolding of the blanket.

He went to the stairs, and he descended. In the kitchen he poured himself three more fingers of bourbon. For propriety's sake, he added two cubes of ice. His hands were still trembling, though now they smelled like the body of the woman with whom he had once shared his life. When she was a girl, she had shaved one side of her head in order to scandalize her parents; she had pierced the same ear in five places. When you're eighteen, or twenty, two weeks becomes a year. He stood in the dark kitchen, his feet on the cold, hard tile, and felt the electricity in his blood. He went to the living room, which was carpeted, and which held a view of his street: the snow, falling onto the cars below. To turn off another's city lights, all you had to do was interrupt the current. Across the street, in a flat similar to his own, a light flickered on: a woman, standing in a room, with pale yellow hair. Everywhere people were going places. Everywhere, anywhere, people were making love, and children. Everywhere people were putting their kids down to bed.

He raised his glass, the ice clinking, and sat in the pale slipcovered chair. Chilled, he draped a throw from the couch about his shoulders. The throw smelled like R—always the hint of orange, and cocoa butter. He nursed his bourbon and turned on the television, which flickered brightly. On CNN, the Newly Familiar Journalist stood giving a taped report of formerly breaking news in front of Sniper Alley, her hair dirty and mussed up, her pale blue flak jacket winking merrily in the cold daylight. He understood, by the state of her hair, they wouldn't have any water, the Bad Guys having shut off the supply. In Zagreb, apparently, certain U.S. officials were unofficially expressing their concern. On another channel the Crimson Pirate was swinging from the rigging of a ship. And on another, a naked woman with implants the shape of preseason grapefruit was kissing a second with equally modern developments. One of these days, they were sure to explode, like bombs.

Q. Why are the girls in Sarajevo so beautiful and thin?
A. Because they never get enough to eat.

Sometimes the world opens up its jaws and eats your heart. In high school girls like those on the television wanted to grow up and be on TV. Bombshells. In Sarajevo, tomorrow morning, which was now . . . in Sarajevo the sky would be full of bombshells. He turned off the television. Look at all the things there are to look at now.

He loved the word, the beautiful name of that city—Sarajevo. Sitting in the dark, he looked across the street. He saw the snow falling which it also did in other places of the world. He saw his father, stooped, shoveling alone the walk, and a young woman in a red sweater with bandages on her wrists. He saw the police coroner's photograph of a fat man in a white linen suit, lying in a staircase off Vatican City, his throat having been slit. He saw Elise, driving breakneck, rowing through the gears into the streets of Stuttgart. She wore fine black gloves. She wore fine, black clothes, and a pale blue cashmere turtleneck, and she placed her gloved hand upon his knee. Soon, she was saying, gently. *Soon we will have you in a bed.* He saw his friend Peter Messinger dodging fire on the city walls of Dubrovnik. He saw the spook David Summerville puking on a linden tree in a cold and darkened park decorated with nameless graves. He saw his son, Gulliver, following a man in a navy peacoat, which he understood to belong to himself—that would be him, Stephen, in the coat, and his son following behind riding his perfect Kettler trike calling *Dad Dad!* and he saw his son eating pizza in a Rome café, the light all yellow and gold, as was Rome's way, the sky full of black sparrows rising. He saw a shriveled figure, draped in black, begging like a supplicant, and he saw a refugee woman, a drugged-out baby at her breast, striking a child with her fist. He saw a thin gypsy girl winking to him in the sunlight—raised above him, as if on a dais, wearing a red cape. He saw his wife, R, weeping on the marble floor of their hotel, her fists bloodied from having beaten her fists against the walls. He saw the blood on the walls and the white marble floor of their hotel and then he saw the National Library going up in flames on account of all the bombshells. He felt the bourbon in his belly warming him to his topic like a hot, wet coal. He felt a draft, descending from the staircase, and another, bleeding through the window.

Sometimes, sometimes you have to bite the world right back. Fuck you, too. Fuck the day and hope it turns to night. Years ago, in Minnesota, when R visited him, he took her riding in the moonlight. The moon in Minnesota could fill a lake, or a girl's hair, with light. At the lake she had taken off her sweatshirt with the crimson initials and then her sheer bra. She had said, kissing him, I'm going to fuck you blind, Mister, and later that night he had taken her riding in the moonlight. *I'm going to fuck you so you can't forget me.* But before she did that they went swimming in the lake, and then she'd had him put her on for size, that was the order of things, and *then* he took her riding. She rode a spirited, soft-mouthed Palomino, and they rode across a ridge where below them grazed the herd—the horses, nickering, ranging on the soft grass, and they had circled around the loose horses in the grass, and then she had begun to call out to him, and he her, and then they had a baby, nearly on the train, but they had done other things in between, they must have, graduate school and first and second jobs, and his father had been buried in the suit in which he had married for what must have seemed at the time for life. To mate, to live with and for another life, a life which might someday rescue your very own—there could be no better sentence, no better conviction by which to live. It was the institution which made us civil, and capable of being more, marriage. Let not, the poet said . . . *let not the marriage of true minds admit impediments*—he was in need of rescuing, he understood this now—because *love alters not when it alteration finds.* He was in need of being saved. He was so in need he couldn't see straight.

After you close your eyes, unless you're dead, they always open up again. The day is like a sonnet, or a pool of water—all of one piece. This he still believes. Here is the day. And over there, here is the dark. Look, Stephen. Look at all you've seen. Look at your son, playing on the snow. Look at your wife, barefoot in the snow. Look at your heart, chewed up and spit out on the snow.

And look how it still beats.

And look at all the things you still might do with it.

A Brief History of the
Twentieth Century in Bullets

- Archduke Ferdinand is assassinated by Gavrilo Princip
  beside the Latin Bridge in Sarajevo, launching the
  First World War and resulting in, among other things,
  the humiliation of Germany by way of the Treaty of
  Versailles;

- The German Nazi Party emerges, bringing forth Hitler,
  the Holocaust, and the destruction of Germany—Stalin's
  Red Army on the ground, American and British bombers
  in the sky;

- Across the sky, out of the fire of Nagasaki and Hiroshima,
  the Cold War is born;

- Tito dies; the Soviet Union collapses; the Yugoslav states
  go to war;

- Rat a tat tat—

Fall 1991—

The House of Scheherazade

Q. Why did the king lop off the wing of his beloved hawk?

A. The hawk would not permit the king to drink from a golden cup, which was filled with poison. (The king lived, the hawk died.)

—

The Montenegrin Reservists came up from the south. Bosnian Serbs, having control of Pigeon Rock on the Bosnian border, came in from the north and the west. Next the JNA—the Yugoslav National Army—rolled through Konavle and occupied the Žarkovica promontory overlooking the city. The Yugoslav navy, long since purged of any non-Serbs, blockaded the sea, and thus was Dubrovnik—the Pearl of the Adriatic—cut off. Then the JNA sent in warplanes. They took out the city's electrical grid. They bombed the Imperial Fort on Mount Srdj, and the telecommunications tower standing just beside it. The hills and villages began to bleed with refugees. As the United Nations Security Council would later describe it, because there existed no main line of resistance, or MLR, there could be no actual front line. Instead the city was surrounded from points on high; the shelling began, as did the siege. Where do you go when you want most to disappear? You go to war.

This was before, this was the start. The inauguration of 1991. Stephen, having recently been delivered to the city by a truck filled with lambs, was living with his recently made friends Marko and Nina in the Ploce district—just southeast of the city walls, up the street from a cluster of hotels. Marko and Nina had a *soba*, a room to let, which is how they were paying for their new house, and Stephen had traveled long enough to know he preferred the sometimes querulous quarters of a private house over the frigid and mini-barred walls of the modern hotel room. Marko had a taxi, which he had now hidden away in the city, and he also had a vending booth—cigarettes, condoms, *Playgirl* and *Swank,* sun creams and counterfeit Ray Bans and postcards featuring topless women in primary-colored bottoms mocking pudgy men. Nina ran the store, but with the tourists gone, the foot traffic of those with money in their pockets had long since dried up. Too, Nina was six months pregnant, and she was counting the days.

Nina, Marko would say, his ear pressed against her body.

And Nina would say, in English for Stephen's benefit, something scolding.

We speak English, Marko would say, looking up. We speak English because we look forward. Forward, you see.

Marko had been approached by the Croatian Guard which had wanted to give him a shotgun and half a dozen shells and the charge of fortifying a last-ditch line of defense a hundred yards out from the city walls. Marko had escaped thus far that service on account of the very few shotguns available and the condition of his wife.

My baby, Marko would say. Baby baby baby.

A planned defense of the city—proclaimed repeatedly by various authorities as one of the world's Great Treasures (they were not wrong in this assessment, just annoying)—was ludicrous. It wasn't merely the lack of a real defending army. At best Dubrovnik was a fragile city. The hundreds of ancient tiled rooftops, each clay tile having been manufactured over the breadth of a man's thigh, to describe the curve—the rooftops would not hold up to the concussions of the shelling. The city walls, at places six meters thick, had been built to hold back men armed with swords and spears. Men on horseback. A rock, hurled from a wooden-framed and oddly slung contraption? If anybody had learned anything from the twentieth century, then the lesson had to be this: artillery destroys anything its commanders hanker to. A shimmering marble promenade—the *pjaca* or Stradun. A clock tower. A palace or cathedral.

Stephano, Marko said to him, as if Stephen were Italian. This will be our greatest opportunity yet.

Stephen said, What's that?

They were sitting on the front terrace overlooking the Adriatic Sea. Nina was sunbathing on the porch off Marko and Nina's bedroom. Sometimes they could hear her singing a song made famous by a Croatian pop star. The latticework over the terrace was woven through with bougainvillea and grapevines. The sun and sea, so quiet and clear.

The deutschmarks, Marko said. The sex. The bad *cevapi*. All gone, but only temporary. Temporary.

And then comes the opportunity?

Of course. I will be rich because of this war. He stood excitedly, and ran inside, returning a moment later with an enormous box. He set the box on the table, nearly spilling his wine. He said, You know what I have here?

No.

American Rock and Roll shirts. Bruce Hornsby & The Range! Nearly a hundred. Size Extra Large. And there's more to come. With strife comes opportunity. And then hard currency like the dollars. Soon we will be rich like Germany. Like Paris. We will have a Disneyland, you watch.

You want a Disneyland?

We are a small country, Stephano. Croatia is a small country.

You aren't a country. Not yet, are you? Don't you need a constitution?

Paperwork. All paperwork. When it is time I will have a fast boat and a big house and I will send my babies to Princeton. To Texas A&M and Old Dominion. And we will have a cellar full of dollars, too. I tell you—

He was cut off by the arrival of one mortar, and then another, which must have fallen somewhere near the harbor. The boats remaining in the harbor were now used for target practice—the water filled with the wreckage, greased over with gas and oil. And these mortars, having landed, exploded, and then it was briefly—oddly— quiet. When they came again, they came closer to home, as if walking up a sidewalk, or a ladder.

Cocksuckers, Marko said, gathering up his T-shirts. You don't get rich by blowing things up! This is not Business! Stephano, come—

They took their wine, too. Nina stood in the doorway to her bedroom, her kimono open, her tan belly poking out. She stood there, looking around, and Marko and Stephen took Nina by the elbows and they scuttled down the staircase to the cellar, which was cool, and where the wine was kept. In one corner stood a box filled with Luke Skywalker and C3PO action figures. There was a second box, too, Obi-Wan Kenobi.

If they destroy my house, Marko said, I will fuck them. Stupid fucking Bosnians. Stupid fucking peasants. Stupid fuck goat farmers. If they blow up my house I will fuck them, the cocksuckings.

Lighting a candle, Stephen caught Nina's eye. He understood her yellow hair had been dyed to look like a movie star's, or a German's. She liked that color, yellow: the color of the sun, the color which might have been her hair. There were dolphins swimming across the fabric of her batiked robe. Her hair was lit up by the light of his candle. He saw, too, that she was terrified, and that she kept her hands inside her kimono sleeves over the roof of her swollen belly.

The fucks I am going to fuck—

Stop saying that, she said to Marko, beginning to cry. And then she said something which Stephen could not understand, and Marko put his ear to her belly, listening, and now Marko was explaining how everything was going to be all right, and then he said, for Stephen's benefit, I will fuck them later after they think that I forget, and now they listened to the intermittent mortars falling onto the city's outskirts and stirring up the dust.

2

They would drink the water from the toilet tanks first. That was twelve gallons right there. Stephen, less optimistic than Marko, and understanding this was going to last longer than a week, began securing supplies: bags of rice; tins of canned beef and fruit; cigarettes. He bought these items now at outrageous prices and brought them home and placed them in the cellar beside a boxful of blue and gold imitation Nike sneakers—size forty-four, or nine-and-a-half?

The next day, the day being quiet and still, and after helping Marko empty the contents of the vending booth, and tape the windows of the house, Stephen strolled down in the sun to the Argentina. The hotel had been built on the cliff which overlooks the Adriatic Sea and the small picnickers' island, Lokrum. The floors of the hotel descend down to the sea, not up, and the highlight of the hotel is its rocky beach. Adjacent to its beach is a private stone courtyard belonging to the House of Scheherazade—a magnificent villa, built by a wealthy Jew for his young wife, subsequently confiscated by the state, later to be turned swank hotel for the likes of Elizabeth

Taylor, and now abandoned. The villa's most striking feature is a pale blue dome.

He went to the terrace, at the back of the hotel, and saw an acquaintance—an EC monitor, taking notes, sitting in the sunshine. The waiter, recognizing Stephen, and not having much to do, set about to bring him a drink. Bourbon, a *dupli*.

Mr. Brings, the waiter said. The ice is all melted!

It's begun, Stephen said to the monitor. What are you hearing?

I have a satellite hookup. Milošević says categorically there is nothing more than training activity taking place. The world, it would seem, does not know we are presently surrounded.

But you have told the world, right?

Oh, I don't think anybody will be listening to me. My work is for when this is done. I work for the European Community, you know.

I don't get it. That's what you guys are supposed to do, isn't it? Report and inform the heads of state?

Stephen, said the monitor, offering him a cigarette. You Americans advised Gorbachev of the coup threatening him. You can take a photograph from space of an automobile and read its identity tag! Do you really think nobody knows what is happening here?

There's no reason, Stephen said. There aren't even any Serbs to speak of. And those that are here are swearing to defend. It's like invading Bali.

Or Grenada.

Yes, okay. Touché. But this, this shit . . . it's an operation premised on spite.

Exactly, yes. Precisely.

The monitor drank from his gin and tonic. He said, ruefully, You know these people in the Balkans. He said, We are cut off from the world now, either way. Washington does not want to hear what it already knows. Russia is stable as a hydrogen bomb. Like it or not, Tito was always the Soviets' first cousin. The U.S. should *pay* the Russians to deploy. Give them a job to do, some *currency*.

The waiter brought Stephen his drink.

So long as nobody is looking, the monitor said, we do not exist.

Stephen said, turning away, I think this is the most beautiful place in the world. Really.

I've been coming here for years, the monitor said. When I was a boy my father brought me here to walk the city walls.

It was a city, Stephen thought, built for a father and his boy. Tunnels and parapets, drawbridges, coves along the sea to play pirate in.

The monitor said, Your George Bush is going to lose the election. Read my lips. You will have a Democratic president and he will order your joint chiefs to stop this. He said, That is an Indian word, isn't it? Chief?

Beats me.

We can't, of course. I mean my country cannot. Kohl is too busy raising taxes in the West to pay for the East. He is too busy eating sausage breakfasts. He said, Do not worry, Stephen. They are not going to destroy the city.

What about Vukovar?

Oh, that is different. The Serbs don't *want* Vukovar. They want to make an example. Like Hitler and Warsaw. It is so common, you know. So utterly provincial.

What next?

The monitor had an awkward, condescending smile, which revealed the gums of his teeth, not unlike a horse. He said, We wait for ITN and CNN to do their thing. We wait for you Americans to get your political house in order and have this stopped by Easter. This *is* Europe, you know.

In the distance they could see two warplanes coming across over Lokrum. Stephen shielded his eyes against the sun for a better look.

Stephen said, NATO?

The monitor raised a pair of binoculars. No, he said. I think not. MIG-21s. JNA.

The aircraft approached, then banked hard, and as the jets passed over the sea in front of the hotel the sea exploded.

The water, the sea—it rose up into the sky. Two great monstrous plumes. The noise was the most terrifying—the water exploding into a cloud of gas. He'd never seen anybody bomb a body of water, as if to break it. In fact he'd never even seen a bomb.

What's that supposed to be, Stephen said. A shot across the fucking bow?

Perhaps they were aiming for us. Very complicated, those airplanes.

Fish, Stephen said. They're bombing the fish.

They are just telling us internationals they know where we live. They are telling us they can kill us anytime. Clever, I suppose.

He watched the monitor make some notes in his notebook. The time, the date. The direction of the wind. They ordered another round of drinks and sat in the sun. Others had gathered now on the terrace to see what precisely had been blown up, though now there was only water, the blue sky reflecting in it.

You would have never known.

3

During the midst of a dirty war it is difficult to keep clean. Dubrovnik—the first republic to recognize the independence of the thirteen colonies, back before the invention of communism, or electricity, or possibly even coal—a city which celebrates water by way of its marvelous fountains, and the first European city to develop a sewer system: here the filth of humanity could not be kept at bay. The sewers back up, the water mains all run dry. Two weeks later, Stephen and Marko were bathing in the sea. Stephen scrubbed at his body with a pumice.

Go wash, Nina had said, waddling to the door and pushing them out. The war is not going to end this afternoon.

Afterward Marko wanted Stephen to come with him to the new harbor. It was a decent walk. This way, Marko said. I want to show you.

The harbor was a wreck, as were the dozens of remaining small craft. There was a man fishing in the greasy water. If you had dropped a flame on it, the water would have burned. Then Marko led Stephen to a square building, and he unlocked the door, inside of which was parked his BMW—*Bay M Vay,* he called it—and a low-slung boat, circa 1940, on a trailer which they boarded.

It belongs to a rich friend in France, Marko said. I have liberated it for him. I have rescued it! Very fast. Two inboards.

It's a beautiful boat, Stephen said.

Yes yes, Marko said, impatiently. It's beautiful. It needs much varnish.

He led Stephen into the cabin, where there was a small galley and two bunks. On one stood a stack of Russian girlie magazines.

Marko said, Nobody has money now for pussy. Maybe later. He said, Stephano, if it goes bad, if the Serbs make a big push, you must meet me here. With Nina. She will not be able to walk fast. We will go first to Korčula. See?

Yes.

If you cannot find me—

We will find you. You'll find us.

No. Do not be American. Do not be sentimental. You know how to drive the boat?

Yes, Stephen said. If I need to.

Marko showed him where he kept the key and the pump to prime the engines. Marko pried at the housing of a vent, inside of which was stacked neatly a thick pile of five-hundred-mark notes.

For Nina, Marko said. If it must be. In Split she can always sell the boat, too. She will not have to, I think. Her mother lives in Split.

Okay, Stephen said.

Not as nice as my house, but bigger. Soon the baby is going to come out.

Stephen said, I know.

Stay near the coast. If you wait out the day, then you can travel at night. In the dark. The navy will shoot at you if it can. But if it comes to that they will have many targets. The gunboats cannot fire at everything. They are too small. Not enough room for the missiles. Marko said, replacing the vent framework, This boat is a fast boat. Fast. It is good it needs varnish. People will not think it is so fast. The owner he stays with us. He is my rich friend.

They went out and Marko showed Stephen where he hid the keys to the taxi. If you have to, take the boat and leave the car. Just leave it. If I am not able to be here it will not matter.

Stephen said, looking at the boat, What do you call the right side?

What?

The right side.

Marko looked at Stephen disappointedly.

A joke, Marko.

Ahh. That deadpan American humor. He said, I have some people to meet. Some business. He said, closing the heavy door, locking it, Okay.

At the Pile Gate, Marko said, Remember the plan, Stephen?

Yes.

Okay then. I am off.

Stephen went through the gate. He looked down the Stradun—the avenue of white marble, resplendent. He stopped at the dried-up Onofrio Fountain. A young girl, twelve, sat in the crowd alone—her head in her hands, crying.

Stephen approached the girl. He said hello, and she wiped her eyes and looked at him blankly. Her feet, shoeless, were dirty.

He said, *Sprechen sie Deutsch?*

She said nothing, then looked at her dirty toes. He held out his hand, which she took, cautiously, and he began to lead her across the promenade.

The girl said, pointing to the fountain, Mama, and Stephen nodded, understanding. He put his finger to her cheek. He told a group of refugees who knew him he would return in a few minutes. Now he walked with the girl, hand in hand, to a house adjacent to a pizzeria—closed for lack of ingredients. He knocked at the door, twice, and when it opened an old woman said, No eggs.

I'd like to shop, Stephen said.

A man came to the door. He wore the black paramilitary uniform of the Ramboesque. Standing there, he was an iconic figure. On one hip he carried a 9-millimeter Beretta; on the other, a knife the size of a fourteenth-century plow.

Yes? said the man, flexing his pectorals, speaking with a tractor-sized lisp. The woman told you the eggs are gone. I heard her say this. You did not hear her say this?

I don't want eggs, Stephen said.

The lieutenant gave Stephen the once-over, as if the man were the doorman at a private sex club in Paris, or Berlin, and now he stepped aside and let them in. He took them through a narrow hallway reeking of diesel fuel which led to a smoke-filled room overflowing with goods. A crate of grenades. Cases of cigarettes, and fruit. Stephen picked a half-dozen oranges, a chocolate bar for the girl. He bought a brick of cheese and two loaves of stale bread. Nina, who could not drink wine on account of her baby, was constantly thirsty. He told the lieutenant he wanted two cases of bottled water.

The man said, unbelievably, *Mit gas?*

Nein.

Okay, okay. More with no gath, you know.

You don't say?

Thay what?

Stephen explained he would be by to pick up the water later, and as he gathered the oranges and cheese and bread, he said, Two Cokes.

The man said something to the woman, who reached into a refrigerator—powered by a private generator, which would explain the rumbling and the fumes—and delivered to Stephen two small bottles of Coke. The girl beamed and they drank them down. After returning the empties, they left the way they came. At the fountain he cut slices of cheese and bread and spread them out on the shelf. He cut the oranges, all but one, and as the women and now two men approached, he looked the other way lest they feel even more obligated to avoid him. He sat with the girl, waiting for her mother, and told her a story from the *Arabian Nights,* a magical one with a clever genie. She nestled up against his side, listening to the rhythms of his voice the way his son once had. When the girl's mother arrived, carrying a yellow knapsack as if going back to school, the girl rushed to her with the orange she and Stephen had saved. She spoke to her mother excitedly, and the woman came to Stephen and took his hand.

No, Stephen said, rising. No no. It's okay.

He said, sitting on his heels, touching the girl's hand, I'll see you tomorrow. Here, he said, pointing to the fountain. Tomorrow. Then he rose and gave the woman a business card advertising Marko's stalled taxi service.

Argentina, he said to her. Stephen Brings.

Stephen, she said.

Stephen, he said. They'll know.

Next he returned to the house of the iconic black-marketer and his wart of a mother. Inside, three men were smoking and passing around a bottle of Joe Beam—long-lost Balkan cousin to Jim. The lieutenant pointed to the cases of water, over which he had draped a greasy towel to conceal their contents, and Stephen paid the man two hundred marks.

Thank you, said the lieutenant. Have a nithe day.

The Balkans, Stephen was learning. He carried the water out— another rich American, doing what the fuck he wanted. The pumice in his pocket banged against his leg. He carried the water through the old city, the water's weight gaining with each hundred yards, causing the muscles in his arms to burn, beyond the water queue, where dozens of people had lined up with buckets waiting to secure their daily ration from the trucks which brought it in. The water was tainted, he knew that. Typhus, cholera, the likelihood of each was becoming inevitable. Imminent? He walked across the old city and up through the Ploce Gate. Through the gate, over the drawbridge, past the House of Scheherazade. When he arrived home, lathered in sweat, he found Nina sitting in the living room reading an American women's magazine. On the cover posed an American woman with American cleavage and American teeth.

Nina smiled sweetly and said, You are clean? Let me smell.

I was. More or less.

Ahh, that is okay. You can swim again tomorrow.

He set the water in the kitchen on the stove which no longer had any gas. He placed Nina's pumice on the small kitchen table. The bougainvillea at the window swayed in the breeze like a song.

The baby's kicking, she called. Come feel.

No—

Stephen, come feel. I am a pregnant woman. You may touch me if I say.

He poured a tall glass of water, *keine gas,* and stepped into the living room.

What's this? Nina said.

Go, he said, handing her the glass. There's plenty.

He watched her drink the water. When she finished, she set the glass on the table and took his hand. With her free hand she wiped the back of her mouth and laughed. There was a faint trace of down on her lip; she had blue eyes. She lifted up her shirt, over the curve of her abdomen, and together they watched her tan, smooth skin flicker. There was something going on in there. Something being made. She took his hand and placed it on her body.

No, she said, not letting go his hand. Here. Feel.

4

A note on the common language: it's the same for everybody—Croatian, Bosnian, Serbian, though the partisans of each prefer to pretend otherwise.

Meanwhile Time, being infinite, slips away for good. To pass the time, he read. He wrote a draft of an essay on Pissarro. Mornings he walked along the city walls. There were Croats on top now, firing off teasing rounds to make the enemy fire back. He checked daily with the young girl and her mother, a few others, if only to provide himself with the illusion he was being useful. He shot no film.

Once he might have: he stood on the terrace of the house and watched a gunboat approach Lokrum. He located his 80–200-millimeter lens and scrambled down to the water to spy on the men on deck. It was a small ship, not much bigger than a fishing boat he had once worked. There was a battery of rockets, starboard and port, but he couldn't make out any actual guns—the name, *gunboat,* having lingered despite the advance of time. The ship cruised slowly to intimidate and to cast thick, black smoke up into the air; it was painted gunboat gray, making it invisible in certain waters. The color of death, it seemed. All that steel, painted to be inconspicuous? The effect was entirely reversed, and he watched the black smoke, the prow and the viscous wake it stirred.

Go home, he'd said to the officer on deck. Get a life.

And then came the cavalry: a fleet of small boats led by two car ferries leaving Split with the intent of breaking the blockade. On one car ferry, there were stacked cases of food and supplies; on the other, some sixty cranky journalists, as well as the new nation's cultural elite, sailing under the protection of those journalists. Outside of Korčula, the fleet was stopped, and searched, but at last the JNA backed down: such is the power of the press once it decides to squeeze. The president of a nation now collapsed, on board a car ferry facing down the navy warships he commands, on the horn negotiating with an admiral back in Belgrade . . . who could dream this up? Meanwhile the boats arrived at dawn, and after word began to spread—like wildfire, like blood poured into a river or pond—the city residents gathered to listen to important speeches about freedom and standing firm. Already in the breakaway state people were learning how to run for office. Standing there, amid the crowd, Stephen saw his acquaintances step off one of the liberating ferries. Everywhere now there were cameras. He knew they would know he was here.

At the cathedral a thanksgiving mass was held in order to permit more important speeches among the prayers. Stephen was sitting outside, smoking a cigarette, as if there were a limitless supply, when Peter Messinger and Elise Kohlhaus and Anna Castile approached.

Stephen Brings! called Messinger. We have been looking for you!

They shook hands. Anna nodded to him, and Elise extended her hand, grasping his own, which startled him.

Do you know where we find a phone line? Messinger asked. Elise needs to file a story. What a circus, that boat. Nobody could translate! Speeches, the Blah and the more Blah, and nobody can translate, and only one line going out—

And me, Anna said. Me too.

Ahna, Stephen thought. Not *Ann.* He said, The Argentina. Business as usual. But the rates are steep. Do you know the way?

Please show us, Elise said, taking his arm.

The crowd thinned as they left it. Stephen, embarrassed, did not know what to do with his arm. Messinger said, admiring the architecture, and then gesturing with his elbows, flapping like wings, It smells here. Bad. No water?

Not enough, Stephen said, growing more self-conscious. He thought, People in America took your arm at the prom, and then strictly for the snapshot. He said, sniffing himself discreetly, The city is an epidemic waiting to happen.

Elise matched his quickening stride. She said, drawing him closer, Peter showed me your cowboys. In Zagreb. They are wonderful!

Well they have not yet destroyed the city, Messinger said, falling behind.

You have been okay? Elise said. Staying here?

Fine, Stephen said. I've been reading.

At the top of the hill he was in his typically lathered sweat, though mercifully Elise had by now let go his arm. Stephen introduced them to the Reservation Director who Stephen knew liked to be called the Reservation Director. Stephen agreed to meet them all two hours later on the terrace, excused himself, and went home.

Nina said, looking up from her magazine, Your friends have arrived? Maybe you won't be so sad? I wish you would not always be so sad.

Well, some people I know.

Should we invite them to dinner? We could have a party for you!

Maybe, he said. They have to decide if they will return with the flotilla.

Oh, of course. She said, Do you think they will?

Yes. Probably.

Then you will, too?

He stood in the kitchen and considered making his decision then. He reached for a bottle of water. Truth is, he hadn't expected to be here as long as he had. He said, Nina, I don't know. I make it a point to never make up my mind until I absolutely have to. I'd like to see the baby. He said, shifting his feet, I'm going to do something very extravagant here. Please don't tell Marko.

Ooh la la, Nina teased. Of course I will tell Marko. She said, There is new soap under the bathroom sink. And shampoo!

He went to the bathroom, red-faced, and stepped out of his clothes. He stood in the bath and poured enough water into the cups of his hands to work up a decent lather. It was good just to wash off the salt from the sea. He shampooed his hair, and rinsed it; he shaved with his father's antiquated safety razor, the double-edged blade fresh. The window to the bath was open, sending in the breeze, and he could see the house up the hill, and the family which resided in it, standing on their terrace, toasting each other and the sunset.

Nina knocked at the door and entered, stepping around his clothes. She had a fresh towel with the Four Seasons imprint.

Nina?

She laughed. She said, unfolding the towel, It is counterfeit. But do not tell Marko I know this. She said, I have been saving it for a special time.

She set the towel on the lid of the toilet and said, checking him out, You will smell like a lily, and now she laughed like a girl and waddled back to the living room. She had left the door open and he could hear her singing. She called to him, interrupting herself: If they stay, we will have a party! Okay?

In his room Nina had also laid out for him a brand-new shirt—Bruce Hornsby & The Range, extra large—which hung like a drape on Stephen's thinning frame. He stood before the mirror and ran a brush through his tangled hair. On the way out, wearing hiking boots and cargo shorts and Bruce Hornsby & The Range (it had that new cotton smell!), he said to Nina, How do I look?

Like an American, Nina said. You are very much an American to me.

Is that a good thing? No, he said, don't answer that. He said, kissing her on the forehead, Thank you.

You shaved, she said, brushing his cheek. Like a baby.

When he arrived on the terrace, he found them—Messinger, Elise,

Anna, and the Texan, David Summerville. Apparently they were playing a game called American Talking Head.

They welcomed him again into their circle. The waiter brought Stephen a double bourbon, neat, and Summerville explained the rules of the game: you can't say something unless somebody has actually said it on TV. He said, explaining, Like this—

Summerville cleared his throat, paused, and said, affecting a speech impediment, Wike that Gweat Amewican Novewist, Wictor Hugo. A twagedy!

The others laughed and guessed instantly the proper authority.

Messinger said in his German accent, pounding the table, Hope is all we can hope for, no Judy? What say you about hope?

Elise said, taking her cue, That's right indeed. In our hour of need, hope is indeed very important for our hoping.

Indeed, Messinger said. A mouthful you said there, eminent journalist—

Read my lips, Anna said, turning to Stephen. I understand none of this.

Elise said, turning to Stephen, We are practicing in order to become BATS. BATS, you are thinking? Big American Television Stars!

Summerville said, Remember when Dan Rather said, Courage?

Yes, Stephen said. I actually saw that. I was watching that one.

How about when Bernie Shaw was in Baghdad the night we started bombing and old Bernie was drunk out of his gourd.

You think?

He was blitzed, Summerville said. Nobody could get him off the line.

God's truth, Stephen said. This is what bugs me the most—

What is that? Anna said.

What bugs me the most is when celebrities wear glasses when their eyes are fine. Then they say, It was a real labor of love.

Celebrity and State, Messinger said. You have no longer any separation of powers. Today every teenager in Berlin wants to be on MTV.

Yes, Elise said, And they say, *It was a lot of fun.* I've been watching, Stephen Brings. Apparently it is very important to have a Lot of Fun while you are making Action Movies.

Taxes, Summerville said. A coming across the aisle.

Elise said, leaning forward to Stephen, Like the Beach Boys.

Before, when I was learning English, I thought they were the Bitch Boys. You know?

Vukovar, Messinger said. Fun fun fun.

That killed it. There was one of those pauses now, the conversational riff having run its course.

Stay tuned, Summerville said. In a moment I'll be back.

Ted Koppel, Stephen thought. God love him. He finished his drink too quickly and ran his fingers through his hair and signaled for another.

Stephen, Messinger said. You have film?

No.

You have no film? Or you have not been *shooting* film?

I haven't been shooting, he said. But I wrote an essay. About Pissarro?

Stephen shifted his weight in his chair. He sensed the men and women wanting to be polite but understanding that he, Stephen, had not been doing what he was supposed to be doing.

Well, Messinger said. Perhaps tomorrow—

I'm not a journalist, Peter.

Messinger said, as if forgiving him for being lazy, But you are here and that is what matters. Still, Messinger said. One war is like all the others.

Why take pictures, Stephen thought, when you don't know what you're taking pictures of? He said, thinking aloud, The story is with the refugees. Everything else is smoke. The story is with the people who didn't make any of this. I'm staying with some people. They know people. There's an ad hoc agency for the women.

Summerville said, The women?

The military situation is all bluff and swagger. Boys, playing at it. The JNA is full of louts in the hills. There is no real defending army. Not yet.

It's the same up north, Messinger said. I think.

They are going to rearm, Stephen said. The Croats. They're coastal, and they're pissed, and the Swiss are creaming at the thought of selling them arms. The Serbs have blown it by not finishing it fast. But then what do I know—

More than you let on, Messinger said.

I do know all the Serbs I meet in the city are defending it. All three.

Elise said, Could you introduce me? To the agency?

Yes. Of course. He said, speaking to the table, not wanting to appear to be picking favorites, I was worried when there was nobody here to see what happened. But now with the press having arrived—Well?

Well, I don't know. It's not good, but it's not that bad, either. The chief danger is the shrapnel and the car accidents. But the reports of the shelling, all that, they've been at best exaggerated.

When Stephen's drink arrived, he said, We can talk about this later. I didn't mean to spoil the party.

Messinger said, after a long quiet moment, To Michel. A toast, To Michel.

They drank. Anna, the earnest one, explained. Michel had stayed behind to travel with a Croat patrol in the Krajina. He had set out several days earlier.

Messinger said to Stephen, You should get a flak jacket. Soon. I know just the guy in Split. Terrance the Armorer. He's Italian but has moved his shop to Split for all the business.

Stephen said, I can imagine.

Messinger said, stifling a yawn, It is dark, and I am tired. I have been working a lot.

Ja, Elise said, laughing. Working on women.

She vamped it up like a proper German, her Ws all Vs, *Vorking on vomen,* and Messinger stood and said to the table, Do not listen to the things she says about me, please. They may be true.

The Germans, Stephen thought—they made great scientists, but they had a difficult time cracking the joke. Perhaps they were just too serious a race. Still, they made great cars. He thought, Some of my best friends are German—

Stephen, Messinger said. Good to see you again. I am glad for your safety.

And now Stephen felt a twang of guilt, perhaps for not feeling as glad to see Messinger as Messinger appeared to be glad to see him. Truth is, he *liked* Messinger: instinctually. And now here was Messinger, disappearing into the darkness. In the wind the candle on the table guttered. There was a slice of lit moon, God's very fingernail, rising into the sky as if to scratch it.

Anna said, finishing her wine, I love the sea. The air. She said, rising unsteadily, I think I will go now and say good night to the sea.

She said to Elise, in German, Leave the door unchained, please, and they watched Anna fill her glass and take her drink to the steep, descending steps which would lead her to the water.

That left Summerville and Elise. Stephen signaled for another round, and Summerville, being sloppy, insisted on paying off the tab, American style.

Summerville said, insisting, I'll just write it off, anyway.

Stephen let him pay. He lit a cigarette, inhaled, sitting back, and said, It's nice to see familiar faces. Then, after he spoke, he regretted instantly having done so, thinking he must sound utterly maudlin. The needy and the damned. He told himself to enjoy the night and to keep his mouth shut. Get a grip, Stephen, and he told himself to leave very soon lest his loneliness cast him further into a pathetic light. At least he had his new Bruce Hornsby & The Range. He listened now to Summerville tell a story about some guy in a casino who lost first his shirt, and then his pants, and he watched Elise lean back into her chair, crossing her fine legs; he watched her reach for the package of cigarettes beside the candle, and say, Yes, this is nice.

Summerville stood and said he preferred to get drunk alone if nobody was going to be listening to his stories, thank you very much, and he made a big show of kissing Elise on the cheeks—French style, he said, parting. For a moment Stephen had considered leaving with him, thus putting a final cap on the night, but he also understood he *wanted* there to be something more in the air than salt and the vague iridescent light cast by that fingernailed moon in the sky. Edward Steichen, the photographer, had insisted that everything was predicated on light, an observation which had never struck Stephen as being particularly brilliant until Stephen understood it was possible also to see the dark.

Stephen thought, watching Summerville walk away, Appetites attract.

And Elise was too everything—and certainly too aware—to pay attention to the likes of either. Americans abroad, how stupidly they behaved. Elise's eyes were watering, he noticed. Possibly she was wearing contacts. Probably he'd offended her by that stupid comment about people wearing glasses. Probably—

You are thinking? she said.

Excuse me?

What have you been thinking?

He said, to bring it to an end, right now . . . he said, for the purposes of building a fence, or wall, I was thinking about my wife.

What is her name?

R.

R?

A family thing.

Her name is R? How striking.

The candle bristled, its flame rising to attention, a good soldier. Well, he thought. That's that.

Elise said, You were frightened. When the bombing started?

I'm a coward, he said. I was terrified, actually. It's my nature.

That's not what Peter says. He says you are a thinker.

Fear is a consequence of excessive imagination. Stephen said, grimacing, I can't believe I said that. Too much teaching. Shoot me if I get blowzy, please.

She said, leaning forward, Tell me about Pissarro. Your essay.

It's just an idea I had.

Tell me.

It's not that interesting.

She said, Stop protesting.

It's about his use of foreground, background. The visual scale.

Okay.

Traditional painters, they'd approach consistently, foreground and background. Like a lens stopped down to create a depth of field. But Pissarro opens up the aperture. He selects what's in focus.

Mm hmmm.

Technology, Stephen said, the mechanics of the lens. Technology did not invent the way we use it. That seems to me the point. People have *always* been inclined to see. Or not.

She was making him talk, he knew, to avoid talking about herself.

So, she said. It is more than a hobby.

More or less.

She said, looking away, briefly, You are going to return with the flotilla?

I'm not sure. He said, I didn't mean to keep you. He said, making to rise, I—

No. It's me. It's been charming, Stephen Brings. That is what Peter calls you. You were blowzy only that once, I promise. She said, And also I would like to apologize to you for being rude. When we first met—

No—don't do this. Really.

You must let me. I was a bitch. On the island? It was about another matter on my mind, but that is no excuse. *Comprenez-vous?*

Tu, he said. Please. And there ends my French. He said, rising to his feet, I can walk you—

No, she said, standing. So okay, she said, shaking his hand, that decidedly firm grip of hers. Not tonight, she said, and then she laughed, deeply, and then she let him go.

She had a strong hand. Had he not been half-drunk—fuck it, he was all drunk—he would have tamped down the emergent erection; he would have bitten his cheek, run his finger along the sharp metal edge beneath the table, perhaps drawn blood. Instead he watched the light from her hair and her arms dissolve into the darkness.

Later he went to the bar inside and talked with some of the ITN crew, learning that the going rate for plundered VCRs in Montenegro was down to fifty deutschmarks. He ordered a final drink, which turned into two—why is it that the *last* one always is the one you shouldn't take?—and talked some more, and he excused himself and took his drink to a stone table overlooking the sea. Late at night, he tended to want a change of subject, and after a while he heard footsteps ascending the stone staircase, and then Anna emerged, her blouse damp at the shoulders from her hair. She had been swimming in the cooling sea. She said, wringing her black hair, Yes?

It's me. Stephen.

Ahh, she said.

She sat beside him on the stone table, their feet on the bench, and they looked at the slivered moon sailing through a bright patch of clouds. He offered her a cigarette, and they smoked their cigarettes in silence.

She said, It's quiet.

He didn't want to say anything.

She said, My husband wants me to come home.

Stephen nodded, pretending to understand more than he should.

She said to Stephen, turning, I am very sorry. About your boy.

Thank you, he said. It was a long time ago.

But not long enough, she said. Maybe someday we will know each other well enough for it not to make me feel awkward around you. I have a boy. I know what a boy means.

It's different, I imagine. For a woman. A boy for a woman is different than a boy for a man.

Or maybe not, she said.

Maybe.

She put her hand on his knee and said, That is one of the mysteries. She removed her hand and shook her hair. She said, laughing sadly, It's the dark.

Yes.

She said, Inside the hotel it is dark.

It's on my way, he said, getting up. I'm drunk, I'm tired, and I'm married. He tossed the contents of his drink onto the grass. He said, You're safe with me.

Oh?

Please, he said. It's a mess in there and it's on my way.

He walked with her into the maze of the darkened corridors, lit by the emergency lighting, and beyond the section which had filled with refugees, the corridors smelling of meat cooked in oil and mold. In one room a handful of men was exclaiming over effete matters of NATO policy. There was a glass, breaking. She took his arm, which flustered him all over again, and they walked on until they passed the EC monitor's room. He felt her hip, the side of her body brushing against his own. Then another door, behind which a couple was making love: a woman's voice, ascending, and a man's—straining, as if lifting a great weight.

Anna said, leaning into his body, Peter. He snorts like a horse.

She said, letting go, taking her key to her own door and fumbling with the lock, When in Spain.

She said, wiping her eye with the back of her hand, The rain in Spain falls mainly on the plain.

Are you okay?

She said, touching his arm, Yes. Thank you.

They could hear the couple's voices through the wall. It was dark, and probable: she pressed him now, rising on her toes in order to kiss his cheek, and once there she lingered, and he felt the turbines in his body lighting up all over again, and he could feel the swell of her chest taking in a breath.

He raised his hand to the top of her shoulder and squeezed it gently.

He said, withdrawing, Good night.

She said, her hand to his chest, We could just rest. Sleep.

I'm sort of fragile right now.

You won't break, she said. You are not the kind to break. That's why some people hurt so much. Because it is so hard for them to break.

I want to, he said. It's not—

That is obvious, she said, pressing her hips into his body, and now she kissed him again, meaning to say good night, and ducked inside her room. He tasted the salt on his mouth, listening for the latch, and returned the way he had come: past the shut doors in all the darkened halls, and the voices, behind them, the voices conspiring their best in preparation to greet the forthcoming day. It had been stupid of him to be so spendthrift with this one clean shirt—and the water, the water he had first used to bathe, and the water he would now require to flush out the toxins. Anna, she too had a boy. When a man loses a boy, the boy also loses a man. So why don't you talk about it? Instead he thought about the dampness on his hand from Anna's shoulder, the water from her hair, the brush of her lips on his cheek, and he walked down the corridor—like a path, or tunnel—toward the patch of light waiting to receive him at its end.

5

That it made sense for Elise Kohlhaus and Peter Messinger to be lovers did not ease the ache and foolish apprehension in his heart, which surprised him, given that for so long now he had thought himself incapable of feeling anything in his heart at all. Like a schoolboy, he thought, waking alone in his bed. Peter, Anna's voice was saying to him. He snorts like horse. Stephen thought, opening his eyes, Where am I? He thought, Grow up. She's just a pretty girl.

He said, You already have a partner.

He said, rising for the day, You also have a headache.

Now committed to it, he drank a liter of water, and a Coke, and then he swallowed three aspirin, and dressed—cargo shorts, hiking boots, Bruce Hornsby & The Range—and walked to the sea, where he undressed, and dove into the water to wash off the bourbon which had seeped through his pores in the night. Even now the sea was cooling: he swam a few hundred yards out to circulate the blood, then floated briefly on his back, the water lapping at his penis, which replied, having finally been paid some attention. Praise, Dostoyevski wrote . . . *Praise makes the man.* He laughed, out loud, and pivoted in the water and splashed like a donkey, and now he returned, swimming fast to speed his return: to blow out the dust in his lungs. He taxied in the shallows, and submerged his face: once, twice. And again.

In America it was illegal to be naked, something about the body appearing indecent. Shame on you. *I see you.* He lay alone on the sunbaked rocks for the sun to dry his shameful body. If you go there, he told himself, you can't come back. That's what it means to disappear. You become unrecognizable.

Q. What are we by nature?
A. We are part of God's creation, made in the image of God.

He used the EC monitor's satellite hookup to call R in Chicago. She wasn't in, meaning she wasn't sleeping at home, and after the machine kicked on—R's voice, cheerful and clipped, faintly winsome—he left a lengthy message, thinking she might wake, less clipped but hopeful, nonetheless . . . possibly she might come swinging in through the door, having heard his voice in the hallway? It had happened before. Still she did not pick up, and so, fighting the static, he said into the machine he would call her in a few weeks, not to worry, that today he went swimming in the Adriatic—

The line went dead. He hadn't even been able to pick his moment.

On the Argentina terrace he found Messinger and Summerville eating breakfast rolls with cheese and sausage. There was a bowlful of fruit worth twenty marks, but then again, as Summerville would have it, who's counting?

Messinger was bright and chipper, having been recently laid, and Summerville said, reaching for a roll, his voice winking, Howdy, Stephen Brings.

Howdy?

Indeed, Summerville said. Care for a snort?

No, Stephen said. Thank you.

Always polite, Summerville said.

Stephen Brings, Messinger said, wiping his mouth with a napkin. Let us go to the city walls. I want to photograph the snipers.

Which side?

Messinger smiled broadly. Oh, I think the side which is closest, no?

Stephen wrapped two pears in a bandanna and on the way they made a detour to Nina and Marko's where Stephen picked up his everyday camera—a Contax II rangefinder. He loaded a roll of film, and Messinger was entranced by the bottom plate, the meticulous and sturdy design of its fit, and said, May I?

Stephen handed him the camera.

Messinger said, There is no light meter.

No.

It is a rock, Messinger said, hefting it. And the lens?

A diamond, Stephen said.

German glass, Messinger said. Zeiss. *Old* Zeiss, he said, returning the camera. But where are you doing your film?

Nowhere. Like I said.

Ah yes, he said, clapping Stephen on the shoulder. Well then, Stephen Brings. Let us go then and be famous men of war.

They crossed the drawbridge. At the entrance to the staircase, Stephen paused to touch the cool stone. They passed an empty card table and ascended the narrow steps and stood on the ancient city walls.

Stay low, Stephen said, pointing. They have rockets. Boom.

Messinger said, I do not like rockets.

They turned a corner, following an incline, and as they turned another corner they came across a gathering of a dozen or so cameras, television and print, surrounding a lone militiaman—a bartender Stephen recognized from one of the hotels, dressed up in brand-new hunting gear. Several of the cameramen were giving the bartender various tips for ensuring the best pose.

No no. Not me, the bartender yelled, pointing to the hills. Them! Shoot them!

Now the man stood in the open and fired blindly into the hills three rounds, and ducked. There was no return fire, which apparently disappointed.

Ahh, said a British voice, clicking. So you want us to shoot them? I see. Right.

Messinger said, So many the brave.

They passed through the gaggle. As they passed, the militiaman rose again and fired several more quick rounds, and this time there was return fire, and splinters of stone, spraying, one of which brushed the back of Stephen's neck.

What the fuck! somebody yelled. They're firing at us!

Fuck, said another. Rat fuck, this is ridiculous—

Stephen lowered his head, turned, and ran on, his camera strap wound tight around his fist, cutting off the blood. He paused, checking a corner, and waited. Messinger had stopped to photograph the Croat militiaman on the parapet giving orders to the press. Then two more rounds struck the wall and everybody went down, kissing the bricks, while Messinger took more shots.

Messinger caught up with Stephen and they went on. They ran along the wall facing the hills. To their left drifted a sea of tiled roofs, chopped up by the concussions of the randomly lobbed shell. They came to a turret well protected from the enfilading line of sight. Stephen took a seat, forearms on his knees, hitching his breath—his back to the wall. He said, From here you can see most. He said, gesturing backward with his thumb, Note Serb flags on yonder hilltop.

There came more fire, potshots, none directed their way. Nonetheless they were awake now on the other side. Messinger, sitting beside him, placed his bag between his outstretched legs. He took out an automated SLR.

Stephen said, Those are serious hilltops.

Messinger said, pointing, A serious lens. He stood, anchored himself, and took several fast shots of the surrounding hills, the bunkers which had been dug in. He turned on his heel and took more of the inner-city rooftops. When he sat back down, kicking out his legs once more, Stephen took his photograph. The photograph of the photographer sitting behind the wall.

Stephen said, May I?

You always ask, don't you.

I try to.

Stephen pivoted for the angle and took one more. He said, returning to his place behind the wall, Otherwise it's not fair.

Here, Messinger said, reaching into his bag, passing to Stephen a warm bottle of Coke. Stephen opened the bottle, its fizz spraying into the hot air.

Messinger said, opening a travel-worn leather album holding several photographs, Here. Look, Stephen. My family.

In one photograph stood a regal woman in a dark dress: beside her, two boys and a girl, rising up the scale of childhood like the triad of a major chord. Messinger said, admiring them, They are my family. My heart's sake.

Stephen said, A man's children are like arrows to his quiver.

Oh?

David. Book of Psalms. Stephen said, They are very handsome.

I live in Europe. We go to the church only to admire the disasters it makes. The churches, I mean. Especially the big domes.

At least you have a sense of scale, Stephen said, passing him the Coke.

Soon, Messinger said, nodding. Soon I will stop shitting around with all this. Become an editor and get fat. You say fucking, I know. But the war coverage, it gets one noticed. People like the pictures.

You are Herr Peter Messinger. Where you go, the others follow.

Messinger said, smiling, ever so seriously, I was glad to know you would be here, Stephen Brings. There is no shit with you. I understood your essays better than maybe you think. He said, pointing to his wife in the photograph, She has taken the children to Paris. She wants me always to come back to her, but Paris is expensive. I love Paris. Who could not? But it is expensive.

They go to school—

Ah no. On holiday, he said, closing the album. More the expense. So I keep gaining notice. Notices. This will be the end of it for me. This, what you Americans call conflict. Always a conflict. So American. He said, raising a Leica, taking a shot of Stephen, What say you now? We are friends?

We will be, Stephen said. Experience and sensibility. Like interests.

My thoughts exactly, Messinger said. And temperament: not the same, but kin. Like you I have very few friends. That Summerville, he is a funny guy, but he has I think a long line.

Stephen looked at him blankly.

Like the telegraph, Messinger explained. A long line must travel a great distance. Things get lost on the way.

He's a big guy, Stephen said. Big brain.

Perhaps, Messinger said. Big like the dinosaur. Too much growth beyond the brain.

Later a pair of Croat snipers wearing black paramilitary gear rounded the corner, and they set themselves up, away from the turrets—the turrets being the most obvious spot to hide a sniper—and using the big lens Messinger got his photographs. After twenty minutes of teasing the surrounding army—a shot here, a shot there—the snipers, having meant only to provoke, packed up and left. When they left Messinger removed the film from his camera bodies and inserted fresh rolls. Messinger gave Stephen a roll to do likewise.

On the way down, at the entrance to the city, the two snipers in black stood waiting for them beside the card table. Behind the table sat another man, big-bellied and officer-like, slicing up a carrot.

Open the bags, the big-belly said.

They opened the bags.

The officer pointed to the cameras. He said, The film.

They made a big show of protest, and Messinger affecting his outrage unloaded all three of his bodies. Then the snipers went through the gear looking for more exposed film. Finding none, they permitted them to pass.

Have a nice day, said the big-belly, waving them by.

Stephen said, later, his film in his fist, What if they had frisked us?

Messinger said, But what is he going to do? Shoot me? They are the same on either side, you know. The exact same. Militia is militia.

Stephen said, I *don't* know. A few weeks ago, the JNA bombed the Adriatic. This war shit, it does not attract.

On the promenade a young man with a brand-new top-heavy bag came running up. He paused a moment to collect his breath, hands to his knees, and asked if they knew where he could find Peter Messinger.

He is back there, Messinger said, pointing to the walls. When you see him please tell him that the old one with the wife in Paris sent you.

The kid lit up. Okay. Yeah, sure. Old one, wife in Paris.

Messinger said, Tell Herr Messinger it is time for him to go home.

Okay. Time to go home. Got it.

They went on to the Onofrio Fountain, and Stephen introduced Messinger to the young girl and her mother, and Stephen gave to the mother and daughter the fruit he had pinched from the hotel. Then Messinger left to meet up with Elise and the rising politician who had built the flotilla on which the distant relatives and the press had sailed, and Stephen sat for a while with the mother and her daughter. They had family in Istria, the mother explained. Here they had nobody. The mother said, We will not be permitted leaving Dubrovnik. The people without friends on the boats must stay. She said, beginning to cry, We cannot leave on the boats tomorrow. All the boats.

Saddened, he went back home, and there he put away his camera and the film. Useless, he thought, locating a place to store it. Later he sat on the terrace facing the sea with the enemy behind him and read a chapter from the *Arabian Nights*. At times, he paused to look up and study the water and the blue-domed roof of the House of Scheherazade, winking in the startlingly clear sunlight. A wave, cresting the day laid out. The dome had been designed to resemble the sky, he understood; it was the sky that made the clean water blue. He sat on the terrace and read from his book while listening to the snipers poke fun intermittently at each other across the sky.

While reading, and before turning to the next page, he thought, Asshole.

Am not, he thought.

Are too.

Am not.

Oh yeah?

Yeah—

Fuck you—

Bang.

6

This is what he knows about Elise Kohlhaus: her father, Philip, is the director of the privately held Kohlhaus Elevator Works in Stuttgart, which he inherited from his father, and which the British and Americans bombed to pieces in 1944. Her mother, Rebekka, was captured by the Russians. Rebekka, then five, and her mother later escaped to West Germany in 1946. Now Rebekka is a pediatrician, very popular, and Elise is the only child, born in the spring of the decade of love.

Educated in Berlin, with stints graduate and otherwise at Oxford and NYU, Elise left an entry-level position with a publishing house to cover the collapse of the Berlin Wall. Being twenty-eight, and child-less, she is young enough to think she requires more adventure than is probably good for her. Elise's hair, pale yellow, falls into ringlets which grow tighter as the humidity begins to rise. She has a small cleft in her chin and a dimple in her cheek; she has abandoned her contacts due to the exigencies of modern war and taken to wearing glasses with metal frames. Also, she has taken to wearing a field cap—a gift to her from a once-smitten U.S. major stationed in Vai-hingen—and, while wearing the field cap, she tucks her hair into a barrette that gathers at the nape of her neck. Her eyes are blue, her frame slight, and following the tradition of all families with military experience—her grandfather, an officer on the Eastern Front, lost both legs at Kursk—she takes meticulous care of her feet.

These things Stephen has learned by way of listening to others, many of whom are unknowingly in love with Elise. Nina had taken instantly a shine to Anna and Elise. Elise was writing about what was happening to the women.

Not for the magazines, she said. For me.

The morning the flotilla was to leave for Split, Stephen went to the hotel terrace, where he felt a palpable tension at the table. Everybody was over-caffeinated and not talking. Obviously Messinger and Elise had been quarreling.

The others, Anna explained, were returning to Split. Elise is going to stay.

With you, Elise said to Stephen.

I haven't said I'm staying, Stephen said.

Of course you are. You can help me. And Nina.

Stephen took a look at those around the table. He said, If you leave now then you know you can.

My point, Messinger said.

Summerville said, There's people getting shot lots of places. Why get stuck here? He said, making a doodle in his notebook, Beats me.

Stephen rose and said he had things to attend to, meaning he did not want to become embroiled in a family matter, especially one belonging to a family by which he had been so recently adopted, and so he promised to meet them later at the harbor in order to say good-bye.

Messinger followed him through the hotel to the street. Stephen!

The sun on the street was bright in Stephen's eyes. Stephen said, turning, shielding his eyes, Yes?

This is crazy, Messinger said. We cannot all of us stay.

I wouldn't know.

If you come with us we would be able to dissuade her. Together.

Stephen thought about this. He removed a packet of cigarettes, offered one to Messinger, and took one for himself. He lit them up.

He said, Peter, the time is not right for me.

Ja, well, Messinger said, spitting smoke. When is it ever?

Stephen said, How badly do you want this? He said, making his meaning clear, If you want me to return, I will, but then I'm going to have to make arrangements to come back, and that will be difficult. Uncertain.

Messinger inhaled sharply, exhaled. He waved his hand through the smoke—as if he were American, apologizing. This is stupid, he said.

Stephen said, I have an exit route. There's room for another.

I worry stupidly, Messinger said. She is not a child, God knows that. The television will be here. With her, you will be safer. Unfoolish. He said, Don't be foolish, Stephen Brings. One does not make friends so easily.

Likewise.

Messinger said, I showed you pictures of my family for a reason. My heart's sake. But that was insensitive of me. I should have thought—

They're your kids, Peter—Your family.

Do you know what I am saying?

Yes.

Then Stephen, please do not pretend you do not.

Peter, I lost my kid. It's a fact, like being blind, or short. But let's not walk around it, okay? Let's please just not always have to walk around it.

Of course, Messinger said. It is like cancer or the AIDS. Nobody knows how to reply. But I will just say what is on my mind. And I will also say, Stephen, do not be foolish. And keep Elise away from the snipers and militia. Okay? No walking along the tops of city walls.

They shook hands, standing in the street, and Messinger turned, and Stephen said, Peter?

Yes?

Will you deliver this for me?

He reached into his side pocket for the letter he had written in Hvar months ago to his son.

Yes. Of course I will. We will meet in Zagreb then, soon. Or Vienna.

Okay, Stephen said. Thanks.

So okay.

—

Say hello, say good-bye: he walked alone across the city to meet Marko at the new harbor. In the garage, Marko was loading a box of pirated software—Quicken—onto the fast boat needing varnish. Marko, like Stephen, was wearing his Bruce Hornsby & The Range. Marko leapt off the boat and said, The cocksuckers.

What is it?

They won't let Nina leave. She does not have a *young* baby. Pregnant does not count. Pregnant is not having a baby! They, he said, meaning the politicians and journalists and priests, they get to leave. He said, Why are you not leaving?

Time's not right. Besides, where would I go?

Marko said, I have some watches coming. Swatch. Very good. Real Swatch, not the fake. Made in the good factory in Poland. He said, Tomorrow we will need to move the boat to another place. Too much bombing here.

Okay.

Fuck the cocksuckers, he said. I am sick of not having a telephone.

They went together to the gangplank of the ferry which would be leading the way out. A crowd had gathered to see the rescuing flotilla off. Stephen ran into Anna, who dropped her bag and embraced him.

She whispered into his ear, Forget everything I said. That night. Please.

She said, pulling back, I was lonely. I am sorry if I made you awkward.

It's okay—

I'm glad, she said. It's not that you should forget. It's because I don't want to be awkward. I try never to be awkward with anybody.

Me too.

Then, she said, beaming. Then stay here and be very safe. Keep Elise safe. I love Elise very much.

I know, Stephen said. Safe journey.

They joined up with Messinger. Summerville, seeing Stephen, waved howdy. Elise was making her farewells. The harbor was now teeming with drama: families being separated all over again. Sister and brother and cousin.

Elise made her way through the crowd, joining Stephen and Marko.

She took Stephen's arm and said, Thank you.

He said, not knowing what to do with his arm, For what?

She ignored the question—or didn't—and gave back his arm. She turned and said hello to Marko. She looked at Marko's shirt, Bruce Hornsby & The Range, and Stephen's shirt, Bruce Hornsby & The Range, and said, arms akimbo, Did I miss something? Was there a concert, too?

Stephen watched her take in the crowd. He said, looking at the hilltops, We should leave. They have a line of sight. Once the press is underway we become a fat target.

They left, and Marko split off at the gate to do some business, and Stephen and Elise went to the hospital, which was dark inside, not having any electricity except for emergency generators. Everywhere now there were refugees with no place to stay. The enemy had been blasting away at the resort hotels—like the one near the old nudist beach, which could have housed two thousand. Three. Elise explained, walking, that she wanted to talk to some people, with Nina, who would translate.

Trust me, Stephen said. You don't want me around for that.

Okay.

He said, Peter and Anna think I can keep you safe.

She smiled, and said, You cannot keep me safe.

I know that. He said, Stay close to the buildings, okay? It's safer there.

When he saw her next, on the terrace at home with Nina, it was obvious she had been crying. Her glasses sat on the table by her note-book—a tablet of paper, unlined, pale blue. On hearing Stephen coming through the door, bearing apples, Nina rose and made her way in her red dress to the kitchen to make coffee—they had some, now, though Nina and Marko never drank it—her belly swinging beneath her muumuu. What was it about pregnancy which made a woman radiant? It was a thing he prized most in a photograph, genuine radiance. Nina's skin, like moonlight, lit up the house.

Stephen, Nina said to him. I was just making some coffee. American style, the way we like it.

They ate a lunch of cheese and bread. The enemy up high began firing from the hilltops at twenty-minute intervals. They listened to the shelling as they ate, and Nina said, They are just trying to scare us.

Elise said, Well, it's working.

A long silence. Nina's baby kicked. Elise asked Nina if she could feel the baby, and Nina beamed and took her hand.

There, Elise said. There!

Nina said, Will you stay with us? It's not la dee dee like the hotel. Don't tell Marko. But we have the room. This way I thought you will not be so lonely.

And then it was agreed nobody wanted to be more lonely than was otherwise necessary in this life, and there was a palpable lifting of the spirits.

I would like the companionship, Nina said. She said to Elise, giving Elise back her hand, Someday you will tell me all about your family. We will have lots and lots of time.

Before Elise could reply, the baby kicked and Nina dropped her cup, which struck the tiled floor and broke.

7

To fall in love is to understand the force of gravity. One never knows where one will land or just how hard. One can fall in love with a cause, Stephen told himself, though of course a cause is incapable of loving one back. A cause might provide one with identity—like a bumper sticker, instant membership and pals—but a cause was not capable of keeping one warm at night or, for that matter, feeling frisky. True to his nature, Stephen distrusted all causes, though he had at times been smitten by various individuals who represented causes directed toward the proper spirit of things. *A woman's right to choose,* R always said. *That's my passion* . . . and it was hard to complain against those who wanted to prevent a girl from having a coathangered abortion, or save the forests belonging to the world. The forests around Dubrovnik. When a shell once lobbed fell into the city, it cast splinters—brick and tile and glass and wood—flying. And he told himself, Don't fall in love, but by now he was free-falling, which he didn't understand. It was the kind of flight he had come to think he was no longer capable of sustaining. At night he lay on the couch, having given over his room to Elise, and at night he felt his blood pumping through his body, through the arteries which led always to his beating heart.

This living hand, Keats wrote. *I hold it towards you.*

They took a small launch to Lokrum and tied up on the north side, tucking the boat between two giant rocks. The island had been shelled, and in that shelling, somebody had taken out the gatekeeper's house. Stephen and Elise had walked around to see it. The roof beams had been shattered. Everywhere, there were splinters.

Stephen said, walking up the path, and hopeful to change the subject, God, I love this place.

Elise said, sadly, Me too.

She was thinking, he knew, about what she'd been seeing. The things she was writing: not the *cause,* but the inhumanity. She was thinking about the way they separated the men to take them off to camps and beat them with clubs. It was easy to break a man's ribs. She was thinking about the way they raped the women. The little girls. The way they killed the livestock and burned the houses and raped the girls in front of their fathers before they took the fathers away to break their ribs. Smash their skulls, the skulls being always smashed last to keep the man alert to the fact his knees were being broken. His ribs and his hands.

Soldiers, she was thinking. Soldiers.

He said, You came here a lot? Before?

Yes, she said nodding. On holiday. My father liked to go to Cavtat.

They walked on to the western ledge. The water surrounding the island was green and blue. They walked along the rocks to the edge of the blue water.

This is not a war, she said.

You know those Yugoslavs, Stephen said. Animals!

She said back, For centuries.

Not like the French.

Not like the Russians and the British and the Italians. She said,

Once you become a defeated people, or have two continental coasts, *then* you become civilized. We are very civilized now in my country. Just like Japan.

She said, negotiating the rocks, which had become tricky, requiring various leaps, The gay men come here. In summer. Dozens of beautiful men tucked into the rocks. Sometimes you never see them until you are on top of them. Like surprises. When I was little, and we came here once, I walked all around them. Besides my father's, I saw my first penis.

Your first?

I was walking like this to a ladder—to that ladder, there—and this boy, he must have been, oh, seventeen. Eighteen? This boy comes right up out of the sea. Like Poseidon! He was so beautiful it made my heart ache.

She laughed and said, I stood looking at him. At all those marvelous complications! I have never understood how men walk. He was tan, *everywhere,* and then he smiled at me. I turned, I watched him walk by. I was in love.

Even then.

Well, I was eight. But eight is not too soon for love. Not if one has love at home. It was not the sexual love I am talking about. It was much more than that. It was the love of beauty. I had seen it. A gift.

She said, Have you ever noticed how people are so much more attractive when they are nude? Not the pretty ones so much—you know what *they* look like. You see *them* everywhere in the shopping malls and magazines. But everybody else? Especially the big people. Big people should not wear clothes unless it is cold. I love the old men drinking beer patting their big beautiful bellies. I love the grandmothers on the beach wearing floppy hats. And the kids. When children swim naked together they do not grow up to have so much shame.

You think?

Oh yes. I learned this from my parents. I'm not talking about the crazies. The people who golf nude. Good grief. But to swim? To lie in the sun?

They came to a fine rock with a long, flat surface, a ledge of marbled granite, and Stephen removed his knapsack. He spread a blanket on the sun-baked rock. Nina had packed for them a picnic: wine from the cellar; and bread; a can of sardines Marko had received in trade for a used pair of counterfeit sneakers; a small brick of cheese. For dessert, an apple to split.

Elise sat on the rock. She lifted her arm, sniffed, and said, I stink.

Stephen popped a cork. Elise undid the laces on her boots and kicked them off. She tugged off her hunter green socks; she doffed her cap. She said, Now I am going to be an American Action Movie Sensation.

Excuse me?

First I undo my hair, like this. Next I take off my glasses, so. She set the glasses on her green socks. She said, squinting, The glasses make me intellectual. So I am permitted to be sexual only once they are removed.

She shimmied out of her shorts; she pulled off her new Bruce Hornsby & The Range, beneath which she wore a navy maillot. She smiled and turned to him, fully, taking him in—meaning she wanted him to be taking her in, too.

Stephen said, I see.

And she laughed, that belly laugh, partly a whoop, and said, But I will not embarrass you. Okay? She said, Also, intellectual women do not swim.

And then she dove in. She resurfaced several long seconds later. She swam out, a strong stroke, and then back in, calling to him from below—

Come swim!

It was a dangerous proposition, given his state of mind. His heart rate. He said, I bathed earlier.

Not with me you did not.

He said, drinking his wine, It's too cold.

Coward, she said. And after I promised you. She said, Stephen Brings, I *always* keep a promise.

She swam back out, splashing loudly with her feet, causing a spray. He stood on the ledge watching her. For a while she treaded water and sang the words to a song by U2. He watched her dive into the water, a porpoise, and resurface several meters later. She returned then, and scrambling up the ladder in the manner of that same boy before her, she said, It is becoming cold—

It's the wind, he said. Not to mention the season.

Her arms and legs were covered with gooseflesh. She shook her hair, wildly, then raised her hands to pull it off her neck, away from her eyes. She stood away from him, her arms wide to the warm sun, waiting to dry. She turned to him and said, As I recall, you have seen me undressed?

From a distance, he said. Mostly.

She laughed. She said, turning her back to him, You are too skinny, Stephen. Losing weight. I can see it on your face and throat.

Now she came to the blanket, sitting cross-legged, facing the hot sun. At times her knee bumped against his thigh and he felt his body shiver. He felt the blood in his veins charging. She put her glasses on and shivered in the breeze.

She said, This is not so bad a place to have a war. Not like Finland.

She began to eat. She knew how to eat with her hands. She said, wiping her mouth, You are going to have to tell me about your family, I think.

How's that?

Family is all. It is the only thing.

You think?

She nodded, swallowing. We are having a picnic. I should know. I should not have to hear about it from other people.

He drank and lay down on his back and crossed his legs. He could feel the sun on his exposed knee. To shield his eyes from the sun, he lifted the edge of the blanket and pulled it over his head. The blanket cooled his eyes and rested just so above the bridge of his nose.

She said, So?

He said, Once there was a king. He had a hawk, which he loved.

This is about your family?

Don't interrupt or I'll forget. I'll get shy on you.

He said, This king . . . the king loved to hunt and he loved the hawk. He went with his men and his hawk to hunt a gazelle. A fine day for hunting, you see. But the gazelle leapt over his head and ran away. He was made to look foolish, this king, before his men. He was made to look foolish by a gazelle. A man cannot abide being mocked, especially a man who is king. What is the gazelle if not an emblem of the beloved? Shame is pride's cloak, Blake says.

Ahh, Elise said. A parable.

The king, Stephen said. The king was ashamed because the gazelle—the sexual object—had leapt over his head. And he was thirsty. It must have been a very hot day for hunting. Very thirsty. So he rode after the gazelle with the magnificent hawk on his sleeve looking for a pool from which to drink. A stream. He was hot, you see. He was thirsty. But he found no water. Riding hard, a gray stallion, a horse for a king, he came to a tree dripping with a silvery delicious-looking fluid. Water, he thought. God's nectar. Or wine, perhaps. Scheherazade, like Solomon, is not always precise.

Stephen sat up and reached for his wine and drank. A trickle of seawater ran down Elise's throat. He lay back down, covered his eyes, and took a cigarette. He could smell the seawater on Elise's skin. Before he could locate his lighter, Elise already had, and she took the cigarette from him, and lit it, and then gave it back. He felt her fingers touch his mouth.

This king, he said, exhaling. He took the hawk's golden royal hawk-cup and filled it. With that dense quicksilver. And the king set the golden cup before the hawk to drink, but the hawk knocked over the cup. The king did this a second time. Perhaps he loved the hawk so much that the king could not bear to drink first? An act of love for his hawk? It was, like I've said, a hot day, the sun fierce. And again the hawk knocked over the golden cup. Then, following the rule of threes, it happened for a third time. And the king, being king, grew angry and drew his sword and in one breath sliced off the magnificent hawk's wing. A great wing. And the hawk rose up, spiraling like a rocket, and pecked at a giant serpent in the tree. The fluid was venom, you see. Poison.

He sat up and looked at her. She had her hand placed to shield her eyes. Two beads of sweat ran beneath her raised arm down her side.

She said, What happened?

The king lived. The hawk died.

She said, I don't understand.

He wrapped his arms around his knees. He said, The king should have stayed home. The king should not have chased after the illusory. The gazelle.

She refilled her glass, then his. Catching his eye, she made her decision, and reached for the top of her suit—rolling the wet fabric over her shoulders, down past her chest, below her navel to her hips. When she had finished, she looked away, smiling gently, and turned to face the water and the sun. She rested her back against his legs.

Elise said, her voice to the wind, I think the gazelle was not illusory. He *saw* the gazelle. It leapt over his head. The serpent, that deceives. The serpent is over his head, too.

Stephen said, To which he is led by the gazelle.

Inexperience, Elise said. He must have been a young king.

Elise said, leaning her weight into his knees, The king loved the hawk.

Yes.

Like a son?

Yes.

How could he live afterward?

He was the king, Stephen said. Kings always live. Or else they are replaced. Without a king there is no story.

She turned and reached for her glass of wine and drank. She set the glass on the stone beside her which caused the glass to ring. She took his hand and turned back to the sea—his hand in her own, swiveling—and then she placed his hand on the top of her bare shoulder. The water of the sea was lapping at the island, breaking over the rocks below, and he could feel the sun's heat on the rocks. He could feel the bones on the top of her shoulder, and the muscle beneath it, beneath the very skin of it, the skin having a faint dusting of salt, and he could smell her skin and the salt from her body, and she held his hand like that with the weight of it resting just so.

She said, What happened to the queen?

8

They worked well in the city and in the house and by the sea. He read her book on the fall of the Berlin Wall and was astounded by the clarity of her voice—she having written this in a language not her own. He marveled at the lucidity of her prose. At her brilliance—meaning *luminance,* meaning *design.* She asked him to read drafts of what she was writing now, and he began to tease her about her idioms, the sometimes formal pitch. And using Scheherazade's Parable of the Hawk he began something of his own, though he was too uncertain to show it. Coward, she teased, and the days passed, and not having a calendar they lost track of the days. Among other things they had each stripped the watches from their wrists. They swam often and lay in the sun nude and when they dressed they confused each other's Bruce Hornsby & The Range. He went to the bookshop on the Stradun and began a crash course on German literature: Goethe,

Grass, and Mann. It is spirit which attracts, he told himself, turning the pages. *Not matter.* It was the pitch of her voice, the light in her eyes when she said, *Why are you looking at me so, Stephen?* He was in love with her, he understood, and he was pretty certain she could be in love with him, but still it went unspoken lest it fall apart for being rushed. And so while he was busy falling in love with her, they were not lovers. Once, when he became too riled up to think, let alone read, he swam off alone far into the distance, where he attended briskly to the call of his physiology, coming into the sea, and when he returned she lay naked on the beach, her hand shielding her eyes, and teased him saying, *Why so far away, Stephen? Why so far?* and then he climbed up onto the warm rock and fell asleep on it as if he were a seal. Later she gathered her clothes to make a pillow for his head and dove into the sea. He knew they had their separate inner houses, both of which were not entirely in order. He knew why she never spoke of Messinger, and so he never asked, and thus they circled each other—birds, spiraling in the sky.

Fish in the sea.

November came and went. The sea had cooled and turned to winter. The wind sharpened all around them.

The night of a fierce bombardment, the night the city was set on fire, Nina's water broke. They were on their way to the cellar, the enemy positions having started up a bombardment in earnest. Shells were landing in the city and along all the streets leading into it. The enemy fired phosphorus shells into the hills covered with oaks, setting them ablaze in the night sky. The moon, full, oranged from the filtering smoke—the air and the sky filled with the smoke of the burning forests. The smoke rose to the orange circle of the moon, to the drain in the sky it made, as if it were possible to escape.

This is serious, Stephen understood, his eyes burning from the smoke.

It was on the stairs—the dark, dusty stairs leading to the cellar—that Nina's contractions began. A doctor, shipped in with the flotilla, had seen Nina earlier that day, assuring her the baby would not arrive for two more weeks, but he had also been busy and rushed and eager to dispense vitamins. Also, he was Greek, and he did not speak English, and his Croatian/Bosnian/Serbian was shaky, and so most of the examination had been done with a lot of nodding. The first two contractions were separated by thirty minutes. Then fifteen.

Nina sat on her heels and wailed. Oh God, she said, finally, the contraction having passed.

Marko had lit candles in the cellar. He had opened two large boxes of Hugo Boss leather jackets, to make a pallet for his wife, and which he covered with several U.S. army surplus sleeping bags to protect their resale value. Marko said, rubbing his hands, They are not supposed to be coming now. I am supposed to be waiting for the good news elsewhere. Locating cigars. Fresh fruits. I am—

There was a blast, this one shaking the joists, and it was the blast, her body's reaction to it, which caused Nina's water to break. Elise took her hand and moved a candle and said, Let me look, Nina.

Nina was in tears, her body shaking with fatigue. She leaned back on her hands and Elise helped her to remove the soaking muumuu. Elise told Marko to find some sheets, and he went bounding up the steps, raising up the dust.

Stephen said, Have you done this before?

God no, Elise said. But I saw my mother once. In a department store.

Oh.

I was nine.

Well then—

Elise gave Stephen Nina's muumuu, which he draped over a low-slung beam to provide a partial screen. He watched Elise and Nina in the shadows behind the fabric.

Everything, he thought. Everything comes down to light.

There was another contraction, and Elise called to him—She's opening! Big! I can feel the baby's head!

Stephen said, I'm going for the doctor. Just wait, he said, taking the stairs two at a time. He skipped the sidewalk and skidded on his heels and the seat of his shorts down the dirt and scree of the hillside to the street. The hotel was a hundred meters. Two? God's truth, he had no idea what a meter even was. He ran now, fast, hugging the embankment. The city was burning, the air full of smoke, and a water truck roared past him, its lights off, nearly killing him for not having seen a whit—the truck shaking the street as it rushed into the flames of the burning city. The air was thick with smoke and then another shell burst on the street, taking out a small garage and the two cars, stacked one upon the other, inside. There was a car on the street also in flames, and Stephen watched the water truck swerve around the flames, clipping the tail of the car, sending the car skidding off to the side as the truck descended into the city on fire.

Oh fuck, he said, running. If I die, forgive me for being bad. Fuck—

In the hotel lobby he looked for somebody, anybody, who might know what he was doing. He ran down the flights to the EC monitor's room, through the darkened corridors, leaping over women and their children gathered in the halls. No voices in the halls: the people there, waiting, terrified silent. He took more stairs in the dark. He sprinted down another hall and banged at a door until somebody from a neighboring room opened up.

The Doctor!

Huh?

Herr Doktor. Wo ist—

The man made as if he held a saw and drew it back and forth. He raised his eyebrows.

Yes, Stephen said. Yes!

The man pointed up.

What floor?

The man looked at him closely, then smiled. He made to drink.

Stephen ran back to the stairs. Flights, more flights up. He should have known to go to the bar first. The indoor bar was empty: he went to the terrace. He saw a table made up of several men. Bottles of whiskey, and somebody smoking a monstrous joint, the air funky with the smell of pot. And there was the doctor, passing the joint to his table partner.

Stephen insisted the doctor come.

The doctor said, When do start?

What?

The contraptions.

Half-hour. No. Forty-five minutes. Three-quarters of an hour. He said, Fuck, an hour, okay! Un hour. *Ein.*

Ahh, said the doctor, taking a drink. He looked at his watch, held up his hand. He held up five fingers, then six.

No, Stephen said, shaking his head. She's in agony. Extreme pain. Too much pain. Pain, he said. It's not supposed to be like this. He said, looking around, Can't anybody here speak fucking Greek?

Silence, and Stephen said, pointing to a man's head, Owww. He said, The head. The head!

Okay, okay. Okay. The head, very serious. Okay.

The doctor said, rising from the table and grabbing a bottle of Bushmills, We go to the head. Okay.

Don't you need a bag or something. Some pills? Medicine?

The doctor smiled and gazed at Stephen as if he were an idiot. He reached into his pocket and pulled out a Buck knife—the type with the brass handle, the four-inch locking blade.

He said, Knife okay. Okay?

They ran, albeit at a slower pace, the doctor stumbling along behind. Once the doctor paused to retch up some whiskey, it having collected in his belly and risen to his throat. The doctor, now refreshed, wiped his mouth and said, *Better. Okay,* and they went on. The hills above them were still afire, an oranged vision of hell—that furnace, slowly dying, as it rose up into the sky. The paradox of fire: the faster it burns, the more it consumes, the quicker it dies.

At the steps he could hear Nina screaming in agony.

He led the doctor through the darkened house. A window, despite the tape, had been blown out. In the cellar, Nina lay draped in a white sheet, crying—the pain lessening on the downhill slope. Lamaze-like, she puffed out her cheeks.

The doctor assumed the position. He took a drink.

The doctor said to Stephen, You?

No.

Ah ha, he said, gesturing to Marko. He pointed to the whiskey and then to Marko. Marko took the whiskey and poured a cupful down his throat.

Elise wiped Nina's forehead with a washcloth she had fashioned from the sheet.

Moon, the doctor said. He howled briefly like a wolf. Big moon. Loony.

Uh-huh.

He said, Baby something. Baby something something, and he twisted his head around.

The doctor said, See?

He gave up on Stephen entirely and spoke in pidgin Serbo-Croatian to Nina. Marko translated: The baby was reversed, twisted. Back labor. Very painful, not dangerous, okay? Great pain. The baby was on the baby's way.

Okay.

Okays all around.

Nina said, squeezing Elise's hand, Like my mother, and Nina screamed.

It's the moon, Nina said, later. The moon has speeded up the baby.

They waited through three more sets, the cellar smelling of blood and sweat and Irish whiskey. The good news, despite the pain, was that the baby appeared eager to get out. There was another mortar concussion. On the hilltops now, from huge speakers, a lunatic was blasting over the city a song by U2. Rock and roll. Everybody loved U2, even the baby: a contraction, with Nina screaming and Stephen rubbing hard as he could the small of Nina's back—he rubbed so hard his wrist began to ache, and as the contraction passed, the doctor told Marko to bring him the bottle. The doctor took the whiskey, had a drink, and pulled from his hip the knife with the locking blade.

American made, the doctor said, looking at Stephen. Very good.

Now the doctor lit a cigarette and took a fierce drag. Then another. He gave the cigarette to Stephen, who crushed it while the doctor poured whiskey over the knife blade and set the blade on fire. When the whiskey had burned off, the doctor said, winking, Too much pain.

The doctor said something to Marko, who said, Too small. She's too small!

The doctor made the episiotomy in a single, deft stroke—a flicker across the flesh, quick as turning on the lights. He said to Marko, displaying his thumb and index finger, A small cut. Very small. Then at the next contraction, Nina, exhausted, her body trembling: then Nina pushed, and wailed, and the doctor caught the baby in his hands. There was no call to spank. The doctor lifted the baby as Nina fell back on her pallet of counterfeit Hugo Boss leather jackets and U.S. army surplus sleeping bags and in a sweeping gesture—like a magician, like an act of God—he placed the baby in Nina's arms. Everybody was laughing now, laughing and crying, and now the doctor cleaned Nina up, waiting for the afterbirth, which came easily enough. In time the doctor gave the knife to Marko who in turn gave the knife to Stephen who in turn gave the knife to Elise who finally cut the cord. She wiped the blade clean on her shorts. She gave the doctor back his knife, she laughed and rubbed at her eyes with her fist.

A girl, Marko said, laughing. A girl!

More drinks. Even a taste, a thimbleful, for Nina—doctor's exclamations. Marko fetched some thread and the doctor sewed Nina up as if she were a button. Just a couple loops. He told Marko to find a warm blanket. Before the doctor left, Marko gave to the doctor a fine counterfeit Hugo Boss leather jacket, which the doctor put on, there at the spot, beaming, and then Stephen led the doctor through the house. On the way out, Stephen grabbed his camera, and now he escorted the doctor up the eerily quiet street—the shelling having ceased, the fires having burned their course—and he took the doctor safely home.

9

Nina and Marko named the girl Stephania Elise. Linked first by accident, they were now bound to this life. Stephen thought, Joy, too, is a thing to have and to hold. At breakfast, having swept up the shattered glass, and with Nina resting, the baby tucked into the bottom drawer of their dresser, asleep on a pile of Bruce Hornsby & The Range, Marko said, Now I will take the leadership. It is my place.

Marko said, First we baptize Stephania Elise. He let his mouth linger over the name. Stephania Elise, he repeated. Next we leave. Today. No more fuckings around.

Okay, Stephen said. High time.

Stephen went into the city to the cathedral to locate the favorite priest. The damage, harrowing while taking place, had been fairly minor. He passed a crew of men securing the scaffolding around the clock tower. He sought out the young girl and her mother at the fountain, and he said to the mother, speaking in German, badly—Do you want to leave? Today?

Yes, said the woman, her face lighting up. She broke into tears once she understood it might be possible. He went with her to the basement of a museum and waited while she gathered their belongings: that knapsack which held, among other things, the family Bible; a transistor radio bearing the Zenith brand, circa 1968; a Sony Walkman and a box of photographs. Then Stephen brought them to Nina and Marko's house, and as they entered, Marko said, What is this?

They have family up north, Stephen said. Here they have nobody.

They have you. They have the cocksucking pussy-ass UN.

But I'm leaving, Marko. Stephen said, Marko, we have the room.

We'll make the room, Nina said. She said, sitting up on the couch, Marko, you will make the room.

The baby needed to be baptized, Marko explained, before they went on the water. On the water, Marko explained, they might get bombed out of the sea.

The girl and the mother stood bravely. The mother said, If there is no room—

Oh fuck there is the room, Marko said. He said something to the woman, and laughed, and then everybody laughed.

When the priest arrived, several drinks were in order first. The actual christening, some of which Stephen understood, took less than two minutes—God, apparently, would abide a rush. At one moment Stephen and Elise swore in the name of God in a language neither understood to watch over the baby, Stephania Elise, and apparently they also renounced Evil, and then the priest opened up a bottle of consecrated Evian and made with the water on the baby's forehead the sign of the cross. One catholic and apostolic church, Stephen thought. *Our bounden duty.* They had a final drink with the priest, thus polishing off the Bushmills, and they had some cheese, and the priest left the house with a new pair of imitation Nike sneakers and several bags of rice.

Marko had made arrangements for a family to stay in the small house to prevent it from being looted. An hour before dark, he left to bring the fast boat around to the landing behind the House of Scheherazade, where Nina and the baby and Elise and the mother and the young daughter and Stephen stood quietly waiting. It was a snug fit, even without a lot of luggage. Marko had to rearrange on the bow two cases of batik silks he was to deliver for a friend. Nina had the baby slung across her chest in an orange sling, decorated with dolphins, and she boarded the boat unsteadily while Marko stood at the wheel, a pair of binoculars to his eyes, waiting, and now he told Stephen to clear the line.

We stay near the coast, Marko said. In the shadows from the moon. Fucks their radar. It will be slow this way. He said, But going out is not so dangerous as coming in. Nobody takes weapons *out.*

Stephen and Elise took their places at the bow. The girl and her mother stood at the stern, overlooking the wake from the thrumming inboards. Marko motored out, as quietly as the powerful engines permitted, and as the dark came, Nina sitting by her husband's side, and Marko standing ... Marko drew the boat further away from the coast, the shoals and the rocks, and slowly increased his speed. The sky darkened and filled with stars, despite the moon, an entire galaxy's worth, and the bow rose slowly to greet the dark.

They made the journey to Split without incident, swiftly and in slightly due course—through the Korčula Channel, then back around the lip of Hvar, then the island of Brač. They followed the light of the moon all the way to Split. Behind him, beside the heady droning of the inboards—behind him the girl and her mother were holding onto each other. He felt the breeze in his hair. He looked at the sky. Before, after he had safely delivered the doctor home, before the sun had just begun to consider rising, Stephen had climbed into the hills overlooking the city. He had climbed into the hills, camera in hand, the shelling having abated, in order to gain perspective—that which the human eye requires most to understand its place. He arrived at a hilltop still smoldering from the fires caused by the shells. The shells, he understood, belonged to the sea. The shells belonged to the sea with the fish and the mussels, with the eons of dead buried therein and with the living skimming across the surface, like boats. So believing, he looked around him at the gnarled blackened trunks of the once magnificent trees . . . *Dubrava,* forest of oaks . . . smoldering in the hot, blackened earth. Across the shoulder of the hilltop a hungover Bosnian Serb watched over him, and there, behind a rock, Stephen came across a sapling which had escaped the blaze. Then Stephen made a thanksgiving prayer for the safe arrival of the baby, and he prayed to God to watch over this new life more carefully than he had watched over Stephen's own son. Far above him a hawk circled into the hot currents above the city; he heard, as if from a great distance, a gasoline-powered generator being fired up. The king, wanting not what was his, saw what he loved most destroyed by his own hand. It was the wanting which displaced most, wasn't it? And the Lord God formed Man out of the dust of the ground. Dust to dust, there on your own hands, and Stephen rose and wiped the blackened soil and ash from his hands while above him the Bosnian Serb stood watching and the hawk circled on a thermal, overhead, each waiting to see what he would do, next, and then Stephen held the camera to his eye and photographed the bitter landscape.

A photographer, he told himself, exists by way of the photographs he makes. Now you see him, now you don't. But he is always, always there.

Everything is made—a body, a photograph, an image of the sky. To see the made thing is to know the maker does exist. On a fast boat somewhere in the Adriatic, sitting on the bow beside this woman, Elise, the wind in his hair, he gazed up at the sky. He raised his knees and wrapped his arms around his knees to fight the cold. He felt the waves breaking at the hull. He felt the boat cresting the seas, and he gazed up at the sky, at the very firmament of being, and he listened to the baby cry.

10

People would say to him you should talk about it. When somebody asked him about it, he would say, What time is it? And then he would say, I have to go. People, they wanted to know what happened, as if knowing what had happened would change what had. As if their knowing could possibly stop the clock and fill the silence and the empty shoes in his son's empty room. As if their knowing might lift his kite back up into the sky, or fill the air with the sound of his voice. What happened was this: the sun was shining. There were sparrows in the air, like clouds, and the plaza was filled with people from all over the world celebrating Christmas. It was crowded and he was looking away, not toward. When you lose a child in a store, say, or at the airport, you think, I wonder if he's lost? Then you feel self-conscious, calling out your son's name, thinking everybody watching you knows you are a careless parent. Then the self-consciousness passes into panic, to match the racing of the heartbeat, and you call out your son's name and the people around you, even in a foreign country, they begin to catch on: they open up their eyes, they look all around, if only to indicate they do not have what you've misplaced. Your son. Then when you find your son, your little girl, people gaze at you smugly and you fall onto your knees and simultaneously scold and hug this blessedly returned creature. You could have been snatched, you say, you could have been lost in Toys. It's the could-have-beens which make you understand anything is possible. Why don't you talk about it? Why don't you try to explain? the people meant. To learn from your mistakes? This is what they also did: they took long rides on the train, the El train, looking at the city lights. They walked on Special Nights with Dad in the cold Chicago night to the corner market for a treat. They looked for birds and squirrels at the park and gave them names: Big Fella, Furry, Hurry and Scurry. What did they want to know? They kicked the soccer ball around. What happened was he turned away and back again in a foreign city. They wrote a letter to Mr. S. Claus explaining this year they would be in Rome. First he turned away, then back, and the market was filled with colors: Christmas colors: red and green, green and red, and then a policeman arrived wearing a white belt. Then another. Sometimes they practiced counting stairs or cars on the street. They called R at the hotel, who arrived, her hair wet from the bath because sometime between when their son had last been seen and when he had last been not she had been in the bath. The police, optimistic, gave them coffee in a station and there were phone calls, and the taking of a description, and then they went back that evening to the piazza amid all the Christmas booths and the booths closed up for Christmas and the people filed out and Stephen and R sat on a cold stone bench in the middle of the plaza listening to water falling in the fountain. This, the great baptismal font of loss: R, her head in her hands; Stephen, his head up, looking in the dark, as if through dark water. Sometimes they made up stories to describe the symphonies: the sorrowful cellos, the friendly flutes. What happened was this: something essential to the making of their lives had been removed, and the darkness of the sky mingled with the lights of the city, and then it began to rain while they waited in the dark. That night. Then the next, and the next after that. On the third day, and having broken several bones in her hands, beating her hands against the marble walls of their hotel, R was given tranquilizers which failed to kill the pain. She sobbed in the dark room of their hotel while Stephen sat silently by the open window.

What happened? she cried in the dark.

Oh God, Stephen. What have we done?

Nocturnes

The Top Ten Wonders of the World:

All manufactured optics, including spectacles and contact lenses and especially the increasingly rare Contax II rangefinder with a Zeiss Sonnar 50-millimeter 1.5 lens.

The carburetor, the train, the act of locomotion.

An automatic, self-winding watch.

A piano, a metronome. Or the *Pietá*.

Moore's Law and the grains of sand which enforce it.

A wineglass or comb.

The art of the locksmith: key, tumbler, hasp.

Antibiotics (and the condom).

A mast, a shovel, indoor plumbing, & electricity.

The Gateway Arch in St. Louis; the Pantheon in Rome; the Taj Mahal; The Autobahn and the Panama Canal and the Hoover Dam; the Brooklyn Bridge. Also the Sears Tower, which started out as a catalog.

—

On Insomnia:

It keeps him up at night.

It's also useful for making observations in the dark.

Exercise, he knows, is the best thing for sleep. The mind requires exercise lest it fall asleep. The body requires exercise lest it not.

A fine tapestry, like a disintegrating marriage, is filled with thousands and thousands of knots.

—

A Brief History of Creation:

Adam, to the lovely Eve, who does not yet need to shave her legs, she's so brand-new:
Lie down with dogs, get up with fibs.
Eve's reply:
Which guys did you name Dog?
Adam, cocking one hip to show off the length of this new penis, and pointing to the sky:
There. See? It flies.
Eve's reply:
Bird, I think. It's more jazzy.

—

On Travel:

Everybody takes it far too lightly. In the old days one sailed across the water and tried not to sink. In the new days one flies across the heavens, often unnecessarily, with people who do not fit well into their seats.

It does not comfort Stephen to know that aircraft blankets, which typically warm him on cold transatlantic flights, are Flame-Retardant.

—

On Grief:

The Psalms of David are helpful.

Grief at least is sweeter than Despair. Rage, far worse, is driven by Shame.

Human nature is not at issue. What is at issue is the ability—desire?—of men and women to restrain that nature.

Grief is preferable to Despair if one has somebody who understands the agent and the consequences of that Grief.

If one does not have so understanding a partner—or if both are grieving simultaneously—they become, Grief and Despair, one and the same.

No light without fire; no smoke without ash; no fire without material with which to commingle and burn. Here beginneth the lesson.

—

On America's Favorite Artist, Tiffany:

She's certainly not a lamp.
Nor a windowpane.
A trick: any photographer will shoot through a windowpane.
Pane/Pain: it's a rule.

—

On Terror:

Like Electricity, like Power, it is a dangerous thing. When it strikes, it strikes always from the sky. It makes the genitals hot.
Why do Men rape Women? Because they can.

—

On the Road to Hell:

The Road to Hell is paved with good intentions and laced with mines. That's mine. No, that's mine. Mine mine mine.

When one steps on a mine, and when one is lucky, the mine takes only the leg which permitted the foot to step on the road paved with good intentions. What one might otherwise call a *Wrong Turn*.

In a minefield, it is always difficult to turn back, especially if one's leg has been blown to smithereens.

The lead singer of a popular band is a man who sometimes rents a house in the city of Chicago. Stephen met him once at a political party fundraiser. After a moment, and after realizing Stephen was not a celebrity, the coked-up rock star turned his back and rejoined the party.

Democracy in action always forms first a committee by which to act.

—

On Solicitation:

He doesn't mind the more traditional sort, wherein one person typically leases a right of passage to his or her body.

What he cannot abide is the latest permutation: the dreaded Telephone Solicitor. Consequently Stephen never answers the telephone. The Telephone Solicitor never leaves a message. For a while there was a lot of ringing until Stephen turned the ringer off.

You're it, he used to say, playing tag.

The Prostitute, naturally, uses the body. The Telephone Solicitor— like Milton's Lucifer, whispering to Eve—relies strictly upon the ear. Other professions which rely heavily on the physical and material nature of the body?

Physicians, Athletes, Ballerinas, Bricklayers and Other Common Laborers. Soldiers, who are trained to kill it.

Once, at a grocery store, Stephen watched—and listened to—a Call Girl in front of the milk schedule an appointment.

Around the world, five hundred, said the girl, who had flame-red hair, picking up her milk. A grand for the night.

Am not—

—

The Catechism of Stephen Brings:

One sees through a glass darkly by way of optical lenses now orbiting in space. The darkness, of course, is the space—the space broadcast between that which is perceived and that which is revealed.

Divine Intervention, like the Old Forms of God, has become a thing destroyed by the Wickedness of Man and the Wonders of Modern Technology. After Darwin, after Freud and Jung, after the splitting of the Atom, after Elvis and the Discovery of the Human Genome, God is no longer the presiding moral authority. With knowledge comes responsibility. Free will is meaningless unless one is willing to exercise it.

Stephen believes to have faith in humanity is also to have faith in God. God did not make Adam in his own image. Adam made God. Adam made God in order not to be so lonely.

At the time it must have seemed a bold discovery—like art, like fire, or the rib cage and the vital organs it protects. Like song. Life from Life, the song goes. One God from one God.

In Stephen's mind God exists so long as Life exists. Consequently, Stephen believes in God because he believes in Life. He believes in the necessity for the absolute and fundamental Forgiveness of Sins.

If God can do anything, can God make a rock so big he cannot lift it?

A tautological question. Frivolous.

If God can do anything, can he split an atom? Can he milk a goat? Can he return a lost boy to his mother and his father? Can he return to the some hundreds of millions of this past century alone their broken hearts repaired? Their hair, shaved off; their teeth, forcibly plucked—can he give that back? Can he make warm the hundreds of thousands of Siberian graves? Can he repair the hymen of Nanking? Can he, like any modern government, rewrite History?

Stephen loves God because Stephen loves his fellow men and women. Even Jesus got to go back home. Stephen loves God because, despite its agonies, what are the alternatives?

In this manner Stephen Brings is a God-fearing man.

Even Jesus, the Son of God, got to go back home.

—

On Kidnapping:

A kidnapped child is not a foundling, like Moses.

The tradition nonetheless goes back a ways. Pluto stole Persephone from Demeter, thus inventing winter. Cold, ice in the heart.

Satan stole Christ, but only for a few days. Just a little visit. God was lucky?

You make your own luck, some people say, usually those who no longer require it. Jack Welch, Rupert Murdoch, that type of guy.

Pick yourself up, Boy. Get on with it!

Lindbergh, that was a famous case. The Spirit of St. Louis and the poor immigrant accused, and consequently executed, and the baby who never came back home, anyway.

How does one ransom the disappeared?

—

The Red Cross:

In Phoenix, a Latina and her two young children were visiting a military air show. Her husband was stationed then on a carrier in the Adriatic. At the air show, the Blue Angels were on display.

There was a B-52 bomber, the wingspan of death, parked on the tarmac. You have to see it to believe it.

The woman's eldest child, a four-year-old boy, stared up at the giant wings and told his mother he had to go poop. The woman took the four-year-old boy to the row of Porta-Potties lined up like soldiers.

The woman set her new baby girl asleep in her car carrier in the shade of the Porta-Potty. She went inside with her son to help him go poop. She held onto him in the dark, foul-smelling latrine and assured him gently he would not fall in.

After wiping her son's bottom, after helping him to wiggle into his short green pants, they stepped into the white light of the Phoenix sun—holding hands, blinking, their free hands to their eyes.

The sleeping baby girl was gone.

The mother wept on television.

The son held onto his mother's hand and watched the Blue Angels in the distance. The jet engines made his ears hurt, and he became afraid, the sky ripping open like that, and nobody ever gave the baby back. The young boy's father was contacted on his carrier in the Adriatic by the Red Cross and granted an emergency leave.

Did you see my baby, the woman screamed. Did you see?

—

On Pornography:

It's there for all the world to see.

It's the smart bomb descending an Iraqi air shaft leading to a hospital or school. It's Colin Powell's very bloody road to Baghdad. It's the Live Chat and the Gentlemen's Clubs. Whack whack, whack.

It's the nightly news. If it bleeds, it leads. It's a rock star named Slash turning on a groupie. The semen on the abandoned torn skirt in the back of a cab. It's blood and teenagers—the lubricant of inner-city vice—straddling the cracks in the streets and the inside look at the celebrity home and the sexual histories of the members of the House made public.

A stockyard in Amarillo. A camp at Omarska.

By the late 1980s child pornography had virtually been eradicated. Then came the Internet and the world's collective need for porn booted-up and brought it back and children by the thousands all over the globe began to disappear. Even in Rome.

It's the snuff film and the slashed throat and the infant caught on tape.

All roads lead to Rome.

www.rome.org

/

/

—

On Adoption:

It's possible somebody bought Stephen's son. An infertile couple in London, or Paris. Millions and millions of lire.

That little boy, he's all mine.

Best-case scenario: a happy home filled with toys, possibly a nanny, or au pair. Weekend picnics on the moors or the coast of Normandy—ski trips to the Alps, though probably that would come later, after the boy had grown some.

The thief would have sold Stephen's son to another, who would have in turn sold the boy to either a pornographer or an adoption agency which—lawyers buttoned up inside, and being lawyers—would have arranged the paperwork to sell Stephen's son to a loving family with the means to bear the cost.

Price, in this case, would be no object.

One cannot ransom that which is priceless.

Perhaps Stephen's son was saved? Like this?

Like so many pennies cast upon a broken plate?

The Return

Scheherazade was called into the chambers of a bitter and black-hearted king. After the king was to have his way with her, he intended to kill her, as he had in fact killed so many dozens of other young women—former virgins, all, prior to their entry into his chambers. A chamber can be a bedroom, an ancillary working space off a judge's courtroom, a particular judicial body or prison cell, a casing for a shell fired from any number of firearms . . . it is a word, *chamber*—from the Greek *kamara,* for vault—fraught with the history of authority and confinement, intimacy and violence. Most likely Scheherazade had deep eyes, raven hair scented with oil, fine silk robes. Perhaps a gold chain adorned her slender waist, resting just so upon the curve of her golden hip. Possibly a golden ring pierced her navel—the nipple, say, or the ear.

Now it is day . . .

Stephen woke, bleary-eyed and thirsty on the chair. A buzzer, sounding and resounding. Where am I? he said, standing. He stood, the scarred muscle in his arm throbbing from the cold, and walked to the intercom. The clock over the kitchen sink read ten A.M. The morning after.

Yes?

Package for R. Metcalf.

Leave it—

Gotta sign.

There was static, that awkward moment when two voices are trying to speak at once through a single line. Stephen said, removing the throw which draped his shoulders, Hang on.

He rushed upstairs to put on a pair of khakis, a sweater. This being the day after his homecoming, and not before, R's clothes were all over the bedroom, the bed left unmade. Clutter. He slid into his old cowboy boots sans socks and came stumbling down the stairs. Her cereal bowl and the knife she had used to trim her breakfast banana were sitting on the ledge of the sink beside the darkening peel. Stephen took the stairs down and greeted the man at the door. The man was wearing the cheerful colors—purple and orange—of the express delivery man.

Stephen signed, and the man said, staring at the bruise above Stephen's eye, Where do ya want it?

He stepped out into the cold air which bit through his sweater. The man was pointing to a loaded skid wrapped in cellophane. The skid, it wouldn't fit through the door leading to the stairs, let alone the hallway leading to their flat.

Stephen said, What's that?

Beats me, R. You ordered it. Where do ya want it? Hey, think fast.

They put the skid in the carriage house behind the building, the first floor of which served as storage for residents and housed the common laundry. Stephen said, finding the key, opening the door, There. He pushed aside two bicycles, pinching the long cut on his hand, and rearranged some boxes. Then he and the delivery man used a hand truck and horsed inside the heavy skid.

The man left, and Stephen opened partially the cellophane: the skid was loaded with signs, thousands, each emblazoned with the logo USAAN—United States Abortion Action Network. Everywhere you went, somebody was manufacturing another acronym, and signs on which to paint it.

Stacked into the skid were thousands of wooden sticks.

This, Stephen thought, your PAC dollars at work.

He lit a morning cigarette and returned to the entrance of his building. He took in the icicled morning air, his sockless feet in his boots beginning to numb, and sat on his heels—his back to the brick wall. Across the street, the eldest Garcia boy had grown, and Stephen waved to him in the cold air, and the boy, wispy-bearded and tough-looking, broke into a broad-hearted smile and waved back. Years ago Stephen had given the boy an old Pentax K1000; they had gone to the park, and Stephen had instructed him on matters relating to film speed and aperture. Don't worry about the focus, Stephen had told the boy. Don't worry about the frame. First you figure out the clutch, then you learn to drive.

You back? called the boy, no longer a boy.

Yeah.

Cool, the boy called. Cool.

Ice, Stephen thought. He loved the way it was always possible to break. He stood, and shivered, and smoked and watched a cab pull to the curb. A woman stepped out in heels and a black, woolen overcoat. She had longer hair than he remembered and was evidently stoned. She stumbled to the entry, her heels clicking sloppily, not recognizing Stephen, giggling slightly. She gathered to her chest the coat to keep it from spilling open. Squinting in the cold light, she recognized Stephen and said, Oh, it's you. I forgot my contacts.

She stumbled beside him, their shoulders rubbing. The last he'd heard the girl was studying fashion design, though perhaps her career in dressmaking had led her elsewhere. He watched her stop on the landing and remove her heels, one at a time, fumbling with the straps. He watched the weight of her heavy, black coat shift in the light. There was dust streaming into the light of the landing. Now she faced the blank wall and opened her coat wide, her back to him, unfolding a pair of black and giant wings.

She said to Stephen, Wanna look?

It's early, Stephen said.

It's late, she said, closing her coat, turning to face him. She clutched the coat closed to her throat, though still one of her naked knees winked in the fragile light. She raised a finger to her lips and said, Shhh.

He waited for her to enter her flat and close the door; he crushed the butt of his cigarette against the tuckpointing; he read the address tag on the mailbox—*R. Metcalf & S. Brings.*

And beneath that, *Gulliver Metcalf-Brings.*

In the kitchen he cleaned up R's breakfast. She had left a note, saying things, reminding him of the gathering to be held in honor of his return. She asked him to pick up some items from the market—including condoms, for example. If he wanted to come by the office to say hello, she would like that. He tossed the note into the trash, which needed emptying—always—and poured himself a drink, which he took all at once, the bourbon burning his throat. He turned on the television to an all-news program: apparently, there was an important development in an important trial. He made a pot of coffee, and drank two tall glasses of water, and then the TV anchor interrupted the important trial for breaking news and a commercial.

When he thinks of Sarajevo, he thinks of the dark. It is cold, and dark, and in the dark nobody is warm. Except when the moon is full, the light on the snow in the mountains, the light is cold and insufficient. Sometimes, a woman is falling out a window; sometimes, the sky is full of thunder: artillery and rockets, and the light they make, God's own static, flashing in the dark night. Sometimes boys are rollerblading on the streets between overturned cars. Always nobody has enough to eat; nobody has enough to drink; always, in the cold and the dark, nobody has enough to give to those who do not have enough. Safely returned to his home, and standing alone in his kitchen, Stephen had a third glass of water. To chase the cold chill in his heart, he went upstairs to the medicine cabinet, located the Xanax, took a tablet, and broke it in half along the scored center with his thumbnail. He started a bath, returned to the kitchen, and poured himself another drink. It went down far more gracefully than the first. He felt his belly warming to the heat. Still, his hands were shaking, and he said out loud, knowing he was speaking only to himself, This is ridiculous.

His voice echoed hollowly off the tile. The body electric, it always shocks. He said, This is not about you. The war is not about you.

He said, pouring a half-drink, If you don't do something about this then you never will.

He filled a large mug with coffee, had the final drink, and turned off the fucking TV. He put on a CD of Beethoven's piano concertos and went upstairs to the bath, past the splintered dent in the door—a hideous argument, so many months ago, which he had finished off by hitting the door. His knuckles had bled, and he had been shamed for life—R, looking at him; she had looked at him blankly, at this wretched man he had become, and said, Well, I'm sure you feel better now, huh? I'm sure that solves it, Stephen. The next morning he called his dean and scheduled a leave for the forthcoming year and left the country. Now, having returned to it, he undressed to take a bath. To avoid looking at the door, he placed a towel over the splintered dent. He slipped into the hot water and lay back and looked through the dormer window across the rooftops of his city telling himself to let it go. *Let it go,* he told himself, and the water was hot, and soon he began to sweat. He closed his eyes and waited for the water to begin to cool.

He had last been home for five months, after leaving Dubrovnik, before going back to Munich, where he spent several days with Messinger and his family, and then going on to the capital of Croatia,

Zagreb, where Nina and Marko had made a new place for themselves and the baby. Nina stayed at home with the baby while Marko ran arms south to Dalmatia. They were rich now, richer than they ever dreamed, and Stephen took a photograph of the baby, Stephania Elise, which was marvelous on account of the baby's radiance—it belonged in a chapel, in a mosque, it belonged in every temple of the world—and he made several prints for Marko and Nina and then a print for himself and another for Elise, who went to Vienna, and then to her parents' home in Stuttgart. She'd be coming back to find him, she said. *This is not a letting go.* At the gate to her train, Elise kissed him on the mouth; she squeezed his hand, silently, and boarded her train. Then Stephen went to Italy, where he learned nothing he already did not know; he visited with a priest on a lone crusade against Internet child pornography—the Christians, they'd never had much luck with their crusades; he considered going back to Chicago, decided against, and went back to Zagreb to spend a nightmare waiting in lines at the Intercontinental listening to piped-in saxophone music by David Sanborn while gathering credentials involving faxes back and forth from his friend at the *Tribune.* Next there was another line with no music and more clerks and rubber stamps—clearing the way, or not—and then Stephen went to Sarajevo.

He stood in the tub, dried off his body with a harsh towel—Chicago, that hard-water town—and put on a pair of jeans he hadn't worn in years. He changed the bandage on his hand; he replaced the blade in his father's old razor and shaved closely, the way his father had once taught him to. The face in the mirror resembled his father's, as well the face his son had been in line to inherit. In the room which served as his and R's office, he went to his drafting table, where R had organized piles of mail, and on which was stacked a handful of large prints. The very print on top was of Elise, wearing a shirt open at the collar—sitting in the sun, facing the sea. This would be Split, where she had shorn her yellow hair in the fashion of a boy. Here she is looking into the eye of the lens: the eye of the world, the needle and the storm. She had needed a publicity photo, and just off center you can see the dimple in her cheek.

Beneath this print was one of the photographs from Biševo—Elise, before he knew her, having risen from the sea, standing alone in the sun. And beneath this the photograph of Messinger on the city walls. Then there were several of refugees in a gymnasium. There was the print of Stephania Elise. And beneath this, as if to footnote, there was a print of his son, Gulliver, striding into the frame, his fine hair in the breeze. He is in the center of St. Peter's Square in Rome. The hair is lit, as if with quicksilver, and it is Christmas Eve, 1989. Just after noon. Though he is only four, there is in the shadows of his small-boy face an intimation of the man he will become. He is willful and bright-eyed, and he is striding across the square on his own two feet.

Also on the desk: the letter Stephen asked Messinger to deliver, another from Sarajevo.

To deliver is also to invite the possibility for redemption? R, he knew, had orchestrated this particular arrangement of his desktop. He knew perfectly well he had left the prints along with several dozen others in a drawer. Wanting to see what he had, she'd been going through the prints, leaving her own along the edges. Also on the desktop, tucked between a dictionary and a lamp, R had arranged a packet of letters Stephen had written over the years, all neatly bound by a purple ribbon which had once dressed R's own auburn hair. And there, on the shelf beside copies of his books, stood a photograph of R, circa 1981, smiling coyly into the lens over a glass of beer. Even then, R was one never to bend.

I see you, she must have said, way back then. *There.*

Give, his father had taught him. *You must always, always give.*

2

Paradox, Stephen had taught his own son to say, so that he might come to recognize it early. His son, he had been four when he vanished, the age at which one begins to understand time moves in cycles. Christmas comes *next* year. Time, like the history of the world, like the living soul, moves in cycles. Four is the beginnings of empathy, the beginnings of compassion. It is the awakening of one's self. It is an awakening, but not yet an articulation.

He had wanted to name his son Thomas, after the Thomas of the Gnostic gospels, but R had voted against, thinking it would mark their child as doubtful. You know, she said. Doubting Thomas?

They followed the standard rules: no names after old lovers; no names invoking the personality of anybody either had ever found offensive. It was so much easier to name a child when one was young—say fifteen, or twelve. They ruled out, too, the environmental names: the Glenns and the Cliffs and the Dales. They ruled out the cities and the states: Georgia, Carolina, Madison and Saratoga. All of his life Stephen's friends had been named Mike; all R's life, her friends had been named Jennifer and Mike. They were countless, the Jennifers and the Mikes who populated the American countryside. And there were other considerations: nothing fakely Irish, the Declans and the Finns. Nothing overly British. Malcolm was excluded despite R's affection for Malcolm because it was built around *mal,* with obvious unpleasant etymological implications.

I know a nice guy named Malcolm, R had said.

It means bad, Stephen said. Mal. Bad. Malevolent. Malcontent. Malvolio, in *Twelfth Night*? You can't give a kid a name with bad at the very beginning of it. Talk about early tracking.

We could call him Rob, R said.

Yeah, great. After a thief. Stick 'em up.

For a while R had been smitten with Calvin until Stephen pointed out that while Cal was a sure-footed enough diminutive, Calvin meant "little bald one." And let's not address the theology, Stephen had said. The entire born-again pro-life movement is going to be patting you on the back.

Well, what then? R had said. Mr. Expert, what?

Names for boys were harder because there were fewer possibilities; in this manner, too, names for boys were easier. This Stephen called the Paradox of Naming. And then, while Stephen was busy inventing theories of names, R had an ultrasound which indicated as great a degree of perfection on the part of their forthcoming baby as anybody in the medical community living in a litigious age would admit to, and during which the ultrasound technician had exclaimed absentmindedly about that shadow of a thing there being a penis, and so that settled it: a baby with a penis was going to be a boy.

There was a sense of panic as the pregnancy passed. Get the name wrong, what kind of parent are you going to be? Toward the end, the conversations were becoming more testy, and they'd spend hours each night with the baby-naming books spread out across the bed. Typically they went back to the *L* name, Luke (which was out, always, on account of being tainted by two soap operas; Luke, which was otherwise a perfect name—having previously belonged to a saint, and meaning *light*), the *M* name, Maxwell (which reminded Stephen of

Maxwell Smart, of *Get Smart,* which was a Cold War comedy about spies who weren't particularly smart), and the fruitful and patriotic *J* names: Jake, Jason, Jesse and James.

Jonas? R had said.

Judas. Christ loved Judas more than anybody will admit.

R said, You can't name a baby after a traitor. Jesus!

Just thinking. I like James. You know. Good, kingly. Goes well with my name. Stephen, *crown.*

God no. No more monarchy. No no no.

Okay. Noah.

No Noahs. Everybody cool names their kid Noah.

Stephen said, Really?

R said, You should read more novels. Also big is Adam, for obvious reasons, and Sam. God, everybody is called Sam now. Or Garth.

Stephen said, Garth?

Uh-huh. Garth. Damn, Garth said quickly under his breath stubbing his toe. It was a dark and stormy night and Garth was feeling randy. Suddenly, Garth rolled over and poked his wife! Oh Garth. Garth, yes. Oh Garth! Yes yes, Oh Garth! Oh do me, Garth!

Stephen said, That's pretty good.

You think? I've been practicing. To show off.

G, Stephen said. Maybe there's a *G* we haven't thought of.

Gawain, R said. G-spot? R said, Are you sure?

We don't have to call him *G.*

She said, spelling it out, we could call him *G-E-E. Gee!* Like that!

He said, We might be rushing things a bit.

He has to be sensitive, R said, rubbing her abdomen. And kind. But not a wimp. No wimps. He can be gay or straight, I don't care, *really.* But he cannot be a wimp and he cannot have a name that makes him into a bully.

He's not going to be a bully.

If you name him Raymond he will be. Or Doug. Doug Doug Doug.

He's not going to be a wimp either. Not with you for a mother.

Praise, R said, looking up. I know you mean that as praise.

Gulliver, Stephen said. How about Gulliver?

There is a time when you know something is right. When you catch another's eye and know, in that moment, you are going to be friends for life with that person whose eye you've just caught. When you take a photograph, and despite the number of frames wasted thus far you know, you just know, this particular likeness is the one you came here for. That this is the image you want to take and keep.

They had to sit on it for several days to let the enthusiasm cool. To be certain. Once, while driving, R said, We can't let anybody call him Gully.

God no.

Three nights later, Stephen woke R in the middle of the night. Or Gull, Stephen said, shaking her. No Gulls. He is not a bird.

R said, rubbing the sleep from her eyes, You always shorten people's names. You call Sarah *Sar*. You call Christopher *Chris*. He hates that, by the way. What makes you think you're not going to call Gulliver *Gull*?

I guess it's not bad. Birds are good. They fly.

Gulliver Brings, R said, rolling over onto her pillow. It was hard to sleep, being pregnant. It was hard doing anything at all.

Gulliver Metcalf-Brings, she said, sleepily. I'll be glad when he comes out to play.

The day came. They had been on their way to a Cubs game—a special treat, what with R playing hooky from the office. A hot day in Chicago . . . the flats heated up, the asphalt on the streets grew soft and began to smell like tar. Gum on the streets, and sneakers, turned soft to the touch. The exhaust from the cars lingered a bit longer, and the traffic stalled, idling impatiently at the intersections, heating up the already stifling hot air. True, it was cooler by the lake. After the game, they were going to go to the lake. All was a go. Especially because she was pregnant, R liked to spend that summer walking barefoot in the foot of the lake. Then, while riding on the train, her water broke, and somebody had helped them to a cab, and the cabby, driving, said *No baby not here,* etcetera, driving through the stalled traffic, blasting his horn, bobbing in and out of all the pedestrians and hot dog venders and then, driving up onto the hospital launch pad— EMERGENCY—where there happened to be a television film crew filming like emergencies, Stephen helped R out and they rush-limped to their preassigned obstetric unit while all the way R continued to dilate.

She was going fast. There was no time for an epidural. R had some Stadol, which eased the pain but also made her catatonic, until a contraction came, and then she screamed, and Stephen did the counting thing: the *wuh wuh wuh* panting he had been taught like a good partner to pant, as if he were actually helping her out, which was ridiculous, what with the Stadol in her bloodstream and that proverbial ring of fire now in flames. You were supposed to hold when you pushed, which made no sense; you were supposed to look at the two little fingers he held up in front of her eyes. Good, good, he said, as if he had any idea. And all of their careful planning—the special birthing room with the hot tub, the bag of sundries including pictures of Stephen and R together at the beach, the Mozart CD which was supposed to raise their baby's IQ by thirty points, the granola bars and Perrier and the warm, blue socks—all of that had been left behind, by the coat tree, right by the door leading out. And now R panted in a dreadful smock: her doc, busy shopping, had called in another, who had the bedside manner of a horse. She kept clip-clopping on her heels in and out of the labor room, careful not to smudge her outfit. Thank God for the nurse, not the Bad Nurse who misplaced the IV, causing R's wrist to swell up the size of an orange, and then a grapefruit, but the *other* nurse, the Good Nurse with red hair who held R's hand and then her leg. She showed Stephen how to hold the other leg (this had not been a part of that partner-education curriculum!) and she showed him how to bend it back as if he were a wrestler intent on pinning her. Harder, the Good Nurse said. *She won't break.* And then the blood, all the blood: he'd seen blood, like when he cut his finger, but he'd never seen blood belonging to a woman that he loved spilling forth from the ring of fire. It was more crimson than anything he'd ever seen, so crimson there beneath the white lights of the hospital room filled with more lights and the machines beeping and a white plastic bucket which read *Sharps.* He could see and then smell the blood and then the baby's head, crowning, and R, screaming now, and then, whoosh, out slipped the baby's head and then his body into the nurse's arms and the well-dressed doc with the bedside manner of a horse clip-clopping into the room said, *You have a baby boy. Congratulations,* and then the Good Nurse slipped the baby to R's breast, right there, and there was that mewing sound of the newly born, and the well-dressed doc attended to the afterbirth and the final contractions necessary to deliver it. The well-dressed doc handed to Stephen a pair of shears, and she said, *Dad, want to cut the cord?* And Stephen said, *Here?* and she said, *Right there,* and he said, *Really? Here?* He had tears in his eyes and was uncertain of his vision. He said, *Here. Right here,* and then he did it, bringing the shears together, and he felt the flesh of that cord caught in the jaws of those metal shears, and then he said, not fainting, I am not going to faint.

Really, he said, swaying. I'm fine.

They cleaned the baby. They weighed him. He was small, just under six pounds, and measured against a point system which, tallied up, declared him to be average (B+/A–). If he didn't get into Andover, or Juilliard, there would always be the historical record to explain.

Stephen held R's hand. He said, his heart brimming, It begins now.

She said, Do you want to go out and smoke?

I'm going to have to quit.

Yup.

Soon, he said.

I know. You can go out now. Just come back. Soon.

So he went out and had a cigarette. On the way back, he stopped in the restroom to wash the poisonous nicotine from his hands. He rode an elevator with a man who was talking on a telephone the size of Maxwell Smart's shoe.

What's that? Yeah, said the guy on the horn. She had the baby. What's that? Nah, I can't complain—

Then Stephen had to go through the security stations to prove he wasn't stealing anybody's baby. He was given a tag, as if he were a record, or a leather jacket in a department store, and then another tag indicating he was the father to Baby Metcalf.

He thought, They got the name wrong.

He thought, They don't know we've already got a name for him?

When he returned to the room, R was in tears. The baby was gone.

What?

They said his heart wasn't going.

What?

His heart. It's not going right. They took him to ICU.

She was bereft, lying in the empty bed, spent. He rushed to the nurses' station and found the Good Nurse. A cardiologist was on the way in from the Cubs game; the tiny baby was on a table beneath a heat lamp. We can't circumcise him now, the Good Nurse said. One thing Stephen knew, the doc with the bedside manner of a horse wasn't going to be getting near his son's penis. In R's room he held her hand. They had to wait, just a little bit more, and R said, What if he dies?

He's not going to die. Babies don't die.

From another room, a woman was screaming, as if she were in fact dying, delivering another baby not supposed to die.

Stephen said, He is not going to die.

Two hours later, he went out for another smoke; there were others out there, smoking in the heat, one in a smock with his arm tied up to his IV. On the way back Stephen passed a man eating a submarine sandwich: this, the cardiologist. The cardiologist said, It may not be his heart. He's not getting enough oxygen through the blood. There was talk of blood and oxygen, a need to top off the baby's crankcase, the only real risks being those of hepatitis or HIV infection, please sign here, we have a fine blood supply these days, and later that night, six hours later, the blood having *finally* arrived in a plastic bag from someplace downstairs, or upstairs, and the Bad Nurse who had trouble with IVs having a heck of a time figuring out how the little gizmo attached to this other little gizmo—Stephen said, losing his temper in the ICU filled with preemies, Is there somebody here who knows how the fuck to do this properly?

The Bad Nurse began to cry, not wanting to be Bad. Another nurse, having taken his point, dismissed the Bad Nurse, and the blood was set up, and Stephen spent the night going back and forth between R's room and the baby's. Once, in R's room, she had said, How's Gulliver?

Naming a thing, it makes it so. Stephen said, The guy says he's going to be okay. He'll need antibiotics before he goes to the dentist. Go figure. Apparently it's just a little murmur. It'll keep him out of the army.

Gulliver, she said. I'm glad he won't be a soldier.

It's just a murmur, Stephen said. It means he's blessed. It means God put his finger there. Right there on his little heart.

He's not going to die.

No. He's not going to die. Stephen said, kissing R on the forehead, He's ours to keep.

And then R said, I want to hold him. I want to hold him right now.

And then the Good Nurse came in and helped R up and took her to the ICU where R nursed their baby. Even in the ICU all the other babies had pink or blue bears announcing their given names, celebrating their arrivals. R said, smiling weakly, Can Gulliver have a name, too? A bear?

Oh God yes, the Good Nurse said. Yes yes.

Gulliver, R said, nursing him. All my life I've wanted to do this.

Gulliver, Stephen said. Gulliver with the magic heart.

Thank you, R said to Stephen. Thank you for letting me do this.

3

Paradox, his son had said. Like when you stick your finger in your nose and get a booger? Like that?

A wave of panic sideswiped him now—No, he said, blinking fiercely, leaning against the sink. *God no*—and when it passed, miraculously, he drank a tall glass of water. The key to riding this out wasn't more substances, but less. A fundamental and willfully engaged act of withdrawal.

He put on a pair of socks, laced up his hiking boots. He stood before the kitchen sink and poured himself a shot of bourbon. Killing time was not necessarily the same as killing oneself. He took the bottle and poured it down the drain.

He went out to the alley, across and down to the neighborhood market, larger than he remembered, and where he bought a pint of skim milk which he drank on the spot. From there he went to a gas station. Like the market, it was a family-owned business; the kid working knew Stephen and loaned him a jerry can. Stephen bought a battery; five quarts of oil, a filter; a gallon of antifreeze; a pack of chewing gum and condoms from the impulse rack. The boy's father drove Stephen back to the alley, past the train trestle, to the garage which Stephen rented. The garage was cold and filled with items packed in boxes ready to be shipped anywhere. For years Stephen had been living his life in a state of perpetual storage—ready, at any moment's notice, to depart for someplace else. Inside, he rubbed his hands together. He turned on the lights and removed the tarp which covered his father's—now Stephen's—sedan.

He had run the tank empty before leaving to keep the fuel from gumming up the injectors. He had also drained the oil, and now, first, he opened a quart and ran a thin coat of film around the gasket of the new filter; he placed the new filter on, spinning it gently. He liked doing this kind of work; he added the oil. He put the dead battery in the trunk and installed the new one. He primed the engine and fired it up. The car, being well cared for, and despite its previous hundred thousand miles, idled sweetly. His one chief extravagance, this finicky car, which he had hoped to pass on to his son. Being in the genes, boys like cars. He let the engine idle and watched the blue-white exhaust billow out into the darkening afternoon light.

He ran more errands now that he had official transport. He drove to the grocery store, also larger than he remembered. America, Land of the Good and Plenty. At the butcher's counter he bought two New York strips and then he went to produce and bought carrots and romaine lettuce and salad dressing, the profits of which went to charity, and mushrooms to sauté for the steaks, and fruit: bananas, apples, kiwis and grapes. The Fruit Santa, that's what Elise called him. When he finally returned home he parked on the street and unloaded three trips' worth of groceries. In the kitchen he folded the paper bags and put away the perishables. He placed the fruit in a bowl, separating the bananas, because a banana in contact with other fruit would cause that other fruit to spoil.

Presto, he said aloud. A symbol.

He drank two large glasses of water and regretted having disposed of the bourbon but congratulated himself for holding firm. Have a chocolate kiss instead. He called R to explain he wouldn't be coming by the office but that he'd be cooking dinner. He took a breath and went up to his desk and attacked blindly the stacks of mail.

R had also left a note, indicating she required several thousand dollars, his share of the rent. No rush on this, she said.

He noticed, not for the first time, that everybody had his name on a list: the DNC, Smith Barney and the Softer Side of Sears, Toys-R-Us. Even the Sierra Club sent him junk mail. What was that? He attached his return address labels—R. Metcalf & S. Brings—to his bills. Having signed his checks, he licked his stamps.

A man who pays his debts is a man who's free to travel. He stood, stretching the small of his back. He went to the bathroom sink, removed the Xanax, and broke another tablet in half. He held both halves in his bandaged hand.

Fuck it, he said, and flushed the Xanax, all of it.

Just say no.

That's that, he said. And then he shuddered through a fierce but mercifully brief wave of anxiety.

He did fifty push-ups.

A wave, once it hit, would eventually recede, just as certainly as another would return. They came, the waves, in sets.

He brushed his teeth. The trick was being clean. Water.

He drank three glasses of water and took a long and thunderous leak.

He did another fifty push-ups and went downstairs to cook.

4

R arrived home two hours late with snow in her hair. He had kept her dinner warm for her. While she ate, R told him about her day, and he listened meaningfully. She stood once, went to the fridge and offered him a beer, which he declined, and she said, Not just one? Why not *one*?

Because sometimes I don't want *one*.

I guess.

He said, Let's make a list—

What kind of list?

Books. Ten Books. You're on an island, or going to be, stranded. A pretty one. You have fresh water and coconuts. You get ten books—

Am I alone?

Maybe, maybe not. That's part of it. You don't know.

Do other people get books?

Yes. But you don't know if you're alone or not when you make your list.

This is stupid, she said, pushing away her plate.

He stood, removed the plate. He brought back a glass of sparkling water for himself and a pen and a pad of paper.

You get ten, he said. What else do we have to talk about? You get ten books. One sex book. One art book. A book of poems, maybe. Maybe an American novel to be patriotic. But it's your list. Whatever you want—

If you pick the books then I don't need to, do I? You do this a lot? Sit around in hotel bars and make lists of books?

Just try it. Ten Books. What do you want?

TV Guide, she said. To see what's on.

Jesus—

No. Okay. Ten Books? What is this, a quiz? A test?

Isn't everything?

Okay. Fine. Give me the pen.

She reached across, took the pen and paper.

He blinked through a wave of panic. He said, hopeful to distract himself, I left a check for you on your desk. The rent.

Don't bother me, she said. I have to study.

He cleaned the kitchen. It was a small kitchen and then, thank God, the jet lag kicked in, and he felt a sudden and profoundly uncommon need to sleep, and he knew this window of opportunity would last at best twenty minutes, and so he said, R, I can sleep now, so I'm going to sleep, and she said, not looking up from her pad of paper, scratching out a line, Uh-huh, and he went upstairs, undressing along the way, and went to bed.

He awoke three hours later—to the sound of his own voice—from a freakish dream: R was going down on him on top of the deck of a ship. It was snowing, and people in Bermuda shorts and golf shoes with spikes were pacing the deck—waiting for the sun, swinging their clubs. We paid for this? somebody yelled. And then, in the dream, R lifted her head and smiled to show him how she clenched between her teeth a double-edged razor blade. She removed the razor from her teeth and, holding his penis at the base, slicing open his testicles at the seam, said she knew he would taste better this way.

She said, You get what you pay for, Stephen. You're the one who signed on—

He had cried out, waking, hitting his bandaged hand against the wall.

In the morning while dressing for work R paused to go down on him, and he felt the silken brush of her hair against his thighs, and he woke a second time, now feeling obligated, and terribly in the wrong, and said, Where am I?

Just lie back, Mister.

No, he said, sitting up. Please.

In the kitchen, dressed for work, she sat finishing her cereal and juice. She watched him as he descended the stairs draped in the blanket from the bed. A purple blanket, R's color. She said, watching him, I know her name is Elise.

He said, You know?

I wasn't snooping, she said. It's in your wallet. I was looking for an address but of course your address book is indecipherable. Pages everywhere.

Elise, she said, and lots of phone numbers. You don't pay attention to anybody's phone number. You can barely make a long-distance call! She said, She's the girl in the photographs. The pretty one. You know, the *naked* one?

He poured himself coffee. He said, Did you find what you want? Did you?

He drank a glass of water, fast. Another day, he told himself. Another day in which nobody could be happy.

Another day, he told himself, and you'll be clean.

He wanted to be clean.

R said, Do you love her?

What? he said, sitting down. He said, I don't really think she's the issue.

Elise, R said, nodding. She even has a pretty name.

She does.

So it is her. The friend in Baden Blitzitburg? That *is* her?

Yes.

When did she cut her hair? Before, or did she cut her hair *after*?

Stephen said, I think we have larger complications.

You mean Adam.

Is he in love with you? Again? And no, actually I mean Gulliver. I mean you and I mean me. But what the hell, yeah, let's throw Adam into the pot, too.

R nodded. Okay, she said, biting her lip. You're not in love with me.

I've known you longer—better—than I've known anybody.

You love me, R said. Jesus, Stephen. I'm not stupid. But you're not *in* love with me. The only time you ever fuck me is when you say good-bye. You don't even want to *kiss* me. You're bored with everything I tell you about that I happen to spend my life doing. And God knows you certainly don't want to *live* with me. With *me*, Stephen.

She said, rising from the table, It's like you don't even live here. Like I'm some kind of port of call. Even before. Even then, you and your need for solitude. Don't bother Stephen, he needs to think. He needs to read. He needs to be alone. Stephen needs and Stephen needs. She said, hitching her breath, And let's not kid ourselves: it's not as if you were a decent father. I mean it's not as if I want to have another kid with you. Thank God we didn't have any spares.

He said, picking at the bandage on his hand, You have more?

She said, wiping her nose, Damn you. Damn you. Goddamn you. People think—We're having a party. For you. Everybody at work thinks we're having a honeymoon and you won't even let me give you a blow job. She said, rising, I'm late for work, and then she said, pushing him a folded piece of paper shaped into the size of a quarter, Here's your Goddamn list.

She stood at the coat tree making her selection, a bright red wool overcoat. She said, turning, I didn't leave you in case you didn't want me to leave you. But you ought to give me a sign, you know? You ought to say, Tell Adam to get fucked and move to LA. And you ought to say that because Adam is also not the issue. You know when I touch you that you actually flinch? We have larger complications, you and your sanctimonious, supercilious—

Look at me, Stephen. I did not leave you because I did not want to leave you. And it's not just about you. It's about all of us. It's about admitting defeat. Giving up? Goddamn it, Stephen, I do not just give up. And that's why you love me. You think I'm a political hack, you think I don't read the right books, okay. Fine. But I do not give up and that's what brought us together, you and me. We do not give up. So if we're going to smash this history of ours into smithereens then we'd better find a way to talk about it. You're good at that. Do some thinking, Stephen. Get to work, okay? Because Goddamn it I did not leave you because I did not want to leave you.

And then she tucked her scarf around her thick hair, wiped her eyes with the back of her hands, and left for work.

5

What's your name?

At least one always has the possibility of returning home, if only for a visit to say good-bye. He wanted to see his home. He bundled up: gray union suit, thick khakis, socks, a maroon wool turtleneck. He rooted through a box in a closet beside Gulliver's blue and yellow perfect trike until he found their skates. A dog, lost, could travel hundreds of miles and still find its way home: its internal sextant leading the way, this way and that: every three or four years there was another dog movie about the lost dog finding its way home. Gulliver had wanted a dog. He always wanted a dog. There were stories about the dog which stayed with a boy lost in the woods. Stories about the dog which pulled boys from icy ponds. Stories about the dog sleeping with the lost boy in the deep snow to keep the boy warm and alive.

Stephen located his wallet, his keys, and headed out with his skates. The Chicago sky, cold and sharp, hovered overhead like the flat of a knife. On the highway, past O'Hare, the planes in the sky lined up for permission to land; beyond that intersection the traffic began to clear. The metropolis, like a middle-aged man, had begun to spread at the hips. A sign of the times. He passed the obscene mall—Woodfield—where once, when it was new, his father had taken him to see John Wayne in *The Cowboys*. All acts have their antecedents. Stephen had cried when John Wayne died, he remembered that. After the movie, driving home in the dark night, his father had explained that Bad Men—criminals, like those who stole the herd and shot John Wayne—men such as these were always afraid of Good Men who followed their convictions. Evil cannot abide Goodness in Men, his father had explained, and Stephen could not follow what came next. Perhaps he leaned his head against the cool glass of his father's car and fell asleep. He was eight, he knew that, or seven. He was just a boy.

He turned off onto Route 59 and encountered a startling array of McMansions—obese houses on tiny plots, cramped like bloated bodies in a common grave. The secret to being happy in America was understanding nothing was supposed to last: not the woods this subdivision had razed, not the houses with granite trim and chrome refrigerators powered by enough electricity to run a turbine. He followed the curving highway and drove into the town of Barrington, dawdling momentarily in the off streets. The stone bank, that former pillar of suburban privilege and stability, had been turned into something else, and soon he was recognizing other places he had visited as a child. Moving on, he saw the horse farm where he had mucked stalls—its rolling whitewashed fences and meticulously groomed paddocks; he saw the large white farmhouse his best friend in the fifth and sixth grades had lived in. A woody, his friend had instructed, was a more mature way of acknowledging one's hard-on. Much better than, say, boner. Anybody could say *hard-on*. Stephen said these words now, driving through his childhood: boner, hard-on, love muscle. It was like being thirteen all over again, and he caught himself beaming into the rearview mirror.

Elise, he said to himself. She *did* have a pretty name.

A man who makes is a joyful man. The road leading to his neighborhood had been gated off to accommodate the newly rich. He did a U-turn, his tires spitting, and returned by way of an alternate route to his old neighborhood, Timberlake. Here, too, had once been timber. It was a quiet neighborhood filled with woods and sloping lawns. Here people had let their children and their dogs run free; they gathered in the summers at the common lake and the girls wore their seventies bikinis and the boys hid their woodies by digging in the sand. They sailed Sunfish on the lake and at night teenagers collected there to drink beer safely—they'd blow some grass, too—in their tight Levi's and long hair and leather bracelets: Dylan on the 8-track, or Elton John. The house in which his father had raised him was for sale. It was a Frank Lloyd Wright–inspired house built into the hillside: long decks, walls of glass. There stood a lamppost at the wooded end of the drive which had involved the digging of a hundred-yard trench to bring it power. One girl, Diane Eckendal—blond, buxom—would wear a white bikini to the lake. On the top was a place with a red heart, which Diane Eckendal had cut out, leaving a faint thread of red material and the shape of a heart which tanned in the sun as the summer passed. When she emerged from the lake her bikini became translucent. You could see the flesh—heart-shaped—and her blond, wet hair, even there, which also formed the shape of a heart. *Memory knows*, Faulkner wrote, *before knowing remembers*. Most likely he was drunk, writing that. Idling in front of the driveway leading to his old house, taking in the lamppost in the woods, Stephen understood he didn't know anybody who lived here.

The girl with the summer-tanned heart, did she grow up and move away, too? At the lake he parked behind some rail ties. He walked down to the surface and sat on the snow to lace his skates. His arm throbbed in the cold, a quarter-step behind his heart, and his fingers numbed—a matter of warming up. He cupped his hands and brought them to his mouth. A puff of steam.

Hockey is a game for boys—that balletic chaos of sticks and pucks and flying wings. The ice, thick and gray, a steel door sealing off that which lay beneath: he was startled momentarily by the tensile brittleness of its surface. He stretched, he blew on his hands, his breath steaming: he took off, toward the other side, dotted with houses and frozen lawns covered in snow and docks locked into place by the ice. There was a young dog—lab variety—snuffling alone on the ice. Stephen's thighs, swelling with blood, like his heart, carried him along the surface of the frozen lake. He blew snot from his nose, one side at a time, cowboy style, and felt the wind chafing at his cheeks, and he skated hard, and fast, working up a fine lather, sweating out the toxins he'd been ingesting: the pharmacological products, the whiskey and the false comfort of nicotine. He felt his first wind go, his second catch up with him, and he felt his eyes tearing in the breeze beneath the sky and then he stopped: hips cocked, gouging his blades into the ice and casting a spray of slivers into the air. Like stars, when light-headed; like diamonds full of light.

This, he told himself. This was what made one capable of being.

It was underrated, joy—like delight, and expertise in something. In anything. One did not always have to be sad, to withdraw, that's what R always said, and believed, wanting Stephen not to be sad. She had a point. She had a lot of points, and he spread out his arms into the falling sky, and laughed, the endorphins kicking in, and he skipped off onto the surface and pivoted, skating backward, and pretended that he, Stephen Brings, was now in possession of the puck, and that he, Stephen Brings, was setting it up. Skating backward, admiring the signature his tracks made in the ice, he felt good, really good, and capable of making great speed.

Jesus, he told himself. Take it.

He said, seeing the sentence coming—a man cannot speak a sentence knowing what it means until he's finished making it—he said, making the next sentence, *You're going to leave her.*

Then he made another.

It's not your fault.

Then another.

And it's not her fault, either.

He said, having found his meaning, *Where to now, St. Peter?*

He paused, gliding, looking back over his shoulder, the same direction he was traveling. Once, a long time ago, in another life, he knew people—and their names—who lived in these houses along the lake. He had spent days digging that trench by himself, but it never had belonged to him. The lamppost. He swiveled, facing the direction he was now skating into, wide-eyed, letting his eyes tear in the wind, his breath steaming, and as he headed back across the long lake he saw the dog—a dog like anybody's—and he watched first and then heard the dog yelp and scamper terrified across the surface of the ice.

Two boys with a rifle, standing on the bank in puffy, goose-down jackets.

Come on, Ginger! called the smaller boy.

And then the larger boy raised the rifle and Stephen, closer now, made out the puff of smoke and the pneumatic thunk of an air rifle firing off a pellet.

Ginger, yelled the other. Come on!

The boy put into the snow the rifle barrel in order to pump it. Having prepared another round, he raised the rifle, aimed, and the dog was hit, again, a dusting of snow powdering off its hip, and the dog yelped and dashed off again, its tags jingling, and now the dog was whimpering, circling, hunkering down for more, and Stephen skated up and sprayed the boys in a sheet of ice.

Jesus, Mister—

He wrenched the pellet gun from the boy and took it to a tree and began to beat it—the tree, the weapon—swinging the weapon by the cold barrel. The stock, being made of plastic, splintered first, and broke to pieces.

One of the boys was crying: the biggest, being biggest. Then, looking at Stephen, catching the rage in his eyes, each of the boys began to run and Stephen spit into the air, Don't you move!

They stopped, being boys generally raised to respect the laws. It's my dog, the first boy said. You can't do that!

Stephen dropped the rifle. He skated over to the dog, who had approached, most likely to protect the boys to whom she belonged. The dog barked twice, uncertainly, as Stephen approached. Stephen dropped to his knees, which caused him to flinch, the hard ice on his knees. He slid into the dog, his arms open wide, and the dog nuzzled Stephen while Stephen checked the dog's body for wounds. The dog had a thick winter coat; there was ice forming in the padded declivities of her paws, which Stephen rubbed out, one at a time, with his cold hands. When he finished, he called the boys over. He checked the dog's tags.

What, Mister—

Stephen said, 14 East Oak. I know where you live.

We didn't mean to hurt her, said the larger boy. I mean, she's not supposed to run away! She's not supposed to do that!

I know where you live. I know your phone number. I know if you point a gun at anything ever again I will come back here and I will find you and I will cut off your thumbs!

The larger boy had begun to sob. He was taking huge breaths.

Do you understand me?

Then the smaller boy fell on his knees and the dog rushed to greet him. Stephen rose, dusting off his knees. The boy wrapped his arms around the dog, his hands digging into the dog's thick fur.

The boy said, crying, looking at his thumbs, I'm sorry, Ginger.

She loves you, Stephen said. You're lucky.

The boys, trembling, each having a hand on the dog's collar—*Ginger*—walked the dog across the ice, and then the frozen ground, and now the driveway leading to the lake. Stephen watched the boys for a long time, until they vanished, and then he went to his car and sat on the ground. He began to unlace his skates and, as he did so, a wave of anxiety rushed him out of nowhere, and he ran his hands through his hair and looked it in the eye. He said his name . . . *Stephen Brings. Your name is Stephen Brings . . .* and he leaned his head back against the car, the panic slowly receding, and looked it in the eye: it was like running away from something: it was like turning to face what you were running from. It was like coming, if you let it, if you called it what it was. The body had a mission, as did the soul, and he sat silently against the frozen door of his father's car, closing his eyes, and as he did so he saw his father, and his lost son, and his wife, R, a woman he loved and pretended to marry for all the wrong reasons. The lamppost—it didn't belong to anybody. It was just a light he and his father had installed at the end of the drive. *Turn at the light,* those were the instructions. In the early dark of winter it was how they had come to set their house apart—a lamp, alone in the dark—and it was odd the way the dark would always cause the light to dilate. To grow and to be more. It was a lesson in transcendence—digging that ditch, tying up the wires. Had Stephen and R not pretended to be married, had Stephen only visited on weekends, they never would have gone to Rome. Christmas in Rome. A trip, it will be fun; we need a trip, Stephen. Take me to Rome. You and me and Gulliver. He had pretended to marry her because he had not wanted his son not to have a father. The gash in the palm of his hand ached bitterly. He had pretended to marry her because, despite loving her, he understood he could love her more. He could be a better man. Light, regardless of its source, belonged to anybody who could see it, wasn't that the lesson? And he saw an image of himself—of the man he had been unable to become, and the younger man he once was, so full of conviction and promise—and he said a brief prayer for the dog and for the boys who would never be able to forgive themselves for what they'd done to her.

They're boys, he said. They're just boys.

He was getting better, he knew that. He finished unlacing his skates. He studied the snow drifting on the ice. Given the right ordnance, it is possible even for water to break. A Soviet-built MIG, bombing the Adriatic Sea; a woman, giving birth to her firstborn in a cellar under fire. A man in winter, regaining his balance, skating across the surface of a lake.

No, he said, turning his eyes to the wind, and wiping the ice from the blades of his skates. You are not going to break.

He said, gaining confidence, Stephen, you are not the kind of man who breaks.

One One Thousand, Two One Thousand . . .

I

You never hear the one that gets you, thank God.

But why is that? Why do you never hear the one that gets you?

Because it gets you.

A bullet's velocity is supersonic. Consequently, the arrival of a given bullet always precedes the sound of its firing.

When a bullet misses, you hear that.

You hear a *crack,* like a ruler slapped against a wooden tabletop; like a paddle, struck against an unruly boy's backside. That *crack* is the sonic boom of the bullet passing by your ear.

Then, only afterward, do you hear the sound of the gun which fired it.

Unless it gets you.

II

The distance of the sniper who fired a given shot can be calculated by counting—*one one thousand, two one thousand*—and thus measuring the delay between the sonic boom passing by your ear—the *crack*—and the arrival of the *bang* which belatedly announces it.

For those unfamiliar with the calculus of ballistics, it may be useful to consider the similarities of sniping with midwestern meteorology. Consider first a midwestern thunderstorm, the kind that shakes the treetops. During such a storm one measures the distance of a given stroke of lightning by the amount of delay leading to its thunderclap.

One one thousand, two one thousand . . .

Lightning, of course, comes from the sky, as does the sniper's round.

III

To locate a sniper, perhaps that same sniper who first missed killing you, his bullet cracking by your ear, it is possible to do this:

- Find a bullet fired by that same sniper into a wall—or better yet a piece of wood, which is likely to have absorbed that bullet's impact gracefully;
- Insert a cleaning rod from your own rifle—or a yardstick, or a radio antenna from an overturned automobile on the abandoned street—into that bullet hole;
- Follow that line of sight to the place of the bullet's origin. Please note this distance may well approach one thousand yards.

—

!WARNING! Do not employ this technique without the benefit of cover! !WARNING!

—

IV

Regarding the lasered scope: one does not see the laser laterally. Rather, one sees its point of origin—red—and its final point of destination—also red—though typically the one being aimed at does not see even that.

SUMMATION & FINAL CAUTIONS

Real snipers do not use lasered scopes.
Remember to count the bullets.
Remember, too, the sniper's motto—
One shot, one kill.

Fall and Winter 1992—

The Goat Bridge

There it is—Sarajevo.

—

The story, Ado said. I am afraid you will be ashamed of me.

Nonsense, Stephen said.

You will have to change my name. You should change it to Mujo—
Muy yo, like that. Like a Tom Dick and Harry.

I'll change your name, Stephen said. But not to that. No American
could pronounce it. How come all your names always end in *O*?

You will not like me. After. I have told nobody.

Jesus—

First, my father was atheistic. I am atheistic. Only my mother is
religious.

Ado spoke these words like a Central European.

My mudder, my fadder . . .

—

The story Ado tells is hardly believable even by Balkan standards. It
begins before the war. The civil war? Ado says, mockingly. The evil
rebellion of the Muslims?

It begins like this, before the war:

Ado is writing freelance for the magazines. He has a heroin problem. A junkie, but he is also writing for the magazines. He is a free-
lancer, which means unemployed in any language; he is writing for
the magazines in Slovenia about Yugoslav rock and roll. He is living
with his mother and his father in Ilidža, a suburb ten kilometers west
of Sarajevo—the way, say, Webster Groves is west of St. Louis; or
Park Forest, just down the road from Chicago. He is living with his
father who is an engineer at Energoinvest—a utilities company, an

electrical concern—and with his mother who is religious, and he is having a difficult time keeping his habit in check. The good thing about the war, Ado explains, is that the junkies either died or cleaned up, but at least they stopped using. After the war begins, there is no supply.

Ado has cleaned up. He has become a responsible citizen and member of the territorial defense. But this story begins before the war, when Ado is living with his parents and loading up the magazines in Slovenia with rock and roll.

One day he receives a telephone call from a woman. The woman has a nice voice. She sounds pretty, he says. If you know what I mean. So she says hello and this and that and things (*tings,* he says) and she says she has been recommended to Ado by some friends of his. Who, she does not mention. But she has heard good things about Ado. He is, for example, strappingly tall, a cut chin, a devotee to Tito's memory and all bone and muscle. He can walk for days, like a camel, without food or water. He has been known to walk for days like that.

The woman says she would like to meet him. She is older than Ado, in her mid-thirties. She says she would like to meet him but that nobody must know. She is engaged soon to be married. Her fiancé is an importer for Panasonic—VCRs, CD players and stereos: he is a big potato importer and makes frequent trips back and forth to Belgrade and to Zagreb and to Ljubljana and to Split. He drives a new Volkswagen Golf made in the Sarajevo factory. He carries wads of cash. And it is not her future husband she is concerned about knowing about this—*This entanglement?* Ado says. *This engagement?*—but rather her mother, who is very religious. The woman on the phone with the pleasant voice is deeply concerned about her mother finding out, and so Ado is to meet the woman only in secret. The woman will not tell Ado her name. The woman instructs Ado, on account of his various recommenders, to stand on the bank of the Miljacka River. She explains, repeatedly, that she is not a hooker.

You don't need to give me money, she says to Ado. No buying of the meals at restaurants.

Jesus, Stephen said.

No, wait—

So Ado goes to the banks of the Miljacka River and stands beneath the pretty lindens. The building the woman lives in is in Grbavica, on the river, a pink and modestly storied apartment complex, one of several. Not the high-rises. It's right across from the bridge—

The Bridge of Brotherhood and Unity?

No, that is further west. No, this is the bridge Suada and Olga were killed on. That one. Right behind the State Museum.

Got it.

So Ado goes to the river in the dark and waits for the signal. The dark, it is a pretty night. After ten, maybe eleven, he can't recall, a woman stands on the balcony, silhouetted by the lights behind her body, and waves.

The wave, Ado explains, is the signal.

Ado, he has not been laid for several months, living with his parents as he does, and being a junkie, and therefore not a particularly responsible type eligible for romance. He strides with those camel legs of his, briskly, across the bridge to Grbavica, which is now controlled by the Chetniks, riddled with snipers like worms in the abandoned apartment towers. But this is before the war. It is a warm October night, thanks to a minor change in climate, and by the time he arrives at the apartment, taking the stairs two at a time, he is in a heated sweat.

The woman answers the door. The lights inside the apartment are out. Through the windows behind her he can see the pale light trembling on the river. It is a small river which rushes gently through the city. He can smell the woman's perfume, all flowers and lust. The woman takes his hand and leads him to the sofa. He can tell by the feel of the sofa that it is made of soft leather.

She says, You cannot see me.

Uh-huh.

No. I mean, you must never see me. We can only be in the dark.

The dark.

She says, removing his jacket, The dark. Then she lifts the sweater off his shoulders, over his head. She runs her hand across his chest. She pinches a tender nipple. She places her free hand along the length of his cock.

Then she removes her clothes, in the dark, and she unravels a condom—with her mouth!—and they fuck.

Like that, Ado said.

I don't believe it.

Neither would I, Ado said, nodding. Who would believe such a thing?

So you fuck?

Uh-huh. She is very hygienic. Clean. Which is good.

And you don't know what she looks like?

Well, I can tell, with my hands. Like somebody blind. I mean, I know what her body feels like. I can see her like that. By what I can feel. You see?

I guess. So then what?

So, after. I thought I should smoke. I thought I should smoke so I could, you know, light a cigarette. I could light a cigarette and see what she looked like!

But you don't smoke.

Too unhealthy. No. Only the smack. But not anymore. Even when there is no water, the war makes me clean.

As a whistle.

Clean. It is better I think to be clean.

Then what.

Well, this is the hard part. You see, it goes on.

On?

For like—six, seven months. Twice a month. She calls, I go to the river, she gives to me the signal. Never when the moon is full.

I don't believe this, Stephen said. You are so full of shit—

No! I would not lie. It is Balkanesque. It is positively true. She likes the younger guys. She likes to fuck. Fucking, she says. It is an art. We are like the bees fucking in the honeycomb, she says. The Art of Fucking?

So you never look for her?

How would I look for her? Sometimes, on the streets, sometimes I wonder if she is nearby. I pay attention to the perfumes. I listen for the women's voices. You never know. At the bookstore. At the clubs. And now, with the war, in the water queues. Maybe that one there is the woman who likes to make the Fucking Arts in the dark.

So—

It is very odd, Ado said. Odd. I never know. And then, the last time, she said, Please, you must be more quiet. But after. After the fucking. We were having the *after* conversation. Why must I be more quiet? She said, Because Mother is in the next room.

That is when I thought this is too wrong. She was most afraid of her religious mother finding out and she invites me to do the Art of Fucking with her mother in the next room? Some people want disaster, I think. Something inside wants to be ruined. I don't understand it, really, but I know what it means. Being a junkie, you know you are ruining yourself. I don't mean to sound moralistic. I know what it means to want to ruin yourself without wanting to. Anyway, this was April. You know what happened after that.

The referendum. The war.

The war, Ado said.

Stephen said, So why didn't you try and find out who she was? I mean, it wouldn't have been tough. Would it? I don't believe this.

I would not lie about such things, Ado said. It is not a point of honor, this fucking. I am not Italian. I am not even Slovenian. No. I thought about finding her. I am not the idiot. I knew what building she lived in. I knew the company where she worked. But then, I don't know. I didn't *want* to know. Can you understand that? I did not want to know who she was.

I guess.

It was better like this. In the dark. It was better just not knowing.

Plate #3

A naked man's torso, his penis fully erect. The pubic hair is lit like steel. There is a drop of fluid on the head, pre-seminal.

Stephen has certain rules. He will take no photographs of dead bodies. He will take no photographs of people—especially citizens—being shot at, and killed, while they try to cross the Eiffel Bridge or Sniper's Alley. The alley is the main boulevard which leads to Ilidža, to the airport and to the western front. Ado is typically positioned at the western front, in front of a meat-processing plant on the banks of the Dobrinja stream. Ado's father was shot and killed several months ago—a soldier in camping gear off duty gathering wood, caught by a random bullet while sitting in the back of a truck filled with wood.

Other things Stephen will not photograph? People in obvious physical pain, such as those engaged in the act of amputation without the benefit of anesthesia; gravestones; or landscapes of the city under fire at night, the tracers lighting up the sky like luminescent spider webs.

These are images he is more than willing to let others take. There is a market for these images. There is a market for the photographs of the mutilated: those images, say, of victims of a surprise mortar, delivered into a breadline. The mortar—it takes only a piece of it, the size of the head of a screw, or nail, to tear your heart—eviscerated dozens in a single blow. These are the images which make one famous; these are the images which are presently being broadcast across the globe; and these are the images Stephen prefers to let others take for themselves—which they can't, given that the image takers are not the victims of that which makes the image. One may lean on another's agony, but one cannot claim it as one's own. In Zagreb, having unloaded his 80–200 millimeter zoom, and having purchased from a recently blinded photographer a tenderly cared for Hasselblad—that crisp, Carl Zeiss glass—Stephen decided strictly on portraiture and figure studies. The Hasselblad, it has a portrait lens which eats light; and so at times Stephen relies on his rangefinders—the Contax and the Leica. What's the difference between a Leica 35-millimeter and a Zastava 7.62 semiautomatic? Nomenclature aside, Stephen will neither poach nor snipe, and he will take photographs in Sarajevo only of those who ask him to. In Sarajevo it is simply impossible to purchase a tripod. There are none to be had unless one borrows from the press corps. Chemicals in the city are equally impossible to locate, as are film, condoms, batteries, fresh fruit and vegetables. And having decided he understood he was going to follow through: he would take portraits of those living—and not dying—in the city of Sarajevo.

He carries with him certain things: his gear, a sleeping bag, a flak jacket he purchased in Split from Terrance the Armored Guy, who also wanted to sell him a barely damaged armored Land Rover with two spares. Business was business and business was booming. Messinger had insisted on the jacket: Messinger, who had been flying in and out of Sarajevo on UN relief flights, depending on the weather and the current state of the alleged cease-fires. While Messinger insisted on Stephen locating a flak jacket, Messinger rarely wore one himself. Choice, it seemed, was the central issue. The Bad Guys—Ado's insistence, *not* Serbs—controlled the perimeter of the airport on the western side of the city; by controlling the perimeter, and then Ilidža, they were able to support the tail of their troops, originating in Belgrade, and circling the northern side of the city. From a military point of view, Ilidža had become a central pivot, which explained the ferocity of the fighting on the western MLR. The eastern front, which terminated at the Goat Bridge, demarcating a three-kilometer neutral zone, was relatively quiet. The roads there leading in were complicated and narrow, and nobody in the war wanted to fight, anyway. While the Bosnians held Vratnik and the old Turkish fort, the Bad Guys held Trebević, the territory above the Jewish cemetery, and then a portion of the city—Grbavica—which bulged to the banks of the Miljacka like a pregnant mule. The boulevard ran parallel to the river, and the residential towers on the banks of the river occupied by the Bad Guys gave their snipers their various points of view. If a sniper could see you in his scope, he killed you, or your friend, or your cat. As for the flak jacket, there was something faintly repellent about wandering around the city in a two-thousand-dollar flak jacket— enough to fund a year's worth of an American IRA; enough to heat your Sarajevo flat through the winter with black-market fuel—when others all around you wearing sweatshirts and blazers were being shot at. Stephen was required to wear the flak jacket on UN flights in and out of the city, which he did, but mostly he kept it folded in a corner of the flat in which he was staying. Nights, he used it for a pillow.

The safest corridor through the city was a road now referred to as the Road to Life. By the time Stephen had arrived, the Bad Guys had taken out the National Library, torching it with incendiary shells. They had taken out the post office which housed the telecommunications for most of the city. The Bad Guys had targeted the Unis Towers, by the Holiday Inn, and the newspaper, *Oslobodjenje,* and the Parliament building. Next to the Parliament building, across from the Holiday Inn, stood the Faculty of Philosophy, which was *not* targeted for demolition. Despite the burned-out buildings, it was not a war: an army could have taken the city in an afternoon, albeit not without a few thousand casualties, a political cost neither side could bear. While the world's attention focused on Sarajevo, the Bad Guys were free to cleanse the rural landscape—Croats in the southwest; Serbs in the east. Cleanse, that polite euphemism for genocide, as if you could put it in your dishwasher.

In the Balkans, everybody looks the same, like trees. Rape a woman and fill her with your seed and it's possible to make your own tree. Even a dog will fuck a tree. This, all of this—it was a kind of barbarism enriched by ignorance and malice, the bread of greed, and in the cities, like Sarajevo, things were a bit more sophisticated, what with all the television networks listening in. Still, the Serbs fired on the hospitals filled with others tending to the wounded the Serbs had already fired upon. They fired on the schools and the parks and the funerals and those waiting in line for bread, and water, and they fired on the old quarter of the city, Baščaršija. In general the Serbs—the Bad Guys? the Chetniks? Those Who Bombed the Maternity Hospital?—were pretty well fired up with all their firing. Light it up, look at all the pretty buildings burn.

The word *top* in Serbo-Croatian means *cannon*. Bosnia, which had at one time been occupied by the Ottomans, carried traces of the reign, its cemeteries littered with gravestones—phalluses, each—of the previous Ottomans. Legend has it the old White Fortress halfway up Vratnik—*the Top,* Ado always called it—once housed a cannon which was fired during Ramadan to indicate the end of each day's fast; some also say the cannon was fired each time the Ottomans killed a prisoner. Stephen is weak on the history of the Balkans, not having heard of them until the winter Olympics of 1984, but he does know, having read his Keegan and Clausewitz and the memoirs of Sherman and Patton and Grant, that artillery belongs to the heights surrounding any battlefield—which in this case had become the city, Sarajevo, now cut off from food and water, electricity and gas.

Q. How does a Bosnian woman keep her money safe from her husband?
A. She puts it in a book.

Stephen lives in a little house: a flat, in a small building housing three others, one for each floor, in the Mejtas district. The neighborhood sits on a northern hilltop above what is called the Big Park. His own building, if one follows a narrow street, leads to an ancient mosque with a wooden minaret and an equally ancient graveyard beside it. He lives on the third floor with Ado and Ado's uncle, Jusuf, and with Ado's mother and an old friend of Ado's mother and Ado's younger sister who are scrambling to find a way out of the city. Ado won't leave; and Ado's uncle, Jusuf, will stay to look after Ado. The fewer they are, the more easily they eat. Ado's mother and Ado's younger sister, who is seventeen, are packed to go.

They can't fly out on an empty UN relief flight because that is illegal, violating either the Geneva Convention or Rules of Engagement. They can't drive out because there are no cars available and because they would be killed within thirty seconds of their departure. They can't leave by train because the beautiful train station—and the track leading to it—has been destroyed. They can't drive out on a bus with a UN escort because the Serbs no longer permit any buses with UN escorts to go. They could try cutting across the airport, at night, like hundreds of others, cutting across the runways to try and escape to the Bosnian-held Mount Igman, but like hundreds of others they would be caught—lit up with UN searchlights mounted on UN armored personnel carriers. Then on the airport runways they would be shot, and killed, by Serb snipers, the UN peacekeepers having spotted them so conveniently.

The question, then: how is one to leave when one is not permitted to leave? Just how are Ado's mother and sister to get out?

The only way out is through the Serb-held part of the city, Grbavica.

Plate #7

A naked woman, pregnant—six to seven months along, the baby having not yet dropped—in the standard pose. Her arm is lowered so that her hand, curved at the fingers, may politely conceal the point of entry between her legs, and which draws attention to the sunlit wedding ring on her finger; the other arm permits her forearm to conceal her chest. The second hand, here, open, reaching across to counterbalance the pose—the hand here is spread like a fan and the ring finger of this hand is missing above the first knuckle so that the tip of her nipple fills its place.

This is how they got in:

Ado, his mother and father and sister, lived in Ilidža. They had a nice apartment. Inside, you could have been in Rome or London or Paris, or Stephen's apartment in Chicago—a television, a stereo, books on the wall. Nearby a neighbor had a dog which always barked. When the wind shifted, you could smell the sulfur in the water from the thermal springs. Ado's mother and father learned the Serbs were taking Ilidža. His mother was a childhood friend of the local police second-in-command. He was Serb, but for many childhood friend-ships held sway: one day she received a telephone call from the friend, who instructed the family to depart for Sarajevo immediately—the family being Muslim. They were to take no more than a suitcase each, lest they appear greedy and conspicuous and ungrateful; their flat, it seemed, was now required for the use of others; to stay would be to die. They were instructed to arrive at the checkpoint leading into Sarajevo by three P.M. the next day—their names already on a list— and told that, should they arrive after three P.M., all would be lost. That night Ado and his father removed the wheels from their small car to keep it from being stolen in the night. That night they packed. They took things like socks and underwear, they took a Canon AE1— Ado liked to take photos, too, like Stephen—and they took a plate, manufactured in prewar Dresden, which had been a wedding gift; they took a copy of Mark Twain's *Life on the Mississippi*. They left: a stereo, Ado's rock and roll magazines, posters, the television and washer and dryer and all their furniture, not being able to fit these items into their suitcases. The Sarajevans have a derogatory word for peasants carrying suitcases—*papak*—to indicate ignorant country folk. Like *hillbilly*. And thus they carried their suitcases to the check-point, their wheelless car having been stolen sometime in the night by thieves traveling with their own spare set of wheels. A man behind sandbags—definitely a *papak,* Ado explained—looked for their names on a list of names. He checked them off with a ballpoint pen. He waved a semiautomatic rifle—Zastava, the same caliber and thirty-round magazine as the Kalashnikov—and then the man with the semiautomatic instructed several others to let the hillbillies pass. It was two thirty P.M., and the family caught a ride on a truck, a cease-fire being in effect, and moved in with Ado's uncle, formerly a welding instructor, now a munitions expert and guard on the eastern front. They learned several weeks later that a new family liked their old home very much, which was how they left it.

In the flat below Ado's there live two girls. One girl, the Married Flirt, is married and very modern. She speaks often about her hus-band's jealousy. She reads the popular magazines from Italy and France whenever she can find them and keeps up on points of fashion. Her husband, who is rarely home, serves as an interpreter and guide for foreign visitors—typically journalists staying at the Holiday Inn in need of a crash course to bring them up to speed. Her husband, the girl says, asks her too many questions. She does not know how long she will stay married to him because of all the questions! She met him—her husband—while driving her father's car and colliding with the man on a narrow street; at the time, she had no permissions. For Stephen, living in the Balkans, things often get lost in translation. Her father might have lived in Visegrád then? The man she married, he told her not to worry, because he wanted a relationship—a very American word, and not money to fix his car—and now they have a four-year-old daughter with pierced ears living with her parents in Budapest. The girl, the Married Flirt, has dyed black hair, plucked brows, a striking figure. She has a pretty laugh. She has a little girl and a jealous husband and she flirts with every man she meets.

The other girl, the Soulful One, comes from a religious family but is not religious and, consequently, she feels separated from and ostracized by her family which now resides in Frankfurt. This girl is fleet of foot, wearing thin sneakers of the type fashionable among American women in the 1960s—Keds. She sings with a choir which rehearses—*repetitions,* she calls it—in the basement of a Catholic church. She invites Stephen often to these repetitions where the choir sings music of all religious faiths. Her favorites are the Negro spirituals. It seems important to her, this showing and introducing to Stephen something beautiful and otherwise not associated with this hideous war which is destroying this once beautiful city. She, like the Married Flirt, is not from this city, but it is hers now. Also the Soulful One likes to read Paul Auster novels and says things like, *We are each a book, and even if you cannot read your own book, because it is too dark, or even if you get lost in your own book, you can always read another person's book in order to find your way out.* Though the Soulful One does not flirt, she is obviously lonely and longing to be loved by a good man. Ado might be a good fit, but Ado is young for his age— randy and horn-dog—and, lest Stephen forget, a former junkie heavily influenced by rock and roll. This girl studies—when she can— French literature; she sings hymns by Brahms; she likes to read novels in translation.

Matchmaking is a dangerous sport. Still, it warms Stephen to see how they all check in with and care for each other. There is also an elderly couple living on the first floor with a handsome dog. Ado is attracted to the Married Flirt, always offering to carry up jugs of water; and now, now that the cold has begun to set in, as has the common understanding that this will not be over next week, or possibly month, now Ado brings the girls wood when he can. Sometimes the girls share things from the husband tour-guide: canned fruit from the Holiday Inn; or whiskey. Once they shared a few spareribs, delivered from a complete rack, which the elderly couple's dog had pilfered from the market. The dog, an Irish Setter, walked into a market, went directly to the counter, pinched the meat, and then carried it home in its jaw for three miles. It had become a legend—this dog, stealing the ribs, and bringing them home.

Stories here fly. In Serbo-Croatian, the word for *quarter,* or neighborhood—*mahala*—provides the metaphoric root for *gossip.* The Married Flirt loves to gossip. The Soulful One pretends not to listen.

Stephen, said the Married Flirt. Do you have a lover?

No, he said.

That is too bad for you, said the Married Flirt.

Ado said, standing tall, Neither do I.

—

Elise was on her way back to the city. She had been everywhere she could interviewing women and children. She'd interviewed a man—it was famous, the story—who'd watched another man who had been forced to bite off the penis of a third. She'd been to Omarska—the concentration camp on the cover of the magazines—when the press pool broke that story open. She was writing about rape and ethnic cleansing; she was writing about the use of rape as a governmentally sanctioned instrument of war. Her articles were appearing in Berlin and New York and Paris. She was due soon to arrive.

Partially to take his mind off her, he spent the afternoon—the good light of the afternoon—at the western front with Ado. First they walked to the looted Blue Winged fashion mall, what Stephen called Neiman Marcus, and then they cut west, hugging the small building, and then on Tito Street they caught a ride with several others inside a small car: the driver, uniformed, turned behind the Holiday Inn. The Blue Helmets—UN peacekeepers—were out driving around in their white APCs. They passed a man on a bicycle with a metal cart hitched up behind him dragging what looked to be hundreds of gallons of water in jugs. Riding his bicycle uphill, the man made slow progress. They were then delivered to the sausage factory—that's what Ado called it, though it could have made bologna, or ham-burger. Dead meat. From here they hoofed it, staying in the shadows of the buildings—and these buildings here were blasted to hell, being fringe to both an industrial sector and a residential area of small houses—until they reached the basement of a burned-out house. Somebody had once lived inside this house with notes and pictures on the fridge. In the basement were mattresses, rotting; a cache of assorted weapons, though apparently not enough to go around: M16s, Kalashnikovs, shotguns, and two ten-round PAP semiauto-matic rifles—each fitted with a scope. We have snipers, too, Ado said, giving him the tour, introducing him around. There was also a stack of Soviet-inspired girlie magazines and sandbags. The home base—three days on, three days off, with the men working in shifts at the front. The magazines were for jacking off to ease the stress. One arrived at the front by following a trench, cut to and under the road, leading to another blasted-out house, inside the basement of which were placed two men on guard. The second house faced the stream which crossed before it. Here was the very point of the territorial defense. Ado, not unlike most members of the territorial defense, being a city boy with a former drug problem, had no idea how to be a soldier.

Ado dressed his feet in sneakers. On Ado's sleeve was a sticker, the kind one places on the bumper of a car—a fleur-de-lis.

Stephen said, gazing at the stream in front of him, I've never been to war.

No, Ado said. As I explained to you, this is not war. This is imita-tion of war. There will be no fighting today. Ado looked over at his teammate, who did not speak English, and said something, and the man, who elsewhere could be teaching high school geometry, or sell-ing cars, retired to the other window. He sat on a wooden box and looked dully out the window.

Ado pointed to a large metal building with corrugated metal sides the size of a Wal-Mart. He said, They have tanks in that building. We keep trying to destroy it, but not with a rifle.

Mortars?

It would take two thousand. It takes thousands to destroy a build-ing. Buildings are hard to blow up. You have to want to. You can make a building burn with one shell—like the library—if you have the right kind, which we do not. Generally factories do not burn anyway. They are places prepared for fire. Anyway we don't have the right kind. We have a tank, you know. Some say two. But I know for sure one is parked in the brickyard tunnel to protect it.

The tunnel?

No no no. The tank. It would be too embarrassing to lose the tank.

Stephen said, pointing to the factory, So what do you do?

We are safe unless real war starts. This concrete is thick. I have two Molotov cocktails and this shotgun for the tanks.

Would they send tanks?

No. You cannot send tanks here without infantry and they would die. If they were going to they would have. They won't send anything or anybody who might be hurt. Mostly this is very boring. Sometimes I am scared. At night. At night I get scared. I am not brave and you cannot do much with a Molotov cocktail. It makes some light, that's all. I am here because my father is dead.

A reward.

It is much worse south, by the residential towers. That is where my father was killed. That is worse. The towers are death traps. Dobrinja, the Olympic Village. What you say the Al Pacino. Fucking snipers everywhere. You are in range of the mountains. It is better being closer to the ground. He said, pointing his finger at a plane, Not like that.

They watched a huge lumbering cargo plane—Hercules—sail into view, cutting horizontally across their line of sight. It had the belly of a whale and, watching, Stephen felt as if he could reach out and pluck it from the sky, he was that close.

Ado said, nodding, Relief flight.

The other soldier mumbled something, to which Ado laughed and said something back.

What?

He said, No pork chops tonight.

Stephen had had no idea they were this close to the airport. He'd thought it was miles away. He said, I have no idea where I am.

Ado said, Half of that food will end up with the Chetniks. We get the MREs from Viet Nam. Powdered eggs. Lemon drink. They get the cans of Dinty Moore stew and cheese and vegetables and gasoline and beer.

And then you buy it back?

War profiteers, Ado said. The war is good for the profiteers.

A story circulating: the formerly bankrupt Holiday Inn had grossed a quarter-million *dollars* in just two months. Stephen measured the light with his selenium meter—a rotating dial, no batteries to run out. The Holiday Inn was a place where he could always get food. Have a *burek,* a nice expensive drink.

Don't smile, Stephen said, setting the aperture. But Jesus, don't try to look like Clint Eastwood, either.

The light fell indirectly from the window. Stephen said, Don't look at me. No. God no.

Fuck you, Ado said. Cheese.

Okay, okay. He slid his camera into the pocket of his coat. He removed a packet of cigarettes and lit one. The tobacco was left over from the destroyed tobacco factory—Marlboro country. The government issued cigarettes instead of currency to its soldiers. Stephen offered one to Ado's partner but the man had fallen asleep. The packet was wrapped in paper from recycled textbooks.

Stephen, Ado said.

Yes.

Can you give me a thousand marks?

It struck Stephen odd that Ado did not use the word *loan,* or *borrow.* They'd had banks here once. Car payments? Then Stephen understood only a rich American would pretend to repay a friend when he knew that he could not.

Yes, Stephen said. If you need it. Of course.

It is not for me, Ado said. I would not ask for me.

I know that. And then Stephen said, trying to assuage Ado's evident discomfort, It's money. It's just fucking money, Ado. You can even burn it.

Plate #9

Two women—one middle-aged, the other her seventeen-year-old daughter—and a middle-aged man wearing a black beret. It is night. Behind them runs a body of water, evident by the ribbon of light from the sky reflecting on it. The women and the man are dressed in winter clothes. The man has one eye closed, as if he has something in it.

Wars are traditionally measured in figures.

Numbers representing those Killed or Missing in Action; those Wounded. But there are other relevant figures in 1992: to wit, 400 grams of food is the amount awarded to each citizen a day by the humanitarian relief agencies; 10 DEM is the cost of a 30-liter container—empty—for water; 200 DEM for a cubic meter of wood; 50 DEM to have that wood delivered; 120 DEM for a kilo of garlic; 20 DEM for a pumpkin; 5 DEM—or a pack of cigarettes—for a liter of milk; 2,000 DEM for safe passage across the Miljacka River and on to Mount Igman, other tolls along the way to Budapest or Split to be determined later.

This is what the Married Flirt tells Stephen. In the First World War, which began in Sarajevo, the ratio of casualties was 15 percent civilians to 85 percent military personnel; in this war, 1992, the ratio is reversed: 85 percent civilians to 15 percent military personnel. So much for a century of progress. She explains to Stephen her husband learned this fact while listening to diplomats talk to each other at the Holiday Inn. She explains this does not at all appear to be news to her. She explains she wants to buy new clothes and party shoes. Like most people who know Sarajevo, she does not like the Holiday Inn.

To begin with: it is monstrously ugly. Yellow, like pus—it is made of metal, square and squat. Local people refer to a local joke. The Holiday Inn, they say, is the only yellow building on the entire planet viewable to aliens from outer space in search of *burek*. The rooms are decorated with a dog-shit brown tile. The cocktail furniture—low-slung chairs and low marble tables streaked with purple veins, like an alcoholic nose—is purple, apparently to coordinate nicely with the yellow and green theme. There is a bar in the center of the atrium, a silver moon of a bar, inside of which stand the nattily dressed and surly waiters. Ado has explained that the hotel was built on an old circus fairground, which accounts for some of the ancillary decor. When the press is on full display, certainly the hotel has the feel of a circus. Writers, camera crews, producers, recognizable personalities and talking heads: to enter the ring, one either comes up through the garage or takes the back door.

He found them, his friends, and they all did an odd combination of American-style embrace and European cheek kissing. Stephen could never get the kissing part down: it seemed something to be done on the TV—at the Grammys, or one of those White House pop concerts—and he had no idea how people ever figured it out. Being raised in the

Midwest, he had been instructed not to kiss people he was not related to. Which cheek were you supposed to start with? Did you let your lips touch the cheek, or was that considered messy? Why in God's name would you press your cheek to another's only to make a kissing sound in that person's ear? Wasn't that loud? And then there was the dreaded kiss-on-the-mouth situation, which terrified him, deeply, and to which he typically replied, being the kissee, by always hesitating before smashing one of his cheeks, probably the improper one, into the oncoming lips of the kisser. Typically he liked to shake hands: there were ways to do it properly, with midwesternly middle-class aplomb. Anna, she kissed him—one of those lips-turned smashed-cheek debacles—and stood back and shook his hand. Then she hugged him. Then she laughed, and Stephen shook hands for twenty-seven minutes with Peter Messinger. He shook hands more briefly with Elise—who kissed him, swiftly, on the mouth.

Stephen said to Anna—partially to change the subject, to suppress a blush—Remind me. I have a photo for you. From the airport. It's very nice.

Okay, Anna said, beaming. I'll remind you.

It's not for you, Stephen said. It's for your family.

For your *loved* ones, Elise said, teasing her.

I'll need to make a proper print, Stephen said.

He waited for people to resume their seats. He took one of his own. So, he said, sitting back. So.

Scotch on the table. A waiter brought him a glass. He poured only a quarter-inch, knowing it would go right to his head by way of his empty stomach. Then it went to his head, like that, and he permitted himself another quarter-inch.

Two photographers approached and introduced themselves to Messinger, who was polite and kind. Do you know Stephen Brings? Stephen understood that in Messinger's presence his own had become inflated. It was not unlike standing next to a senator, or general—the less you said the more cachet you seemed to have. It was nice sometimes not to feel snubbed by the important journalists and waiters. The photographers and Messinger talked for a moment about Michel, the French reporter Stephen had met with the others on Biševo, and who had been killed in the Krajina by his guides.

They found his body, Messinger said. Shot in the back of the head.

Stephen felt his stomach turn. The reporter had been murdered for his supply of emergency cash—strapped to a leg, the small of his back. Stephen had thought the guy was back in Paris playing with his kids. It followed that the guy's family was . . . what? Your husband dies, father of your two kids . . . what? Explain that. Apparently his wife had been pregnant. The wife was going to name the forthcoming baby—a girl—after her father.

Eventually the conversation began to break apart into separate groups. Anna asked Stephen a question about the government. There was some talk about the Canadian General who insisted the Muslims were shelling themselves to make the Serbs look bad. Very naughty, those Muslims. There was talk about the trees, the water queues at the brewery and the supply of flour at the bakery. General laughter at the incomprehensible incompetence of the United Nations. Also, sometimes there was gas; sometimes there was not: what was important was that you never knew if there would be gas and, thereby, heat for your home. People were making stoves out of metal crates at the technological institute, and ordnance—a generally hit-or-miss proposition.

The photographers made to leave, and everybody paused politely to say good-bye. Messinger smiled, demurely, and said, I'll see you again soon, I'm certain—meaning they could leave now and he would not take offense and that, further, he really wanted them to leave now. Enough already.

Then Stephen heard a voice, calling—Stephen! Stephen Fucking Brings!

Summerville, striding across the atrium in his boots, a sheepskin vest—the Marlboro Man. He strode up, half-cocked, drink in hand, and clapped Stephen on the back. His breath was a flamethrower absent the spark.

Hey, Stephen said, recoiling. How's the spy business?

Spy schmy, Summerville said. I am a reporter for an important daily. I am a writer! Give me liberty or ring me a bell!

Okay. How's the daily business?

Beats the dog out of me. God's truth, Stephen Brings. I have no idea. He said, taking a seat, Where's the hootch? Elise? Pass me the hootch, s'il vous plaît. Stephen, he said. Fill 'er up?

A pinch, Stephen said. Really. Whoa.

Whoa, Summerville said. You've passed the Palomino Hotel!

Excuse me?

Me, I like that *šljivovica*. Helo vitz ya? That stuff, Steve. From pears?

I thought it was plums.

They make liquor from grass, too, you know. Grass. Like ethanol, you ask me. Put it in your tank and go. He said, When's this beauty pageant? Got to see the Beauty Pageant. Grass hootch, go figure—

Have you tried it? Stephen said.

Elise said, taking Stephen's arm, I brought you a tripod. And film. She said, pulling him close, This time I am staying.

I'm glad, Stephen said. He said, looking at her, Really. Now he looked at Peter Messinger and felt clumsy, and so he stood, and walked to the bar, and Messinger rose to follow him. At the bar Stephen overheard an American woman explaining to an American man the way she felt. *I feel he's just not listening to me,* the woman said. At the bar Stephen asked the nattily dressed waiter behind it for several rounds of *travarica* and paid for the drinks.

Stephen, Messinger said. While we are alone—

Stephen looked at him.

Elise has asked me to deliver to you a message. She is staying.

I feel, the woman was saying, *that he doesn't care at all about the way I feel.*

Okay, Stephen said, stepping back.

No. You misunderstand. She does not want to come between us. I am here to tell you she cannot come between us. Do you understand?

No—

I am a married man with two children. I love my children. Shit, I love my wife. It has been over between us since Zagreb. Before Dubrovnik, even.

Your wife? Stephen said. Oh God, Peter. I didn't know. I'm so sorry—

No, he said. No, of course not my wife. Ahh, Messinger said, shaking his head. A joke. You had me.

Well, Stephen said. Not exactly.

Maybe, said the man who had been listening to the woman. *Maybe you should try and stop feeling so much?*

The waiter presented a tray filled with several shots of viscous liquid. Stephen said, taking the tray, Isn't this embarrassing? Faintly?

Messinger said, properly serious, But that is why I am speaking to you.

Okay, Stephen said.

She is like a sister to me, that is all.

Got it, I think.

What about me? said the woman. *Me!*

This is not a permission thing, either. It is not a thing like that.

I understand. Well, no, actually I don't. But I'm on the page somewhere. It's a big book. Stephen said, holding the tray, Are you free tonight?

Yes. If it is not cold out.

Bring Elise, he said. Bring Anna. Don't bring Summerville, okay?

At the table they passed the drinks; they made a toast, and Summerville said, What kind's this?

The herbs, Stephen said. *Travarica.* Cheers.

Anna said, rising, not touching her drink, I need a toilet.

There was shelling now, incoming: it was always incoming, but it looked to be incoming in a distant part of the city. Ado would have been able to tell you where down to the block. Now a tremendous noise from the street, metal on metal, and they ran with several outside to the barrier protecting the lobby from sniper fire. Facing the State Museum a UN APC sat like a water buffalo. There was an overturned Volkswagen Golf on the street, its wheels spinning, the engine stuck in gear. From beneath the car were scrambling two journalists, their ID tags flapping in the breeze. They left the car where it stood upside down and raced to the barriers. There was no fire whatsoever.

Above the ridgelines a pair of F-14 Tomcats ripped open the sky as if it were a cotton sheet.

—

A half-moon. The enemy had intensified the shelling and the sky was deeply reddened from several buildings having caught fire. The smoke drifted thickly. Stephen listened to the clatter from the people clattering at the bar. He said to Messinger and to Anna and to Elise, We are going to meet my friend Ado.

Okay, Messinger said.

They crossed the street in the dark past the overturned car. On the sidewalk of the Faculty of Philosophy they passed a dead dog. Once across it was less dangerous; they had only a little way to go to the State Museum—the airport side. There was a bunker there, right before the river. Ado met them and led them to another bunker. In the bunker Ado introduced Stephen to the commander: a big man with a Kalashnikov and radio set. The man said hello with a British accent, and then there were other introductions, and Stephen introduced his friends to Ado's mother and sister and friend of the family. The girl's hair had been shorn, her chest bound in order to flatten it. By tomorrow morning they might be on Mount Igman. The friend of the family carried a suitcase, inside of which he said he had a flashlight. They waited nearly an hour, smoking, sitting in the cold dark behind the bunker and then the radio fired up, and the commander did some talking, and then there was talking from the other side. If you looked you would have seen nothing on the other side. They could hear the river rushing, and the branch of the river, to their right, also rushing. Then two men went to the stream on the right and passed through a culvert running beneath the road in front of them: they watched a man with two jerry cans scramble down the bank on the other side of the river. In the dark they all looked alike. The man representing the other side carried the jerry cans across the river, which was cold, the man obviously cursing the cold water which ran to his knees. Now he turned back and picked up two more cans and returned. Then there were boxes to be carried across. A fire line had started and the supplies were being passed man to man, and to Stephen and Anna and Messinger and Elise, up into the bunker and now to a trench leading eventually to the bed of a truck. This went on. Ado appeared and said to Stephen, They want to say good-bye to you. Stephen went to the culvert, in which he could stand freely; the water was ice. He made out Ado's mother and sister, the friend of the family, who could have been any man. The sister was crying, and she hugged Stephen, and Stephen hugged her mother, Ado's mother, who said something to the man. The man said to Stephen, She wants you to tell Ado not to be stupid and get killed. Tell him not to do the drugs when this is over.

Okay, Stephen said. I'll convey the message.

She wants me to tell you thank you. He said, rubbing at a speck of dirt in his eye, So I am telling you this. Thank you.

Be safe, Stephen said.

And then the man said to Stephen, We've said good-bye to Ado. The man said to Stephen, touching Stephen's arm, God bless.

They turned and walked to the river's edge. At one point Stephen took their photograph. Having made their farewells, there came the anticlimax of more waiting. Nobody stood now on the other side. Ado arrived with Messinger and Anna and Elise, and Elise wrote down some last-minute contacts; she made a duplicate set, one for the man. A rule of the trade, the sharing of contacts with those traveling to foreign lands. In the cold water their feet had turned to ice. There was more shelling in the old part of the city. Somewhere a machine gun, large caliber, was having its say. *Wa wunka wunka wunka,* sliding like a metronome on its hinges, counting out the beats, legato. Then a burst of rapid return semiautomatic fire. Another house on fire. Then a man, a different man, stepped out from the shadows and stood on the opposite bank. He put his hands on his hips. He did not carry a weapon. The man looked right at the place where they stood, and nodded, and Ado said something which must have meant, Go.

His mother looked at him.

Ado said it again. He was crying, which made him say it more harshly than he intended.

And then the friend of the family and the woman and the girl made their way across the cold water.

Plate #12

A large window, interior, shot from below. The window is covered with plastic which, in the light, casts a white glow. A naked woman—muscular, lean, with short-cropped hair—is standing on the sill, her feet stretched out to each corner of the sill for balance. She is on her tiptoes. Her hands, too, are stretched to the far corners of the window. Thus her body is a silhouetted X and toward the center of the photograph one can see the light shooting through the cleft of her genitalia and the fine hairs surrounding it, lit like steel.

Bosnia is among other things a study in bridges. There is the Bridge on the Drina, which later became a book. There is the Stari Most Bridge, or Mostar Bridge. In Sarajevo there is the Goats' Bridge.

These ancient bridges, Ado tells Stephen, were built by the Ottomans. They were built with eggs in the mortar, Ado says, proudly, which explains why they have lasted for hundreds of years.

The bridges, the mortar mixed with eggs. In Serbo-Croatian, the slang for testicles is eggs. *Jaja.*

It is the Soulful One who tells Stephen the story of the Goat Bridge. Though there are two versions, the official version illustrating the uses of philanthropy, the other is the story everybody loves to tell. It is a story of possession. It is, she says, the poetic story.

Once, the story goes, there were two billy goats. The goats stood across from each other—the Miljacka River between them. Each wanted to pass; neither wanted to give the right of way. This was when Sarajevo was known as the Golden Valley. Probably the goats knew there was gold nearby, awaiting two philanthropic brothers to discover, given that all wars are about money. The goats, like men, they refuse to give the right of way. Like men, they begin to fight, like spoiled goats: they hurl themselves at each other in the middle of the river. They hurl their bodies into the bodies of each other. The battle lasts for days. Neither wins, each dies. The goats die with their horns locked, each to each, and become the bridge itself.

It is like all of Bosnia, says the Soulful One. We are turning ourselves to stone.

In the early morning Stephen went to a funeral at the Lion Cemetery, which before the war had been considered all filled up. Across the way a soccer field had also been made available to accommodate the newly dead. Behind the cemetery, just up the road, the few remaining animals in the zoo were starving. For the cemeteries no stones were being cut for the fresh graves. After the funeral Stephen made his way to the Holiday Inn; he was hungry, not having eaten for two days. At the Holiday Inn he entered the conference room and joined up with Messinger and Summerville. Elise and Anna were doing something on three UN diplomats flying in. Then the diplomats were flying out. The traffic in the conference room was light, and Stephen had stale bread and salami. Water. He ate and drank slowly, lest he cause his stomach upset. The more slowly he ate, he was learning, the more quickly he could fill himself up.

Summerville said, removing a laser pen from his sheepskin vest, See this?

Uh-huh, Stephen said. It was one of those things rich people bought in mail-order catalogs for their equally rich partners: the kind of gift one gave to one who could not possibly be in need of anything.

Here, Summerville said, his eyes lighting up. Watch this.

He turned it on and pointed the laser to a group at a table across the room. People there were talking heatedly.

Just look how far this sucker goes, Summerville said, pointing it.

He landed the red laser dot on a man's chest. The man was wearing one of the twinkly blue UN flak jackets. The dot lingered on his chest—

Jesus! somebody screamed, diving for the floor.

Two others at the same table looked up and saw the dot and tackled the man in possession of the chest Summerville had located.

They threw the man on the floor, who was oblivious to the reasons why, not having seen the dot.

Snipers!

Where?

Which was a good question, given that there were no windows. Summerville tucked the gizmo into his vest, patting his chest, and then others saw him, and some laughed, and others expressed their disgust. One glared to prove he could. The men at the table across the room resumed their places.

Honest, one of the men was saying. I swear to God.

Messinger said, yawning, I need something to do.

Me too, Summerville said. Before I get killed.

You aren't getting killed, Stephen said. Everybody likes you too much.

Messinger smiled, broadly. The luxuries of coffee and tea, of tobacco—his teeth needed cleaning.

—

All wars are about money, which is to say, *currency*—the pound and the yen, the dollar and the crown. The mark. On the way to the Goat Bridge, in a borrowed armored Land Rover, they pulled to a stop behind a tunnel. They left the Rover there with two guards, behind the tunnel, beside a place where two mortars were stored for safekeeping. They began hiking a steep, narrow and snow-covered road. It was hard going, but then it began to decline: Messinger, Summerville, Stephen. To their left there stood a giant stone, like something out of Monument Valley, the kind climbers would spend a day on with hundred-dollar ropes and brightly colored carabiners, only this giant stone was white, like marble in the light, and Stephen said, They call that Granny's Tooth.

The rock? Summerville said.

Yeah.

Summerville said, You ask me, looks more like Grandpa's schlong.

Summerville began a story about a steer his father once told him to castrate. Ah duh, Summerville said. I kept looking, you know?

All around them were hymns—natural and fabricated—to the penis: the metal posts around the presidency, what Ado called *dick-heads;* the minarets; the ancient gravestones, sprouting in the parks like genetically engineered mushrooms cast in stone. Freud, apparently, had spent some time in Sarajevo. No surprise there. The newspaper building, now burned to the ground, with only its elevator shafts intact—it resembled painfully a giant stone dildo. But beneath it, every day, the people there still brought out the paper.

Rock, Scissors, Paper . . . what was the name of that game?

Or did you just call it that? *Rock, Scissors, Paper.*

The name of the paper was *Oslobodjenje,* just another word for *Liberation.*

Serb, Croat, Muslim; Rock, Scissors, Paper . . . Each, Stephen thought, is capable of killing one but not the other. To build the city, the city had required each; and now to destroy it, too. They walked on through the cold snow. Bosnia: the Land before Time of Identity Politics. In Sarajevo multicultural had actually meant a part of the city's design—the *mahalas,* the streets all leading in to the center. The celebration of the common ground. Here in the valley there were rocks and snowcapped mountains and forests. It was the landscape of a fairytale, Narnia or Middle Earth; it was something rich, and magical. Alpine without the familiarity of chocolate and watches. It was beautiful and cold.

Messinger said, I think Yugoslavia is doing now what Western Europe finished in '45. Establishing the borders. Identities. The history of Europe requires that each nation have a dominant group.

This history of Europe, Summerville said. This history of yours *requires* the US of A to come over here every twenty years and fix it. It's getting old.

He's got a point, Stephen said. This is Europe, not Kansas.

Messinger said, Everybody has to be able to get along? How is that?

No third world? No Middle East? Africa makes Gaza look like California. The world's a toilet and there are always too many people taking a shit all the time.

Pretty goll-dang pessimistic there, Summerville said.

This, Messinger said, sweeping his hand across the landscape. This is nature's way of clearing the ground. The twentieth century is the century in which man makes his own plagues.

Condoms, Stephen thought, might help to check the spread. He had no condoms. Perhaps a word with the Pope was in order? What good was technology if you couldn't improve people's lives? A little food. Employment. Not so many mouths to feed by way of a rubber satchel full of sperm. As the New Democrat had reportedly said a few thousand times in the past three weeks, *A place called Hope.* Stephen was hopeful about the new president, who promised to do something about the war; who promised to provide health care—about time; who promised to make the world a better place and to lay off the chicks.

Is that where that expression came from, *getting laid*?

And what, really, were the antecedents of the phrase *blow job*?

And where did *come* come from, anyway?

He had sex on the brain. This is your drain; this is your dug on drains.

Stephen said, shaking it off, How do you make a person want less than he or she doesn't need?

So, Messinger said. You are a socialist, Stephen Brings.

Maybe. I know what we have now, this unchecked free-enterprise firestorm, isn't working. Where there's a Will there's an A-Plus-Plus. What, we're suddenly going to get smarter?

Well, Summerville said. I'd rather have a bottle in front of me than a frontal lobotomy.

They approached the command house, which Stephen had been told belonged to a Serb to explain why it had not been shelled. Its setup was similar to the command center in the west, though much quieter and, thereby, more cheerful: a place to sleep, a place to light a fire, snow on the roof. The obligatory stash of porn. Dozens of stacks of wood, each neatly bound up with twine. Nobody was inside, so they walked down the hill to the Goat Bridge.

The bridge stood sparkling white in the sun—at each base a hollow circle, one for each side of the river, architectural conduits. If the river flooded, the water would rush through the bridge and not wash the bridge away. The two circles in turn quoted—the figure eight, toppled to its side—the arch of the span. You could lie down in the center and stretch your arms across its width. The design, so simple, so elegant, leading the way to Istanbul. The thing about an arch—it wants mainly to come full circle, to complete its revolution, wherein lies the secret to its strength. Beside the bridge was a plum orchard, long since plundered, and across the way a stand of apple trees. A blasted-out house across the bridge. During pleasant times people came to picnic at the river.

Q. How does a Slovenian woman keep her money safe from her husband?

A. She puts it between her legs.

There were five or six soldiers arguing over something. There was a mortar set up. Jusuf, Ado's uncle, was speaking loudly and holding a shell in his hand: fresh gray paint, narrow, long as the hand which held it. He was telling somebody something who was making adjustments on the pipe. Seeing Stephen, he waved, and then returned to yelling. Now Jusuf stepped over and made introductions.

That's a bunker there? Summerville said.

Yes, Jusuf said. The front line. Cross that line, you go to Serbia. Ha ha ha.

Really?

Well, you know, he shrugged.

Summerville said, Where's the enemy?

Asleep, drinking. Who's to know? We cut wood this morning; sometimes they cut wood, and we buy it, and then we sell it. Free trade, Bosnian style.

I saw it, Summerville said, removing his knapsack. The wood.

Ah ha, Jusuf said, pointing to his eye. Very keen. He said to Stephen, Now we are making a test. You are in time! We had to bring the pipe.

It was a test because nobody was certain how to make a shell work. Over the past two weeks they'd been having a lot of experiments. It was thought best to test here, in a neutral zone filled with mountains and woods. So, okay?

No Man's Land.

Somebody wearing a Bon Jovi T-shirt said something. Another kid had a mohawk and two Nike high-tops and pieces of metal in his nose and lip. They were ready to go, tapping their feet. Jusuf went to the pipe. He said, turning around, First you hear the *wump.* Then the *ssshhhh*—the whistling. Then the *bang.*

Okay.

But we should hear only the *wump* and the *bang.*

Messinger said, Not the whistling.

No. Jusuf said, pointing to the bunker, There. Not the whistling.

The others had taken their places in the bunker. They knelt there, in the bunker, eyes wide.

There there, Jusuf said, smiling. Please. His teeth were in need of fixing. It was the kind of thing an American took for granted: an adequate supply of munitions, decent dental care.

They joined the others in the bunker. Somebody called out something, loudly, and Jusuf called back, grabbing his balls, laughing, and then another in the bunker said something—What? Summerville said—and Jusuf said something, pointing to the bridge: serious now, checking the projectile. He had a wooden box full. He set a shell in the box, closed his eyes, and picked another. *Eenie meenie . . .* Having made his choice, he grinned, shrugged his shoulders, and dropped the shell into the pipe.

The projectile detonated, *wump,* and Jusuf ran and dove into the bunker with his hands over his head. Once there he scrambled, smiling, clapping Stephen on the back, and they began waiting for the *bang.* They waited some more. Messinger was taking pictures. Somebody farted, the silent deadly type. Ugh! said another, and Summerville said, *One who smelt it dealt it,* while they waited for the *bang.* And then came the *ssshhhh,* the whistling, and then everybody ducked headfirst into the floor of the bunker as the shell exploded some fifteen meters in front of them—taking out, among other things (like Summerville's knapsack), the pipe which had fired it.

Plate #16

Two women's faces, in the dark, illuminated by a single flame.

He met Elise at the Eternal Flame. The Eternal Flame had long since gone out, its eternity presently cut short by a lack of gas, but still it was a good meeting place in the center of the city. By way of the Eternal Flame the city honored the dead from the Second World War—just another sequel. If only those in charge had waited a bit to build it, the Eternal Flame might resemble something else. The Eternal Bonfire, say. The Eternal Furnace.

He took Elise for a walk, which today was dangerous on the open boulevards, given the snipers. He told Elise how Ado liked to call the snipers *snoopers,* which he pronounced *snoper.* Ado called them snoopers because they were always snooping into your life, get it? Stephen pointed out to her the various ridgelines marked by cut timber. He took her to a small café which was open but which today had only tea to serve. The thing about Sarajevo, he said. Everybody shows up for work. It dulls the edge of boredom.

I can imagine, Elise said.

I can't.

Elise told him a story about two girls. She kept her voice low. They were blond and pretty, the girls. Blue eyes. They were abducted, their names having been on a list, and taken to a barracks, and locked in a room with twin beds. Probably, the barracks had been a hotel. That night men came to rape them. One of the girls, the oldest, seventeen, would not stop screaming, so after the tenth or eleventh time, the man then raping her stood up and drew a knife and stabbed her in the mouth. She didn't die right away. Her younger sister, silent, listened to the men raping her—grunting, cursing, spitting. They smelled like brandy and goat shit. Her sister was bleeding from the mouth and throat and she was bleeding from between her legs. After a while it stopped. Her older sister died. In the morning a man old enough to be her father came and put the younger girl in the front seat of a truck and drove her home. Now the girl is pregnant and wants to die.

Elise said, They can't gas the populations. So they humiliate them. When you rape a girl you rape her family. It is obscene.

He nodded. He lit a cigarette. Ado had said to Stephen once, Why don't you ever ask if I have killed somebody?

Elise said, What are you thinking?

Nothing, he said. It's awful. It's just awful.

She said, leaning forward, What is the worst thing you have ever done?

Excuse me?

You know. The most terrible thing you have ever done. What is the worst?

He thought a moment.

Elise said, If we are going to be lovers I should know.

He said, You mean on purpose. They're little things in this light. They're just stories.

Everything's a story.

Not over here.

Elise nodded. She said, I have to tell you something now. Before we continue. I had an affair with a married man.

Peter.

I should have told you. She said, It is over. I told him to tell you.

He did.

After Dubrovnik. I told him then. I knew *in* Dubrovnik but I had to tell him first. To be right. But I was not right to you. I should have told you.

It's okay, he said. I knew.

Because I did not want to hurt his feelings. Later. I should have told you.

Okay.

She said, leaning forward, Do you believe in Evil?

I didn't used to.

But you do now?

Yes.

I have a theory, she said. About the big things. I don't mean the small things—the shameful things, sleeping with your friend's lover, or husband. That's venal. That's a lot of soup spilled in your lap. I mean the evil things. The Hitler-Milošević things. She said, taking his hand, I know why the big things happen.

He sat there and felt the warmth from her hand. She withdrew, slightly. Now she took his hand with both of hers.

They happen, the big things, because we don't forgive the small things. Because we don't forgive ourselves.

Pride, Stephen said.

Mm hmmm.

Pride always carries a mirror, Stephen said. Like vanity.

Mirrors break, Elise said. She said, I am the mirror. She said, pointing across the room to a young woman reading a book, She is the mirror. Those girls in the room reeking of goat shit: they are the mirror. The mirror is the other person we don't forgive ourselves for looking through.

Welcome to hell, Stephen said.

Stephen, she said. I want you to be able to tell me everything.

Are you certain?

Everything, she said. Everything in time.

Plate #19

A boy—he could be anybody's—sitting on the steps leading to his building. He is wearing rollerblades; the plaster of his building has fallen off in sheets, the walls are riddled with bullet holes. At the boy's feet are thousands of pieces of shattered glass. He is staring right into the lens.

Names, like faces, change. They met Ado in front of Egypt, across from the Ferhadija Mosque. The street was filling with people out for a walk. Anything to get out of the house. Ado kept watch of the women, the Sarajevan women, who reminded Stephen of blooded horses: chests out, eyes straight, lifting their proud hooves. They were women proud to be admired by the men who pretended not to look. As it grew dark, Ado took Stephen and Elise to a club on the Obala Boulevard, which kept changing names. First it was the Obala of the Franz Joseph, then the Obala of Stepa Stepanovic. The Obala of Fill-in-the-Blank.

Yugoslavia, Ado said, shaking his head. In America, when the Democrats win, do you change the Boulevard of Davy Crockett to the Boulevard of Daniel Boone?

An F-16 passed low overhead—a bully on the playground, pulling at a girl's hair. They cut through a courtyard where there was a water queue. Overhead somebody had written on a wall a message not to drink the water. This water was for washing, not for drinking, but that didn't stop the thirsty from drinking it. The bar, which they entered from the back, was already filled. There was a generator roaring on the outside, and inside the music pumped like a dragon's heartbeat.

In the bar there were soldiers in their rock and roll T-shirts and actors and professors and former students and a handful of journalists; there was beer, as if by magic; there was a man dancing on crutches, having recently lost most of his leg; there was a bald kid with a shotgun; there was smoke in the air, and dance lights cutting through the smoke. Stephen told Ado to tell Elise the story of the Unknown Lover of the Dark.

No, Ado said, blushing deeply. I cannot!

Stephen said, Of course you can. Who else are you going to tell?

After more prodding, and beer, Ado told Elise the story. He had to shout the details which Stephen pretended not to hear.

What? Stephen said.

Oh shut up. I am telling to Elise.

Elise put her hand in Stephen's pocket, listening. All around them people were dancing in the dark while Ado told the story.

Elise said, laughing, Oh Ado. I don't believe it!

Ado said, looking hurt, Who could believe such things?

I don't believe it either, Stephen said. But God it's a good story.

Maybe she is here, Elise said. The woman?

Ado made a joke. He said he could go to all of the women in the club and ask them each to make the certain sounds: *ahh haaa* and *oooh.* *Eeeh,* Ado said, swaying. Things such as that. He could run his fingers across their faces? Smell the perfumes? By curfew Ado was too drunk to stand. The doors locked, and the party went on, given that nobody could leave now until dawn. Consequently they danced and they drank and they ripped it up. Elise danced with her arms in the air, her sweater lifting, revealing the flesh of her pale stomach. Later, Stephen stood behind her, his body pressed into her by the press of the crowd. He could smell the perfume on her neck, sandalwood and lily of the valley, and the oil from her hair. He put his arms around her, his hands on the silver buckle of her belt. She took his hands and slid them slowly up her body, over the warm flesh of her stomach, across her breasts to the center of her chest. She rocked her body into his to the rhythm of the music. When she felt the length of his penis asserting itself against the seat of her jeans, thrumming with the music, she turned and put her arms around him and opened her mouth, kissing him.

Soon, she said.

In the morning they woke Ado, who, unsteady, drank a beer and went to meet his unit. They walked through the empty morning streets, the sun not yet up. They went through the park and up the steep hillside, past the Ottoman graves and the linden trees. It was a long climb uphill, and in his building, on the stairs, they passed the Soulful One and the Married Flirt on their way to work. Hello

Stephen, they called, their voices winking. At the top of the stairs, Stephen and Elise entered the flat. In the ceiling there was a hole the size of a small car. The windows to the living room had been blown out. Most of the furniture remained in good repair, though the walls were scarred with the results of shell fragments.

Elise said, Oh—

It's fine, Stephen said. Not like they're going to hit the same place twice. Besides, now the light will be better.

A skylight. For your models.

As a temporary fix, they hung a blanket over the windows; they nailed another to cover up the hole in the ceiling. They rearranged things and Stephen said, Are you hungry?

Yes, Elise said. Where is the bed?

—

An erotic encounter, writes Octavio Paz, *begins with the sight of the desired body. Whether clothed or naked, the body is a presence: a form that for an instant is every form in the world.*

Naked, then, she took Stephen by the hand. Naked, she ran her fingers across his throat. Then he kissed her throat, and she let out a sigh, and he felt that sigh vibrate against his mouth. He kissed her eyes. He kissed her navel.

She said, coming up for air, Which is the best way? For the first time? How is one to know?

He said, I don't have any condoms.

She said, I do. At the hotel. She said, sitting up, This way.

They sat facing each other, atop his sleeping bag, her legs around his hips, and she said, sliding her body onto his, I have condoms at the hotel. Then she arched her back, and he buried his nose into her neck and hair; she drew her nails along his spine; she breathed into his nose.

Q. Why does the act of love require movement and repetition?

A. Because the body wants to do it again and again.

As does the heart, which beats inside of it, and the voice which rises to give its assent. This, the encounter . . . *the engagement* . . . it affirms the heart's desire to make. It affirms nature's desire to join, to participate in that field of energy and light which makes it. So affirming, it transcends, and thus it is possible to make the body one with the body of another. All music has a rhythm, even fire, and all lovers believe in the possibilities of love, which is and always will be an act of faith. To love well is to know the power and grace of a god: it is to join in that field of energy and light all gods first require if only to describe. Spin a wheel on its axis, drop a coin into the sea—to delay the passage of time—to frame the moment, there—they made love in a single pose. They measured their bodies with their hands. Then they closed their eyes and then they opened them. She held him tightly. He kissed her mouth. She bit his ear.

—

Stephen, she said, in between sessions.

He said, Do you know what you said? A while back?

What?

Ja. You said, *Ja.*

She laughed, hard. Then he laughed until he was in tears. After a while neither could really breathe, and so he tried particularly hard to give it a rest.

She said, getting up, reaching for her jacket and her boots, *Wo ist die Toilette, Bitte?*

—

He stood at the window and watched her pee in the snow. Then he stepped outside, wearing only his boots, and did likewise.

—

She rested the side of her head on the palm of her hand, elbow cocked. She put her finger to the mark she'd made on his ear. She said, kissing his shoulder, Now I've made a mark.

You did that a long time ago.

On Hvar.

I kept watching you. And then we kept meeting—

She said, It is like Ado's story. Nobody will believe it.

They don't have to. They don't have to believe a single word.

She said, I did not want to do this unless I was certain.

Certain of what?

Certain I could forgive myself for breaking up your marriage.

He said, We have things to talk about. We have things I need to tell you.

About R.

About R. And my son.

What was his name? I should know his name.

Gulliver. His name was Gulliver.

Plate #22

A man and a woman, each wearing only a transparent shroud, facing each other. They are standing in profile in the center of the Goat Bridge. The landscape is white with snow. They are standing on the cold stones.

Music, especially that deriving from the voice, is best experienced live. A song remembered is like a boy's shadow: he sees the form, but not himself. Song remembered is not song felt.

They had some nice days which followed despite the war. They picked up some UNHCR plastic to cover the windows and the hole in the ceiling, which vastly improved the light. They went to see *Hair*—standing room only—and they went to the Holiday Inn and joined in a party there, and then they went up to Elise's room, and they took off their boots, their jeans and thick sweaters, and Elise draped her underwear on the doorknob, and they made love drowsily inside her sleeping bag. There was an odd wave of hopefulness in the air: perhaps the sides were going to talk things out? Then Peter Messinger arranged to show Stephen the Serb fortifications on the ridgelines, the Old Austrian Fort, and they took a brief trip with a television crew to Pale: at a checkpoint on the way back, the guards refused to accept their bribe and let them through until Stephen showed them first his faculty ID and then a membership card to a Bally health club. In the city, Anna and Elise interviewed a passing-through entourage of diplomats who spoke diplomat-speak while expressing hopefulness while surrounded by their seven bodyguards packing 9-millimeter Glocks. There was a drag race between two reporters in separate Yugos on Tito Street, and one of the reporters burned out his engine, which caught fire, and rolled to a stop in front of Tito's Barracks. Summerville had scouted out a woman recently turned to prostitution whom he now promised to deliver safely to the other side—by which he meant the West. Paris or Berlin. He was a guy with connections. He said, What good are they if you can't save a pretty girl? In the bar there was a visiting rock band carrying a lot of guitars looking mournful from their hard life on the road.

Life under the big top: all was pleasant given the general conditions, but then the enemy destroyed a neighborhood on the western edge, Otes, obliterating it with thousands of shells over a period of two days, and the hopefulness vanished like that. UN flights stalled. The smugglers and war profiteers raised their prices. Sniper activity increased. Then like a flat stone an outbreak of enterocolitis skipped across the city and everybody came down with the shits.

Ah shits, Messinger said to Stephen. Messinger took Stephen up the stairs several flights to a room. He opened the door to the room but the wall behind the door had been blown away, which made entering feel as if you were stepping into another world—a magic kingdom, where it was cold.

Messinger said, pointing at the distant timberline, I am getting out of here. I want a toilet that works.

So soon?

It is not going to change. We have the gist of the things. If people like me leave the younger ones will have more chances. All the motors on the cameras. Snap snap. It is a different world, Stephen. Nobody aims anymore. My pictures, they go on the same page as the tampon and the dishwasher. This war will make many of the young ones. It will establish them. When you are young you think, Oh God, please let my pictures appear in the same place as the tampon. But I am no longer young. I no longer care to sell the dishwasher.

Stephen said, Will you take Elise?

But I don't understand, Stephen.

To Zagreb. She needs to go to Zagreb but she won't leave. You know—

I don't think Elise will want to leave you.

I don't want to go yet. Not yet. I'm not done.

What are you doing? You never show me anything.

A project. Something to finish before I show it. I'm slow. I don't want to go yet. I said four months. It's not time.

It is not going to get better. Stephen, you cannot make it better here.

Stephen looked out through the massive hole in the wall, across Sniper Alley, to the dark mountains. He said, I know that.

So?

You know how everybody hates the press? Motherfuckers, you know? I mean, Evil Press, always trying to be rich and gain notice at the expense of the people they talk about. And there's a side of that, God knows. But for all those people who hate the press, especially here, in Sarajevo—if it weren't for the press and the UN this city would have been obliterated months ago. Erased. Like Tito's wife from the photographs. She never did exist. Sarajevo would not exist.

Yes, well—

Stephen said, I *know* I cannot make it better.

As you say, you are not a journalist.

I don't want to leave. I don't want Elise to stay just because I am.

This is slightly ironic, I think. I will speak with her. We are like brother and sister, only for the fact that I of course am much older and we used to be lovers and then she does the tearing of my heart in pieces. You are putting salt into the wound of my old man's heart.

Really?

No, Stephen. No. But of course you are right.

—

That night shelling erupted throughout the city. Like lambada, Ado said. *Boooom, boom boom boom boom.*

Stephen and Elise and Ado went to the cellar in his building. They were joined by the Soulful One and the Married Flirt and the old couple who lived on the first floor and their dog. The shelling lasted throughout the night.

There must be a push somewhere, Ado said.

I wouldn't know.

They had a candle: a wick in oil, burning slowly. There were no real candles left. People had stolen candles from the churches and cathedrals. A candle is romantic only when there is air to circulate; otherwise, it eats up oxygen.

Okay, Stephen said. Favorite Movies.

Dirty Harry, Ado said.

The Married Flirt said, *Top Gun. The Way We Were.*

Das Boot, said Elise. Or *La Femme Nikita. The Young Lions.*

Plenty, Stephen said. Anything by Fellini. *The Searchers.*

Dirty Dancing, said the Soulful One. And then she sang from that movie—*Baby! Oh baby!*—and Stephen's skin goosefleshed.

The Married Flirt said, Favorite Places to Do It.

There was silence.

You know, she said. The Lovemaking!

There was another silence, then an exploding shell. Then laughter.

Anywhere, said Ado. But of course.

Me too, said the Soulful One.

A boat, I think, Ado said. I have often heard good things about the boat.

Elise said, Oh, a train. Always a train.

Stephen?

I agree, he said.

More laughter, which rang hollowly. Even though they did not speak English, the old couple joined in. They sat huddled in the corner. The couple had no children to either lose or care for them, but they had their dog, which trembled beneath the shelling. And more shelling. Another hour passed. Then two. Elise took his arm and said, once, I'm frightened. *Really.* He had now a throbbing headache. It was going migraine, he could tell by the clouding of his vision; he needed air. Then at one point Stephen walked up the stairs to the third floor. He checked the new plastic on the windows, the hole in the roof. He went to the roof and looked out over the burning city. Everything, once again, was on fire. The houses and the streets and the people who had made them. He stood on the roof and looked out across the fires and the red and burning sky. People often confuse the sublime with that which is tender, and pretty, which is a mistake, because this was neither tender nor pretty: it was fierce and terrifying, apocalyptic. It *was* sublime. And this little city burning in this little pocket of the world—this was just a token, Stephen knew, of that which made the world. Likewise it was a token of that which will most likely destroy it.

He reached into his pockets and gathered all his loose change and flung it at the sky.

Fuck you, he yelled. Fuck you all to hell.

There was a sudden lull, then, and he could hear the coins landing on the rooftops—falling, tinkling like rain.

—

In the morning the dog would not go outside. The man of the old couple tugged on its collar, but in the doorway the dog stood locked like a mule. The man cursed and the woman cried. He did not hit the dog, but he cursed it, viciously, and yanked on the collar, while Stephen stepped out and turned to call to the dog. Still the dog would not budge, and now Elise entered the doorway, with the dog, and Stephen was crossing the deep yard when a shell—that whistling, first—landed behind the fence. Diving, he hit the ground while the shell exploded all around him. He had been saved, though he did not know it, by a tree, and when he rose—it was silent, except for the loud ringing in his ears—dusting himself off, he felt a wetness. Great, he thought. Pee in your pants. Pee in your pants in front of all the girls. Way to go, Steve, and his ears were ringing, bells in a cathedral, and he knew he was walking in a circle, a tight circle, checking the surroundings, the bark of the tree, and then he stopped to rub the wetness from his crotch, hoping to make it bleed into the fabric while he began nonchalantly to walk back to the house, which was difficult, given the trembling in his legs. He smiled, widely, and said, waving his hands, No problem.

Elise stood in the doorway, her mouth open, and made a slight cry. She pointed to his waist.

Fuck, Stephen thought. Fuck, and then he looked down and saw that the front of his khakis was soaked in blood. There was blood on his hands. And then, standing there, he undid his belt and dropped his slacks. A fragment had sliced across the glans—bleeding like a ripe tomato. Ginzu knife, he thought. $9.95. Collect them all. He thought, getting dizzy, What, now I'm going to faint? He said, loudly, No big deal. All in one piece. Really, and then he began to laugh. He laughed, really hard, and he was trembling and having difficulty hitching up his pants. Goddamn it, he said, trembling, God fucking damn it, and Elise stepped into the yard to help him do the belt while the old man and the old woman went to their apartment to find a bandage.

The dog, standing in the doorway, knelt down upon the mat and licked its paws.

—

He went with Elise to the Koševo hospital complex, which was bedlam. No plasma. No antibiotics. No anesthesia. Everywhere there was blood and misery and the indecent wail of human suffering. She spoke with people while Stephen waited in the basement. People were being delivered now by taxi, the drivers covered in blood. When she returned, she slipped Stephen two sealed packages.

They're sterile, she said. Take them.

She said, Don't argue.

His arm had been cut, too, tearing his favorite sweater. She took him to a doctor who sewed up in less than three minutes the top of Stephen's arm. The doctor used blue sewing thread. Then he taped the arm, and Stephen said, Thank you, and the doctor said, You are welcome.

They left and made their way to the Lion Cemetery. It was painful for him to walk, but at least his headache had cleared. Fog blanketed the mountaintops, making them safe. The giant stone lion at the center of the cemetery had been chipped and torn by repeated shelling. Its tail looked as if it had mange.

They sat in the curve of the statue's pedestal, the lion above them, looking out at the radio tower. Stephen said, pointing to a ruined building, The maternity hospital. They wanted to kill the babies.

Elise curled into his side; they watched the cold morning drift across the ruined Olympic complex.

Stephen said, Ado comes here. Before the war he'd come here and get high. It's a good place to meet chicks. You know, those suddenly available.

He's a boy, Ado.

Really. Once I watched him help a girl find a grave and by the time he was done he had her address and was dropping by twice a day to fetch her water.

She laughed. She said, I like him.

Stephen said, I used to read to my son. Gulliver.

Mm hmmm.

A book about a magnificent lion turned to stone. Just like this guy.

She said, I should read this book.

He comes back to life. It's a happy ending.

She said, taking his hand, I have to go to Zagreb. I'll stay with Nina. See the baby.

Okay.

I don't want you to stay so long, okay? Finish what you need to do.

He said, There's not going to be a happy ending here. The city is destroyed. Even if it ended now, right now, the city is destroyed. Stephen said, I want you to send a fax. To R. Tell her I'll call her in a few weeks and that I'm safe and well. Will you?

Yes, Elise said. Of course. She said, Stephen, promise me something.

Yes—

Promise me when I'm gone you'll pay attention to the dog.

Plate #26

*A man, dressed in a sweater and corduroys and socks, no shoes, seated in a chair. He is holding to his chest an open book. His hands are arranged so that one can just make out the title—*An American Tragedy.

Two days after Elise and Messinger caught the two o'clock flight out, Anna came by his building.

Oh Stephen, called up the Married Flirt. You have a visitor!

There were shoes at the door of his flat, and boots, in keeping with the tradition of Ado and Ado's family. Stephen was photographing a Serbian woman whose family lived in Belgrade. The woman, Biljana, had come to Sarajevo because her husband was a Muslim. Her husband was famous for having destroyed several tanks with an RPG. Each time he took out a tank, he'd pierce his ear. He had not left the city because he wanted to take out tanks and because his grandmother needed somebody to care for her, and then she had died, his grandmother, from a heart attack while walking up the stairs. On the sixteenth floor, she sat down, and somebody found her, rolling down the stairs to the landing. It took several hours to locate some petrol to put into a car and by the time they had there was no point in driving her to a hospital. Everybody in Sarajevo was dying for a lack of something.

Biljana was a striking woman—statuesque, in the manner of Botticelli's Aphrodite, though Biljana's hair, unlike that of Botticelli's model, had been shaved close to the skull. Less hair in the breeze meant less target to attract a sniper in the hills. Biljana was seven months pregnant. On her way from Belgrade to Sarajevo, somebody had cut off her ring finger with a pair of metal shears. Before permitting her to pass, the border guard's officer returned to her the ring so she might place it on her other hand. Stephen had fixed tea, and she was sitting on the sofa, when Anna arrived at the door beside the shoes.

I was lonely, Anna said at the door. And Summerville won't leave me alone. She said, May I come in? May I watch?

We will have to ask Biljana.

Yes, Biljana called. Of course.

I brought presents, Anna said, taking off her shoes.

She had brought three bananas from the Holiday Inn and a bottle of German wine—light, and very sweet. Though it was early, the light pouring in through the plastic sheeting was fair. It was not a cold day, but it was cold inside the apartment. The light caused one to expect it to be warmer.

Biljana rose, and stepped into the room Stephen used for sleeping, and changed into a robe. She emerged from the room and said to Stephen, Where am I to stand?

She had modeled before the war in Belgrade and Ljubljana for the magazines. She knew how to stand. Anna poured the wine into coffee cups.

Anna said to Biljana, A boy, I think. He's going to be a boy?

I think so, too, Biljana said, laughing, stepping back. She removed her robe, the scent of her body billowing out across the room as if caught in a small breeze. She had to be six foot one, Stephen thought. She weighed more than he did. Biljana laid the robe over the back of a chair.

Stephen drank some wine, which tasted warm, having been carried through the city beneath Anna's coat. Anna sat on the sofa, watching, sipping her wine. Stephen said to Biljana, testing the light, Who do you want to give this to?

Pardon?

This picture. It helps sometimes to know who it's for. He said, moving her arm into place, Can you open your fingers? Like a fan? There.

What do people say?

Here? Usually they say . . . I don't know. It doesn't matter what they say. It's best *not* to say. Look, this is the thing. It's not for the person who *sees* it. It's for the person to whom you *give* it. It's for that person only. So, you have only one person to give this to. Who is that? Don't say. Just know. Who is it for? First thing that comes to your mind.

Okay, Biljana said. I know.

Okay, Stephen said. There you go.

They took some other poses: Biljana, seated on the floor, her arms behind her for support; Biljana, standing on her tiptoes, her arms to the sky; another of her torso, arms also raised, out of the frame. When they had finished—it did not take long—Biljana put on her robe and drank a final sip of wine. Leaving, she kissed Stephen—cheek, cheek—and exited the apartment fully dressed with her robe tucked into a shopping bag which read *Saks Fifth Avenue.*

Anna said, Will you take one of me?

Yes.

Not for your thing. Your project. Just for my husband. Our children.

I have something for you already, Stephen said. You're at the airport, coming off a flight. The sun is in your hair.

No. I mean, you see. Like her.

Pregnant?

No no no. Stephen Brings, you are teasing me? She said, finishing her wine, Someday I would like a photograph—a beautiful photograph—the kind you make, of me in the nude. No, not nude. *Naked.* Even if I am not beautiful. That's the beauty, isn't it? The likeness? I am not a model like her, like Biljana. But someday I want a photograph of me for my husband. Who is one to ask?

You must have friends, Stephen said.

Yes, I suppose. She said, Elise and I are very close friends.

Yes.

She said, I think she will be good for you if you let her be good for you.

You know I'm married, Anna.

Oh, I don't think so. I know. *I* am married. *Peter* is married. My family, I am going to meet them in Bonn. My husband, he works for the government.

I knew that.

Some things will never happen and other things will. She said, Will you do something with me today? Will you help me pass the day? Always when I am away I get lonely and feel dark and then I don't know how to pass the days.

Me too.

I want you to do something for me.

Take your picture—

Yes, that. But not now, that's for later. I am not a part of this. I might be part of the description, but I am not what needs to be described. You can take my picture this summer when you and Elise come and visit us in Spain.

It sounds nice—

We'll go to the beach. To the mountains.

Maybe. I'd like that.

You will have to bring Elise or my husband will think we are lovers and spoil it. He's much older than me and becomes jealous easily, which is stupid. There is no man I could possibly love more. He mixes up the fucking with the loving. You will have to bring Elise. Promise.

Okay. If she'll come with me. I promise.

Anna smiled, having made him promise. She said, He is a man. Typical. Do you know Spain? I want to show you Spain. You and Elise, together. She said, I am glad we were not lovers. That one night.

Oh?

She laughed. She said, I like you more as a friend than a lumpy pillow in the dark. As a lover, I would have left you for my husband, or you would have left me, angrily perhaps, knowing I would not leave my husband. That is how one knows one is married, I think.

It's a new experience for me, Stephen said. I'm not used to it.

You mean Elise.

Yes.

Stephen, you must be very certain not to mix up the fucking with the loving.

I won't.

Because otherwise you will have more heartache.

—

That night he and Ado and Anna went to Skenderija—the Youth Complex Hall now turned UN Barracks. To get there they had to cross the Eiffel Bridge, which was tricky—*Pazi,* the sign read. *Snajper!* They had a small window between dark and curfew, and once across the bridge Ado led them to the trash receptacles used by the UN troops. Beneath, a shopping mall, with no products left to sell; above, guard posts sandbagged and filled with peacekeepers keeping track of those shot by snipers, keeping track of shells coming in. They were meticulous, the peacekeepers, at keeping count.

If abortion is murder, Ado exclaimed, then masturbation must be genocide!

At the trash receptacles, Ado selected the correct dumpster and leapt inside. He started going through it. He tossed things out, lots of raw garbage fetid with the stink of rich food. There were empty packages which had been delivered to the troops, boxes and boxes; there was office paper of the type one finds in offices. The only thing UN troops wanted which they could not get through the mail, through the incoming flights, was girls. There were a few pimps, running them, but mostly for the Big Guys. Ado was not a Pandarus, a pimp, but, he said, I know people. It's a small city. In a small city you get along by exchanging the things people do not have. He shrugged and said, The same as in the big city.

Sometimes, he said, he came here looking for guns; sometimes fresh food. Sometimes other things. Once he found six rocket-propelled grenades, just like that.

Ah ha, Ado said, tossing out several boxes, each of which was sealed, and inside each was a pair of boots. NATO boots. Much better than the Chinese boots which never fit. These boots varied in sizes in the European manner and the leather was really leather and of course these boots were not made inside a prison by somebody who did not even have a pair of slippers!

Somebody told me there might be boots here, Ado said. And look at the things we have found. Boots!

Will they fit?

I have very big feet. Like a camel. Two humps.

Ado knelt to the ground and removed a worn sneaker and put on a boot. Yes, he said, looking up, beaming. The boot fits. Who could believe such a thing?

How much does a boot cost? One that fits?

A boot like this? Oh, I don't know about such things as that. A boot like this is not so popular because it must be so big.

Uh-huh, Stephen said. You know what they say about guys with big feet?

Uh-huh, Ado said, lacing up the other, proudly. I do too.

Plate #28

A young man with a mohawk and pieces of metal studding his nose and lip. He is naked save for a single Nike high-top sneaker on his foot. He is leaning on a crutch, having recently lost his right leg just above the knee. There is also a ring piercing the head of his penis. He stands extending his middle finger in the classic pose: Angry Young Man.

An acquaintance, a professor, asked Stephen to give a talk to his seminar on the relationships between literature and photography. The professor explained it would be a useful distraction for everybody. Afterward, the professor would take Stephen to a dinner being held in honor of an American Diplomat's Birthday. The location of the dinner was top secret. They would arrive by way of a windowless APC. On the way, inside the APC, the professor said, That was more useful than I thought it would be. Thank you, Stephen.

The professor had done part of his training in the States and was highly regarded for his work on Dreiser. Clyde Griffiths, like Theodore Dreiser, was typically misunderstood, especially by Americans; the professor, his teaching load having been radically reduced, was active elsewhere in his efforts to save the city. The professor said, My grown children, they will leave as soon as it is over. But I am here. They will plant me here with the other stones.

Stephen said, You could go to any university in the States.

I suppose. But here I am of more use, I think. He said, Tell me about your project. You are trying to document the war?

No. Not hardly.

Then what?

There is a rule, Stephen said. I call it the rule of the shrink.

The psychiatrist.

The rule goes like this: whenever a shrink listens to a patient talk about anybody—his mother, father, his partner—the shrink is taking notes. The shrink takes notes here especially because here the patient is really describing what's led him here. To this shrink's office.

I see where you are going, said the professor. Like Jack Burden in *All the King's Men*? Like Nick in *Gatsby*?

A version of that, yes. When Sturges photographs a naked family on a beach in France, he photographs himself. He photographs his love and wonder for that family. For what made that family and for what brought him here to it. He photographs everybody wearing clothes.

So—

So when I photograph a figure of Sarajevo, of the other, I photograph also the self. Not just my self. Any watchful self. It may be a complete disaster. But I want people *not* to see an other. I want people to see the self they've made.

You could do this anywhere, said the professor. The Sudan. Bolivia. So why do you do this here?

Driving in, the first time, I passed that sign. That graffiti. *Welcome to Hell.*

Yes.

Hell, as I understand it, the real hell, not the fire and torture of the priests to scare the children—the *real* hell is permanent separation from God. Hell is being separated from that which made you.

The professor said, cautiously, This must cause God some pain, too.

Maybe. Stephen said, If I were God, yes. It would cause me pain, too.

I see.

I never knew that, Stephen said. I never knew that until I just said it.

Well, said the professor, pleased to have been of some use. Then I would like to volunteer. If you will have me, I would like to be photographed by Stephen Brings and visit your Chicago. The professor said this word, *Chee ka go,* as if he'd never been there.

When they arrived, they were led into a cellar, the doorway of which was protected by a platoon of UN troops. Inside, past the descending stairs, they entered a large room positively glittering. A chandelier the size of Rome, a rug the size of Baghdad, and in a much finer state of repair; there was a snazzily dressed fellow playing the ubiquitous Petrov upright; there were butlers carrying flutes of champagne on silver platters and women wearing thousand-dollar dresses with brooches pinned like medals to their chests. Stephen, shabby in his one sport coat and threadbare turtleneck and blood-stained khakis and dirty boots, felt adequately out of place. He needed a shave, a haircut. He needed a hot bath with some soap. Everything here in this room, unlike the rest of the city, was clean like raw steel: the glassware, the silver, and the jewels blinking like Christmas beneath the chandelier. Too, there was some reading of Wordsworth, in honor of some British chap particularly keen on Wordsworth, apparently all seven and a half million words' worth: some clapping, some glad-handing. A speech with kudos and false yuk-yuks. At the dinner Stephen was seated by a concerned Italian movie star who said to him once during the course of the meal, Pass the salt. There were several courses to the meal, and a half-dozen forks with which to negotiate it. The food was too rich to eat, and so he nibbled, politely, when he could. He felt light-headed and never finished his first glass of wine. Obviously he had a fever. When the American diplomat clapped his hands, a Moroccan manservant appeared, in uniform, as if from nowhere. As the dinner party began to wind down, Stephen became entangled in a conversation with an Intellectual.

The Intellectual said to Stephen, So, you are here for fun?

Excuse me?

The man was drinking a glass of red wine, not his first; in his free hand he held a tumbler of Ballantines. He had a cigarette tucked behind each ear—one of them, the cigarettes, was French. The man's suit, which had seen better days, was nonetheless of a superior cut to Stephen's outfit.

Fun, said the Intellectual. On safari. War tourism? You wish to understand our humiliation and suffering. You and Bianca Jagger? Joan Baez and her hippie songs?

Stephen's professor made a step to intercede, which Stephen did not understand, and which consequently failed. The Italian actress strode across the carpet on her Italian legs. The circle formed. The professor made a second attempt to rescue Stephen when the Intellectual called out—

You Americans! What could you possibly understand? What could you possibly know about suffering!

The professor turned and said something to Stephen. The American diplomat, pleased to have turned fifty, clapped his hands for the Moroccan manservant who appeared wearing white gloves.

A French woman in a navy silk dress smiled in sympathy.

Stephen said, What?

Our city, said the Intellectual. Our security, our basic necessities. While your airplanes fly every day over our rooftops! Degradation, said the Intellectual. That is the coin of this realm. Denial, that is yours. Of the United States. The Intellectual said, pointing to Stephen with his tumbler of scotch, Go home. Go home and eat your supper there. Play your guitars *there*.

The circle parted, and the professor guided Stephen, and helped Stephen with his coat, which smelled of woodsmoke and sweat and manure, and Stephen said thank you on the way out to somebody he did not recognize.

Outside an APC was filling up with departing guests. It was cold, and their breath steamed in the cold air. Stephen's side ached, as if he'd been struck by a downed power line, and his legs felt dangerously weak; the glans of his penis, having healed, felt nonetheless tender; the muscle in his arm throbbed in time to his cold heart. The wind blew against the fabric of his khakis at the knees, which *also* hurt. He was dizzy and trembling and made off to enter the APC when the professor held him back, stamping his feet in the cold, nodding to a second vehicle.

It is not you, Stephen, the professor said, shivering, taking again Stephen's arm. It is not you.

A tiny red dot sailed amid the stars across the sky. Mars? A satellite spy?

So, the professor said, letting go. So now we go home to the dark.

—

That night in the dark he had a dream in which he drove across the United States. He started in Manhattan and took the GW bridge and cut across Pennsylvania by way of the turnpike, then Ohio and Indiana and the Skyway past the abandoned Falstaff brewery: stopping for lunch in Chicago, he kissed R on the cheek, and she introduced him to her husband and his two teenage girls. R said twice during the course of lunch, We have to stop the Cycle of Violence.

She had grown older and more sad, though perhaps this sadness was just him, Stephen, driving into her life this way uninvited. Blasts from the past, when were they ever welcome? In her office hung a framed print of Stephen's which she removed from the wall and now returned to him. The space on the wall where the print had hung, it was described by a rectangle of missing soot—the passage of years. Then he shook hands with R's husband and drove past the refineries in Denver, doing ninety, the flames shooting up into the sky. In Nevada he realized it was odd, driving across the country without having yet encountered any traffic, and sometimes in the mirror he saw the face of a child—wide-eyed, silent, looking out the window. If flying was this, it felt like flying. At times he drove faster than the distance his lights could illuminate. Everything is light, he said.

I need to sleep, he told himself, because I'm going faster than the light.

You need to get there, a voice said to him, one which sounded like his father's. You need to get there. Then you can sleep.

I need to sleep, he said. I really need to crash.

—

Elsewhere in the city that night in the dark somebody turned on the gas. Zoran Jovanović, having awakened from a dream in which he drove a car into another on the Road to Life . . . having awakened from this disturbing dream, he sat up in his cold bed. The air smelled funky, as if it needed washing. Then Zoran reached for his cigarettes, and struck a match, and blew himself to oblivion.

—

Stephen ran to the window. There was a man in flames below him on the street. The man in flames was trying to put the flames out in the snow.

—

Stephen! called a neighbor from below. There's gas! They've turned on the gas!

Plate #32

A woman in the sunlight descending the ramp of a UN relief flight. The woman wears a white shirt with sleeves rolled up exposing her bare arms. She is wearing khaki shorts, socks, and hiking boots. The light shines on her knees, the sun and the wind fill her hair.

Life is preceded by the same silence which follows it. O, says the mouth, opening into the cold. The city was cold and silent, and he walked across the city in the cold night air. The mountaintops were covered with fresh snow. The sky filled with an ambient light. At times he cast a shadow; he listened to the steps of his boots echoing off the buildings—as if the streets and passageways were mere canals through which he was traveling. The voyage, he thought, is always uncertain, and all too brief. Despite its moments of turbulence. The scars of the bomb in the pavement: the concrete rose, the dragon's footprint. Earlier he had listened to a choir rehearse in the basement of a church. The basement had filled with the voices of the choir which now were lost to him. Song, like hope, always takes place in the moment which it fills.

He decided to cut through the Kamerni passageway, beneath the chamber theater, which was complicated by the dark. During the day, in the light, one could see the nuclear-bomb shelter with the vault-like door built in Tito's day to protect the population. So much for planning; so much for telling the people what the people wanted to hear: crawl into a vault, all several hundred thousand of you, and you'll be safe. In the passageway, he held his hand before him, a blind man, and stumbled in the dark.

That you? said a voice.

He stopped. A red light—the laser beam—on the wall beside him, circling. The light blinked, as if to give a signal. He felt his heart race belatedly into his throat.

Summerville's voice laughed in the dark. Over here, Steve.

The light blinked once again.

Stephen said, You are going to kill somebody with that thing. Somebody is going to kill *you.*

Nah, said Summerville's voice. Not me.

Stephen's eyes adjusted to the dark. He said, Maybe you shouldn't be so overconfident.

Summerville was sitting on a crate with his elbows on his knees. The passageway smelled like urine and smoke. Summerville said, lighting up a cigarette, the flame blinding Stephen all over again, What'cha doing, Pardner?

Going home.

Me too, Summerville said. Got lost. He said, holding out to Stephen a bottle which smelled putrid, Want a hit? A belt? Wanna snort?

No, thanks.

Gover something. Govo, nara gova. Something. Summerville said, Beats me. Got it from a peasant for thirty marks.

Really.

Tastes like shit, you ask me.

You okay?

Yeah. Me, I'm okay.

That stuff will make you blind.

Sit in the dark, you don't notice.

They listened to the clatter of a woman's heels clicking on the stones.

Stephen said, Don't turn that thing on. Do not do that. Just keep it in your pocket with your dick.

Lighten up, Steve.

They caught the woman's perfume as she strode by the two of them. From the look of her, she'd been at BB. The club to be, BB was it.

Summerville said to the woman, You speak English?

The woman, leaving behind a cloud of perfume and nicotine, said, lying, No.

Summerville laughed. Too bad, he called to her, laughing. Too bad!

Shit, the woman said. Bye-bye. And then she was gone onto Tito Street.

Stephen said, making up his mind, You can't stay here. It's cold. Curfew is coming. You'll end up in the clink.

I'm too drunk to go anyplace. He said, Besides—

Come on, Stephen said, lifting him up. He took the bottle. Stephen said, emptying the bottle in the passageway, This represents a massive failure of intelligence. You know that?

Summerville said, You think I'm a spook, Steve? A ghost in the night?

No.

That's perceptive of you now, isn't it. Everybody feels bad for the Bosnians. But I'll tell you, it's the Serbs who are fucked for life. I'm not even a journalist. My cousin, he edits a rag in Abilene. I send him letters; he calls me a reporter. Not the *Gazette,* I'll tell you that. Not the *Daily Planet.* Summerville said, I'm fucking nobody.

You are who you are.

You know you can get credentials that will make you anybody you want? Want to be born in Moscow, change your name to Vladimir, I know the guy. How 'bout Argentina. All you need is cash. Cash makes the ghost.

Yeah, Stephen said, catching Summerville's weight. A big fat one.

Watch your tone, Steve.

Then don't breathe on me. Jesus.

They had to cross Tito Street, where the light returned. They had to enter the park. Several times, going uphill, Summerville asked for permission to rest. Twice, he stopped to vomit. Jesus, he said, vomiting. Fuckin' A. This is a big fucking park. Then they'd start again, passing by the gravestones—those turbaned stone penises, glowing in the light. They passed beneath the giant trees.

Too bad that girl didn't speak English, Summerville said. Know what I mean? You know what I like? I like 'em real. Real girls. You go to any strip joint in America all the chicks have fake jugs. I'll tell you this, Steve, the milk of human kindness most certainly does not run through a fake jug.

Gotcha.

He said, It's not supposed to last. That flower of youth thing? He said, You can't make *that* last. That's why it's so fucking precious, don't you see?

I do, actually.

Say, you hear about the tunnel they're digging?

No.

You can see the scar marks in the porno films. You know that? Nah, you don't watch porno films. Too good for that. What is that? Me, I like the real thing. Nice thing about Europe, people still appreciate the real thing. Too bad they don't all speak English. I mean, too bad for them.

Uh-huh.

Thing is, I feel for these Serbs, you know. No matter what happens, they are going to become the fucking piranhas of the world.

Uh-huh.

That's right, Summerville said. Mean-ass fucking fish!

Got ya.

Not like your German pals. Oh no. Kill a few mill Jews, all is fine, we're best pals. The Krauts, they have industry. They have fi-fucking-nance. Technology. What the fuck does Belgrade have?

I don't know.

Exactly. Nobody does. And once the smoke all clears and the dumb-fucking dumbfucks get off the hills and go back home nobody will ever talk to a Serb again.

They had made it to Stephen's street now, which was steep, uphill, and very narrow. Walking with a drunk man, it slowed your progress. Stephen knew he did not have the strength to spare to be doing this. Summerville said, You hear about the tunnel?

No.

Somebody's digging a tunnel, Summerville said. Supposed to go under the airport. Top secret. Digging it right under the fucking UN. Very hush-hush.

Then maybe we shouldn't tell anybody—

Say, speaking of secrets. You like that girl? Really? The girl whose daddy makes elevators?

Elise.

That's the one. She's a looker, that girl. Kraut and all. He said, I was married once. Just like you, you know? Kids.

I didn't know.

Didn't like the life. Didn't like people who thought I was good. Thing about being a dad, your kids think you're good. They think you're better than you are just because you want *them* to be good. Me, I'm not good. I'm bad, Stephen Brings. I felt bad pretending all the time. I like to fuck and run.

There's always rehab.

More times than you can count. Not like you. You are good, even if you are getting some on the sly with Elise. Fräulein Kohlhaus? You should check out the busted elevators in the Holiday Inn. Jesus. Don't take offense. God knows I'd be in there pitching. Your pal, Messinger, he knows the score. He said, Jesus, where the by-golly fuck do you live?

It's not much more.

I like that Anna girl. I'm friendly friendly. But they don't like me!

They don't trust you.

How's that?

You lie.

Well. Just a little bit! Me, I like that Anna girl. Woman, excuse me. I like a girl with natural jugs. Milk of human kindness. I like girls who are already married and have suckled a babe or two. Who know what a man is like. Cuts down on the lying, you see. Not the pretend man. The real stinking snorting beast of a motherfucker.

You're not as bad as you want people to think you are. You're not even as bad as *you* think you are.

Just go dry out, huh?

And stop lying, maybe.

Clean up and wash away the sins of the world? You know that line in church, Christ died for your sins? Christ died for your redemption to save the blah blah world? I always think, *Everybody* died for your sins. *Everybody* died for the sins of the world. That's the fuck of it, you ask me.

They reached the door to Stephen's building. From nowhere came the lonely and metronomic sound of a man chopping wood in the dark. He could smell smoke in the air. The sky was bright.

What'cha looking at?

The light.

Well, Summerville said, swaying. La dee da. Looking at the light. He leaned heavily on a post. Then Summerville turned and put his cold hand on Stephen's shoulder, and said into Stephen's ear, sadly, *Boo.*

—

In the morning Summerville went out into the yard to retch. Ado and Stephen stoked a fire in a metal stove and heated up two cans of Hormel chili. When Summerville returned, he dug into his pockets and fished out a jar of aspirin. He said, looking at the chili, Just like home.

You should eat, Stephen said. After last night.

Stephen's own sides were blistering; his fever had intensified; standing, stirring the pot, he'd felt weak at the knees and wanted to fall back into his sleeping bag and sleep. The blisters on his sides felt like fire. It felt like a dripping hot fire.

Summerville said to Ado, taking a place at the table, You're that guy. You're that guy who does chicks in the dark?

Ado looked at Stephen, who shrugged. Stephen said, It's a good story.

Woman, Ado said. One *woman*. Be sure to tell the whole world. Ado said, At least I do not drink the liquors made from the shit of animals.

What's that?

Let it go, Stephen said.

Summerville said, elbows on the table, It's unbelievable, that story. The Affair of the Dark.

I know, Ado said, nodding. Such things.

Summerville said, So you guys have any condoms around here?

No, Ado said.

No, Stephen said.

Me, Summerville said, I've been using the same for a week. It's getting old, if you know what I mean.

Stephen said to Ado, Anna's flying out today.

Lucky Anna, Ado said.

Okay, Summerville said. Okay. Let's do Favorite Pop Stars.

U2, Ado said.

Stephen?

He set down his spoon. He pushed away his plate. No, he said. I can't do this anymore.

Bread, Ado said. You need some bread. I'll get some today.

David Gates, Summerville said. The Guitar Man! *Mm hmm mm hmm Baby it's hmm the Guitar Man.*

Stephen said, Would you give it a rest? Please?

Summerville said, taking Stephen's plate, You should get on that plane with Anna. You're not looking too spry.

What about you?

I'm working on that girl thing, Summerville said. I'm going to give that girl her freedom.

Oh, good.

Summerville said, For once I'm going to do something right.

Lucky you, Ado said, rising. He took his plate and set it in the sink which had no water. He said, I would like to say good-bye to Anna.

They arranged to meet at the Holiday Inn. Ado said he would bring home some bread. Summerville asked which way Ado was going, and they went out the door together, regular pals. He listened to their boots thumping down the stairs.

Later, when Jusuf returned from his shift at the Goat Bridge, Stephen heated up some water for tea. Then Jusuf hooked up a radio attached to a car battery and for a while they listened to pop music from Armed Forces Radio piped in from Bonn.

—

They stood outside behind the Holiday Inn with the burned-out Unis Towers standing guard. The ground, everywhere, was littered with broken glass. Following the rules, Anna wore a flak jacket. She kissed Ado good-bye, cheek to cheek, and she placed into his hand a fistful of marks.

No, Ado said. I cannot—

Yes, Anna said. She had tears in her eyes. A Blue Helmet was talking to another Blue Helmet at the APC which was going to deliver her to the airport—a flight to Split, and then to Zagreb. Given the distance she'd spend more time on the ground than in the air.

Ado said to Stephen, I am going inside. I will get us a drink.

Anna said, wiping the tears from her eyes, This is stupid. I'll see you in a couple weeks, right?

Right, Stephen said. He was fatigued from the walk over. His right side especially ached and he felt as if he'd been branded with an iron. He was dizzy and hot.

I'm going to go to the Esplanade, Anna said. I'm going to burn my clothes and take a bath and walk around in one of those cotton robes and order salmon! Meet me at the Esplanade, Stephen. Me and Elise. Okay?

Okay.

Say it again, she said, shivering in the cold. Promise. Say okay, Anna. I'll meet you at the Esplanade.

He saw a shadow pass, a bird's. Her hair was tied up. The wind kicked up and tossed her bangs. She wiped her eyes and was smiling now, and she said, Well, say good-bye for me, will you—

And as he reached to embrace her, he heard the crack, the sonic boom of the round passing by his ear, while Anna's face exploded.

—

He wiped the blood from his eyes. He knelt on the ground, screaming, cradling the back of her head in his hands.

—

The blood stayed in his eyes, blurring his vision. It was hot on his fingers, the blood, and he pulled Anna's body behind a dumpster reeking of shit. The Blue Helmets at the APC arrived, automatic weapons in tow. There was a cab, nearby behind an overturned bus, and they waved the cab down. They put Anna in the cab and Stephen climbed inside and held her. It was only a few hundred yards to the Military Hospital. At the hospital he was told she would not die. Her lower jaw was missing, as were several of her teeth. She would not die so long as she did not stay. She needed, said somebody with blood on her clothes, to be stabilized.

—

He stayed with her the night. In the night she slept courtesy of humanitarian morphine which had arrived on the incoming flight she was to have departed on. In the morning Ado brought him bread. They used a phone set up at the Holiday Inn to contact Elise and Anna's husband. Ado had made arrangements with people to have an APC pick her up at the hospital. The APC picked her up, and Stephen took the ride with her to the airport. There was a film crew arriving and two others departing. The departing crews helped Stephen get Anna on the plane. Across the tarmac a handful of red and green tracers fired across the darkening sky.

Plate #36

A naked man—tangled hair, a scar across the muscle of his arm—facing the camera, holding in his outstretched hand a photograph. The man holds the photograph with his thumb and forefinger. The photograph is obviously the size of this photograph. In the photograph the man is holding there is the figure of a small boy. The boy is striding across a plaza: behind him, a woman, her head cocked, admiring the architecture of St. Peter's mid-stride. In the back-

*ground, opposite that woman, three young priests in black
cassocks stroll across the plaza. They are laughing in the
sun.*

Ado met him at the Holiday Inn. Stephen said, I hate this fucking
place.

Go.

Stephen said, looking up, I'm sorry. It's not fair. I know I can go.

Ado said, Stephen, we all can go. The question is *where* we go.

Thank you, Stephen said. For before.

She did a story about my friends, you know that? Came to the
trenches and then she sent my photographs to her magazine in Spain.
My photographs. I am a photographer now in Spain. Someday maybe
I will be like you.

—

They had more drinks despite the stiffened blood on Stephen's
clothes. The sky was too bright to walk safely in. Summerville arrived
by way of an armored Land Rover with his girl on his sleeve. She had
pressed clothes. A miraculously clean white cotton shirt. She was a
beauty—Balkan features at their best: a little Turk, a little Austrian,
throw in a pinch of, what, Greek? Chinese? Why were the most beautiful people always of mixed ethnicity? There was a lesson there, a
moral. There was an understanding which could grow common.

No more drinks, he told himself. Then again, the drinks quenched
the fire burning at his sides.

Summerville said, Steve. I'm sorry. God, I'm sorry. Is she going to
be okay?

I guess.

Summerville said, Those things I said, you know. I was cocked, you
know? I didn't mean any of those things I said.

It's done, Stephen said. Let it go. Really.

—

He ate a fistful of bread. As the afternoon began to darken, as he and
Ado were making ready for the walk home, two soldiers came running
in through the back door. They had been looking for Ado.

Having found him, they spoke urgently.

Ado said, rising, Stephen, I must go.

Where?

To the river.

Why?

Somebody wants to talk to me. War profiteer. He insists on talking to me. It's probably nothing. A jokester. A funny guy. But the commander says I must come. My commander.

They had to make it across the street to the museum, which was dangerous in the light. We do this at the same time, Ado called. Okay? At the same time!

Okay.

Okay.

They bolted across the street, across the median and the tram tracks, and then the other half of the street. Once they reached the safety of the other side there was a sense of anticlimax. As if all that effort—the running, the panic—had been for naught. They hit a trench and made their way beneath the bridge to the river. There were two soldiers, different soldiers, with a wireless radio. Everybody had been waiting. The commander appeared and tapped his watch.

The commander spoke to the radio, announcing Ado's arrival. Across the river the buildings facing the river were blasted into ruin. Gutted by fire. By looters. Nothing inside but men behind sandbags with automatic rifles standing guard. Snipers, their barrels poking through spaces meant for bricks.

Ado spoke into the radio. There came shouting from the other side.

Ado shouted back.

More shouting.

Fuck, Ado said to Stephen, pointing to the handset. This fucking guy.

Then, more shouting, and Ado slammed down the radio. He was trembling. He rubbed his eye with a fist. He swung his arms and hugged himself in the cold.

What?

He asked me if I was Ado.

And?

I said I was Ado. He asked me if I was the same Ado who is the Ado who fucked his wife.

Stephen looked at his friend. He felt a chill in his heart. He said, feeling his chilled heart quicken, Really?

I told him to go fuck himself.

Shots fired on the other side of the river. A man in a fourth-floor window stood in the window and fired his weapon into the air.

Then another voice shouting Ado's name across the river.

Ado! Hey Ado!

And a woman's body in a green dress thrown over the side of the building. There was a telephone cord wrapped beneath her armpits; there was blood dripping from beneath her dress down her legs to her bare feet. She swung in the cold against the ruined building. She was alive.

And then there was another voice, screaming. Ado's.

Inside the tunnel, one of the soldiers beside Stephen raised his rifle and aimed across the river and fired at the woman. He missed the first time. The second time, he hit her shoulder, and she swung slowly around.

Then another cursed and shoved the soldier aside, aimed his rifle, and shot her in the head.

So that she died.

—

Later that night Stephen said, Was that her? Was it her?

Ado said, drunk and in tears, I don't know.

Ado said, his hands shaking, Maybe.

—

Ado said, wiping his eyes, I think so. I think it must be so.

Notes

From *War and Peace;* from the page where my father stopped reading:
  "When the apple is ripe and falls—why does it fall?"

Notes for Lecture on Triads and Unisons—
  A major chord is made up of three notes. CEG makes the chord C.
  This harmonic arrangement can be adapted to matters of literature and visual composition, depending upon one's knowledge of the
language, or key, that one is working with.
  A simple literary triad might involve the words *key* and *lock* and
hair, as in Alexander Pope's "Rape of the Lock." Study the common
things of this world long enough and things reveal increasingly what
they have in common: namely, the language by which we describe
them. This search for detecting forms of order and arrangement,
always, is the work of all artists, regardless of form.
  Art joins; war, like pornography, separates.
  Bosnian, Croat, Serb—this the great triad of Yugoslavia . . .
  Fuck Pope. Won't work.

3

The artist uses the pun to connect that which *feels* disconnected. The
artist—the hand of God—employs the pun to deflect attention onto
the feeling of wholeness and interconnectedness aroused by the work.

Pun is the wrong word: a fusion of meaning, a verbal pivot—this device provides just another way of looking.

For example: A common triad of photographic expression in Sarajevo involves images of *glass* and *eyes* and *boots*.

The eyes, you see, are the windows to the soul. Here the windows are all shattered, thanks to the men in boots. A man's boot—or a woman's shoe, a child's sneaker—is designed to protect the human sole. This language has become increasingly iconographic and, consequently, clichéd.

Prose writers and poets often work with triads, which merge, or join with, other triads—a common root holding them together; but then prose writers and poets have the luxury of narrative—melody—with and in which to make their jazz-like discoveries. Jazz-like for the way words and their meanings permit various notes to bend—to make a sustained sixth, for example. To improvise and syncopate and bend the form to provide tonality.

Each composer signs his or her name by way of a signature.

Likewise, photographers often develop bodies of work which embrace thematic unisons.

—

A unison—two notes, the same, though played on a stringed instrument in different places—is a prime interval. A common photographic unison in Sarajevo involves images of blood and images of bread. Sometimes the images of bread are soaked in blood. The image—its scale—is a consequence of a shared historical context. Namely, the breadline massacre outside the Austrian Market on Ferhadija.

One Sarajevan photographer, Kemal Hadžić, is taking photographs of the city's empty morning streets, glistening with rain, and the sewers which collect that rain. The photographer goes to the Holiday Inn and exchanges the film he has shot for chemicals and more film with members of the foreign press who, in turn, publish the photographs of the photographer under their own names.

Other unisons?

Sebastio Salgado's photographs of migrations in seas and waves and all those people drowning therein;

That French guy's books which always have naked women and cats. Ugh;

James Nachtwey's photographs of dead bodies which leverage among other things the implications of the word *lie.* Dead bodies, or those bodies in the state of dying, don't tell lies. (Rather, governments which cause dead bodies do.) Eventually all dead bodies lie down. This becomes in effect one's resting place.

Peter Messinger's photographs of convicts and industry—that which makes the bars—and the ways in which he repeatedly frames those photographs, thus confining further the subjects while, concurrently, releasing them.

—

Take theater. Our understanding of which is premised on Shakespeare's observation that all the world's a stage. Even in a *theater* of war. This theater/play unison is gaining currency in Sarajevo. Show the photographs of Mladen Pikulić and Milomir Kovačević. Here the children are at play with guns, acting out the scenes. On the surface we see pictures of children at play wearing cardboard flak jackets and kitchen pots for helmets, and we are deeply moved; below the surface that feeling is charged and informed by the relationships amid our collective understandings of the words *theater* and *play* and *stage.* *Play,* in this case, is the pivot which connects one meaning with another, which charges our feeling with understanding, and vice versa.

Harmony, the heart of the triad, means different things to different people.

Unison means *all together.*

4

A Quiz:
  Q. What was the prophet Mohammad's first command to the
      faithful?
  A. *Iqra.* Or, *Read.*

A Parable:

Montenegrins are treated by way of Yugoslav humor roughly. They are lazy, this is the pith of it. Where does a Montenegrin woman place her money to keep it safe from her husband? Under a shovel.

One day the Diplomat of Montenegro was talking with the Diplomat of China. The Diplomat of Montenegro was quite serious about declaring war. We are going to declare war, said the Diplomat of Montenegro. Montenegro, of course, is a small region of, let's say, three hundred thousand. Be that as it may, the Diplomat of Montenegro was very serious. He said, We are going to declare war on you in China!

The Diplomat of China said, kindly, That would be unwise. We are a big country.

How many do you have there, anyway?

A billion, give or take.

Ah fuck it, said the Diplomat of Montenegro. Too many graves.

6

Militarily Speaking:

Q. What is the Common Ground?

A. The Battlefield.

7

The Stars:

In the old days one honored the king, the dictator or president, as a way of honoring the people. In the old days one looked to the stars.

Lightning, it came from the sky, and gave us electricity. Something to plug into. Then came modernity, industrialization, and light pollution. In these vast modern cities of suburbs and malls the stars disappeared from the sky.

So we had to find our stars elsewhere. So we had to turn on the TV.

There is a star up in the sky for everybody, my father used to say, pointing to the night sky. At the time there were billions in the sky.

Go out some night and look. What do you see?

∞

God is light. A young boy when you place him on your shoulders is also light. The heart beats lightly just before it begins to die, or wake. A ship's wake is typically filled with the light of the sun or the moon or the darkness of the sea. To wake is, in all things, the test and end and means of art. To wake is to celebrate the dead. To wake is to return. To wake is to open up your eyes and see the light.

9

From *Ways of Seeing,* by John Berger:

"To be naked is to be oneself.

"To be nude is to be seen naked by others and yet not recognized for oneself. A naked body has to be seen as an object in order to become a nude. (The sight of it as an object stimulates the use of it as an object.) Nakedness reveals itself. Nudity is placed on display.

"To be naked is to be without disguise."

10

Worst Dental Stories:

A catalog, from last night:

I told my story—the abscessed molar, leading to an emergency root canal in Guatemala, leading to a hospitalization in Panama City.

Summerville told a story about a bull, lots of pulleys and ropes—for the bull, not the tooth—eventually involving a small sledge, which did involve the tooth.

Anna confessed that her husband refused to go to a dentist who was not a woman. If he must have his face plastered up against another's chest, then that chest had best belong to a woman. Anna is always having to call to make sure the dentists and hygienists are female! Very embarrassing, apparently, but an embarrassment she tolerates. This condition of their marriage is prefigured too by a particular incident. Once in London her husband needed two new crowns, which he had done there. After fitting them, the dentist (this one male) left the final work of sealing those crowns to the assistant (also male) who proceeded to glue them on. But in so gluing the assistant reversed the crowns—accidents happen—so that the wrong crowns were attached to the wrong teeth. Apparently Anna's husband's jaw is still a wreck, though this incident—the permanently bonded crowns to the wrong teeth—took place years before the birth of their child.

Messinger told a story about a man he knows blinded in one eye—permanently—on account of the dental assistant–in–training sneezing with the ice-pick thing in her hand.

Ado said, Who would believe such things?

King me, Gulliver used to say, playing checkers.

11

On Graves:
Q. Where do they go?
A.

12

From *Camera Lucida,* by Roland Barthes:

"The photographic look has something paradoxical about it which is sometimes to be met with in life: the other day, in a café, a young boy came in alone, glanced around the room, and occasionally his eyes rested on me; I then had the certainty that he was *looking* at me without however being sure that he was *seeing* me: an inconceivable distortion: how can we look without seeing?"

13

A transcript of a conversation regarding the pizzeria Chuck E. Cheese
which features among other attractions a brightly lit arcade: the conversation which follows took place between Gulliver Metcalf-Brings,
then Age 3.2, and his Best Friend, Liam Smith-O'Connor, Age 3.1, on
the way to Humboldt Park in the backseat of a red 1987 Jeep Chero-
kee. In keeping with the laws of the state, both boys sat in their car
seats. They sat each like a king upon the throne.

Liam:	I want to go to Aerrnn Cheese.
Gulliver:	What's Aerrnn Cheese?
Liam:	It's where you live.
Gulliver:	No. I live in Honore Street.
Liam:	What's Honore Street?
Gulliver:	My neighborhood is Honore Street. I live in Honore Street. What's Aerrnn Cheese?
Liam:	I want to go to Aerrnn Cheese. You get a cup with coins in it.
Gulliver:	I live in Honore Street. Do you want to ride my bike?
Liam:	What's Honore Street? I want to go to Aerrnn Cheese.
Gulliver:	What's Aerrnn Cheese?
Liam:	It's where you live. *L.* You say, *L.* It's where you *live.*
Gulliver:	No. I *live* in Honore Street.
Liam:	What's Honore Street? I want to go to Aerrnn Cheese.
Gulliver:	You can ride my bike. After I show you, first.
Liam:	I don't know how to ride bikes.
Gulliver:	That's okay. I'll show you. What's Aerrnn Cheese?
Liam:	I told you. You get a cup with coins in it.

14

From *The Mind's Eye,* by Henri Cartier-Bresson:
"My passion has never been for photography 'in itself,' but for the
possibility—through forgetting yourself—of recording in a fraction of

a second the emotion of the subject, and the beauty of the form: that is, a geometry awakened by what's offered."

15

A Catechism:
    Q. Why do you believe in God?
    A. Because without faith the only thing left to believe in is what's on television.
    Q. What's wrong with celebrity?
    A. Not everybody gets invited to the table. In the old days everybody had a chance to be redeemed.
    Q. If heaven is a myth, can't Hollywood whip one up?
    A. It can. Problem is it will last typically under two hours.
    Q. Do you *really* believe in God?
    A. Yes.
    Q. But don't you want to be a star? Don't you want to see your name in lights? Don't you want to have your picture taken?
    A. I want back my son.

16

Another Parable:
    Once I watched a movie about Thomas Edison. The movie starred Spencer Tracy. My father loved Spencer Tracy. He said, Spencer Tracy, he's a good man. How my father knew this I have no idea. My own thinking is that Spencer Tracy is a *weak* man: back always hunched, mumbling through his teeth, scamming on Katherine Hepburn, whom my father also admired. In the movie about Thomas Edison we are to understand that Spencer Tracy—Everyman—is under a terrible strain to be a genius, which is why he invents the electric pen. He invents the talking machine, or phonograph, and thus the recording industry and Madonna. But the *real* thing he invents, the utterly amazing thing, is the electric light. Spencer Tracy in the manner of Thomas Edison found a way to make the light of this world electric.
    At the end of the movie Spencer Tracy in the manner of Thomas

Edison delivers fraily a speech imploring humankind to bring science and humanity into balance. It is an effort to join, to bring together, the elements of this world lest it turn to ash. What is fire if not the essence of consumption? I think my father admired Spencer Tracy because Spencer Tracy exuded an air of humility; my father, after his wife died, my mother, never married again, and was lonely for the next thirty years, what with my not being able to fill that place in his heart my mother had. My mother died; my father died; I will die.

My father died knowing that my son was lost.

Maybe he'll come back, my father said, before my father died. Maybe he will find his way back home.

17

From *On Photography,* by Susan Sontag:

"A capitalist society requires a culture based on images. It needs to furnish vast amounts of entertainment in order to stimulate buying and anesthetize the injuries of class, race, and sex. And it needs to gather unlimited amounts of information, the better to exploit natural resources, increase productivity, keep order, make war, give jobs to bureaucrats. The camera's twin capacities, to subjectivize reality and to objectify it, ideally serve these needs and strengthen them. Cameras define reality in the two ways essential to the workings of an advanced industrial society: as a spectacle (for masses) and as an object of surveillance (for rulers). The production of images also furnishes a ruling ideology. Social change is replaced by a change in images. The freedom to consume a plurality of images and goods is equated with freedom itself. The narrowing of free political choice to free economic consumption requires the unlimited production and consumption of images."

18

The Stripper's Last Word:

First, she takes your eye. She places herself at a distance so that you may observe her fully—she appears, always, to be admiring you the way you are her. Now she places her hand to her breast and raises it to her mouth. She licks the tip of her breast, the nipple, which incites arousal on the part of the viewer.

She puts her hands on your shoulders and draws you in; she puts her breasts into your face, her nipple to your eye.

Spit in the eye, she thinks. *Take that.*

19

On Meaning:

    Q. What does Stephen mean?

    A. What does anybody mean?

20

On Teeth:

In this part of the world the officials do not attempt to match unidentified bodies with their dental records, though still the snipers in Sarajevo often aim to hit the jaw, at least on a man. For a woman, the snipers seem to prefer a breast, as if to eat it.

21

Note to Self:

    Q. How do you exit the program?

    A. Hit *return.*

The Return

The field, writes St. Matthew, quoting Christ . . . *the field is the world.*
By definition fields are typically enclosed—a field of battle, a field of
wheat. And that which encloses—a highway, a fence, a set of theoret-
ical constructs, a shield bearing a Red Cross, or the circumference of
a coin . . . that which encloses is also that which defines. Like a book
caught between its boards, like a body dressed in linen, a field is any
given area visible through the lens of humanity, and that which
occludes this vision—malice, or ignorance—is that which also
describes the limitations of the human eye. For a photographer, depth
of field—or perspective—is measured by manipulating for a given
image the amount of darkness visible—a phrase from *Paradise Lost.*
Thou shalt not worship any graven images, we are told, because
God—and any god, at that, including the god of free enterprise—is a
jealous God. Sometimes it's enough to make the people of this world
wonder: this human failing, jealousy, so carelessly attributed to the
divine.

What happens when a boy disappears?

When a man has a boy, things happen, and in this manner Stephen
evolved into another man. He no longer smoked in the apartment,
lest he put at risk his baby's health; then he quit smoking, like that,
should he die prematurely on account of it and leave his child
stranded. He chewed gum and gained weight and went to the gym
and pumped iron like a college sophomore until the seams on his
clothes began to split. He gained weight, and mass, and strength.
Sometimes, going through a door, it was difficult not to brush against
the jambs.

And it was nice, what happened next: R and Stephen's union had
been based on a youthful sensibility they had each outgrown, and
then it had been reborn into a union based on adult heat, and now,
after the arrival of Gulliver, they traveled slowly through a kind of
second honeymoon. They lay in bed, and they talked in bed, and in the

bed they brought their perfect baby with the magic heart to sleep between them. And the figure which had so often come between them over the years, R's old college chum, the guy who'd since become a vice president, had been relegated to the past. In the past the guy and R had played house together until R decided she liked Stephen, even though she didn't *really* like Stephen—he was becoming too set in his thinking about matters which disagreed with her own; and he was, well, kind of snobby. He was, well, *so certain*—but Stephen, he was more sexy in the irresponsible bohemian sort of way. He was, unlike the vice president, often unavailable, and this lack of availability was essential in understanding Stephen's relationship with R. R was a woman who wanted a man most when she did not have him. She liked the challenge of it. Look at what I can do, she said. She liked the getting of her way.

R's way, which meant *my way or the highway,* and which made a union with Stephen problematic given that she could not always change his course. She had a nasty habit, for example, of correcting one's English; mid-sentence, at dinner, and typically in front of others, she'd stop him and recommend changes to his diction.

No, you mean *reveal.* Not *betray,* Stephen.

Yeah. Thanks.

Too, and conversationally, she had to be at the center, which was fine so long as one didn't have anything to say. More and more, he just bit his tongue, and after a while he began to be really bored. It became boring, like arguing about the First Amendment, or talking about the Oscars, this constant need to be at the center of the world. Look at me, R seemed always to be saying. *Look at me!* But with Gulliver, that hunger to be always at the center shifted perceptibly. The baby was now the center. The baby was what they looked at. And Stephen began socking away money for his son's college fund; he began taking fewer trips for himself and instead went to visit other college art departments for the honorariums. He came home earlier from the university than he used to, and he avoided the pretty students who took nude pictures of themselves, especially the ones who stopped him on the lawns in spring, and then he began avoiding anybody who was female. Anybody at all, should he be giving off the wrong signals.

I have a son, he told the world. Stay away.

Then he found out R was doing all over again the college chum/vice president during lunch while their baby was at daycare, and he blew his top.

What the fuck, he said. Are we not grown-ups?

It's nothing, R said.

Indeed.

You don't give me what I need, R said. He at least needs me.

He said, Buy him a vibrator.

She said, You don't think I'm smart anymore.

He said, Get another master's degree.

She said, You used to think I was smart and now you don't listen to me.

He said, I still think you're smart when you aren't being so stupid. What, you want to marry him? Not *me,* okay. Fine. But *him?* You want *him* to raise your kid? You want to marry a guy who goes after *partnered* women with a kid?

No, she said. No. I want you. But I want *all* of you.

And he said, Well, fuck me, R. Just fuck me blind.

And then he left. He kissed his son good-bye and went to Texas and spent eight months working on a ranch. The flyover, that's what people in the media called anything between New York and LA. He went to Texas and disappeared into the flyover.

Weekends he didn't visit home (a Chicago hotel, so that he might see Gulliver), Stephen went with the cowboys to the strip joint in Amarillo where the skinny girls who did meth with teased hair and gapped teeth danced in front of the fat, married men just like the real strippers on TV, and they'd get all liquored up, as was the fashion, and back at the ranch Stephen would take a cold shower in order to wash off the smoke and cheap perfume. R began sending letters, asking when he was going to return. There was a girl on the ranch, the owner's daughter, who was sweet on Stephen, and they flirted with each other patiently—like horses circling in a corral, high-stepping up to nuzzle each other's heads. Aside from this love of horses, what did they have in common? The girl was pretty in her jeans and boots. Stephen thought, What do we talk about in ten years? He thought, I am not a cowboy. Though sometimes when he and the girl went riding he thought about becoming one. He could change his life and become something other than what he was. People did that, right? They changed? At night, though, he missed his son. Sometimes he and the girl went riding to a reservoir fed by a tributary of the Red River. He'd chew on a blade of grass. The girl, being a cowgirl, knew how to seat and collect her horse. She'd chew on a blade of grass and gaze at the dusty points of her booted toes, and then one day on the bank of the river she said, out of the blue, I went away once. To college. I'm not doing that again.

I know, he said.

You're going to go away, she said. You're just a tourist. That's okay. Okay.

She said, You should go back home to your wife and son.

She was right, too. Gulliver was growing up and it would be useful for Stephen to be around more than every third weekend in a hotel. He wasn't going to be an absentee father. Enough said.

So he went back and forgave his wife, who in many respects, especially emotionally, *was* smarter than he was, and he said, This doesn't have to end.

I've been saying that for months, R said. What, you finally read your mail?

And after a while they were happy again, and Stephen's book came out, *McClean, Texas,* and two or three people in two or three circles took some notice. In the book there is a photograph of the pretty girl in jeans seated on a mustang. She has the horse's reins in her teeth; she is tugging at her gloves; the neck of the horse, preparing to buck, is curled up tight as a muscle. That was a real success, that photograph, and it had now become a part of the permanent record: first, he was going to leave R, and then she became pregnant, so they partnered up. Then she had an affair with the same guy she always had an affair with, and he left her, but only temporarily, because he knew R wasn't going to marry the guy she'd had the affair with. That's *why* she'd had the affair. To accept what you had was to admit failure for not having what you did not.

People said about old lovers that so and so was like a brother, or a sister, and this made sense to Stephen, despite—or perhaps because of—the twinge of incest the sentiment evoked. It made sense, though: *family.* He knew R better than he knew his father, whom he never really knew at all. Once, when they were twenty, Stephen had nursed R through a bout of food poisoning so severe it had caused her while vomiting to shit all over the floor. That, she had said. That was love, your not leaving me after that! And she had nursed him, too, when he was in need of nursing. He could be a needy guy, he knew that, especially when the light was bad. The dark winter skies. And too, she had been his first girl: the first time, doing it, having no idea where to go. He was nineteen and all ribs and terrified out of his mind. They were at a house R was watching for the weekend. A rich couple's house. R pretended it was theirs and walked around, at twenty, in a green silk robe which belonged to the married woman now off in Vienna, or Rome, and they drank two seven-dollar bottles of champagne (because she was twenty, and he was nineteen) and they watched cable TV because it was new then and had sex on it. Then she leaned back on a set of pillows, as if she were a courtesan, and the robe parted like the parting of the sea, and she took Stephen who could not stop trembling and undid his belt and slid off his clothes and pulled him inside her body—and he had thought, going there, She's smarter than me. She knows everything.

She was sexually experienced; he was sexually naïve. Her pubic hair was gold, like an old, Roman coin, and she had a mole beside her navel he used to call the North Star, and then she taught him the location of other constellations, and certainly marriages have been formed on shakier platforms than that. They liked the same books, they worshiped the same teachers who had taught them how to read. Too, he loved her body, all lonesome highway and curves. He loved the way she carried her body, like a boxer, on her toes. He loved the way she'd stand in the cafeteria at the ice cream table, hip cocked, as if to express all the sexuality of the world into a single dish.

Why did she become an abortion-rights activist? Because she could.

Because this, according to R, had become her passion.

Fair enough, he supposed, but it spelled trouble from the start. Not that Stephen wasn't pro-choice. But it spelled trouble, this career track of hers, if only because it required her to spend time in circles which would not give Stephen the time of day. Then she took to referring to Stephen in public as her *partner,* lest anybody even *think* they might actually be married; she went to poetry slams celebrating anger and injustice; she talked about the Cycle of Violence, because she knew a lot about it now, violence, having become officially left of center. Having a child had made Stephen move simultaneously to the left *and* to the right, while R, as her reputation and stature grew, set up a permanent camp along the left bank of the Chicago River. She'd say things like *Tax the rich motherfuckers* in order to get a laugh; and she'd say *Corporate Welfare* as if it were equivalent to child molestation, and as if her office (and her salary) were not funded by the revenues of corporations. In a restaurant she'd look at a table of men she did not know and say, *Two o'clock: Fat White Men Alert.*

He thought, Why is she becoming so hateful?

And one day he said, I think you should start listening to some of the things you say.

And she said, What, now you're suddenly for capital punishment?

He said, Can you imagine if I said something about *fat white women* at a restaurant? Can you imagine what you would do with that? What, pray tell, does being fat or white have to do with being an asshole at a restaurant?

Pray tell?

I don't get it, he said. This boilerplate speak.

Pray tell? she said.

You used to think for yourself. Now you dish out the propaganda.

Pray tell?

She had a point. To help her make it, he stopped going to restaurants where R met up with the Women, which meant Stephen and R also stopped eating meals together. When he came across her friends, at the El stop, at the bookstore, they began to give Stephen the evil stink-eye. He was one of *them*. One of *those* who wanted to give his son trucks. Probably he wanted to start a *Take Your Son to Work Day, Too,* and he was tired, really, of the stale and bitterly clichéd drift down along the politicized banks of American prosperity. Identity politics, he reasoned, were at their core selfish, premised on the *getting,* and not the *giving,* and he and R, they were splitting at the seams like his shirts. He went to the gym, he lifted his weights (typical man); he stopped smoking and gained weight (*great, now I'm a fat white male . . .*) and came home early to pick up his son at the daycare and take him to the park. At the park, they chased birds. At the park, they threw pebbles into the puddles and the snowbanks. At the park, he'd lift his son into the sky, like a bird. At the park, they became imperfect father and beautiful son.

And then R had an idea. They should go to Rome for Christmas. They should go to Rome and make up for all their arguments and make up some vows, too, and state them, albeit privately, in St. Peter's Cathedral. *Or maybe at the Forum?* It would be fun, a trip to

Rome. A lark. She loved Italian food. She wanted to travel more. She said, at the supermarket in the aisle for bread, Take me to Rome, Stephen, and I'll love you forever.

You've always loved me forever, he said.

Yes, she said. But I'll show you how. She said, lifting her shirt, flashing him like an undergraduate, I'll really show you how.

And she had laughed. She had laughed and put her hand to her heart, as if it hurt, laughing so hard like that, and Gulliver said to Stephen, Why Mommy laughing like that?

She's happy now, Stephen said.

Why she happy?

Because we're going to take a trip.

This is what happens: a man has a son, he becomes a man. He becomes responsible for something other than himself. He becomes the guardian and the caregiver and the very voice of God. He becomes the father he once had but never knew in order to assume responsibility for all the risk of the world. Having only one life, he must understand that to live out this life he must also live with the decisions he has made long before the arrival of this understanding. So living, so *accepting,* he becomes older and wiser and a source of light. Then he kisses his mate in gratitude for this thing he holds in his arms which weighs seven or eight pounds: this life, which will grow into a boy, and then someday a man.

He kisses this woman and says, He's perfect.

He looks like you, she says.

Like us, he says. He's made of us.

2

The recent storm. The anxiety, thank God, was finally passing—

He felt the wind kicking off the lake through his tangled hair. Passing by the Wrigley Building, which he might have visited, he had stopped to admire its skyline before walking on. The sun was out in the blue Chicago sky. He did stop by R's office, Michigan and Madison, and there he said hello to the Women, and he hugged R's bangle-wristed boss, a local politico of whom he was deeply fond, that power scarf and set of heels notwithstanding. In R's office, he kissed R on the forehead. He said, shutting the door, knocking his bandaged hand against the knob, I haven't been very easy and I want you to know I know this.

She said, So, you've been busy thinking?

Sometimes I want it to be okay to be happy. So yeah, I took a walk—

Her phone rang, and she said, looking at it, I should take this. She said, picking up the phone, This is R.

He stood, waiting, and R said into the phone, Can you hang on a moment? Thanks. She placed her hand over the phone and said to Stephen, Tonight. Okay? People are coming tonight—

I know.

She said, I'm glad. I'm glad you've been thinking. But I've got to take this.

Okay, he said, and he left.

On the way out Cheryl at the front desk teased him about his tangled hair. There was a photograph of his behind the desk. He knew that here there were no secrets. The people here knew R's lover, and how he dressed for work, and what they ate for lunch. Stephen felt suddenly exposed and shy, as if he'd been caught sneaking out of a strip joint by a neighbor or, worse, colleague, and walking to the door, he saw R's bangle-wristed boss talking on the horn from behind her desk. She caught his eye, and waved; she turned and came around her desk and closed the door. In the elevator, he understood that R was going to become that woman. Ten, twelve years out, she'd be a mover and a shaker. R, she'd make the ideal congressperson. A good one, really. It was a comforting thought, actually, and he was proud of her, R, and the things she would do because she believed in them. Stephen believed in God, or at least he tried to, and Providence; R believed in Social Justice, and Equal Rights, and Equal Opportunity. These were possibly far more useful things to believe in if only because they were more practical. These corridors of power, having been bequeathed to her, they were hers to make.

He caught the El, walked down the dirty North Avenue toward his street, taking the wrong one. Get a clue, he told himself, laughing. He found it, his street, and he saw the Garcia boy chatting it up with two girls. Yo hey, the boy called to Stephen, looking tough, and Stephen waved and said hey back. He turned the key and passed through the door. In the living room several messages blinked on the machine: the first from a woman who was on the ground. On the ground, that meant she was typically in the air? The woman spoke for several minutes into the machine about the forthcoming rally at the Schaumburg clinic presently under siege by the whack-job from Kansas. The woman would not stop speaking. He checked his watch and still she kept speaking. She repeated, before finally signing off, *Okay, R. This is Lynn and I am on the ground.*

Other messages for R about the shindig tonight. The final message was from his publisher, to whom Stephen owed a call. He made the call from the kitchen sink and spoke with the assistant who put him through.

Stephen? We need an afterword!

Really?

Really. Especially from you.

That ought to boost the sales.

It's not about the sales. It's about posterity and publicity and *then* it's about the sales. Slut yourself out, Buddy. Give me a couple thousand words.

What about?

About Sarajevo. About the fucking war. What do you think?

I don't know anything about the fucking war.

Tell me why you did it. Just that. Give me a thousand words. Five hundred? Do it for me, okay? He said, By the way, your pal, Messinger?

Yeah?

He sent an introduction. How's that!

I don't know. How is it?

Well, he writes like a German, that's for sure. Lofty lofty. They have trouble locating some of those verbs over there, don't they? He sure seems to intend for you to be taken notice of, which you should be, but I'm partial.

I wish you hadn't asked him for that.

Oh, grow up. He said, What, you wouldn't do the same? Don't be precious. Look, when can you get it to me?

How long can I have?

A month. A month. Oh, six weeks. But no extensions, okay?

Okay.

You got a fax?

No.

Stephen, *everybody's* got a fax. Give me your fax and I'll send this—

No. Let me wait till I finish this—whatever. What *is* an afterword?

Whatever you say it is. You're the man, here.

Okay, Stephen said. But it's going to be short—

Say, he said. There's a girl here. Ahem. Woman. Elise Kohlhaus. She wanted me to deliver a message. Straight from the horse's mouth, so to speak.

You've met her?

She delivered Messinger's essay personally. Had a lovely little lunch. Quite dainty. She asked me by the way to deliver a message to you personally.

Which is?

Okay. Now I've got it written down. It's very precise. I got to get it right. Here. Wait. Jerome! Where's that notebook? The one. The one with the papers and the lines. Not *that* one, the *other* one. Okay, say something. You, Stephen. No heavy breathing there. Shame shame. Okay. Okay, now here it is. Are you ready? Let me know when you're ready.

I'm ready. Shoot.

Nope. You're not ready. Not for this.

What?

I don't think you're ready.

I give up, Stephen said. I'm not ready.

It says, Ahhhem. It says, and now I'm quoting directly, Stephen. It says—*Stephen, come live with me and stay with me and spend your life with me.*

Stephen laughed. He poured himself a glass of water.

Hey, you out there? Aren't you girlfriended or something? This seems serious, if you know what I mean. He said, By the way, she's at the Dakota.

I know.

You know? You know! What am I? A secretary? What, she can't call and leave a message? Oh yeah. Oh yeah. What am I thinking? I see. I get it, Stephen. Your *girlfriend* doesn't know!

Eh heh.

Stephen, he said. Stephen Stephen. You can't see me, but I'm shaking my head here. I'm shaking my head! Now I'm sighing. Hear that? Sigh. Now I'm going to let you go because I'll bet you got some things on your mind.

Thanks, Stephen said.

Okay, Stephen. Think fast. Be brilliant.

Okay.

Okay?

Okay.

Right on, Stephen. Type type.

3

Spend, she had said. *Spend your life with me.*

Everything comes down to currency—even Time, being infinite, because of course a person's time is not. Before he made the second call, first he had to do the math. He took a tall glass of water up to his desk. To stall he checked the bandage on his hand: the purple scar, the loading up of it with ointment meant to heal. He returned to his desk and pulled out the statements from his father's—now his—broker. By all accounts a recession was taking place and the past two years had cost him. For the miscellaneous expenses, flights and chemicals and the biannual new suit of clothes, not to mention that new suit he'd just bought in Germany, he permitted himself a budget of eleven K which he would need to fund with various windfalls. He'd still have to put himself out for hire. But it was doable: certainly he'd lived cheaply before. He said, looking at the papers across his desk, You're going to do this, aren't you?

He said, Stop pretending.

He'd be giving up health insurance—which he never used, anyway, not wanting to be tracked. He'd be giving up the funding of his pension. He'd have to scramble to fill in the annual two-K gap for his IRA.

He could live in his father's farmhouse; if he lived in Europe, he wouldn't need a car. He lit a cigarette and placed his second call. A career in academe, it takes years to build: years to get even a first job. Post–grad school, his first job had been as a sub-minimum-wage laborer in a California Mountain Resort—digging ditches, skimming condoms out of hot tubs, arranging boulders to compliment Resort Lifestyle Landscaping. For seven months he worked with (and took pictures of) those who worked just like himself beneath the sun— mostly illegals, a few convicts, those who couldn't afford to insist on anything. Later Stephen hitched a ride to Massachusetts, and there in Gloucester he got himself a job on a fishing boat, a topic recently in the news thanks to a catchy pop song by a pop star describing the plight of those who worked the industry, and that job had led to the photographs which eventually became *The North Sea,* and then he hunkered down in an overworked and underfunded art department in South Dakota, and there he paid off his student loans in two years. Once paid he was a free man. By now R was calling, so he went to Chicago. For two months he did a stint as a coroner's photographer for the Chicago police—which, like everything else, he'd done for the experience, and which was dreadful, photographing murder victims, bloodstains, various points of entry. The scenes of the crimes, they always smelled, a terrible fact he'd never considered: the photographs went into files, which went into boxes, which went into warehouses for the unsolvable, and this work had led to various contacts with the press and that led to other things: all the while, he'd thought, he was just taking a break from academe, believing that his place was there, teaching to the future, and finally an overpriced but nonetheless respectable institution had reached out, so to speak, and he took the train to the suburb, through Rogers Park and the concrete canyon to the land of big trees and yards and fern bars packing fifteen-dollar cheeseburgers, and there he did the things one does to make certain one gets the cushy job. And so he was hired and, after his book of essays came out, tenured and promoted: on the third day he went through a terrible crisis and took an unpaid leave, and then another unpaid leave, and now his new dean had been leaving messages with R about Stephen's coming back. Stephen could have spent months on the matter, he knew this. He could have pumped the school for a raise. Certainly an office with a window.

He made the call. The new dean's secretary answered, who had no idea who Stephen was, given that life always goes on, thank God. The new dean, who was actually a guy named Dean from Media, said over a speakerphone, Stephen?

Hey, Dean. Dean Dean.

Haven't heard that!

Stephen said, Are you on a speakerphone?

What's that?

You sound like you're in an ice rink.

Oh, it's okay. I'll talk louder!

They did chitchat, then, while Stephen held the phone a foot away from his ear. The chitchat, this too was a rule.

Then the dean said, unfathomably, So, Stephen. How's the kid? And Stephen said, before he quit his job for good, Fine.

4

What do Stephen's fishermen and cowboys and now Sarajevo portraits all have in common? The books all document a disappearing way of life. All ways, he supposed, disappear. In the sixties *The Way* was a Bible cheesily translated—Jesus for the folk in denim and beads—and when Stephen finds that now, next to his King James and *Book of Common Prayer* and *I Ching* and *Rubaiyat of Omar Khayyam,* his first edition of Fitzgerald's *The Beautiful and the Damned* and his Standard English Classics' *L'Allegro, Il Penseroso, Comus, and Lycidas—Stephen, hey baby. R.*—and his G. K. Chesterton's *Orthodoxy* and his Fowler's *Modern English Usage . . .* when Stephen locates this book, *The Way,* with pictures of soulful kids on the cover contemplating the meaning of their souls, he knows he will never let it go. This book, like the others, a gift; this book, and however badly paraphrased, a gift from his father.

To Stephen Sellers Brings, his father had written. *A son to be proud of on the Day of his Confirmation. April 15, 1969. From his Dad.*

This is his Special Box—a carton full of essential odds and ends marking his life. A sheathed K-Bar knife with rosewood handles; a stone from Omaha Beach at Normandy; his grandfather's gold pocket watch, circa 1902; a woman's comb once belonging to his mother, and which still smelled of the oil from her hair; this handful of books; a lock of Gulliver's hair; his father's slide rule; a copy of his own book of essays, *The Poetics of the Line and the Art of Sight,* which he had signed and given to his father . . . *To Dad, whom I hope always to make proud. Love, Stephen . . .* and packets of letters and postcards, mostly from R. There is a blue mussel shell from Elise, in which she had once poured a spoonful of mineral water, and then raised to his lips; there is a champagne cork; there is a paper bird, indigo, also from Elise, with a note which instructs the reader to pull the wings apart and blow; there is an unopened string of condoms, like tickets for the carnival. And here a birthday card for Stephen's thirtieth birthday from R writing in her profoundly circled and fisted script—

R being a lefty—thirty reasons why she loves Stephen . . . *Reason #4, You like it when I wear only socks. Reason #12, You're thinking. Reason #22, You love coffee in the morning with me on the wrinkly blue sheets. Reason #28, You're still thinking* . . . There is a snapshot of R and Stephen as sophomores in the college library preparing for an exam. There is a cassette tape with a recording of Gulliver having a conversation with his friend, Liam, in the back of R's Jeep. There is a small red car Stephen bought for Gulliver at a gas station outside Paris. These are the things in his box.

He had bought the condoms in South Dakota—a small town, adjacent to the very small town in which he lived and in which he was constantly running into his students and colleagues—in preparation for a visit from R. To avoid being spotted, he had driven one town over. At the grocery store, the only game in town, a girl he nonetheless recognized from the campus had rung him up. He had thought about buying other products to conceal his real mission, but instead he thought, Screw it. I'm a grown man. I'm a university professor . . . and the girl said, holding up the condoms, Five thousand dollars, please.

She said, shrugging, Law of supply. She said, giggling, making a big show . . . Paper or Plastic?

She said, Do you need any help out?

Enough, Stephen had said, sufficiently embarrassed—So much for being a grown man, etcetera—and the girl said, catching his eye, Well. Have a nice day!

Then he laughed, like that, and she laughed back, and he drove back to his furnished attic apartment on Main Street, and R arrived, with champagne and cocaine, and later that night the kids of the town cruised up and down Main—Dairy Queen to the Square, and back, and then again, like toddlers running circles through the largest rooms in the house—and he and R had spent the night going at it. This way, that way. They never did use the condoms. Once she put him on his back and descended, squatting on her heels, flexing, and said, You know when you get ready to come?

Yes?

Don't.

And maybe it was the cocaine—he'd done it twice, if only because he wanted to do it more, and nicotine was hard enough to give up, thank you—but he never came, and they kept going at it like birds in the sky over the dark yard, all that rough strife, with the springtime windows open and all those kids' cars going by with their radios *whump whump whumping* and the headlights, like beacons, and R, coming like a banshee, and those beacons casting shadows through the gauzy drapes amid the light of his room. In the morning, the day was full of birdsong, and R said, rolling over, and not having any birds near her apartment in Chicago, only panhandlers, Why are they so loud?

What?

The birds! It sounds like an ava thing.

A what?

An ava thing! It sounds like a zoo!

She didn't get pregnant that trip but he understood she wanted to. She was thirty now, she explained. Do you know that?

R, sitting at the window, brushing her hair. You could move to Chicago, R said. We could play grown-up?

And thus they began the extended conversation involving trips to Omaha—a wedding of a common friend—and Minneapolis, another wedding. The brides and the grooms, those who R claimed didn't know any better, they were melting like icicles. They did a trip to St. Louis and then to Nashville where they wandered around the lonely-hearted downtown. These were trips, sometimes funded by Stephen's giving of various presentations, of decidedly carnal exploration. He thought, while tugging off R's underwear in a rental car, Okay, let's try it, this playing of house, and see what happens.

What happened was clear from the start. What happened was R and Stephen did not play house particularly well—theirs might have been a romance now premised on carnality and trust, punctuated by the long-distance thrill of reunion, but it was no longer a romance built on sensibility, and certainly it did not have the juice, the coal-oil burn, for longevity. Despite their history together. Still one does not let go easily, despite the volatility and the flames (because, you know, those flames *are* hot)—and now there was a kid on the way, a baby, and what were they going to do?

R said, I've had two abortions. I'm not going to have a third.

She said, doing the math in her head, Who'd be a better father than you?

I don't know.

She said, I don't want to be alone.

He said, R, everybody is alone.

She said, But I don't *want* to be. Stephen, she said. Let's partner up.

Like that?

What? You think there's somebody better out there for you? You think there's somebody who could know you better than I do?

He said, Well, there might be somebody better out there for *you*.

She said, But that's not the point, is it?

The point was, like all points, endlessly disappearing. The point was: she had let herself get pregnant because she was thirty and it was time to have a baby. And as if shopping from a catalog, she had selected Stephen to be her partner in this and all like matters.

Stephen's middling career of romance—the women: he was genuinely glad to have been there: the awkward courting pauses (*Oh, you like Lyle Lovett! I love shrimp. Do you like shrimp?*), the thrilling introductions to each other's bodies—kiss and breath, hair-in-the-face, sigh—and later, in the clear light of day, the awkward retreat. The pulling away. The conversations, the explanation. In South Dakota, surrounded only by students and the waitresses where he ate his meals, and the cute girl at the Wal-Mart, and now the *other* cute girl who teased him at the condom/grocery store, where Stephen always returned now to buy lots of other things he didn't need . . . in South Dakota, Stephen had been lonely. He dated one girl with a storybook name, Polly St. James, but after only two weeks she began picking out houses with picket fences and then she began dropping by Stephen's attic apartment unannounced with a wok. And so he had stepped away, always, as he always did. R might not understand him—or he, her—but she respected what she didn't understand. With R, because of their relatedness (it always felt incestuous, listening to R discuss a book, or a lover's technique, all in the same breath), because of their mutual and fundamental trust—that's what it came down to, a trust, like a bank account with a big, fat line of credit— with R he had always been able to return and stand in line and cash his checks. In general, though—and wasn't this the lesson of the taboo?—one should not marry a sister. They, the sisters, were supposed to be taken by another, like God.

Taken. Do you take this woman? This man?

And if so, where?

They hadn't done the vow thing; they hadn't even done the Justice of the Peace thing. Instead they spent a weekend in French Lick, Indiana, and there they spent most of the first night in a warm pool of water smelling of sulfur. R drifted on the warm blue water with her three-months-pregnant body—Not yet broken in, she called across the water. Still like new. *Well, kind of* . . . and the water was blue, like the light in the Blue Grotto off Biševo.

He thought, R would like Biševo. He wished he'd taken her there.

He stood alone in his office. He stood alone going through the items of his box. All points endlessly disappear, he thought. It's a law of geometry, the final lesson of optics. On a camera lens, as in mathematics, infinity was transcribed thus: ∞

Taken.

Look at an explanation long enough, and even the reason to explain will disappear. Glass houses, who isn't sitting by the window? Gulliver, too, had been taken. Look at an explanation long enough, or a wave in the sea, and all you get is lost—

Hey, called R's voice. Where are you?

Up here.

She pounded up the steps—that aerobic sensibility. She turned the corner and said, balancing on her toes, God. You look great!

It's the suit.

Well, you should get some more of those. She said, kissing him, What are you thinking about?

Infinity. Its expression.

There you go. Of course. She said, Me? I've been shopping. I got apple juice. So, you know, people don't have to know. So you can pass.
Cover up all that shame.

Don't try that shit with me, Stephen. I'm not ashamed. Fuck you. I just thought you wouldn't want people asking you all night long why you weren't drinking and saying atta boy and telling you stories about their Uncle Joes.

Okay, he said. Thanks.

Thing is, you gotta get it. It's all in the car. Hundreds of dollars' worth of hootch. No nipping. I'm not going to be one of those pathetic co-people.

The co-people?

I've been hitting the self-help section. You know, to understand better. And not just the Dare to Let Yourself Grieve schlock. I'll tell you this, the more I read, the worse it seems. Everything. Like *I'm* supposed to be better.

I used to think you were a drunk. In college. Always getting blasted. I was going to talk with you about it. I was very serious.

And?

You stopped getting drunk.

I liked to have fun. It was sexy. For you, it's never fun. It's work.

More or less.

She said, having confided with her coworkers, Self-medicating. You're probably bipolar. It's becoming quite chic, you know. Yin and Yang, Light and Dark.

So that explains it. A Manichean vision.

Up and down? She said, looking at the cut over his eye, You're not going to tell me, are you?

About what?

About what happened. Before you came home? I know something bad happened. Did you get arrested or something?

No.

She said, touching the bruise, It's a lot better now. She said, You know, whatever it was, whatever happened, it's okay. It's okay, Mister.

Okay.

She said, Well, whatever. That's the thing I wanted to say. And I didn't want you to confuse my anger and whatnot with something else. You know?

I know.

She said, You've got the box out. The Special Box.

Yeah, he said. I'm supposed to write something. An afterword, whatever *that* is. I'm supposed to figure out why I went to Yugoslavia.

The book, she said. It will be nice to see it. You might show it to me sometime, you know?

I didn't know you wanted to see it.

Of course I want to see it. I'm just scared of what I'll find there. Then I'll be scared I won't reply the right way. You can be a little intimidating, you know.

Uh-huh.

No, she said, taking off her blouse. I'm going to take a hot bath and put on a party dress, okay? No more sniping.

He flinched at her use of that word, *sniping*. He said, Okay.

I've got a new one. A party dress. Just for you. She said, looking at her watch, The caterer people will be here in twenty minutes.

You got a caterer?

I got a whomper raise. I got a man I need to do some pleasing to before he leaves me. Also, the DC Power Chicks. So be polite. No fisticuffs. Stay away from Welfare Reform and Foreign Policy, please. No smoldering stories about the Balkans. And no saying of the word *dyke*. Okay?

Can I say *black*? Or do I have to say *African American*?

Black is okay among friends who know you. Elsewhere, it's best to go polysyllabic. Unless you're talking to somebody who *is* black. Then you *have* to say *black* because if you say *African American* you sound stuffy and insecure.

R turned to fire up the tub. There was a towel covering the dent in the door, which she left open; her marvelous hair shimmered in the light.

True story, Stephen called after her. This guy, this talking head, he used the word *clearly* four times in the same sentence. I counted.

Clearly, she said, coming back. Clearly you were teasing me. That question about *African American*?

A little.

I like it when you tease me. But not in public. She said, stepping out of her long skirt, You're not the only one who's been doing some thinking. You know, you're not the only one who can be a bitch. Patient, know thyself?

She stepped out of her underwear; shrugging, she lifted off her camisole in one breath; she held her clothes in her fist. She said, Look. I know you're thinking about leaving. I know that.

She set her clothes on his desk beside the stack of prints. She fit her body into the general description of his own, tucking the backs of her hands into his belt, her finger descending the length of his fly, and kissed him. She'd been doing this to him just so for years.

She stepped back, brushing her hair from her eyes, and said, I know you're thinking about leaving. I know. I want you to know, it's okay. It's okay. I don't want you to leave, but it's not as if we've been happy together. And if you leave me it's not because of somebody else. God knows that's not why I'd leave you. This, she said, is about us. It's about us and the family we used to have but don't have anymore. It's about us failing and fucking up.

It's complicated.

And simple. She said, hitching her breath, Look. If you leave, I don't want you feeling bad. That's the message. I don't want you feeling guilty. We've had enough bad feeling to last a dozen broken-hearted marriages. So don't do that.

Okay.

She said, shivering, crossing her arms, You're packing. I know that. Either way, it's time you went back to the doc. But you know that, too.

More or less.

Ever since you came home, you've been packing. Doing inventories. You keep looking at the books on the shelves and the pictures on the wall. You're planning your next trip only this time you aren't going to come back.

You know I never know anything until I do it. You know that.

You are the most inexcusably temperamental man I know.

Delicate.

She laughed. She wiped her eyes and said, You could keep me company in the bath, but you gotta bring in the groceries before the thieves get it all. I left the door wide open.

She said, dipping her toe into the bath, Just so you know I'm going to soak and smell real pretty and make you want to stay.

5

Q. What is an incubator?

A. A safe, Gulliver explained. An incubator is a safe warm place you put baby animals who don't get sat on by their mudders.

After one always follows another, like numbers or ducks. They came, the people to the party, to the table decorated with linen and borrowed silver; most of them Stephen did not know. There was Susan with the Nose Thing, and her lover, Jennifer Something; there was the new Assistant DA and his wife, who were important; there were the two doctors, Michael and Mike; there was R's bangle-wristed boss with a mighty power scarf, and who kissed Stephen, European style, and proceeded to give him advice about all manner of topics; there was Dana of the Recent and Bitterly Divorced, mother of Liam, Gulliver's playmate; there was a friend of Stephen's from college, Jack, who now taught in the sculpture department at the Art Institute.

Thirty-five, Stephen thought, and I have *three* friends.

He had friends now abroad, at least. Another friend was a freelance reporter who had thrown Stephen work back when Stephen first came to the city. The guy was eager to talk to Stephen about Stephen's trip. Instead the guy listened patiently while a woman who knew a lot of things explained to him and Stephen the underlying ethos of the current Balkan crisis.

You knooow, the woman was saying, staring at Stephen's bruised eye. You knooow they've been killing each other for centuries.

Next the woman began to lament the current state of crime in her city. The nation's capitol, she said. She said, most sincerely, My God, it's become a regular war zone! The violence!

Uh-huh.

Apparently she had all kinds of plans to stop the Cycle of Violence. Education, it seemed, figured prominently in her plan.

Stephen said, I think it's so important to teach people not to be violent.

Oh, but that's my day job. Not my *passion*. Well, not my *passion* passion. She said, I'm actually writing a novel? It's a novel about how our lives are shaped by the themes of our lives and desires? The city becomes a symbol of the themes, you see. I'm calling it "Life on the Ground."

Good title, Stephen said. You must be Lynn.

Why yes. I am! And you?

Stephen, Stephen said. Friend of R's. We go way back.

She said, I'm looking for an agent.

Stephen said, looking for an escape, Like for a house?

She laughed, very understandingly. Well, sort of, Stephen. My book is going to be character driven, I think. She said, thinking aloud, Very.

Neat, Stephen said.

Stephen's friend gave Stephen a wink, asked him to call, and ducked out lickety-split.

The woman said, watching the friend vanish, And what do *you* do?

I used to teach.

Me too!

But not anymore. I've been having a lot of what you writer types might call flashbacks.

Oh, I see—

Very vivid, the imagery. So I'm between things. Until the pills kick in?

Things, she said, knowingly. Well. Well well.

Stephen made off for more apple juice. It was easier to enjoy a character-driven party when one was actually taking part in it. He stood in the corner of his living room nursing his apple juice, biting his lip, and watched the party.

Well, Jack said, sidling up with a martini the size of Naples. How's tricks?

Fine.

Lots of people here, Jack said. You're going to need new digs.

R wants to get a three-flat. Our own. Rent out the first two floors and become landowners. The gentry. She's been looking. Humboldt Park.

Danger.

The place you can afford, Stephen said, that's by the crack house. You spend a hundred K on the building and another two rehabbing it and that's with the plastic doors. Then the guy who's been there since 1944 gets screwed.

Jack said, Hey. You guys doing okay?

No.

I'm sorry, Jack said. I love R. God knows she knows what she wants.

And doesn't. Everybody loves R. I mean, look at her—

Too bad. For both of you. Jack said, confidingly, Depakote. R asked me to tell you. They're doing cool things with that now. Really—

Stephen said, Can't we talk shop? Compare departments? You should tell me about the novel you're writing.

She got to you, too, huh?

More or less. Stephen said, Just so you know, if she comes back over here, I'm stepping out.

How'd you like to be a character in that fucking book?

I have a new rule, Stephen said. No talking to anybody I don't want to.

That's a good one, Jack said, shifting his weight.

Yeah, Stephen said. Simple and elegant.

I'll tell you this, Jack said. I think there's a lot of estrogen in this room. I'm still trying to figure out why R invited either of us.

The DC Power Chicks recently on the ground had by now collected in the center, holding court. R stood at the ring, lively and sexy in her party dress, laughing a lot. Being R. She kept brushing her thick hair from her eyes and laughing. Stephen stood quietly, admiring her figure and her poise. Then Susan with the Nose Thing, catching Stephen's eye, wandered over and told a funny story about her new dog, which she'd named Taxi.

Really? Stephen said.

Really—

When did you get him?

I don't know. A week ago?

And you named him Taxi?

Yeah, she said, nodding, stirring her drink. She explained she liked to go out to the street and call his name. Taxi! He has big ears, she said. Big and floppy. She said, This way I always get a cab!

Jack left next. Stephen spent some time with R's bangle-wristed boss, and he was finishing off his fifth glass of apple juice—*So,* R's boss had said, now tipsy and loud. *How's the Not Drinking?*—when he decided to step out.

Take a drink, he thought. Take a knee.

He took the front stairs. On the porch he stood in the cold wind and lit up and studied the light. One thing he loved about Chicago, he loved the light. *Light dwells within light,* Christ had said, at least according to the Gospel of St. Thomas. From across the street, at the Garcias', drifted music and laughter. He could smell the woodsmoke from their chimney which reminded him of the woodsmoke in the air over Sarajevo. It was cold there; it was cold here. He felt a wash of lingering jet lag, the sagging of the eyelids. He'd been back a week and somehow it now seemed years. Perhaps they too were having a party—the Garcias. The center of his hand ached deeply in the cold: the scar, it was one made to last. He listened to the crippled dog, barking, and then came a child's voice: calling out to the dog, inviting it in. In the light you could see the metal staples in the dog's hip, reflecting. The snow on the ground had a glazed sheet of ice which caused the light to bounce. Now he heard a set of heels and turned to watch a woman walking down the salted walk. His neighbor, the same he'd seen the other morning stepping out from the cab. She was wearing the same black overcoat and a red scarf which matched her hat. Her heels, they clicked and clicked against the walk. As she approached, she slowed her pace, the rhythm of the clicking slowed, and Stephen recognized her perfume in the cold air.

Hey, Stephen said.

Hey, she said, coming to a halt. I didn't know you were back. She said, awkwardly, So you're back?

For a while. How's school?

I finished. All done.

Congratulations, he said. That's great.

I guess.

He said, We're having a party.

She looked up through the windows to the people in party clothes, behind the sparkling windows, the lace drapes, and said, Looks that way.

He realized she could not recall his name; nor he, hers. Distance could be like memory that way. A peal of laughter rang through the air—R's voice, calling out. They both looked up at the open door. Stephen said, R would love to see you—

No, she said, pleased to have been invited. But thanks.

Okay.

Well then, she said, turning. It was good to see you.

You too.

Thanks, she said.

Hey, he called after her. By the way, I like your hat.

Really? she said, touching it. I made it.

It's cool. Anyway, 'night.

'Night, she said. See you around.

6

The Garcias' house burned that night. A hot coal, spitting up through the chimney onto the shingled, sagging roof, and igniting.

Nobody saw it happen. It was late, R asleep, slightly drunk, and Stephen below, having changed into sweats and having cleaned up and having fallen asleep on the couch. In his sleep he dreamed he saw lights flashing against his eyelids. He dreamed he heard sirens, and he thought he was dreaming about places he'd been before, and he thought it odd the way the sirens sounded like American sirens, not the sirens of Europe, and then he saw a woman on an island, wind in her hair, and that woman became Elise, standing in the sun in front of the blue sea on the island of Biševo, and she was saying, *I've been calling you,* and he said, *I know,* and then he heard R's voice, exclaiming, and he thought this was going to be one of those dreams, the fight dreams, which saddened him, and he woke. He thought, listening to the sirens, Somewhere there must be a fire.

He raced upstairs. R stood at the window, her face and disheveled hair and her bare arms illuminated by the light of the fire.

The house was in flames. There were trucks on the street and men shouting. R turned and dressed in jeans and sneakers, a sweater, and they ran out through the front door. The street had filled with neighbors. The family, the father and mother and grandparents and kids, six or seven in all, screamed when the roof fell in. The crippled dog stood inside at the window and a fireman with an ax was trying to get at it. Once he'd broken the window, reaching for the dog, the dog attacked. The fireman fell back off the ladder, cursing, with the dog's jaws locked on his sleeve. Falling to the ground, onto its stapled hip, the dog cried out, letting go, and two of the kids ran to the dog and calmed it and began to tug it away, but now the dog spooked and turned and attacked one of the kids, a little girl. The dog bit her hand, and face, and then a fireman hit the dog with an iron bar and killed it.

They stood on the street in the cold air and felt the heat from the flames reaching into the dark sky. The sight of a burning house, it's bigger than most things which take place in a person's life. R said, crossing her arms, My God, look at it. And it was pretty, and magnificent, he thought, those orange and purple flames billowing into the sky: fire, like the sun's, was the first source of light. Then fire became two sticks, a little friction, in order to warm the first tribe. And then there was the beating of the drums, with more sticks, for the giving of thanks, to be followed by a couple of misunderstandings, a few wars, during which fire then became the signal to aim, to kill another at a distance. First with the arrow, then with the round: the distances grew, and the spears became the muskets which became the ballistic missiles, and then the distances grew too far to see. Or too close.

After a fire consumes, there's smoke. The dust and the ash linger in the air. Standing before the fire, Stephen watched the flames reflecting off R's face. The firelight lit her eyes and flickered in her hair. A woman stood alone, crying. There was a man, also crying, and several children holding hands. A fireman with blood on his jacket carried a bewildered girl in his arms. The wispy-bearded boy paced before the fire with his camera. The people on the street were shielding their eyes watching the man and the woman crying, the flames behind them, and now R said, turning to Stephen, shielding her eyes, You have something to tell me.

He said, I quit my job.

Oh.

I didn't want to say anything before the party.

Uh-huh. She said, So you've already made up your mind.

Yes.

When were you going to tell me?

After the rally.

You're not going to stay. I knew you weren't going to stay.

We want different things. I always was a compromise for you.

And me?

We're different.

She said, Go to hell.

You should let me go. It's not right to try and keep me just because you don't want to lose me. That's not a reason to fight. It's not good enough.

Not if we're not happy, she said. We used to be happy.

We were kids. We were eighteen. Siblings.

I know. She said, beginning to cry, I'm really going to miss you.

Just walk away, Renée.

She said, wiping her eyes, laughing, God, you used to love that song.

I still do.

I don't want you to go. I mean, I want you to be able to come back. This is different. It's not fair. You start to get your act together and you leave? We're just starting to recover. We could *still* have a life, Stephen. It's not fair.

What kind of life? We keep trying to change the other. We can't let the other be. It's not right.

I know. I was supposed to be able to fix it. Together. With you.

When you look at me, Stephen said, all I see is the boy we lost. And you, too. Because you didn't just lose Gulliver—you lost me, too. And I lost you. And Gulliver lost us. And Gulliver *is* us and you can't rescue me and we can't rescue him. I can't rescue anybody.

You did. After. You did. A little bit.

He's not coming back.

How do you know?

I just know. He's gone. He's not coming back and it's not our fault.

No? she said, turning her face back to the fire. You're wrong. It is.

Letters

The Farmhouse, Vermont; 1982

R, R, R,

Hey. I'm safe. Thanks for the loan of your phone and thanks for feeding me. Old flames, two ships—

I got a job on a boat in Gloucester. At first the smell was hard to get used to but I'm getting used to it. I kind of like it. I like the way the engines rumble. As long as they are rumbling, everything is safe. They've given me the scut work, which is fine, given that it won't last forever. Fish guts, everywhere. When we lower the booms, birds into the sea, the ship grows wings. It's a sight.

You can reach me at my parents' farmhouse in Vermont, where I've set up a darkroom in my father's old bedroom. I've hooked up the answering machine you gave me. Thanks.

Why is it I am always saying thanks?

There are seagulls here everywhere. I never really saw before how graceful they can be. Like hawks, only white. I love to watch them sweep across the water. Then lift, magic. I suppose all flight is a form of magic. One thing I love to be is transported, especially along the surface of the water. Like that.

I left for you a book I like under the bed.

S

—

From the Badlands, 1984

RRRRRRRR,

Hurry.

S

—

Dear Gulliver,

You don't know me but I'm your dad. After you were born, I held you. I also stood by while you were circumcised, as was my duty. I hope someday you forgive me that. Your mother thought we shouldn't, and I thought you should look like me, and she said you already did.

That's called a penis joke, by the way, which liberated women like to make often at the expense of men. Truth is, it *was* pretty funny. And then I said I was serious, and your mother said, Oh, I guess you're right, which believe me is not something she says very often.

I hope someday you know me better than I know my dad. I love my dad, I am proud of my dad, and in general I have always obeyed my dad, but I do not know him. He is more like a figure than he is a bodily presence. He wants to know you, by the way. He keeps demanding pictures, as if I worked at the mall.

Listen to your mother. She is always right.

I took some photographs of people praying in a big cathedral today. Your mother permitted me to have you baptized, which allowed us to introduce God to you. But your mother and I have not yet figured out how to introduce you to God. To religion, which tries to describe God—like poetry, or chemistry. Mostly you know God when you speak to God. Which is what you do when you pray.

Tomorrow my dad and I go to Paris. I collected these stones on Omaha Beach in Normandy—once the place of a great battle. I will tell you about soldiers after you turn five. Your grandfather, who was there at the time, most likely never will. But I will tell you that he was very brave, that he was one of the first to cross the Dragon's Teeth of the Hurtgen Forest, and that this is why his knee hurts when it is cold out.

The water here is too cold to swim. There are giant, furry cows chewing the rich green grass on the dunes behind the sea. Today, I saw a fighter jet with Dutch markings sailing across the shoreline. Seeing me, standing alone on the shore, the pilot dipped his wing.

Dad

—

Dear Gulliver,

I had to have an emergency root canal. Did you brush your teeth? Swish and Rinse? A root canal is when a man in a big digger truck drives into your mouth to build a great big canal like the one in Panama, which is the big lock the big boats go through in our *Big Book of Boats.* In Guatemala, which is not too far from Panama, there are many digger trucks to do this work, but they are also rusty. It is very important you brush your teeth so that someday when you go to Guatemala you also do not have to have a root canal. So please don't ask your mom for more than one piece of candy a day. A rule is a rule. I will be home soon and we can go to Buckingham Fountain and look at the lights. Also, your mom tells me we need to go sneaker shopping.

Dare I eat a peach?

Kiss your mom. Brush your teeth.

Dad

—

McClean, Texas; 1989

Dear Gulliver,

Today I rode a quarter horse and above us there was a hawk drifting through the blue sky. A great horse sails across the land the way a hawk does the sky. Also today we began to brand and castrate the calves. I will tell you about castration when you are fifteen.

This is why cowboy boots look so funny:

The long part which covers the shin and calf is to protect you from thorns and cacti. Also, when afoot, snakes!

The pointy toe is to make it easy to slip in—and out of—the stirrup, which is the dangly part of the saddle, in case your mount—that's what cowboys call a horse—throws you, and drags you all the way to Dodge (in Kansas, ask your mom to show you on the placemat).

The front of the sharp heel is to catch the stirrup, for balance.

The back of the sharp heel is to dig into the dirt after you've roped your calf or wild mustang—something your father cannot do at all.

But when a *real* cowboy ropes a varmint, the cowboy leaps off the horse and grabs that rope and digs those sharp heels into the dirt to bring that varmint to a standstill. *Varmint* sounds like a bad word, but it isn't. It's one you can use.

Some cowboys wear spurs on the back of their boots, which are sharp pieces of metal, to dig into the sides of their horse, though most of the cowboys I know do not use spurs because they hurt the horse. City folk, just so you know, do not like cowboys. Not because city folk are bad. I think city folk don't like cowboys because they secretly wish *they* could ride a horse. Everybody wants to learn to ride and to love a horse. To ride a horse—it is a gift, like walking.

You may also notice lots of city folk like to wear cowboy boots. Your mom likes especially that purple pair because they make her look pretty and almost tall.

The fancy stitching is so you look real sharp.

What do you do before you cross the street?

Dad

P.S. A real cowboy always measures the size of his horse w/ his hands, not his feet.

—

Chicago, Illinois; 1990

Dear Gulliver,

There is something magical about the mail—the way you slip a letter into a box and then the letter travels through the day while you wait for the letter with all those hieroglyphics to reappear inside another. Airmail.

I put your name today on the mailbox—it is beneath your mother's and my own.

Your mother washed all your clothes today, including the Special Blanket with the Green Frogs. For dinner we had your favorite, Rice All Over the House. There is an agency in Washington DC which is trying to help us find you. The police in Rome still look; they tell us not to lose hope. Thousands of people have your photograph. It's one I took of you at St. Peter's. You are wearing your moose sweater and warm plaid pants. What a beautiful boy, they say.

Fear, the Buddhists say, is what blinds us. Your mother is brave. Your father is trying to be more like her.

I stripped and oiled your trike—there was a lot of sand in the bearings. There is also sand in your brown shoes. When you come home we'll dump out the sand together. Your shoes are by my old cowboy boots beneath the French Guy's picture of the Blue Lady.

Dad

—

Rome, Italy; 1990

Dear Gulliver,

I saw the television show today—the one your mother orchestrated with her friends in DC. An entire segment devoted generally to missing children and specifically to you. Your mother sent to me the videotape. Apparently you are good for ratings, and now there are hundreds of pounds of viewer mail. Most of the letters so far are kind. Only a handful appear to be from quacks.

There is no trace of you in all of Rome. That is the repeated conclusion of the investigator. In fact there is no trace of you in all of Italy.

In the video there are shots of your room with all the toys picked up and the park where we go to take pictures and there is a long, moody montage with sentimental music involving the narrow staircase you like to play on with your digger trucks. There is also a shot of our mailbox with all of our names on it. Your mother is very well-spoken and cries only once. She is wearing the blue sweater we bought for her birthday at the Big Store downtown. Field's.

Marshall Field's.

The sky in Rome is full of sparrows. This evening I went to St. Peter's Basilica and lit another candle. I watched the Papal Guards do their changing of the guard, which they do every night. I looked for you in the dark.

Dad

—

Chicago, Illinois; 1990

Dear Gulliver,

I never knew I wanted to have a son until I learned about you. Until your mother took my hand and put it on her body and told me you were so.

— 227 —

Sometimes I am afraid of finding you. I keep writing to you in case I do.

A song of lamentation is made with notes, like these I keep writing to you.

Your grandfather, my father, died this morning. He was sitting in his den in the big brown chair. He had been reading a book he loved very much. I have marked the place.

My father believed you would be returned to us.

Gulliver, I do not know how people bear the loss of those they love. I do not know how this is possible.

Dad

—

Hvar, Croatia; 1991

Dear Gulliver,

Everywhere I go people know all about you. I met some people on an island today and they asked me all about you. On this tiny island is a small goat-keeper's house: but there is also the Blue Grotto, which is a cave fed by the Adriatic Sea. The sun lights up the cave so that everything inside the cave is translucently blue; inside the cave, I swam in the cool blue water. I could see my body floating in the blue water. I think whenever possible you should swim naked with others who are also naked. In this manner only will you be seen as others are seen. Shame is a consequence of concealment, never revelation. Your mother taught me this.

Where are you? Why can't I see you?

Last week I thought I saw you in Vienna. You were feeding ducks in a park with two other boys. Then your mother called out your name, and you ran to her, and she lifted you up into the sky. You were laughing. She kissed you.

I stood on a balcony today and watched some people dance in the moonlight. Tomorrow I have decided I am going to go to a city named Dubrovnik which has thick castle walls. The city, it was once a great fortress. There is soon to be another war in Europe.

If that *was* you, kiss your mother.

Dad

—

Dear Renée,

It is as bad here up close as it appears to be from far away.

When bad things happen, one turns away. That's what I always do. When my father died, I told myself, Don't look there, and poof, he went away. When Gulliver vanished, I looked—outwardly—but I did not look inside myself. I made him go away, too.

You are braver than I; I've always known that. It's why you always forgive. It's why you never stop hoping. You check the mail. You get on the phone. You keep the place safe and warm, should he show up tomorrow, or the day after next.

By not looking, by turning away, I've lost part of myself. My history, my life. I've lost my father *and* my son.

I've lost what made me; I've lost what I've made.

To not look anymore is to become willingly blind.

—

I thought I saw him in Vienna—a year ago. He was with some boys and a woman who looked to be his mother, who *was* his mother. What I'm telling you is that if that was him, then he was happy. He was loved.

And that's when I understood that we don't want to find him. That *I* don't want to find him. That's when I understood that either he is with a family which loves him or he is not. More than anything I want him snuggling up with somebody on a sofa. I want him saying, *Read to me. Dad? Read this.*

I've seen what happens to the orphans. I've seen what people do to them. If he is not with a good man and a good woman on a sofa, being read to, then do we really want him to be alive? Do we want him alive and suffering just so we might find him? How are we to find him?

—

It hurts, this looking, and I am trying not to blink. Meanwhile the only time I feel alive anymore is when I am unaware of feeling anything—when I lose myself to a moment, or to a book, or to sleep. It's like sex: you're out of the body only while you're having it. I miss you, that out-of-body partner of mine. I miss us losing each into the other's self. That sense of transport. And God knows I miss the body and soul our out-of-body experience made. That perfect boy with the magic heart.

—

There are war junkies everywhere and the city is under one massive fucking. *Welcome to Hell.* Today an old man on the street tried to sell me his coffeepot. He was sitting behind an overturned bus; the bus provided a screen from snipers, as did several cars stacked one upon the other. *Spiders,* people call the trucks that stack the cars. I gave the man sixty marks, all I had in my pocket, but one can't buy redemption. One has to earn it. When I refused to take the pot, he gave me a pen. He put the pen in my hand. He closed my fingers around it and would not let me let it go.

Then I understood I had to take it. I could not give and walk away with nothing. Who could bear that? That humiliation? If one gives, then one must let others also give.

It's a shitty pen of Communist vintage celebrating the '84 Olympics—obviously treasured, this being among the last of his possessions. Perhaps it was a gift. The ink keeps skipping, I do know that; this pen will be a possession I treasure long after the ink runs out. When winter comes people will burn their books for fuel. It's barbaric, the daily threat to survival, and the means required here to survive. People carrying their own excrement in bags to find a place to bury it. The children, scavenging; the boys and the girls being pimped out to the UN troops who are here to save them. The black-marketers skimming off the relief only to sell it back to a bankrupt population.

—

I've been opening up my eyes. It hurts, this looking. Sometimes there is a tremendous fire in the sky; sometimes I can't stop from shaking, but I am not afraid. Not anymore. Accident, I've decided, does not derive from Fault: nobody *intends* to wreck the car, or plane. Sarajevo, this obscene war, is the last (please, one hopes) great disaster of the century which made it. The Holocaust, it took place in a chamber—first in the courtrooms, then in the camps. Fire: it requires oxygen to breathe, fuel to burn, and people always forget. This disaster has been caused by those who saw it happening and looked away. Why must suffering always be caused by those who also suffer? Don't those who also suffer ever learn?

—

Evil, I think.

Like most academics, the members of my generational tribe, I used to think Evil was a quaint little word to describe the consequence of unenlightened self-interest rubbing up against the common good.

Now I think, Evil took our son. And now I see it everywhere. Evil, dressed in the body of an old crone, hitting a toddler with her fist. The woman is not the Evil which takes advantage of her weakness. The Evil is instead what is now inside her. And then the Evil flutters, out her eyelids, and then the Evil soars across the burning sky, and then the Evil is thriving in the hands of a Serbian peasant mounting a heavy machine gun—*the death planter*—strafing leisurely a residential tower, floor by floor, as if to paint it.

Evil. It's not a disease; it's not a misunderstanding; it's not a Point of View. It's a fire which consumes before it kills; it's the ice in the soul which will not thaw. It's the weak-willed heart.

Evil, it's not a person. It is what a person does.

As is Good.

—

What do I know? I know the twentieth century began in Sarajevo and I know that is where it's ending. I know the twentieth century was not America's Century. It was Everybody's. And maybe it is the century which will finally teach the residents of this world that the sacred will not protect the living from what the living do—and will continue to do—to one another. Rather, it is the work of the living to protect that which is sacred. It is the work of the living to protect the libraries and the schools, the chapels and the parks—and all the living souls, gathering therein to speak. It is the work of the living to protect that which all the members of the choir hold dear, and close, lest its mission perish.

—

It is a mistake to call this war an accident. Fault is an act of will, a break in the tectonic plates which hold this world together. This war in Sarajevo, it prefigures what is yet to come. The wars forthcoming against cultures and civilians—the wars of the weak against the weaker. Nobody is safe. The world is not a vault—though it will most certainly be our tomb—and in the next century, millions more will die, horrifically, and they will die because we did not pay attention. Because we did not open up our eyes and look.

We should stop going to the Vatican and to Mecca. And we should start making our pilgrimages to Sarajevo and to Jerusalem. If people in Ohio knew what Sarajevo looked like, if they could see it and touch it and walk on all the broken glass, the people of Ohio would not permit this to go on.

Having been there, I know. This morning I went to the Shrine of the Seven Brothers, and said my prayers, and dropped my coins. Then I went to the basement of St. Anthony's and talked with a priest. After a while a woman came in to sing.

—

I dreamed I was driving my father's car across the country. I knew it was a dream when I realized there was no traffic. You were in Chicago, and happy, and I was having a conversation with my father. When I checked my mirror, there was a boy in the backseat. My father always said Gulliver would come back to us—but maybe he meant something else. Maybe he meant Gulliver will come back to the world.

My father has come back to the world—his ashes, spread across that field in Vermont, along with my mother's—and I do know that I am talking with my father more than I did when he was alive. I think I'm talking with my father because my father wants me to know that he has found him. That Gulliver is no longer lost. Isn't this the essence of faith? That no matter how one perishes, no one is ever lost? I think my father wants us not to feel so lost.

—

Things unseen.

I was awakened from that dream by an explosion. There was a man in flames on the street, and by the time several of us had put them out, he had died.

—

What I miss most is the future: I miss not being able to see him now. To see the boy and then the man he would have grown into. The shape of his eyes, the length of his hands. The sound of him singing alone in his room.

Accident is not an act of will, but Fault is. Just as closing your eyes can also be an act of will. What I'm saying is I'm trying here to open up my eyes but I can't see you anymore. I just can't see what it was we wanted to become.

We should be able to do that, at least that. If we can't see our son, shouldn't we be able to see at least that which made him?

Look, if something happens to me, it is not your fault. If something happens to me, read this again. It is not your fault.

I miss you,

S

—

Zagreb, Croatia; 1993

Dear Gulliver—

I know where you are only when I whisper.

Dad

Winter 1992–93

The Appian Way

In mathematics, as on a camera lens, the symbol for infinity is this: ∞

—

Having found his place in the field, he was now on his knees. He was on his knees retching behind a tree into the snow.

His stomach, three days empty, his legs too weak to hold him—the muscles in his torso were convulsing, as if by electrocution, and he was spitting up bile. When he finished, he wiped his mouth with the back of his hand. The old couple's dog, seeing he was finished, stepped out of the stairwell to see if anything had been left behind.

It took Stephen seven minutes to make it up the stairs to the door of his flat. His side was burning. He fell onto his sleeping bag, holding his side, and said, I am not going to die of the flu.

Testing the measure of his conviction, and purposely forgetting many details of the century, he said, People in the twentieth century do not die of flu. Americans especially do not die of flu.

Depth of field, he told himself. *Depth of field.*

And then he disappeared within the tumult of his fever.

2

He woke to the sight of Elise, her hand beneath the back of his head, another holding to his lips a bottle of water. The water was spilling down the sides of his mouth. He was coughing. At first he thought it was a dream.

Where am I? he said.

Ado's, she said. You're burning up. We have to get you out of here. It's just the flu.

Then he was asleep, and through his sleep, amid the fevered dreams, he could hear her packing things up.

The next time he woke, or remembered waking, he was in a room at the Holiday Inn, which was freezing, the window having been shattered and covered with a mattress. He was on a small bed beside a machine for pressing pants. His luggage and gear were packed.

Sometime Ado came into the room.

Later, she said, It's still dark. Shhh.

She said, We catch tomorrow's two o'clock. We have to hope it is not canceled. To Zagreb.

She said, I can say things because you won't remember any of them. You are very sick.

He said, in German, Why did you find me?

Weil ich Dich suchte, she said. Because I have been looking for you.

The two o'clock was postponed to four o'clock on account of weather. They huddled at the airport. A Canadian gave them as much water as they wanted. In Zagreb, a cab to the train station. Only four hours to kill.

He said, I need a shower. A bath.

The concierge at the Hotel Esplanade opened a room for Stephen and Elise. No, Stephen said to Elise. Wait.

He went to his bag and removed a pair of khakis and socks, a sweater. Something clean? He said to her, I have lice. I need some chemicals.

She said, nodding, The Holiday Inn. Anna spread them to me. I spread them to you. The linens.

I didn't know—

The linens, she said. It's nothing. She took the clothes downstairs; he began to undress: a sweater, his two shirts, his union suit. He fell trying to remove his socks which had holes in them. In the shower he fell again. A bellhop appeared with a bottle of lindane smelling like petroleum—the Esplanade, you could get anything there; a couple chicks, a stinger missile—and then the bellhop disappeared. He washed his body, his hair. He put on a cotton robe and Elise returned with hot tea. She said, Something to eat?

No. I can't.

She made him drink water, which he threw up on the quarter-hour. The housekeeper brought his clean clothes; the concierge said there was nothing to charge, and Stephen left the concierge several large bills, as always, and thanked him, asking that he leave something for the housekeeper, too.

Of course, Sir. Very good.

The concierge said to Elise, Safe journey, Ms. Kohlhaus.

Old world, new world. The doorman held open the iron doors. They took their bags and made it slowly across the few hundred yards to the train station. On the way they passed a sign leading to the chic underground shopping mall which read *No Dogs, No Bicycles, No Firearms.*

It was sleeting in Zagreb. He would remember that.

Stephen said, I didn't get to say good-bye. To Ado.

Elise said, He came to say good-bye.

I don't remember.

You were asleep, she said. Don't worry. He knows you love him.

The train, a night train, would deliver them to Munich, and they rode on the way in a sleeping car. The *Schlafwagen.* They lay on their backs in the bottom bunk, their heads by the cold window, rising often to endure repeated border checks. The Croatian guards, new to the game, were the most cartoonish.

Said the baby-faced guard with the Uzi, his partner at the ready with a drawn 9-millimeter Beretta, Perhaps you have something you wish to declare?

No.

Perhaps you have some drugs? Some other illegal items?

No.

Perhaps before I search your bags you will wish to make some declaration?

Stephen said, What are you waiting for? A bribe? Search them or get out.

Elise said, pointing, He is sick.

He is American? This is his American passport?

Stephen said, What are you. Sixteen?

Yes, Elise said. That is his passport.

And why are *you* traveling with an American?

Because we are lovers.

Ahh, so. I will not intrude further. I am glad you are not smugglers.

Then there was the other side of the Slovenian border to endure. It was obvious everybody took him to be a junkie. Then Austria. The Austrians were polite, cheerful and precise. They came in teams of three with headsets, checking the database on a laptop. They went their way, whistling.

In between stops Stephen dozed in and out of nightmares. I should have said good-bye, he dreamed saying. Anna was shot.

She's in Bonn. With her husband. I saw her. She is fine.

I found some of her teeth.

Sometimes, he cried out; sometimes he rose to fall onto his knees in order to retch into a bucket of ice. Elise would hold a glass of Coke to his lips. It was real glass, not plastic.

Once he said, somewhere in the mountains, It's too bad I am sick.

I know.

You are supposed to make love on a train. In a sleeper.

We will have more trains. We will travel the world by train.

Not the United States.

No. Not the United States.

Australia, Stephen said. And Russia. I would like to cross Russia on a train. It's cold there.

Italy, always.

To Spain, Stephen said. When we visit Anna next summer. I promised.

You did?

Yes.

So did I.

He laughed. He said, I'm not so hot anymore, am I?

Not so bad. But you need water. Your clothes are soaked again.

Later, dozing, Stephen said, Gulliver loved trains. When he was very little he called them *dues*.

Du, Elise said.

It sounds like him. The tracks beneath. The rocking. It sounds like when he was born. Like his heartbeat hooked up to the monitor. Just like that.

She said, later, You are very weak.

I never get sick. It's a point of pride.

Everyone gets sick, I think.

He would not remember entering Munich in the morning. He would remember leaving his pillow, soaked with sweat by the cold window, and removing the case. They took a cab to a garage on the edge of the city. It was bright and clear and cold. Elise said, paying the driver, My car is here.

It was a small silver car with an enormously powerful engine. The Germans, he thought. They love to drive. She took the car to the lip of the autobahn and shuttled into the fast lane and did not look back. She said, at the speed of some two hundred kilometers an hour, Do you want some music?

Is it okay if we don't?

Of course. It is not too long a drive.

Not with you driving.

She laughed. She said, flashing her lights, My father calls me Gordon Johncock.

The racer.

The racer, she said. First I will take you to my parents' house. Did I tell you my mother speaks with a Texas accent?

How is that?

She studied there for a while. At Rice.

And your father?

He is a businessman.

I know that.

I don't know if he will be home or not, if that is what you mean.

I'm not likely to make a good impression.

I have already made that. She said, taking his hand, It is important for you to know: my parents love me. Because of that they will want to love you.

He shivered, fiercely, and she said, Shhh. It will be all right.

Could you pull over please. Right now?

He threw up on the side of the autobahn. It was early afternoon. Soon they were making a winding descent into the bowl of Stuttgart. It was a city set in a bowl. Grapes on the side, the vineyards of the Neckar Valley. She squeezed his knee and said, downshifting, Soon. Soon we will have you in a bed.

The houses on the hilltops had red tile roofs. She pulled the car into a driveway and pushed a button for the garage.

We're here, she said.

Work, say the Germans of Stuttgart. *Save. Build a little house.* The house was spacious with a view of the city below. It was located not on top, where the winds blew, and not below, near the downtown's perimeter traffic, but halfway up the hillside: quiet and safe, modestly proportioned, guarded on either side by trees. Inside the furniture was rich and used and well lived in. There were walls of books. Elise led him to a hall, then a room—the guest room—and said, pointing across the hall, A bath.

A blue silk robe hung on the back of the door. She sat him on a chair; she started up the bath. He watched her by way of a mirror pour a dose of the chemical rinse into the water. When she returned, he said, I feel better already. Really. I can do this by myself.

I don't think so.

She stood him up. Let's take these off. She said, lifting his sweater over his head, Do you want me to burn these? The clothes?

Not the sweater.

It is made of holes.

It's my favorite.

She opened the window to his room just a slice. Stephen leaned on her shoulder while he struggled with his socks. His khakis, ripped and torn at the knees and the seat, were stained with blood. He stood, gaunt and shivering.

I stopped having any strength, he said.

Shhh.

He remembered undressing his sick father much in the same way. She had gotten down to the gray-ashen skin of him. She inspected the knotted scar on his arm. Looking at his raspberried sides—each appearing as if he'd slid naked across a hundred yards of asphalt— she said, Stephen, what is this?

I don't know.

Your knees are shaking.

I know.

She led him to the bath. The lindane made him cry in pain as it brushed against his sides. He sat on the lip of the tub. Elise scrubbed at his hair, and then the thatch of his genitalia. She inspected briefly the pink scar on the tip of his penis. She drained the tub, and as he sat on the lip of it, she ran the shower faucet along his body, rinsing him. She stood him up and rinsed the tub. Then she washed his hair, twice, with a rich shampoo. She helped him shave with a freshly bladed razor she used for her legs and arms.

She said, shaving him, I shaved my whole body. I was certain you would be mad at me and never speak to me again.

He said, Just the face, I think.

She said, laughing, Mm hmmm.

She poured oil into the warm water and he slid into the tub.

He said, I've never been this clean. Squeaky. I'm squeaky clean. Bath time, that was my favorite. With Gulliver. He had this perfect body. Pure boy.

She brought him hot tea. When the water cooled, she warmed it again, and poured more oil into the water which smelled of sandalwood. Then he fell asleep, hard, and when he awoke, the water having cooled again, he saw Elise and an older woman dressed in the classical German manner—dark skirt and jacket, white blouse: beautiful fabrics, perfectly cut. She had the same features as Elise, only very dark hair; her glasses sat perched on her nose, and she stood looking down on him as if he were an interesting insect or plant. He understood she was gazing at his penis, the tip of which was bobbing just above the waterline. Then the woman said, realizing he was awake, simultaneously raising her gaze while extending her hand, Hello, Stephen. I am Rebekka.

He reached with one hand to cover himself and slid his body deeper into the water; with the other hand, he shook her own, which he made wet.

She laughed, a burst, and reached for a towel, which Elise handed to her. Well, Rebekka said. That injury appears to have healed satisfactorily.

I am very glad for that, said Elise.

I would think so, Rebekka said. It should be a lesson to both of you to stay away from shrapnel. Why do young people think it discriminates? But that is for another time. She said, turning to Stephen, You are very ill?

Just the flu.

She said, I think it might be more than that, no? *Like* the flu, correct? Will you show to me your side? Is it very painful?

Yes.

Will you show me now please? She and Elise helped him stand, and Elise gave him the towel to wrap around his waist, and Rebekka said, looking at one side and then the other, Ah so. Yes.

This is embarrassing, you know.

I am a doctor. Nothing embarrasses a doctor. She said, putting her hand to his stomach, and pushing, There. Is that okay?

Okay.

But it hurts?

Okay.

While Rebekka checked his lymph nodes, she said, Well, maybe flatulence. Unexpected. Maybe *that* embarrasses a doctor. The dropping of one's forceps, that of course embarrasses. Especially during a surgery. Right into the liver, say. Whoops! Very embarrassing. Now she told him to turn around in order to listen to his lungs, which she did without a stethoscope. She said, turning him back around, looking at his side, Well, you look to have the herpes.

Excuse me?

Here, she said, pointing to his side. The blisters. They are very painful.

God yes.

It is like the chicken pox herpes only these hurt very deeply.

What?

It is quite serious. Your immune system has failed you. You have probably been anemic for weeks. Too long at the war. No vitamins. We are going to get you many vitamins, among other things.

Elise handed him the blue silk robe. Rebekka said something in German to Elise, which Stephen did not catch, and Rebekka left the room.

Your mother, she's a pediatrician?

Elise laughed. She is the director of pediatrics at the hospital. Do not worry, Stephen. We are not a family of quacks.

I didn't mean—

Stop being sensitive, Elise said. She took him to his room, where she had laid out pajamas and wool slippers. There was a pot of hot cocoa. Elise said, pointing, Rest.

Later, as he sat alone in his room in a deep chair in pajamas which nearly drowned him, all legs and arms and cuffs, Rebekka knocked at his open door.

Yes?

Hello, Stephen, she said, entering. I have spoken with a colleague.

She placed a glass of water and two packages of medicine and a single pill the size of a horsefly on the table. She said, The good news or the bad news?

The good news.

She laughed, like her daughter. You are an optimist. I like you already. So: you are not going to die.

The bad news.

Mmmm. I think maybe the medicine may make you want to. You have what you call shingles. That's why you are so weak. The herpes blisters—

You keep saying that. Herpes?

Not *that* herpes, of course.

Thank God.

God has nothing to do with it, I think. Take these three times a day. It will hurt. It is a very powerful antiviral medicine. Ten days. Also, these for the pain. Then the misery will end. I promise. She said, But if it comes back you will need tests from my colleague, but he and I do not think it will come back. But for the next three weeks, rest. Real rest. No working. Four would be best.

You're kidding.

No, I am not the kidder in this case. This is very serious. You must rest.

Okay.

Stephen, she said. Do not worry. It is not contagious. Nobody gave it to you. Such an odd expression. Who would give away a sickness? And you cannot give it to anybody, anyway. It is all your own.

When she said that word, *anyway,* he caught the Southwest in her accent.

She said, catching his eye, And it is not sexual.

Okay.

We have a flat nearby. My husband uses it for the business guests. After we know you are feeling better, you can be there. Though you are always welcome here, too.

Thank you. I'm not used to. Well, I am—

Elise showed me your cowboys. Did you know I lived in Texas? They reminded me of Texas. So big and barren. In the apartment you will have more privacy. It will be a good place to rest and to reflect. Personally I like to read my Henry James there. It is very nice. The light is very nice. You will see.

Thank you.

It is an ugly building. But when you are inside it, you do not notice the ugliness. You see instead the view *from* the ugliness.

Okay.

Elise, Rebekka said. She had to meet with somebody. Errands. Her editor. I know not what. Also she had to go to Munich to fetch things from her flat. My husband, Philip, he will be home for the weekend. He wants to make certain you feel welcome and told me to say so. Also, the telephone, the fax . . . they are in the den. You must have many calls to make. So please feel free. But *after* you take your medicine. *After* you begin your resting.

That night, the painkillers having kicked in, he removed the cuffed pajamas and slid naked into the bed: firm, trimmed by two feather pillows, a down quilt tucked into the envelope of a silken cotton sheet—the duvet. It was the bed of a European. One made specifically to comfort.

—

On the third morning of Stephen's stay, Philip introduced himself: an enormously tall man, which explained the depths of these pajamas. Bald, he wore wire-rimmed glasses and a beautiful wool suit. Fifty-five, Stephen guessed, the same age as Messinger, which meant Philip would be twenty years Stephen's senior—not old enough, really, to be his father. Philip said, ducking through the door frame, extending his massive hand, Stephen, I am Philip Kohlhaus.

Stephen rose from the reading chair, and Philip said, No no. Sit. Please. Thus they shook hands—Stephen half up, half down in the man's cuffed pajamas. Like Rebekka, Philip had a solid grip. Philip said, I have just come by to say hello. We will have time to talk later. He said, Do you play chess?

Yes.

Marvelous. He said, But I am off. Please come out. Please come out for some breakfast. Or shall I ask on your behalf to have something delivered?

No, Stephen said. Please don't.

Having been so far removed from a steady diet, Stephen still wasn't hungry. The first few days of the medication went by unremarkably. At times he felt as if his stomach had turned into a hard, smooth stone—one which would fit into the palm of his hand should he feel the need to pull it from his body. The blisters began visibly to recede, though still he remained unfathomably weak.

One night Elise had helped Stephen in the bathroom, where he had fainted standing at the sink, knocking his head above the eye on the way down. There was minor swelling, and a bruise, and she helped him from the bathroom to the bedroom, where he had sat dizzy in the reading chair. Sometimes he regretted not having the strength to read, but not enough to think about regretting it; instead he sat in the chair and reviewed the spiraling currents of his life which had brought him here. Too, there was the consequence of taking nourishment: the food, entering his digestive tract, and then passing through as if he'd swallowed a cupful of broken glass: this was the real source of agony. The food he ingested now passed through his body with inexplicable speed, its rate of passage increasing each day. And as that food passed through his body, he endured a new kind of electrifying pain. It was like having hemorrhoids, and then having those hemorrhoids doused with alcohol, and then set afire, and then having that fire doused with gin and salt and mercuric acid. His ass throbbing like the heartbeat of a rabbit had become an unbearable source of constant pain.

Rebekka, always the hawk-eyed doctor, said to him on the fourth morning, You are not eating.

It hurts, Stephen said. He was sitting—uncomfortably—in her husband's massively cuffed pajamas. Oddly, the robe fit him well. The robe, he thought stupidly, was meant for guests.

It is not unlike the chemotherapies, I think. No embarrassments. I know where the pain is. But you must have food. Broth at the least. Chicken broth.

Okay, he said. But no bread. Please. No bread.

He spent a lot of time in the bath, soaking in cool water; each day, the pain grew, phenomenally, worse. He thought he must have a cancer. He thought surely Rebekka had no idea what she was talking about. On her mother's instructions, Elise ran out to the Apothek shop for a hemorrhoidal cream, which at least broke up the pain for three-hour blocks, though when it returned, it always returned more viciously. Sometimes, during those blocks, he read from a novel in bursts—an epical novel, complete with a descent into hell, and the founding of a new kingdom—lying flat on his stomach, and as the days passed he now found himself able to concentrate. As the pain grew, at least his mind was gaining strength along with it; at least his mind had returned to him, as had his will to kill this motherfucking pain. Fuck you, he said to the pain, gasping. Fuck you. And by fighting the pain, he knew that he was coming back, even if physically he was still a weakened lamb. On the eighth morning Elise helped him to the bathroom. She stood by him as he peed, as he washed his hands and face and brushed his teeth.

She said to him, by way of the mirror, You're better. It is in your eyes.

That afternoon Elise went downtown and returned with several packages. When she returned, packages in tow, she knocked at the door of his room, gently, lest he be asleep.

She said, How's your bottom? Am I disturbing?

No. Please.

She said, entering, I have come to announce that my father admires you and my mother adores you even if you are not eating.

He said, What's this?

I took your measurements. Some clothes.

He shifted awkwardly. Really?

Don't get nervous, Stephen. It is unbecoming.

She removed the packages: an indigo turtleneck of cotton and lambswool; white, brilliantly white underwear, of the thigh-hugging sport-brief variety, made from incredibly fine and seamless cotton; a pair of black twill jeans. Socks.

She said, I could make you into a German, maybe? We will need to find you some black shoes, I think.

I can't speak the language.

That will pass. You must work on your cases, though. I wanted to maybe buy you a coat but I was uncertain of the kind you might like.

I'll need to reimburse you.

Oh God. Stop stop stop. She sat quietly on the foot of his bed. She looked away, and then at him. Okay. So reimburse me. Pay me back if you must pay me back. If you want, then okay. So yeah. But soon it will be Christmas and you cannot pay me back if I choose to give to you a gift. That I will not permit.

I'm sorry, he said. I'm sensitive to gifts.

Stop it. At least with me. Just stop it. Grow up.

—

It wasn't just Stephen. People were recovering all over Europe. Anna had a second surgery on her jaw which looked to rescue it completely. There would be a scar on her cheek, where the bullet had entered, and she would likely set off airport security screens on account of all the metal used to reconstruct her face, but that would generally be invisible. Modern medicine, a wonder of the world. Messinger was in Paris with his family. Summerville was in and out of Sarajevo, doing what he could to rescue his girlfriend, whom he now intended to marry. In Zagreb Nina was raising her baby, Stephania Elise, and Marko was making his fortune smuggling arms from Italy to Dubrovnik, which were then funneled into Herzegovina. In Sarajevo, people were not recovering, but they were not perishing as rapidly as they had been: Ado and his uncle, Jusuf, were doing well as anybody might expect, and Ado's photographs of his comrades at the front were appearing in Spain and England and Italy. He had legitimate press credentials now. His career had been made.

They were a family of chess players, the Kohlhauses. One night Elise's father, nursing a cognac, defeated him easily. There was a Beethoven sonata on the stereo, a log on the fire. It had taken Stephen a while to discover what made the house feel unusual. It wasn't the fireplace or the furniture. It wasn't the coffee table smothered with magazines. It was, instead, the absence of a television. Elise worked in the kitchen wrapping tins of Christmas cookies for friends of the family; Rebekka worked late at the hospital.

Later, after Philip had gone to bed, after Rebekka had returned home and taken her two glasses of wine, after the house had settled in for the night, Stephen called R in Chicago.

She said, Are you okay?

Yes. Fine.

You sound funny. Guilty. I got your friend's fax.

I've been sick. I'm staying with some friends in Stuttgart.

The same friends? Friend?

Yes.

She said, Where is that? Austria?

Germany. Baden-Württemberg. They make Mercedes here. It's on the train station, the emblem thing.

That's interesting. She said, So are you coming home?

No. Not now. I wanted to wish you a Merry Christmas.

Okay. So you've wished it.

Stephen said, Are you still seeing Adam?

Sometimes.

Is it serious?

Sometimes.

Is there news?

No. There's another bill from the Italians. Just the bill.

Okay. Write a check from my account.

I already did.

Okay.

Okay, she said. So I have your permission. Is that what you want?

I wanted to say Merry Christmas.

Then he heard a voice—not R's, not a woman's. He said, He's there now.

Yes.

All right. Well, be sure to say hello. He said, Will you—do you have a place to go? For Christmas?

Yes.

I'm sorry for calling at a bad time.

It's your house. It's the first time I've heard from you in months. Well, not counting the fax. And the letter.

R, he said. For Christmas. Don't be alone, okay? Go see your parents—

Do you want me to come there? To Baden Whatsitburg? You haven't been shot or anything, have you? Stephen?

I just don't want you to be alone.

She was crying. She said, I'm going to go now. But I'm glad you're safe.

When he hung up, he went to the kitchen and poured a glass of water. Elise was waiting for him in his room. She was sitting on the bed, lotus-like, wearing a white transparent cotton nightdress. He could see the exposed nipple of a breast, and she caught him looking at it.

She said, frowning, Are you going?

No.

You are not going?

No, he said, taking her hand. I want to stay.

Good, she said, standing. She took him by the hand and led him to her room. At her door, she said, rising on her toes, I forgot to get you pajamas.

I never wear them.

I know that, Stephen.

She kissed him at her door and said, Good night.

Three days after Stephen had finished his course of medicine, and with Rebekka's permission, Elise took Stephen downtown.

We'll walk down for the exercise, Elise said. We can taxi back.

A bright day despite the clouds overhead, the brightness elicited by the snow on the rooftops and lawns. Elise's family, he had learned, lived on Dilmannstrasse. They walked down, past a lone tall residential tower, striped in green, which could have been in Split or Sarajevo or Chicago. It was the location of the flat Stephen would be borrowing. Next they walked by offices for the Max Planck Institute and picked up a pedestrian path which wound down through a hospital campus, delivering them to the university's two glass and steel towers. Now Elise led him through an underground passage, beneath the highways, and they emerged back on the surface on a street which led them to the Königstrasse.

It's so clean, Stephen said. I'd forgotten what a clean city looks like.

The Königstrasse had filled with walkers charmed by the hustle and bustle of a forthcoming Christmas. Elise took his arm, the way European women do, and he felt suddenly displaced. It was the kissing thing all over again. They strolled away from the Hauptbahnhof and stopped at a café nearby the stone-pillared Börse for chocolate. They sat on the second floor, overlooking the pedestrian avenue. The restaurant, like all of the city, was impeccably clean.

We could be on Ferhadija, he said. Across from the Economy Park.

Do you know why all the buildings look so new? Because the buildings *are* new. Well, not *all*. Almost 20 percent survived in some part. The Allies, the bombing. My father's factory—the Nazis made my father's family manufacture parts for trucks. The bed part and the fences to keep things in. The drive shafts. By the end of the war my grandfather made treads and skirts for the tanks, but it was too late. The factory was destroyed over a weekend by a flight of sixty-two bombers. The Allies had so many they didn't have anything left to bomb. So they sent sixty-two bombers to make sure they destroyed the factory. In case one or two missed. So maybe there is hope for Sarajevo. I don't know.

What does Peter say?

Ach. Peter is a cynic. He is a great photographer. What does he know?

Stephen said, What does anybody know?

I think it will be bad there for a long time, Elise said. It is too per-verse. Like Greece after the war.

I hope not.

The problem with stupid people is they are stupid. She said, It was not serious with him, you know. I am not a little girl. It was a little exercise.

I know.

And you are not too old for me.

You're certain?

She beamed, and popped that laugh, and said, nodding, Oh yes.

I've been feeling frail. My hair is turning gray.

You've been sick. Seven years is not so many. When you are forty, I will be thirty-three. That's very good for you! And when you are fifty, I will be forty-three. Blah dee blah dee blah. It's meaningless. Plus I am not so impressionable.

He laughed. I hadn't noticed.

She said, taking his hand across the table, I want to tell you some-thing.

His heart raced. He said, bracing himself, Okay.

She said, bringing her other hand to bear, squeezing his own, My parents are going to have a party. For New Year's.

Do they— Should I leave?

No, no. It's *for* you. For you not to feel so lonely. To introduce you to friends. If, that is . . . if you are still here. Later you can move into the apartment. And rest. And work. I have to go to New York, but not until January.

For your book.

Yes, she said, nodding. She said, sipping her chocolate, For my next book I'm going to write about something else. I'm tired of the raping. The rape. I want to write instead about sex. Or something about the body. Medicine, maybe. She said, laughing, catching his eye, But I think I have sex on the mind right now.

Why's that?

So coy, Stephen. No. Seriously. Without sex a self cannot be. It can-not grow into a mature self. That's the crime of it, the rape. That's its horror. I'm not talking of the impregnating of Muslim women with a Serb, or a Serb with a Croatian—the washing out of the bloodstreams? That is too literal. Too common. No, it is the *smaller* emblem of it. The psychological damage that is so irreparable. The taking away of the sexual self. The turning of another into a husk. Milošević, he is one of those priests who fondle the little boys. It destroys one's faith in humanity. It makes the soul into steel.

Stephen lit a cigarette. On the walls were black and white photographs of movie stars in steel frames. Below them, a sea of holiday window-shoppers.

She said, You know Berlin? The ruined cathedral?

Yes.

Some call it the Rotting Tooth. A reminder to us, our evil country. But that's not what it looks like to me. To me I call it the Syphilitic Penis.

She said, taking one of his cigarettes, Didn't those people pay attention to what made them? To what *made* Yugoslavia? To what we did to the Russians? The Jews? To what the Russians did to us? To the women of our mighty cities reduced to gathering all the broken bricks? How can anybody rape another? I do not understand why even after the atrocities of the Nazis—okay, okay, of the *Germans*—I do not understand why it is satisfactory for the Russian army to rape the German women. Kill, okay. But rape? You see my interest. My focus.

I do.

She said, Eight in ten Berlin women, raped, repeatedly, in front of their children? Twelve-year-old girls, grandmothers. Two million illegal abortions in 1945? The Russians didn't capture Berlin to capture Hitler. They did it to capture us. To kill our German soul. The war was over. Stalin had won!

Stephen said, My father was part of that. He was there. Not in Berlin—

Everybody wanted to surrender to the Americans. At least we hadn't bombed *their* cities. They had chocolate! This, this third war, didn't these stupid people pay attention to the first and to the second? And what if it does spread? What if it does spread into Greece? Macedonia? What if Russia decides to quit democracy and aid the Serbs against the NATO peacekeepers? This thing could still explode. One plane shot down. Then another. Then what?

She said, People, I think. People need a frame to hold themselves together. God knows they cannot do it by themselves. They need a context. Something to contain themselves. Like a tree, one you must train.

Germany, she said. We have our frame of guilt. Like Japan, which is reinforced by America's forgiveness for committing the unconscionable. Before the wall came down we were beholden and guilty and small. The Russians were framed by their poverty and conquest, that cold peasant smugness, and now that they have collapsed, they are framed by their poverty.

And the French, she said. The French are framed by their arrogance and defeat, which they will never get over, being French, and the British are framed by their arrogance and great sacrifice. A fallen empire. The Suez Canal, South Africa. The Italians are my favorite, I think. They are framed by their lack of resources and warm sea climate and their love for children, which they mistake for industry. Everybody loves the Italians. It is impossible not to.

And the Americans?

The Americans are framed by what has always framed them. Their bounty. By their lack of struggle, which makes them good in the heart. Americans are never bitter, just annoying.

She said, Yugoslavia, it could have been a real nation. Tito dies, move to Sarajevo, build a multi-religious capitol. They have had forty years to prepare. A brand-new democracy. Instead they fall apart because they have no frame. Or because the frame of their leaders is one of selfishness and fear and separatism, and that is the frame which always implodes. Like the Middle East. Boom.

She said, looking around her at the photographs of all the movie stars, Most beautiful woman. It's okay. You may have more than one.

Anouk Aimée. In the race car movie. She's the film editor—

Yes, she said. *A Man and a Woman.* I love that movie.

It's the editing, Stephen said. It describes by how it splices.

Well, Elise said, laughing, she's also very beautiful.

Later, back outside, walking through the mall, it began to snow. Big, white, deliciously fat flakes drifted in the sky. The snow, looking up at it—you could not tell if it was rising or falling.

She said, taking his arm and cocking her head, Favorite second career.

He said, A luthier.

She said, Dentist. She said, What is a luthier?

He who makes guitars. Or she. Cellos, he said, A dentist?

Got you, she said, laughing. Actually a cook. Chef. A *real* chef in a marvelous restaurant. But I would have to be very good at it. And no tourists for customers. No no no. I would be a chef only for people who know how to eat.

They stopped at a crowded booth and ordered hot wine, the cups of which steamed in their hands. A handful of drunk men stood singing nearby. The wine was sweet, and they went on, and there was a book-store which specialized in art, and Stephen purchased a copy of his North Sea photographs—120 marks, which smarted.

Back on the street, Elise said, A coat. You need a new coat.

He said, gathering the collar of his pea coat, The stores are too crowded.

They stopped at an art and office supply store, where Elise picked up several brightly colored file folders she was partial to, and while she was busy Stephen purchased a Rotring mechanical pencil—brushed in silver, not chrome. Outside, they walked to the old town, down toward the church. There was dark now, and snow swirling in the lights, singing and laughter in the streets. They stopped at a crowded booth for more hot wine. She said, We will have to take a cab back. The wine is making me sleepy. She said, I want to buy you a warm coat. It will be my gift to you. To keep you warm. She said, rais-ing her eyebrow, For when you go back to the Windy City.

They walked through the crowd to the church. There, he stood still a moment and looked up at the sky, and Elise said, What is it?

I was thinking about Gulliver. Christmas Eve. That's when I lost him.

She said, taking his arm and pulling him close, I did not know that.

4

On Christmas Eve, after Elise's parents had returned early from a party, they all sat before the fire and exchanged gifts. Elise's father, Philip, gave Stephen an antique brass-handled magnifying glass; Rebekka gave Stephen a navy scarf. Philip and Rebekka spent sev-eral minutes exclaiming over the book of North Sea photographs. Elise kissed Stephen, and then, as he was seated on the floor, she sep-arated his legs and snuggled her back into him, placing his arm on her shoulder, bringing his hand to her heart. She was delighted with the pencil: its weight, and balance. Elise's parents gave her a leather folio for her trip to New York. And then Rebekka and Philip retired to their wing of the house.

That night, after he had slipped into his bed, Elise came to his room. She stood in the doorway in her white cotton nightdress. She said, May I come in?

Please, yes.

She shut the door and stood in the light from the street and the snow and removed her nightdress, which she hung on the knob of the door. She rushed to the bed, lifting the duvet, and slid in beside him. She wrapped her arms around his chest and said, I was cold.

She ran her hand along his ribs. She said, Stephen, I want you to tell me.

She said, Tell me.

—

And so he told her. He told her the story of the American couple with the strained pretend-marriage; he told her of the couple's trip to Rome which was supposed to ease the strain. They did in Rome, he told her, the things one does. At the airport, upon arriving, they walked by a half-dozen carabinieri in the process of removing by way of a fishing pole an unattended duffel bag. They stood in line for a cab and went to their hotel near Vatican City. The staff at the hotel was proper and punctilious and coldly impolite. They went to restaurants, and after the first day, Stephen learned to watch out for dog shit on the cobblestones. The wife of the couple, he said, asked her partner to buy her a beautiful pair of leather boots. At the Vatican Museum, Stephen lingered over the Gallery of Maps. They had taken that spiraling staircase so out of place. It was crowded, the museum, and hot, and they—the couple and their young son—were constantly being pressed by the sea of pilgrims. In the Sistine Chapel, the young boy did the Hokey Pokey, having recently learned it in preschool.

Exhausted, they were expelled out onto St. Peter's Piazza—the great collection plate of the people, Stephen called it. He took photographs of his son, and of his partner, R, holding their son into the air before the fountain. Three young priests in black cassocks passed him by. That night, the couple arranged for a sitter, and then the couple walked to the Trevi Fountain and made a wish. Stephen wished to be more happy, to be more content with this life of his, and later they went to look at the Pantheon in the moonlight. They returned home, tired, and went coldly to bed, neither feeling happy.

Gulliver had been fussy that night, he remembered. Gulliver was jet-lagged and did not like the strange bed. He did like playing with the bidet. He called it the Magic Fountain.

Stephen said to Elise, All roads lead to Rome. We had been heading there since we first met.

Go on.

We had done the ruins, which seemed fitting. The Castle Sant'Angelo and the Pons Aelius. Nero's baths. The Tomb of the Scipii. The Spanish Steps and the Colosseum, the House of the Vestal Virgins. Keats's House. We'd done the things one does. We were in the Piazza Navona. I liked the fountain—those beautifully sculpted bodies. So sexual, the bodies and the water. The Fountain of the Four Rivers. We were having a drink and there was a gypsy woman in a long red coat— like Santa, one of his vixen helpers. White fur at the hem. She stood on a bucket, and the coat clung to her body and draped to the ground, and she did various pantomimes, and a crowd gathered. There was a radio set up blasting sexy music. Very Latin. R was turned on. It's hard to explain: the foreign setting, the beautiful light, the woman in red, the music. And R and I, we hadn't made love in months, and then it was as if the ice between us was melting away, and she was whispering.

Go on.

Some details I'll spare you. A general rule.

Tell me. Tell me all.

So there they were: Gulliver, the boy, sitting on the man's shoulders, laughing and looking at the pretty lady in the bright red cape. R had Stephen's hand beneath her sweater. And now an older man— Italian—trim Italian suit, brash, introduced himself to Stephen. R, using Stephen's thumb to tease her nipple, while Stephen turned to answer the man's questions—

You are a photographer?

Excuse me?

The man explained his name was Antonio. The man explained he was the Paparazzo of the Empire.

One thing led to another. R gave Stephen back his hand. The man introduced the couple to his bodyguard—a handsome boy. Conversation on the way to a café, laughter and a drink. Another.

I knew you were a photographer by your camera, the man said, pointing. In Rome I know all the photographers. I am the Paparazzo of the Empire.

And then the man invited them to his flat for more conversation.

So you go?

Yes, we go. We are world travelers. This is our adventure.

Inside, inside the apartment, it's a hymn to celebrity. It's a vast apartment filled with photographs of every conceivable star. The galaxy. The royals from Monaco to Jordan to England. There's Fergie, pudgy and topless on a beach. Diana in Versace. There's Tom Cruise and Nicole Kidman in opening red-carpet gear at Cannes. Even Anouk Aimée, a set still. We are told that this man has done more drugs and had more sex with the famous stars than anybody. He is, you see, the Paparazzo of the Empire.

Then the man pulled out some ecstasy. He shared politely. The handsome bodyguard. R, who sallied forth up to the rail, as if she were at communion—the tablet on her pink tongue. I pulled Gulliver aside to look at the photographs of the pretty people. The hundreds on the walls. Distant family.

I said, It's time to go.

R did not want to go.

I said, It's late. Gulliver is tired. I am tired.

Oh Stephen, said the man, suddenly electric. Have some wine!

Go, R said, drinking wine. Go. I'll get a cab.

Oh nonsense, Stephen. It is not far. Come and kiss your pretty wife. I will escort your pretty wife personally!

R, I said.

I'm in Rome, Stephen. I'm in *Rome*.

So, okay.

She kissed Gulliver, and I placed Gulliver on my shoulders, and we walked back to our coldly impolite hotel. On the way we stopped to look at the moonlight on the pretty buildings. At home, a bath, and he played with the Magic Fountain, shooting up the streams, laughing, and I read to him books and tucked him into bed. I sat on the edge of his bed and looked at Antonio Bianchi's card. It had his picture; it read *The Emperor of the Paparazzi*. When R returned, at dawn, she had wine and condoms and spermicide on her breath.

Was it his, or the bodyguard's, I will never know. If I guess, it's the bodyguard's. The old guy, he's busy with the camera. He's snapping shots. Of that night she will remember only the sexual compromise. You cannot play around with ecstasy. People, they assume photographers are obsessed with sex, but one does not make love with a lens. The lens may be a shield, but it's not a dildo. A lens requires distance. What is the paparazzo obsessed with? Money.

Go on.

She's angry with me for not being what she wanted to make me into. She is a feminist, class of 1978, thanks to a conspicuous lack of women professors at her small college; thanks to the example of her thrice-divorced aunt and sacrificial mother who gave up her career to raise the children, etcetera, and who would otherwise have been a great something-or-other. R is the feminist caught in the wake of those women who had nothing and who made their way from nothing, but she is of a generation of replacements, only she is not yet aware of the changes on the battlefield. It's no longer enough just to protest—

She is not honest with herself, you are saying.

Something like that. What troubles me, Stephen said, is that she could do so much. Instead she becomes a replaceable part in an ordinary political machine. Wanting to be loved, she does what those around her want her to. And so they have these differences, the couple, but despite these differences they love each other. They have a history, years of growing up together, and now the fact of this beautiful child. She's on a trip, feeling frisky. She's tired of the distance the man keeps and she's eager to break it down. She breaks people down to make them laugh, agree, to make them all her own. This is something she is good at, something people love her for. So why won't he?

In the morning, he lets her sleep. He puts a glass of water beside the bed and two aspirins. He takes the boy back to the Colosseum. On the way, they talk about Roman soldiers. There are men at the Colosseum with red skirts and golden swords. The men make funny faces and cry out in fake pain, and they delight the boy, who is in love with soldiers even though he has never once been permitted to watch any on television. But he is a boy. He is enchanted by the uniforms and bright weapons gleaming in the light and the sounds they make sliding in and out of scabbards. The soldiers, they make those funny faces to him, and he laughs into the sky. He laughs in peals, like bells.

The streets, they are buzzing with scooters—giant gnats high on gasoline. The boy explains when they go home he wants to have a scooter too. But a *quiet* scooter. One not so noisy, because the scooters scare him, the noisy ones. The man and the boy, they talk about scooters and nifty sports cars and make their way back to the Piazza Navona. On the way he, the man, is trying to decide if he should cut short the trip. R, his wife, she's in the bath. She's got a case of morning-after. She's crying bitterly into the bath. It's over, now. She's got a good reason to make it over. This ridiculous act of infidelity she will never confess. Or will. The partnership, the union, it burdens her like a tax. It's not the first time she has wanted it to be over; it's time to humiliate the cuckold. She thinks she can make it over now for good so long as she tells him precisely what she's done. Stab him in the heart's faithful core. Twist the blade.

He stopped speaking. He reached for a glass of water and drank.

So, Elise said, gently. So you go back to the Piazza Navona.

The narrator, Stephen said. The narrator should tell you the man in question is one who loves women. He is neither a philanderer nor a pervert, but he loves women. And she's back. The gypsy girl. He watches her in an alley remove her jacket and slip on the red Christmas cape. The dazzling white hem. It's this sudden, awkward intimacy. And she is startling. The eyes. The cheap makeup surrounding. She has that gaunt figure of the proverbial and fetishized gypsy. Now she's talking with a man. The same handsome boy. The bodyguard. The bodyguard is handing her a wad of bills.

He thinks, So they are friends. He thinks, All great cities are made smaller by their common circles. Now the girl enters the square. The man, the narrator, he should have left right then. He should have picked up his son and gone back to the hotel. His wife could have confessed her sin, or not; he could have forgiven her, which he would have, much to his wife's surprise; or he might not have, depending if he sensed from her a genuine desire for dissolution. By not forgiving her, the road to separation would be more clear. More direct. The word *unite* has never been far removed from the word *untie*. A mere slip of the tongue, or pen. They'd have to work out only matters of custody.

Instead he should have gone to St. Peter's. He wanted to photograph his son with one or two of the Swiss Guards. The *Pietá,* the most beautiful sculpture in all the world, that is in St. Peter's. He thought a picture of the Swiss Guards with his son would protect his son for life. Guardian Angels, Soldiers of God.

And then?

And then I hear that beating Latin music. The girl is on the elevated platform, toes together for it being so narrow. A paint bucket, draped over and concealed by her red Christmas cape. Her hips are tucked. I take out the camera, check the light. I tell Gulliver to come with, to stay close, because I have to let go his hand and in crowded places we always stay close. That's the phrase, *Stay close.*

Eyes sharp.

I wanted to see her up close. I wanted to look.

So I crash the line, dump a handful of lira into the collection plate. I'm on my heels, shooting up at her elevated figure. Always the serious artist. She gives me a sexy pout. She shakes her finger at me. She is actually flirting with me. She is terrifyingly angelic and marvelous. She has caught my eye and now she keeps it to herself by pretending to give it back. She twists that red cape like a skirt. She's a matador, and Gulliver is standing right behind me, looking sharp.

Only he isn't. He's gone. Like that.

—

Antonio Bianchi, the police assured me, knew nothing. He was of the paparazzi, well respected, not a *pornographer* or *pederast* or *ransomer.* Three months later, he was found in the stairwell of his building, dressed in a white linen suit, his throat having been slit. The police determined his throat had been slit in the dark by somebody who knew him well.

The bodyguard had also disappeared. Some speculate there might have been a quarrel between the two. Truth is, if I saw him, the bodyguard, and having never photographed his face . . . if I saw him I wouldn't recognize him. He was beautiful. Anybody can be beautiful.

The wife, Stephen said. The wife never forgave the man for losing her son.

In Rome, he said, you walk by the old lepers. It's a thespian-influenced form of panhandling. Very creative. The bent, crippled figure, hooded in black, twitching. You are supposed to give her money. That summer I went back to Rome. I learned of the assassination of the Paparazzo of the Empire. In my crueler moments I like to imagine somebody taking a picture as it happens—the knife, coming across the throat, just a bit more firmly than a kiss. A girl's ribbon, or silk scarf, blowing in the breeze. The blade would be sharp and handled by somebody very close, preferably a lover. Somebody holding the camera would have to use a flash. The flash, hitting the blade, would bounce back into the lens, into the eye of he who held the camera, blinding him. Her? The eye of the first beholder. A picture like that, a snuff picture, it would be worth thousands. He must have had a thousand people who wished him dead. Who could wish otherwise on a paparazzo? They are leeches. They suck the blood of the public figure and then they sell it. They are parasites.

You? Did you?

I just wanted my son. I wanted to ask him what he knew but arrived too late. That summer, amid the tourists and the faithful, I watched a girl in sneakers and shorts and a halter top put on the black robe of the leper. I followed her to her place, to a spot beside the McDonald's at the Pantheon, where she struck the pose. Got down on her knees, her face to the cobblestones, twitching endlessly.

Nothing is what it seems, I said.

And then I went home, and then I came back, almost a year later, and still the bodyguard was gone. Perhaps his throat had been slit, too. Perhaps his body had been dumped into the Tiber. People forget, why shouldn't the river? I never saw the same girl, though I saw many like her. The brothels in Europe are filled with pretty girls from the Ukraine and Slovakia, Romania and Hungary, and the girls are all protected by their bodyguards. The brothels are filled with girls who are not permitted to leave on account of their bodyguards who protect them with knives and guns and who keep them safe by locking them up at night into their rooms. So much for Wars of Liberation. Sometimes the guards permit the girls to call home to their families. Nothing is what it seems. Not the War on Choice; not the Sexual Revolution.

And then I went across the Adriatic to Hvar. I went to Biševo. I went to the Blue Grotto and swam in the blue water and I saw you. You were diving into the sea. It was the first time I took your photograph.

He said, The first time I saw you, you were naked.

As were you.

Mirrors and veils, he said. The veil is the key to all deception.

He said, rolling over, now facing her . . . Once. Once a clerk at an airport asked to see my identification. I showed it to him, and the clerk said, I am protecting you in case somebody has stolen your ticket.

I said, No. You are presuming I am a thief.

I said, Presume anything you want, but let's not lie about it.

The veil is the key. The veil is the key to all the secrets of the world. The veil is what keeps you warm; in the house of God, it keeps a woman's hair in place. It is the essence of all that is erotic which is the essence of that which creation permits. The veil is the fabric which conceals the face, the body; it's made of the same fabric as the shroud. It is the emblem of an act of vision. The veil describes what one permits another to see of oneself. The eyes. Why do the eyes tell all? Because they *see* all. I lost my son because I looked away from him for a moment. Because for a moment I was entranced by a woman wearing a red cape.

That's what I found in Rome. I found out that God holds a mirror from the sky but I am the one who holds the veil. I found my calling. My calling is to remove the veil, or to hold the veil in place, but either way, stay or go, it is I who must choose to reach. To keep it there. To take it away.

Elise said, almost a whisper, Why did you stay with R? After that?

Because if we had split up then Gulliver would not have had a place to come home to.

But you are never there.

No, Stephen said. One thing I am not is ever there.

—

In the morning he was awakened by Elise, sitting up in bed, watching him. He stirred and rubbed at his eyes. She was squinting one eye to focus. She said, We all have a frame. A frame that holds us. My frame is my parents and their love for me and my love for my parents. Their love for each other.

Okay.

Your frame is your lost son and his heartbroken mother, whom you love but cannot love enough. Not her heartbreak, but your own. You can change that. You can change that loss to love.

She said, That's what my parents did. When their son died. Leukemia. Even my mother the important doctor could not save him.

I didn't know.

They had to fill that loss. That void in the heart. They had to love to fill it up with more. They had to have me.

He said, You can't fix me, Elise.

I don't want to fix you. I want to love you. I want to know you will forgive me in advance of all I do wrong. I want you to know that I will forgive you likewise. And then I want to spend my life with you traveling the world.

What are you saying?

I am saying you cannot disappoint somebody who loves you.

You don't know me well enough to love me.

Then how am I to reply to your love for me? That is a silly premise, Stephen. It does not hold. A love which is new does not mean it is a love which will not last.

Most don't.

Some do. She said, I *know* the essence. I know there is more to know that I want to spend my life discovering. You are afraid you will disappoint. You are afraid you will never be forgiven because you will not forgive yourself.

Something like that.

You do not believe that two people can be perfect for each other. That love must not always be the acceptance of things which diminish that love.

I've never seen it.

I have.

Your parents.

Yes. Also others. Anna and her husband. I know two women who have that love with each other.

My father had that, I think. With my mother. I don't know.

She said, There's time. I can wait. Love does not vanish unless you make it. But you must look at this: I have never met a person like you, and I know you have never met a person like me. I know because only my life could have made me. I am not a dewy girl looking to be laid, especially by an American. This is not a passing infatuation. Do you understand? A crush?

She said, reaching between his legs and grabbing a handful of testicle, Like this?

When she let go she swung out of bed. She picked up her nightdress, and she said, opening the door, I'm going to use the toilet. After we'll make breakfast.

Okay.

And then, Stephen Brings. Then we are going to break the fast.

5

As Stephen grew stronger, his spirits rose. For breakfast he ate bread and a tomato and a slice of Gouda and he drank two cups of the most delicious coffee ever brewed in the history of caffeine. Following Rebekka's instructions, he drank mineral water by the liter. Next he moved into the tower apartment with his gear and set up shop. The apartment was on the seventh floor, sparsely furnished, facing the rising hilltop. There were a French bed and a table in the center room, a wooden-framed self-standing mirror, a pocket kitchen which would serve well as a darkroom; there was a bath built for two. The light was warm and there was a rich, dark carpet, a fine reading chair in the manner of Eames and a shelf full of Henry James and John Hawkes and William Gass.

It's perfect, Stephen said.

It was snowing again. The sky white like flowers. In bed, before the windows, they watched the snow swirl into the wind in the sky. Elise said, looking out the window, I have always liked this apartment. There is no need to draw the drapes.

He noticed, for the second time, she had shaved her body. And he thought, A woman who smiles at you when you begin to rise, knowing she has caused it: it is a confluence of power and desire, which allows for trust. He watched the upturned corners of her mouth. He felt the laugh bubbling in the back of her throat. He thought, She has you now. Look at what she can do.

He said, Ten Books.

She laughed. She said, Well, *Anna Karenina* I think is in order.

Perfect.

She said, The usual suspects. *Emma. Middlemarch. Orlando.* Kundera, she said, shifting her weight on his lap. Don't you want to come?

Not now.

She laced her hands behind his neck, arching her back. What if I did?

Do you?

Not just yet. But fairly soon, perhaps. Before the sun comes up, certainly.

Promise, he said.

She said, brushing his tangled hair from his eyes, We have a lifetime to do this. Oh fuck. We could read, doing this. I have never done that.

Nothing technical.

Mm-mm, she said.

Nabokov?

Yes. And maybe a little Anaïs Nin.

The Story of O?

Doubtful, she said, laughing. Again that laugh, which traveled through her body, and gripped him. But *The Kama Sutra,* she said. God yes. We would have to have that. The walking of the crab and such. The squeezing of the horse?

Later, while she slept, he spooned her body and buried his nose into the nape of her neck. Simply he could not get his fill of her. He ran his finger across the declivities of her ribs, he placed the flat of his hand against her navel and felt the rising and falling of her breath. He repeated in his mind observations she had made. *Why is it,* she had said, *that children always appear older in a photograph than they really are? What is that radiance? That lack of self-consciousness?* She said she preferred skiing to bicycling. She preferred Beethoven to Mozart. She said, *Have you ever noticed that a man's penis, once fully cocked, resembles a loaded gun?* She preferred long letters always to the telephone. Without the answering machine, she said, we would be compelled to answer. *Ugh.* She said she preferred to drive rather than to be driven. She preferred to wear her hair short now that she had made it so. She preferred winter to summer only if it was possible to ski, and she preferred a pencil to a pen because with a pencil it was possible to erase. She preferred modernism, she supposed, to postmodernism; film to television, which she refused to watch on account of the commercials. Italy to Greece, Spain to France. Berlin to Paris. She didn't care for London at all. New York City, she supposed, to Detroit. *Just checking.* She said she preferred nude gay beaches to nude straight beaches because at the gay beaches the men were beautiful and preferred not to look at you but rather to be looked upon. A man like Stephen, one thing he was pretty certain of was his ability to love a woman not for the way she looked, but rather for the things she saw.

This honeymoon, this unexpected adventure of the body, it was like absorbing into the bloodstream a finely manufactured opiate—it freed the mind; it loosened the heart. *Ich komme,* she'd say, coming. And then she'd say, later, maybe at a café, *Ich will dir einen blasen,* and wait for him to translate, laughing, and it wasn't simply this spilling bucketful of sexual display which freed him: that manic thrill of travel, and discovery, the there-and-back-again of the erotic imagination freely exchanged. *Behind,* Elise said. *Sometimes I like it from behind.* The blind cry in the midst, the arching of the back, the breath in the ardent, tangled-up kiss? Sometimes she liked him to come on her breast. Sometimes she'd put his cock in her fist and say, *No, No, not yet, Stephen,* and he'd bite his tongue, and then hers, and then he'd come without ejaculating and she'd let him go all over again. Because it wasn't the love which had set him free, it was the possibility to. It was the pauses, the rests—like in music, or after great exercise: the space and pauses between the sentences and the heartbeats, the ranging of the eyes across a field of vision before that precise moment of their locking into focus: the fine ribbon of light circumnavigating the aureole, the blue-white vein throbbing at the ankle, the scar on the knee the length of a penny. There was always the hint of sleep in the waking eye; and the curve of her hip, silhouetted against the skyline.

He thought, watching the snow fall from the sky, Sex is about the body only insofar as it has nobody else to mind.

He thought, Thinking makes it so.

—

In the morning she awoke and pulled the duvet up across her chest. She sat up, hanging onto the duvet, and said, Will you make the breakfast?

Sure.

He swung out of bed: the heat was on, the room toasty, the windows fogged with condensation. He went to the kitchen and poured juice from a box—those Germans—and began water for the coffee. Waiting for the water to boil, he smoked a cigarette at the window. He opened a fresh brick of coffee. He stepped out of the kitchen and saw her, sitting up, the quilt covering her body, and said, Are you cold?

She held the quilt in place and said, looking at him, No. Why do you ask?

Nothing, he said. He stepped back into the kitchen and called, Toast? With cheese?

No. Meat.

Never both. He made a three-egg omelet to split. He poured the coffee; he set the tray. Then he brought the breakfast to the foot of the bed. In bed, she insisted on holding the duvet to cover herself. She ate with one hand. She made a big show of it, always shifting her coffee or juice from one hand to the other, using her chin to pin the quilt in place. Once, when the quilt began to slip, she cursed under her breath. She raised her eyes and caught him looking.

He looked away, at his coffee, which was hot.

She caught his eye again. She said, You look perplexed, Stephen.

I was just wondering what's with the sheet thing—

And then she burst into a laugh. She threw aside the quilt and pushed aside the breakfast tray and grabbed his shoulders and pinned him on his back. She said, laughing, pinning him, her ribs shaking, You should have seen your face. I mean—

She howled now. She howled and held her ribs. She said, shaking, Really. Boy oh boy!

Very funny.

She said, shaking, wiping the tears streaming from her eyes, Boy oh boy. Did I get you!

—

After a while even the most ardent lovers come up for air. So they did other things. Stephen, for example, wrote an essay in the manner of Andrew Marvell exploring the relationships between body and soul. It wasn't right, the essay, but he was eager to be trying to explain the state in which he found himself. Elise met with her publisher and editor about page proofs and publicity matters. In summer there would be a tour through Austria and Switzerland and Germany: together, Stephen and Elise marked up a map with places to go and to stay. They took a day trip to Baden-Baden and did the spa, parting at the lobby, going their separate ways through the various stations where Germans of hardy stock with beefy hands attended to their bodies. They met, naked and weak-kneed, in the center of the pool beneath a spectacular dome. There was an old couple nearby, sitting on the lip of the pool, holding hands. There was another couple, younger, and another. In the pool the water was blue and rife with minerals. Also they attended a reading at the American Center by an American poet nobody in America had heard of, but should have, and they ate at the Rathskeller, and they picked out a suit for Stephen in a tony shop off Calwerstrasse and lingerie for Elise in a basement shop with an arched brick ceiling—where Elise pulled him into the curtained booth, while the clerks spoke through the gauzy curtain, and Elise said, undoing his fly, kissing him, Do you dress to the right, Sir? Or to the Left? When Stephen blushed, she laughed, by the bellyful, and said, Oh Stephen, sometimes you should see yourself. She said, turning him to the mirror, Look, Stephen. Just look at us!

For the doorknob, he said, looking at the piles of lingerie. No?

They ate delicious pretzels; they walked up to the top of the hill, and back, to build strength in their legs; they returned to their bed, or to the bath built for two, and made love; they read books together in bed, and in the bath for two. Stephen was partial to the effects one could generate with the magic wand of that handheld faucet, perhaps Europe's greatest and most underrated prize; why wasn't this a standard device in every American bath? Shame, shame—and so, reading, taking turns to adjust the temperature, they could fill an entire day. Once, she made him lie back, and close his eyes, and then she used three of his razor blades to shave his body.

He said, Elise?

She said, laughing, Trust me.

It's not that I don't trust you—

She had his calves resting upon her shoulders. She said, squinting, I am in a delicate place just now. You should not make me laugh so hard, Stephen.

Or sneeze.

She laughed again. She said, Next it will be your turn.

And then he shaved *her* body, which was little more than a touch-up job; still he shaved all but the tuft she'd asked him to leave for decoration. The arms, he understood, they could be a tricky proposition, and when they had finished, they stood in the toasty room and slathered each other with lotion and gazed at each other in the free-standing mirror.

Like babies, she said, kissing him.

And then they dressed and went into town and met Philip and Rebekka for dinner, during which Stephen learned more about Helmut Kohl than he could possibly ever keep straight. And so the days passed, and they attended the symphony, and the ballet. They took the subway to a movie theater which showed films in English and sat in wooden chairs belonging to a former grade school; they strolled in the dark; and alone, learning the city, Stephen worked on his German.

And as his health improved, as his strength grew daily, certain elements of his chemistry began to assert themselves. Whether it was the food, or the surprising lack of stress, or the heady state of being deeply in love, he wasn't certain, but he had somehow slipped over the equatorial line circumscribing his moods. Among other things, he was reading breathlessly: book upon book, now often through the night. He felt it unnecessary to sleep for more than three or four hours, usually in the morning, while Elise also slept, whereupon they rose together to plan their days. Next he began to print, working in long, dedicated blocks; he wrote letters to the owners of galleries who knew his work. And now he was taking notes: he saw the next three projects unfold before him like a flower in the course of a single night. He'd do something about foreign workers in Berlin. He'd do something in Moscow as it struggled to embrace free enterprise. He'd write a book about—a study of—light, and he'd ask the physicists at the Max Planck Institute to help, and they would help because didn't everybody want to help? And as the speed of his mind accelerated so too did the speed of his speech so that he was often asked to slow down so that he could be understood. Then, the final proof of it—he mastered, finally, his understanding of the German dative case. Like a lightbulb, clicking. *Den,* and *Der*! He was on. He was on fire—his mind, his heart—in a way he hadn't been in years. He was, as they say in the helping professions, high.

The night of the New Year's Eve party, the knife's point of the most recent wave having passed, he thought it odd how people used that expression *clean as a knife* always forgetting that a knife remains clean only insofar as it is never put to use, so what's the good of that? Take note, he thought, settling in to a very pleasant cruising altitude. Sit back and enjoy the flight. Ladies and gentlemen, the captain is pleased to announce that lithium is a place for those afraid of elevation. He was alive: his senses—his eyes, so sensitive to light; his hearing; his sense of smell: it was as if he had been finely bred to put these things to use—a dog, say, looking to flush drugs and bombs, or birds. And he was sexual, this suddenly teenaged physiology of his, in ways he hadn't been since he first discovered sex, alone in his bed, at the very complicated age of thirteen. That first, solitary orgasm, in which he had felt as if his spine had sprouted a dragon's wings and taken flight out of the small of his back, taking along with it his ribs, and pelvis. And then the semen, the entire flooding Mississippi River of it all. He'd had no idea what had been inside of him, what his body had been making. Terrified, he had touched the pooling river of it in his sheets. He had held his fingers in the air and looked at it in the light.

Mostly Dead, says Miracle Max. *I said Mostly Dead. Mostly Dead is not All Dead.*

And here he was alive like a current. Like a flaming sun. And so the night of the New Year's Eve party, and in order to adjust his trim, he nipped into his supply of Xanax. To be used sparingly, he'd taught himself, lest he have to kick. Then he dressed in his new suit. Never had he ever worn so fine a suit of clothes. It made him feel rich, or at least faintly important. At Philip and Rebekka's house, he and Elise were the first to arrive, and Philip said, shaking his hand at the door, Stephen, may we speak a moment?

Well, yes.

Philip led him to his office, a room which Stephen had yet to enter. There were two chairs off to the side. Two empty snifters, a bottle of cognac. Philip poured, he made a toast, they sat and admired the liquor's bouquet.

Stephen, Philip said. I say these things not to stick my beak in.

What is it?

We can arrange a work permit. You could work for my company—

I can't imagine being any use to you.

Oh, we could have you shoot the annual reports or something. If that's not beneath you.

Not if it's for you.

But that's not the issue, I think. We could arrange something with the university where I have some relations. There will be people here tonight. Or perhaps some magazine associations.

I have a job, Stephen said. In America.

I mean only to discuss a way for you to stay. I did not mean—

No, Stephen said, placing his hand on Philip's arm. It was the gesture he typically made to indicate gratitude and warmth, though it struck him, mid-gesture, as out of place. Who was he to gesture in this man's study? Suddenly he was nervous, which irritated him. He had made it a point in this life not to be intimidated by anybody, fuck 'em, and, well, here he was, crossing his legs, sniffing at the cognac to hide his face behind the glass.

He said, I understand, I think.

What I mean, Stephen, is that we should not permit immigration to be a deciding factor in any matter.

You are kind to worry.

This is not worry. One does not worry for the likes of you.

To offer, then. To help. I know I can't stay in your apartment forever.

It is free to you until spring. In spring we can take up the matter again. If you are here.

Thank you.

Philip said, looking at a photograph on his desk, I hope you are here. You have compelled me to address my game. He said, Are you a good teacher?

I never met one who said he wasn't.

Philip laughed. Yes, I suppose. I suppose you want to grow.

Yes.

A company, it grows. We are in Brazil now. And soon Chile. I would not want to be a part of something which could not grow. Which could not make me change. In this manner I think we are very much alike. Others, too.

Stephen nodded.

I did not want, Philip said, my daughter to fall in love with a man who has commitments elsewhere.

I take your point.

Do you?

Yes.

I am very hopeful to know you well, Stephen. He said, rising, The guests?

Stephen thought, following him out, Well, at least he didn't say, *That's my last son-in-law on the wall, looking as if he were alive.* They joined the party. There were tall Germans everywhere in tailored German clothes. When introduced, they spoke English to save Stephen embarrassment. Stephen met, among others, friends of Elise—two of whom had come up from Munich, and the elderly lesbian couple from Heidelberg, and a friend from the America House. Elise, wearing the Little Black Dress, a platinum choker at her throat with a small emerald pendant—she said, fingering it, My grandmother's. She said, taking his hand and putting it to her warm waist, Are you happy? I am very, very happy. What did my father say? Tell me later, please. Her perfume, sandalwood and lily of the valley, bloomed off her chest and throat. She kissed him, they parted to mingle; mingling awkwardly, Stephen popped another Xanax. He stood in the corner, sipping his wine, sipping, fearful of getting drunk, when Rebekka approached him and said, You are fine? You are not bored with all this?

Not at all, he said. It's splendid.

She brushed a bit of lint from his shoulder, and then she stood beside him and proceeded to describe the various guests. She laughed, just like her daughter. She said, We will have fireworks at midnight. It's the tradition.

He shifted his weight. Elise stood across the room, laughing at something her father had said.

Rebekka said, Stephen?

Yes?

This was not a bad idea, was it?

What?

The party, of course.

No. No.

And then she kissed his cheek, and Stephen said, I think I'll step outside.

Outside on the porch, he took in the hillsides surrounding the city; he stayed out there as long as it was socially permissible, and then others stepped out to smoke, and there was interesting conversation as far as interesting conversation went. Now he stepped back inside for a bit of food and became involved in another interesting conversation. There was a scientist from Uganda and his wife wearing bright and cheerful clothes. There was a young German novelist Elise had gone to school with, whom Stephen liked instantly, and his Venezuelan lover. The hour approached, and the clock struck midnight, and now everybody was kissing and shaking hands.

Come, Elise said, kissing him, leading him to her parents' bedroom, another room he had yet to enter, and out onto a porch overlooking the city.

She said, The fireworks!

He had been expecting lights and flowers shooting up into the sky. Roman candles. But that is not what happened. Instead it was just fireworks, packages of dynamite, the noise of them lit off by all the neighbors—detonating like guns. Big guns, little guns. No need to aim, given the occasion. Soon the air began to smell like smoke, like cordite, and the smoke rose up from the Neckar Valley and then there was a low-flying aircraft sweeping over the city checking for fires. And now he was shaking, listening to the detonations which kept firing across the city in the dark, and he drank down his flute of champagne. Elise refilled his glass. He drank that down, too fast, and he took the glass from her own hand and set it on the railing. He put his arms around her and held her tightly, breathing in her perfume, and the smell of her beneath that, and she held his arms tightly, and then she said, *Happy New Year, füsser,* and he said, *I don't want to go,* and she said, *Don't.*

They rejoined the party to pay their respects. Outside they looked at the sky. They breathed in the cold, winter air, which felt cleansing now, the smoke having cleared. He took her hand and they set off, briskly, and he said, Sometimes I get excited. Worked up.

Really?

No really. Really. Like I'm on speed.

I hadn't noticed.

Okay, okay. But see then I come down.

She said, What are you trying to say?

He stopped walking. They stood beside a tall tree, the residential tower overlooking them. There were parties all around. Music, blasting from a house, with people dancing on a porch. Women's voices, pealing from pale throats in silk blouses. Men, laughing. Elise said, gathering her coat to her throat, shifting her legs, Yes?

I'm not always easy, okay? I'm not always happy happy.

You are trying to scare me.

No. I don't know what I'm doing. I eat, I feel the fuel kicking in, I can't stop. It's intoxicating and exhausting at the same time. But sometimes I can't stop when I want to. And then it's not fun. Or I crash hard, he said. I'm not good at stress. Little things. Like meeting new people. Or driving in traffic. Parties terrify me, actually.

Why didn't you say so?

Because I can manage. Because I'm not a fucking cripple. Thing is, what a lot of people take for granted I don't. And here's the deal. It's getting worse. As I age. It's getting harder for me to slow down. In my twenties people thought I was goofy and alive and whatnot. I was moody. But it's harder now for me to slow down and then speed up. It's harder for me to find the center. Like a bubble in a carpenter's level? To find it you have to be able to hold it steady.

He said, I have never told anybody this. Anybody.

What?

Well this, *all* of this. This thing I have. This whacked-out swinging state of grace and abandon. It killed my mother. She was my age. The age I am now. My father, it broke his heart. She was charming and then she was oh so vivacious and then she was dead. Do you see? It broke my father's heart.

She . . .

He said, I did that once. I can't do that again.

Oh Stephen, Elise said. She put her arms around him, holding him. She said, stepping back, looking him in the eyes, You're stronger. Your mind's alive. You're not used to it now. Like too many sweets.

God, please do not tell your mother.

She said, taking his hands, You're cold.

No, I'm shaking. He shook himself like a dog, shaking it off, and said, You need to understand the whole package. I can cut it off with exercise, with physical exhaustion. I used to burn it off with booze, but that's dangerous and I'm too fucking old for that. But it dulls it. At least it used to. But—

Just tell me.

I think I need to walk, he said, walking.

She followed, her steps skipping, and they approached the tower's entryway.

She said, It's two A.M. Should I come? Do you want me to come?

No, he said. No, please.

He saw her to the elevator, kissed her, and stepped out of the building and now he really began to walk. Fast, a pace that swallowed up the yards like a long-legged horse down into the city. He passed a drug dealer in the subway. *Tssst.* He went to the church and looked at the sky. There was a warning beneath the roof of the church to watch for falling sheets of ice. Then back, and across the university campus, then back, now off to the Schlossgarten, then back to the Hauptbahnhof: he was breathing fast, too fast, along the Königstrasse and on to Schillerplatz—the sun was rising now, rising into the sky—and there was a television tower here, too, just as there was on Hum in Sarajevo—and he headed for Wilhelmsplatz. There were people on the streets now. A happy drunk with a monstrous bottle of wine, a new pair of shoes. And he, Stephen, telling himself, *Find the center. Just find the fucking center* and now, walking, his mind slipped back to Ferhadija, in Sarajevo, and he saw shelling from the hilltops which might have been from one of these, and he saw kids on rollerblades going off to their abandoned schools, or the water queues, the breadlines: the world, since when had it become so porous? Its borders had dissolved like sugar or salt into a glass of water, like semen into a hot pool, and he thought *Who am I?* and he thought *Why am I?* and there was a backhoe, in reverse, beeping alarm as if preparing to dig a grave. There was a fifteenth-century mosque with a fountain now dried up. There was the Chicago Water Tower standing like a minaret and the lions of the Art Institute and the Börse and the Vatican with its mighty obelisk and there were all the capitals of the world and then there was the woman he was approaching: a woman, dressed in a black cashmere coat, having made her own pilgrimage, making her way home after a late-night party—her tall, thin heels clicking; her black, waist-length hair and her perfume billowing into the cold morning light. She was crying, tending to her eyes with a white handkerchief; she was walking home alone in the rising morning light in order to start the year off right. To get it under way, the entire whole of it. Probably she intended to catch a train. And as they approached, and then passed, they were

subsequently separated by way of their direction. By way of their profoundly independent lives.

—

When he returned, it was after seven. He could hear Elise in the bath.
There was a breakfast laid out waiting to be made. She stood in the
center of the bath, rinsing herself with the handheld faucet, soap
pouring off her limbs. He stood in the doorway, his face flushed, and
said, I'm sorry.

Are you hungry?

Yes.

She set the handle down; she turned the lever to stop the drain.
She said, stepping out of the tub, reaching for a towel, Get in.

She said, drying herself, watching him undress, You spend all your
life taking care of other people. You think I don't know this. Okay.
But you can take care of me only when I need to be taken care of. I
don't need that now. Sometimes, yes. Three years ago, yes. Maybe
next year, who's to know? But I know the whole package. Just one
rule.

Okay.

Never lie. Not to me. Never, never lie.

He stepped into the tub and slid in. She poured oil into the water.
She held the faucet over his body. She said, Agreed?

It cuts both ways.

Agreed, she said. To you I will never, never lie.

We should seal this somehow. With a toast. A kiss.

After breakfast, she said, kissing him. We will seal it then.

6

This was the real gift: the way they worked alone together. Not the
same, but similarly, and always side by side. Never before had he
known somebody he could actually work beside. And so they
exchanged ideas—exchanged, as opposed to espoused—and he read
the work she wrote in English—It always comes out different, the
language, she said, and my idioms are always backward and upside

down—and she pored over the prints scattered now throughout the flat, looking for points of order, for unexpected moments of unity.

This, she said, pointing to the two shrouded figures on the Goat Bridge. This is my favorite. This will be your cover, I think.

Why?

Well, it is beautiful and stirring and provocative. But that's not the reason. They are *all* provocative. The reason is because it is about us. Because it is about the two of us meeting on the bridge.

I still don't know how I got there. To that bridge.

Well, she said. Perhaps it came to you?

One night, walking up the hill to the flat, Elise said, Come meet me in Manhattan. I would like that very much, Stephen.

If I leave Chicago I'll have to go somewhere. That's when my mind shuts down. Where do you go when you don't know where to go?

You can go anywhere, she said, stopping, turning to look him in the eye. Always the eyes. She said, And you don't have to come to me. I can come to you, you know.

I have a place in Vermont. An old farmhouse.

Well, so you do have a place to go then.

If I go, for good, then—there are other issues.

Your son.

Always my son.

I see, she said. Really I do. She said, not entirely changing the subject, I want you to meet me in New York. It puts a clock on the matter. A structure. She said, I think you are afraid to go from one lover to another. The rebounding. You are thinking it is not proper.

Well, it isn't, is it?

If you were happy and in love with R, of course not. But if you were in love with another I could not be in love with you. It would be a different experience. Not the experience of this. She said, Two years! How much longer do you require? I do not like this doing things because that is what the magazines say one should do. It's like shopping in the stores with the bad music always going on. The airport televisions blasting American news broadcasts. The billboards in the train stations? Everywhere you go people are telling you how to think and how to behave—

To sell. They're selling—

Well *you* should not be buying. The best movie is always the most popular when the best movie is supremely banal. People are sheep. Bahhh. But I think nobody can tell you what you are supposed to do. You should follow the road you like the scenery to. Your heart's beating. What took you to Yugoslavia? What? You went there because it was the right thing for you to do. To find something out. She said, taking his arm, leading him up the hill, And look what we have found. I think it would be stupid of you to be a stupid sheep and give that back. To let that go.

She said, People always *know*. But they do not always *act*.

They walked now in silence and he listened to the rhythms of their shoes beating in time against the pavement. As the residential tower came into view, the wind picked up, and Elise's scarf began to blow in the wind. She said, You know that's the secret of Sentimentalism, which is always false, and grotesque. Sentimentalism, Capitalism, Formalism. The *isms,* they are the sticks that instruct the sheep how to behave. Like Hitler telling the good German women to put on the dirndls while he fucks the teenage niece. Never mind the ruined cities. What Sixth Army? What Africa Corps? Oh look, the Schwartzes' house is empty, and look at all the pretty paintings and the nice piano they have left behind! And the silver! Otto! Otto, come look at all the pretty silver!

She said, Like Leni Riefenstahl, so brilliant and corrupt. She became the sheep as much as anybody. She wanted to be the Leni Riefenstahl.

She's brilliant.

And stupid, Elise said. Like Good and Evil, Brilliance and Stupidity are not mutually exclusive, I think. Everything is propaganda now. That is what we Germans made and what you Americans have perfectly corrupted. The only way to be safe is to turn off the radio. The only way to be safe is to filter out the noises. Elise said, I think nobody can tell anybody what to do. Don't you see? Not your father, not your mother, not your neighbors, and certainly not your country. Not even your lover, Stephen. That's the great mystery. The people are sheep and they want to be told what to think and what to do so they don't have to be responsible for what they do. That is the heart of it. Cowardice in the face of existential anguish. The heart of it is there are no rules.

She said, taking him by the shoulders, There is only trust. There is only the taking of real joy when you are offered it.

Messinger arrived. Hermes, didn't he have wings on his feet?

Stephen, he said, shaking his hand. Elise, he said, kissing her: cheek, cheek.

She laughed, her hand to her belly. When Messinger reached to close the door behind him, he grabbed a handful of Elise's underwear (namely her bra), which he passed to Stephen, who put it in his pocket.

Oh, Stephen said. Thanks.

Messinger said, removing his coat, looking around the toasty apartment, Well, this is quite the lovers' nest. Yes?

Elise removed her bra from Stephen's pocket—*That's mine, I think*—and placed it beneath the pillow on the bed. They had coffee, then, and drinks with their coffee. Messinger had brought brandy, which they poured into thick-bottomed glasses, and Elise was in and out, packing, listening in when she could. She was leaving the next day. Meanwhile Stephen showed Messinger his new work, nervously, while Elise pretended not to listen in, and while Messinger admired it.

Messinger said, So, Stephen. You have a signature. Even when you do different things. He said, One can always spot your signature, Stephen. You always pull away at the moment of the looking. You direct the eye elsewhere so that the person has to *want* to look. You complicate the subject and then you layer it. Riddles and paradox.

This, Messinger said, pointing to the photograph of Biljana. The pregnant woman, okay. Then the wedding ring on the wrong hand. The light on the ring. Ahh, the missing finger? The nipple, the space it fills. So quiet. And this—

He set before them the print of Elise naked at the window—her body a silhouetted X. This, he said. This is splendid. The woman at the plastic window. Why is the window plastic? you make us ask. Because the metal bombs have blown out all the glass. Then you place *her* body in the window to fill it. The sex organs, shockingly de-eroticized. Another space to be filled. Another window. Her body just another target: an emblem of what they've missed. Messinger said, It is what I have *always* liked about you. It is good it is not about the war. It is good that it is about more than just the war. He said, and this praise coming from Peter Messinger struck Stephen to the quick, It is your best yet.

Yes, Stephen said. I think so, too. But it's nice to hear.

Peter said, I think Americans confuse humility with a lack of self-confidence. But you, Stephen. You do not lack confidence. Your strength lies in your humility. In your understanding of the task you face.

Sometimes, Stephen said.

So you see, Messinger said, laughing. I *did* read your essays. Messinger said, his hand to his chin, *The Goat Bridge*. That is what you will call it?

I still haven't decided.

Your publisher will not like that. Goats. Too many goats, he will say. Goats do not sell books.

Tell me about it.

Stephen, Messinger said, studying the print, the shrouded figures of Stephen and Elise on the bridge. You do not see it?

See what?

Nothing, Messinger said. My mistake. I thought something dumb. Messinger said, It is to be a marvelous success, which is not important, because as you know it is important all by itself. And if anybody asks, *I* like the title.

Later Messinger said, crossing his legs, I was very sorry to hear of your friend.

What friend?

Ado. The one who— The one who knew the woman?

What about him?

His uncle, I forget his name—

Jusuf.

Jusuf, yes. Messinger said, You do not know this then?

What?

Jusuf was killed. A mine. I am sorry, Stephen. I thought you knew.

Stephen sat on a chair. He put his head in his hands and took a breath.

It was very fast, apparently. His legs were gone, Stephen. The blood poured out of his body. I am certain he felt nothing.

Where?

Past the border at the No Man's Land. Where you showed us at the bridge. He was collecting wood. Messinger said, I am going back there, you know.

When?

No, Elise said, entering the room. No. You have done enough, Stephen.

I've done nothing. There is no reason for Ado to be there. His family is gone. He shouldn't be there. He could be, he could be like us. Like us, going wherever. We could get him out.

We could arrange the credentials, Messinger said. But not a visa—

Once out he'd be fine. A refugee. Not Croatia. We fly into Italy, Ancona. We could put him on a flight with us.

You are trying to save people again, Elise said.

I'll go back. Talk to him.

With me, Messinger said.

Yes. With you.

It's bad there, Stephen. It's bad there again.

In and out, Stephen said. Quick.

7

To travel fast he lightened his load; he went to the DHL office and shipped hundreds of dollars' worth of shipping: the prints, a duplicate set; the excess camera gear, which he could insure. The slides he kept with himself in case the plane to the States with his possessions exploded en route. Then he caught the subway with Elise to the airport. Before passing the security gate, Elise said, Don't forget. And stay near Peter. He is too old to want to get killed. People only *think* he is brave. It is part of his charm.

Okay.

She said, kissing him, Come back, okay? Just please come back.

—

They caught an APC at the airport to the UN post on the boulevard. There they hitched a ride in an armored Land Rover to the Holiday Inn. Messinger got them a double room with blown-out windows: a push underway, it was getting crowded, and the hallways, also crowded, reeked of shit. Messinger said, I am going to part with you now and go down to the bar. The light is gone for the day.

The cab driver who had helped get Anna to the hospital, he was there. Stephen had brought gifts and he gave the driver a bottle of whiskey. The driver lit up and took Stephen's arm and dragged him to the underground garage. Nobody paid for a cab anymore. The cabs were the ambulance corps.

Okay, the driver said, opening the door to his cab. He pushed Stephen inside the beat-up Volkswagen and said, Okay, go. Okay. We go. So, Stephen! Where we go?

The driver torched the tires, spinning out onto the boulevard—in the near-dark, no lights. They went to Jusuf's building above the Koševo complex. The girls were there: the Married Flirt, the Soulful One. Stephen lightened his load further and distributed bricks of cheese and coffee and a liter of olive oil and a carton of cigarettes and a ten-pound bag of pet food for the dog.

Where is Ado?

He is at the front, the Soulful One said. On shift.

The Married Flirt took the cheese to her kitchen. The dog, having saved their lives, and knowing it, followed her into the kitchen for a slice of cheese. The room smelled like burning newspaper.

I'm at the Holiday Inn, Stephen said. Will you tell him?

And then the driver took Stephen back. When Stephen tried to pay him, the driver said, No no no. No. No.

Stephen said, leaving a hundred marks on the seat, For the petrol.

Okay okay, said the driver. Okay. Petrol. He said, pointing to his watch, Tomorrow. Okay? Okay? Super. Okay, Stephen!

Inside Summerville was entertaining a group of British journalists. Cowboy stories. Bull and Cows. He said, seeing Stephen, Steve!

They had a drink from another bottle. Stephen gave Summerville a box of condoms, quantity one hundred. How is it, Stephen thought, that this man never ages? Probably because he was always pickled. Summerville had been preserved, as if in formaldehyde. That night, they stayed up late, drinking.

Summerville said, Steve oh Steve. Even Stephen, he said. God it's good to see ya, Pardner. It's a regular Comanche-land out there. You know? Lots and lots of Indians.

Later Stephen went outside. He had a smoke and took in the cold night.

Trust, Elise had said. *Trust,* which was an expression of power. The ability, however illusory, to keep things safe.

—

In the morning he met the driver who put him in the car and drove him down the boulevard. There were shots fired at them. The driver said, facing Stephen, Boom boom. Ha!

The driver delivered him behind the rotting road. Stephen left, and then he made his way crouching to the collection point.

There, somebody said, pointing.

Ado was standing in front of the stream. He was throwing rocks.

They embraced. Stephen removed a bottle of scotch and they had a drink. He said, Where are all the Bad Guys?

Hiding.

Excuse me?

They are hiding from me. They know I am angry.

I am sorry, Ado. About Jusuf.

Also there is the cease-fire.

Since when?

Ado said, You know, we are all family. We are a family of the manic-depressives. We go up, we go down. We drink together and tell each other how much we love each other and then we cut off each other's heads.

Ado bent to gather a handful of broken stones. He measured them in his hand, and then he lobbed a fat one into the dirt and rubble behind the icy stream.

Ado said, The men who placed that mine, they lived here, too. By the bridge. This side Serbia. That side? Death. I am sick of the death.

We can get you out. That's why we came. Me and Messinger. We can make you a journalist and then you can, I don't know. Messinger could get you work for the magazines. You could work for NATO, or the UN—

The UN, Ado said. The UN is nothing more than the woman who fakes the orgasm. It is all shouts and lies.

Ado threw another stone. He said, Stephen, I am in love.

What?

That girl. Just a girl I met at the cemeteries. We are lovers. Not the fucking lovers. The *real* lovers. You know? My heart, it keeps going boom boom boom.

He took another rock and threw it. He said, taking another, catching Stephen's eye, I am looking for the mines.

I see.

Ado said, I am going to explode all the mines.

—

Messinger flew out that afternoon after making Stephen promise he would do likewise the next day. No more pictures, Messinger said. We have taken all the pictures. And then they walked by the presidency, past an operating television camera, aimed at an intersection to catch the latest victims on tape.

The camera crew, not wanting to be a target, was nowhere in sight.

—

They stood in front of an old bridge above the dam. The night was falling. It was a small bridge, made of battleship gray metal, though in the dark it looked plain black. The wooden planks across the bridge had long since been removed. Ado and his beloved, a young woman with hair cut like a boy's, and Stephen—they stood above the dam looking down at the water. The young woman did not speak English, but she admired with Stephen the light on the water. The river shimmered in the fading light, its currents the cut and size—the same dimensions—of the stones paving the old town. He'd never noticed this before. Everything, Stephen thought. Everything reflects.

Ado said, I wanted to show you this.

He stooped and took off his jacket to make a shield and shone a light, briefly, in the dark. The light illuminated a circle, graffitied onto the metal beam, inside of which was the first letter of the alphabet: *A*—the universal symbol for anarchy.

Ado said, My friend Natasha put that there. She was older than me. Eighteen. Very sophisticated about the ways. I was seventeen. We went to movies together. We were punk rockers. What did we know? We liked the rock and the roll. She's dead, too.

Ado passed his silver flask. They had a drink. Stephen, he said.

Yes?

Where does a Serbian wife put money to keep it safe from the husband?

I don't know.

Neither do I. Not anymore. Blame it on the Field of Blackbirds.

The Battle of Kosovo—

Thirteen eighty-nine, Stephen. Thirteen eighty-nine! Shouldn't we be over it by now?

I know.

Stephen, he said. I cannot go. I am here. I told you about the Balkanian humor. We cut off our fingers, we put knives into our heads, and we laugh. You know why we are the committing suicides? Because we are afraid to help each other. Because we are afraid to ask for help from each other.

You could come back—

This is not the heroic gesture, Stephen. This is my life. Where would I go? Where? I would not know where to go. The people that go, they are the brave ones. To leave everything they have ever known! I could not be a refugee. I am not strong enough for that. So instead this is my life to prove that we can be here and live and get drunk and make fun of our hangovers in the morning.

Ado—

Stephen, this is not your tragedy. You cannot stop this tragedy. You cannot make the tragedy better and have the nice American ending.

I know that.

My life is to prove that we can live here again and be the family we once were. Ado said, scooping his arm around his beloved, We are going to be married. When it is over. We are going to be married and have seven babies.

What if it isn't over?

Everything is over, Ado said. How else to begin?

—

Alone he walked back to the hotel, cutting through the city, which could have been a city anywhere. He was cutting through the market behind the destroyed National Library when he felt a shudder, a flickering sensation—a knife along his ribs, a hawk's shadow. He turned then and saw huddling in the dark the shape of a figure, draped in black, watching him. Stephen had felt its presence; why otherwise pause? Why otherwise stop to feel it? He stopped. He turned on his heel and looked at the figure draped in black. He took a step toward it, opening his hand. Then he took another step, as if to ask permission, and then the figure spit.

He wasn't scared. He wasn't particularly angry. But he knew, looking at this figure in the dark, the fear in its eyes, he knew with the same certainty that the earth is made of dirt, the oceans cold and deep—he knew that his son was lost.

8

Zagreb is a dirty city. The air chokes with its history of complicated industry. The streetcars scream in the canyons of the buildings they run between. There were whores, dressed in black, hanging out at the fountain beside the train station, and as he passed them they spoke to him in German, and then they mocked him, for not replying, and he went on to the hotel. He recognized the concierge. He was the same who had once shown Stephen the great and whispering ballroom. When you stand at one end, you can whisper to another. You can hear the voices of everybody in the room. And if you stand alone in the very center, and strike the flat of your hand against your chest, it sounds the same as a rifle shot.

He would not remember much of this last stay. He was drunk by the time he entered the marbled lobby, but he did not know he was drunk—the Xanax in his bloodstream having masked the effects of all that scotch. He swayed a bit, perhaps as if overly tired (he had not slept in three days), but he did not slur. He shook hands with the concierge, and tipped him heavily, and the concierge then picked out for Stephen a corner room. The lobby, all that glittering marble, the very slabs of it—he stepped into the whispering ballroom and stood beneath the dome and whispered his son's name. Then he went up the wide stairs and then to his room, down in the corner, and inside the room swaddled in pink drapes he dropped his bags. He pulled out a bottle of scotch and poured himself just a little glassful. He took, what the hell, another of those little pills. They really weren't that big. Then he took another.

That night he wrote his son a letter and walked the city. To Bana Jelačiča Square. He sat on the ledge of a fountain and watched refugee children play with a paper boat. He went to the cathedral and had an argument with God. He went to a dog park full of dog shit with a tiny iron boy pissing from a fountain. Even in the middle of the night, there was a woman exercising a massive Dane. Then he walked to a bar. Amazing, a city full of bars. He was lost now, somewhere in a pedestrian mall, and he overheard a pretty girl speaking to her date, in English to prevent others from understanding what she said, *Maybe later I will let you fuck me;* and later in that same pedestrian mall he had a brief conversation with the statue of a man wearing a topcoat and black hat, each of which could have belonged to his father back in 1955; and now he was in a Hard Rock Cafe, which felt like home, as it were, being hard and made of rock. And then he was out, again, stumbling among the pilgrims and pedestrians. He passed a man playing a guitar in the cold, not badly, and put into the man's instrument case a wad of bills. God played the guitar, one could be fairly certain of that. In a mixed state, Stephen had no idea any longer what anything was worth.

He said to the man playing the guitar, Have you seen my son?

Ehh?

Keep an eye on your children.

Then the man said *Ahh* and played a few bars of a song by Crosby, Stills, and Nash. *Teach,* the man sang. *Teach your children* . . . Like that?

Stephen would never recall this moment. He would not recall stumbling into a stone wall and bruising—cutting deeply—his forehead. There was blood in his eyes now. He saw some cops with machine pistols standing outside a massive building which looked to belong to the Federal Reserve. More iron bars. He walked by, his hands in the air, his eye bleeding, and said, American. Don't shoot.

They called for backup, not wanting to leave their post at the bank. There were warlords and other thieves afoot. He was less than a thousand yards from the finest hotel in all of Europe, home to the Magnificent and Whispering Ballroom, even if that fine hotel had been requisitioned by the Nazis: there was a history here in Zagreb. *With undying affection,* Omar Sharif had written on his photograph framed upon the wall. There was history everywhere there was a history or a tomb. Then a new cop came to haul Stephen away, and on the way back to the hotel, they laughed a lot and stopped for drinks at a disco filled with handsome men dressed in black. Then they walked by the whores in front of the train station, and the cop said, laughing, *Make love, not whore,* and then, inside the hotel, the cop asked the concierge to help him to deliver this particular package, and Stephen said, No. No delivery. Just water.

Water, Sir?

Water is the only cure for alcohol poisoning.

Indeed, Sir. Very good. Water.

The cop left after Stephen tipped him. Stephen drank a bottle of water. Then another. To Althea, he said, from prison walls. He said, Stone walls do not a prison make. Four days, five days, what was the point of sleep? Sleep schmeep, he said to his friend Summerville. He said, Water, and he drank another tall glass of water, and he opened up the bottle of pills, took six more in his hand, and gave the bottle to the concierge, saying, Whatever you do don't take these.

Excuse me, Sir?

You'll disappear.

Then he left the building and became lost all over again.

He returned a day and a half later, cold for having lost his jacket. *Stephen,* Messinger had said. *Do you not see it?* Somewhere along the way in the alley of a visionary stupor he had finally seen it. And seeing it had made him feel naked and small. Meaningless. Utterly bereft of consequence.

Q. What do you call a young goat?

A. A *kid.*

His son, he told himself bitterly. Not a kid, not a goat. His son. And it wasn't the grotesqueness of the pun that chilled his spine; it was the fact that his life's work had led him so blindly to it. In a cold alley he placed his back to a wall of stone, he sank to the ground. Somewhere a woman was singing. He made a fist and struck his own jaw: once, twice. He couldn't feel it. He tried again. He couldn't feel a thing.

Put it to rest, you say. Go to sleep. Let go, let God.

God isn't in the details; God is in the syntax. Muslim, Christian, Jew—if God made the world, then let God worry about the errors in translation. Lost, he'd been faithful to this pilgrimage, and thus he'd been led here to the inexpressible core of human understanding: to the ecstatic, sublime, poetic heartbeat of the living world. And from this distance, he knew it to be timpanically scored. A big stick, and an even bigger drum: the sky the vibrating hide now of some other-worldly creature. And the hand, holding that stick, striking the instrument which filled his own heart with blood.

The heart's beating, the first act of violence.

Several hours passed before he rose to his feet. The numbness having faded, his chest began to ache. It filled his lungs, it pooled like near-frozen grease into the small of his back. And his mind refused any longer to hold still—it filled instead with the flashes of where he'd been, what he'd seen, what he'd thought he had forgotten—and the only way to hold it was to make it will his body to act. To appeal to the mind's vanity: see, I can make you do whatever I want. Stretch out that leg. Get the blood flowing. Lean on a wall for support. Get up. Just get the fuck up. Just get the fuck up and fucking go.

Stephen, somebody called, but he was alone on the street.

He'd been stumbling all his life. All those years of study, and still he'd been unable to see it by himself. That white-stoned bridge, the last of its kind. *The Goats' Bridge.* Walking, briskly, he was able at last to focus. His body and his spirit—they'd become separated, as if by a hyphen, and he began to shape an argument as if it were a brief. Discovery, he began. Even the discovery of something no longer present—or not yet here, or right in front of you all the time—wasn't this too a gift? Wasn't this proof of God's very order? His son was lost. His son was part of something else. His son belonged now to the constellations, to the currents of the tide, to the air that he breathed. He couldn't help it. He believed in the need for God, and now, stumbling alone in a darkened foreign city, he understood why he had always needed to believe.

Because he, Stephen Brings, was a creature of need, and because only God was big enough to fill it.

Like hunger, it was the need which made up for a lack of supply. Need, that which motivated the body to go forth and forage. Need, that which inspired one to do good works. Need, that which inspired one to give and forgive. He stepped through the iron doors of the Esplanade and skidded on the floor. Food seemed in order, no? After so long a forty days and forty nights? Truth is, he was scared any longer to argue. You weren't supposed to argue with God. You were supposed to praise. And give thanks to. You were supposed to do good works and not fuck up and turn the other cheek. He went to his room and showered and came down in clean clothes and ate half a croissant.

Stephen, he said to himself. You're fine. A rough patch. All done.

He said, making his point at the bar, I demand my right to water. Water water water.

He also drank a Coke, two of them, with a lemon, no ice, and he said, I am very clean now and presentable. And then he went into the dome of the Magnificent and Whispering Ballroom and stood all alone listening to his voice.

I'm clean so why am I not clean? and he said into a rising sea of swirling panic *Oh fuck not again* and then he left the domed room and struggled up the red-carpeted stairs falling only once. On the way to his room he got lost and passed a woman wearing only jeans and spiked heels. She was carrying a bottle of champagne, and two glasses, squinting at the room numbers as she wandered down the hall. Obviously she had misplaced her glasses. Once inside his own room, he stripped off his clothes. He went to the bathroom and got his kit and removed the double-edged blade from his father's razor. First he held the blade to one eye, then to the other, thinking he'd start off with a lid. Then he drew a line in his hand along the lifeline and closed it. And then he worked on it some more, the lifeline. That map across the desert of his palm. He built for it first a stream and then a river. Then he heard the voice of his lost son calling *Dad! Dad, wait! Wait!* and he wrapped his bleeding hand in a towel and hit his head against the white-tiled wall and curled up into a ball and wept.

—

Look:

The word *camera* derives from the Greek *kamara,* for vault; from the French *chambre,* for chamber, intimate and public; from the Latin *camera,* for arched roof, which is in turn kin to the Latin *camur,* for curved. Even before it was discovered, the camera has always been little more than a room with a curved ceiling, as is the space beneath the sky. A hallowed dome.

And the glass shaped into a lens? An instrument of vision, ground from matter, like sand and stone. All it takes is fire.

If war isn't self-inflicted, then what is? And how does one make peace with oneself? And just how is it possible to heal? Even if he couldn't answer, he could still fall asleep. He had to fall asleep, he knew; he had to be out of here by six the next morning, just so many hours away, because he had to go. The flight to Zurich, a final layover, then home. He lay naked sweating on the featherbed. Why hadn't anybody said anything? Somewhere, anywhere, somebody was fucking. He lay on the sheets and sweated saying *Sleep, sleep you must sleep* and then the phone rang and it was R.

Hi, he said, sitting up. Hi! God I'm glad you called.

Hi, she said. How are you?

Oh, a little sleepy. I'm fine. Really.

Really?

He heard a knock. He said, R, can you hang on?

Of course.

There's somebody at the door.

Go see. I'll wait.

He walked toward the knocking, and there was a royal blue door, and inside the door an enormous closet filled with light blue clothes, and a large red and white box with *DHL* on the side, and inside the box sat a small boy.

He said, back on the phone, R? R! There's a boy in my room. There's a little boy in my room!

What's his name?

What's your name? he called.

Francesco, said the boy.

He says his name is Francesco, R. Francesco!

What a pretty name.

Why didn't we think of that?

It's a great name, Stephen.

R, he said. He must belong to somebody. Somebody must love him. Somebody will think I took him? I have to find who loves him.

He hung up, and dressed, and he took the boy's hand and they went down to see the concierge. The concierge, a different one, this one with a German accent, said, But he is not my boy. Why do you ask?

He must be somebody's boy?

Why are you to worry? You have the boy.

He stepped outside through the iron doors. He held onto the boy's hand and he thought he'd go to the police. The police, he knew, would be watching the bank. They would be watching the bank to keep it safe. The safes inside would be filled with notes and bonds and precious stones. Outside, there was a vast lawn, a soccer field's worth, ample enough to welcome a thousand graves, and standing on the field were all these people he knew applauding him. His father. His mother, wearing a red sweater with white bandages at the wrists. There was a girl he had been sweet on once. There was Elise, standing next to R, talking and laughing together.

He said, Well—

We are here for the show, Stephen!

What show?

Your show. It's a surprise. Your first retrospective. Are you surprised?

And then a warplane came flying slowly overhead and everybody looked up and waved and then the plane crashed into the top of the dome of the Hotel Esplanade. Pretty flames filled the sky, like ribbons on a package, and everybody cheered.

Then, then the boy was in the back of a small car. A convertible.

The boy was laughing, holding onto his sides. He called out, Taxi! Taxi!

It was time to leave. He needed to get into the car and go.

His father said, his arm around Elise, I'm so glad he's finally learned to take, too.

And R said, kissing Elise good-bye on the cheek, He's found him.

Who? Stephen's mother said.

Himself, Elise said, explaining. He's found himself.

And his wan mother said, shivering in the bright sun, I never did.

And then the phone rang, like a whisper, and then a bell, and Stephen answered it, and there was a voice now rising up from beneath him, calling up to him through all the flights, and he said *Yes?* and then the voice said to him, calling,

Your wake-up call, please.

Ten Books (Gulliver Metcalf-Brings)

A list, prepared by his mother, R—

Go Dog Go
Mike Mulligan
The 1988 Catalog for Harley Davidson Motorcycles
Green Eggs and Ham
The Family Picture Book in the Bottom of Mom's Desk
Go Dog Go
Where the Wild Things Are
Madeline
The Wion, the Witch, and the Wardrobe
My Dad's
Fireman Small

The Return

The day breaks—

Like a man's heart, or a wave. All over the world people are rising and welcoming the day. *It's been a long time. Where've you been?*

The kids, like the fish in the sea, are all in school. They're opening up their books.

—

To live is to participate knowingly in the spectacle and amplitude of light.

He felt light-headed and awake. Hungry.

He rose from the bed. He showered and dressed in his black jeans, his indigo turtleneck, and then he made a bowl of cereal and ate two plums. He drank a tall glass of milk.

R was out—a note on the table—attending to matters of the rally in Schaumburg. She wanted to say good-bye, not like this. She'd be back at one. Please wait.

—

Packing was easy given that he'd always traveled light. He opened one of the boxes he had shipped from Germany and located a duplicate set of prints which would make up the contents of this new book. He went through them, pleased—not for what he'd done, but for what the portraits made. Elise was right. He'd call it *The Goat Bridge*. Then he closed the folio and took the photographs upstairs and slid them beneath the bed.

—

The signs for the rally were still in the storage room, having been long forgotten. They would need to be returned, the signs, perhaps to be saved for a rainy day. There was always certain to be the need for another rally.

He sealed up the box he had opened, and several others; he made two trips to the shipping store and sent the boxes on to Vermont. He was eager to see Vermont.

His father's—now his—farmhouse.

The snow on the trees.

—

He saw the wispy-bearded boy across the street in front of his burned-down house. The boy had his camera. He was taking pictures.

Hey, Stephen said, crossing the street.

The boy looked up. Hey.

Stephen said, You're taking pictures?

Yep. The boy said, It's okay. We were going to move anyway. To my grandmother's. She has a bigger house anyway.

I didn't know that.

Yeah. He said, pointing, I mean, it's just a house.

Stephen said, I wanted to say good-bye.

You're moving, too?

Yeah.

The boy nodded. Cool, he said. He kicked at a charred beam. He said, pointing with his camera, The light's not right. Not yet.

It will be, Stephen said.

You think?

Well, I've never lost my house.

The boy said, smiling, It's just a house. Only the dog got killed. We were lucky, man. You know? I mean, it's just a house. This kind of thing, my dad says—happens all the time.

—

This is something Ado once said:

When I go across the street, and there is the sniper, I always go with somebody else. Never alone. I run at the same time as another. This way there are more targets and everybody has a better chance. This way, if I am killed, I know I have helped to save the other person from being killed.

He said, It is always best when they shoot at me and miss. This way, they are powerless.

—

He drove to the lake. He stood before it, cold, the wind kicking through his tangled hair. Certain places he'd been he'd go back to. He'd go back someday to Panama, and to Chile. He'd go back to Sarajevo—not soon, but later, when the time was right. He'd go back there often. And he would go on to Gaza, and to Moscow, but he would not come back here to Chicago—the city and sprawl into which he had been raised. He was grateful for the place, for the fact of his being raised here; he appreciated its resourcefulness; he was thankful for the cold water and the whitecaps on the lake and the clarity of the air and the light. But he knew he would not come back, and so knowing, he removed the bandage from his hand and dipped his hand, his wrist, into the water. The water parted icily to receive him, and when he withdrew, the water resumed its place. He tasted it, the water. He turned his back and went back the way he'd come.

He was thirty-five. He was no longer young. Nor was he old. He was instead a man yet to do what lay before him. Thirty-five is a turning point for a man: reaching it, he either grows stronger than he already is, or he begins to weaken and to die. He is either all he will ever be, or he is charged with a desire and conviction to be more.

Either way, and like God, he is and always will be all alone.

—

He was thirty-five. He was glad to be alive. It was a given, it always had been: the greatest gift one can give is to sacrifice one's life for another.

Q. How is one to know at any given moment, right now, that this is the moment of sacrifice? The moment of one's destiny?

A. One never knows, though perhaps for those to whom that moment is delivered, perhaps for them that moment is deeply felt.

He had not been able to save his son. Certainly his son would want his father now to save himself. His son would want his mother to come here in the summer and walk barefoot in the lake she loved. In summer, when it was warm. There are sacrifices measured by the breadth of the surface they cover, and there are sacrifices measured by the depths they penetrate. And all sacrifices required first the act of diving in.

Like the act of self-resurrection, the act of sacrifice required first an instrument of will. It required first an understanding of one's place. It required a given life to save.

He turned, looked back at the lake, and then he made his way.

2

It is day. Time to get going.

Any road, even the most ancient, will take you either *to* or *from*.

He called Elise at her hotel.

Stephen!

Can you meet me?

Of course. Where?

He gave her directions to his father's—now his—farmhouse.

He said, I'll be there late tomorrow. Late.

Not too late, she said.

He said, There's no insulation. It'll be cold.

I don't think so.

The key is under the mat. There are sleeping bags in the big room. Bring some long underwear. You can build a fire to warm it up.

—

He went up to R's desk and turned on her computer. It was a Macintosh, named after an apple—an operating system which relied on folders and icons.

He opened a new folder, then another, then another, and then several more. Before putting the folders into each other, a kind of collapsing accordion of intent, he labeled the folders thus:

Stephen's Work
No Snooping
I'm Serious, R
Please don't Snoop
R, you're Snooping!
I'm grateful to you, R
But you're still Snooping
Am not
R too

And then, for the final folder, he labeled it, *Got you!*
And then he created a document for that final folder which read—

I left for you a book I like under the bed. Afterword to follow.
Love, S.

—

She arrived a little after one, slightly breathless.
I was afraid you'd be gone.
No. Not yet.
She said, taking off her red coat, What about the books?
Oh, I don't know.
She said, Come on. They went to the bookshelves then, and she said, I want this one.
Okay.
You can have this one.
Okay.
She said, stopping, God, I do not want to do this.
He said, R, keep the books. Later, if you move, if you're packing, if you want to get rid of some, if you want to clean me out of your life, you can send me some. Or not. There's always libraries.
Where are you going?
Vermont. I'll set up there. And then I'll be going back to Germany.
To Elise.
Yes.
She said, wiping her eyes, Okay. She said, Maybe someday I'll

meet her. I'd like to meet her. Maybe. I mean, if you love her, I'd like to meet her.

I left contact info on your desk.

She said, I'm going to move. I'm going to find a new place. Maybe I'll do that three-flat idea.

Okay.

I'll send you my new address. When I do that.

She said, shaking her head, I don't want to meet her. I'm sorry. I just don't want to do that.

And then she stood and pushed aside the books and hugged him. She said, I'm really going to miss you, Stephen. Really.

She said, pulling back, I've got you something.

Really?

Yeah. Uh-huh. She went to her purse and removed a package. It was wrapped in blue paper. She said, Go ahead, Mister. Open it.

Inside was an address book. Leather bound, beautifully tooled.

It's lovely, he said. I've been needing a new one.

For years, she said. Years and years. It's in case you get lost. So you always have someone to call.

He held her then. He said, holding her tightly, Thank you.

She said, releasing him, Time to go.

—

Ado said, There will be no happy ending.

But then Ado didn't understand that the decision of when to end— a story, a song or life—was just a matter of God's particular editorial design. End a story anywhere you want, you make it happy or otherwise. Bitter or sweet. Conclusive or not.

He started up his father's—now his—car and drove away. Traffic was light. He crossed the Indiana Skyway, and then the state of Indiana. He gassed up in Ohio late and in the dark. By the time he hit Pittsburgh, he was growing dizzy, and so he stopped by the side of the road and did fifty push-ups and drank a Coke. Then he did fifty push-ups more. He spent the next day crossing the dark state of Pennsylvania. I-80, in the dark, under the gray skies—he drove fast across the longest state in the world. By late afternoon he was in the tangle of Connecticut, this state's legislators having recently decided its bridges were unsafe, now engaged in the process of rebuilding each. The lanes narrowed dangerously and unexpectedly at each crossing. There were men and women working at the sites, wearing hard hats, waving him through. Then, past Hartford, he took the highway up through the middle of Massachusetts, and then he crossed the border into Vermont.

His father had been born in Vermont. His father had fallen in love with a girl who would become Stephen's mother in the state of Vermont. The Green Mountain State. In Putney he stopped at the general store for the makings of a breakfast.

—

Elise, having seen his lights in the dark, stood at the door bundled in long underwear, a dark scarf, and a sleeping bag. She walked in big boots across a field of snow to his car and wrapped her arms around him. Then she led him inside the house. In the big room, there was a fire roaring.

She said, I've brought to you a coat.

3

He took her to the small school in western Massachusetts where there stood a new library named after his mother, Arscilla Brings. He wore his new overcoat, loden green, which reached to his ankles. Inside the library Stephen introduced Elise to the librarian and they all exchanged words. They met an old teacher of Stephen's, now deaf, who teased him loudly in precisely the same manner he had twenty years ago; there were two boys sitting in the big chairs looking at the women's breasts in the foreign magazines. Then Stephen went to see his books on the shelf his father had made. They were there, his books, and he touched them each on the spine. Then they went to the cafeteria and grabbed some coffee; they went outside and sat on a wooden bench in front of the library to drink their coffee. A bell had rung, and there were boys and girls, their cheeks red from the cold, racing across the lawns to make their classes.

He said, My father built that. With his life's work.

It's a beautiful building. We should all be so lucky. A library.

He said, Do you like kids?

Very much.

Do you want to have some?

She said, laughing, Well, not tomorrow.

But in general?

Well, I would like to have one, she said. I would like very much to have one.

If you have one, you have to have two, in order for the one not to feel so lonely.

Two, she said. Okay. Two.

And if you have two, you need to have three.

And just why is that?

Because if you have three, then you have more to keep *you* from feeling lonely. After you are old and all alone and they have flown the coop.

Elise said, I would like to start with one. With one. Not so soon.

Okay. Stephen said, We don't have to have any. It won't change—

Oh Stephen, listen. You would like to. *I* would like to. Listen to what we are saying.

Yes. He said, I would like to. Maybe.

What?

I don't know if I can do that again, he said. You should know this. The children.

I don't know.

We don't have to, Elise said. Some things we don't have to know. Some things are just given.

—

He drove her to the falls nearby the farmhouse. The rocks were covered with snow and ice. He said, stamping his feet and overlooking the ledge, In the summer you go skinny-dipping here.

Is it cold?

Sometimes. Mostly it's a garden. Lush and green, waterfalls and moss. Dragonflies, skimming across the surface. Blackberries. It's difficult to imagine.

Not too difficult, she said.

He said, How do you feel about marriage?

Yes.

Really?

Yes, Stephen. Yes.

Really?

Oh yes, she said, laughing. *Ja?* She said, *Yes.*

He said, warming their hands in the pockets of his new coat, If we have children, I would want them to know God.

She said, They will know God. They will know God because they will know who made them.

He said, taking her arm, There's a storm coming. He said, leading her back to the car, I wouldn't want to leave forever. I would want to be able to live here, too.

She said, It is beautiful. I love this Vermont. I want very much to do the skinny-dipping with the dragonflies beside the mossy boulders, but not I think when it is so cold.

In summer. In winter there's good skiing. Not alpine, but good. It's a good place for children to learn. Maybe we could adopt, too.

Elise said, Some of us, some of them?

Maybe.

She said at the car, stamping the heavy snow from her feet, My turn to drive. You will have to tell me the way.

And then it began to snow.

—

The snow fell heavily that night. They took the thin roads and drove slowly back to the house. In the field across the field leading to the house there were two Morgans standing beside the barn. The horses had thick winter coats and black tails and heavy beards. In the morning the owner would hitch the horses to a sleigh. He would feed the horses, and then he would brush them out, and then he would put them into harnesses with bells.

And then Stephen and Elise went into the house in which his father had been conceived, in which *he* had been conceived, and they lit a fire. First they lit a match and then they lit a fire. And then they turned off the lights and opened up the blinds.

And that's what they did.

Like that.

Afterword

I've told this story before, I'll tell it again:

When I was a boy I often saw my father naked. He was a widower; I, having no mother, was raised by him alone. We had an old shower in the basement, with a pipe sticking out of the wall, and in that shower he would wash my hair and behind my ears. When it came time to rinse, he would remind me to close my eyes, lest they burn.

These images are not for children but for their parents.

—

When my own son was three, shortly after Easter, his mother had to travel on business and left me alone to care for him. At the time I remember feeling irritated—a pressing deadline, and I remember I was working late that night; my son, being distressed by the absence of his mother, wanted to sleep in our bed. I put him there and returned to my study. Later, sometime after two, I heard a *thunk,* and then my son's terrified cry—he had fallen, you see, out of a strange bed. He was inconsolable. He refused to leave my side. I'm cold, he wailed, inconsolably, hugging himself. *I'm cold.*

—

The love of form, writes the poet Louise Glück, *is a love of endings.* These images were each given—and not taken—in the city of Sarajevo during the second half of 1992. Presently the city is still under siege and like many I do not know what is to happen next. But I do know that each of the figures herein is animated by and charged with and beholden to a spirit I can neither fathom nor fully grasp. What is the study of the body if not a yearning to reach the soul?

—

This spirit I am referring to belongs to those who recognize it. It is, among other things, that same spirit which once blew into my household and made my son cold; it is also that same spirit which implored me to set aside my work and to comfort him.

—

The study of war is also the study of peace. These, then, the figures of a peace the world has yet to make.

—

First, I hold them each in awe; then I let them go.

—*Stephen Brings*
Stuttgart, 1993

Author's Notes

The Siege of Sarajevo, which began 2 May 1992, was lifted 1,395 days later on 26 February 1996.

There are many moving accounts of the war—inside and out—which have informed this novel. To direct the reader to the authors of only a few: Roger Cohen, Zlatko Dizdarević, Slavenka Drakulić, Ferida Duraković, Misha Glenny, Roy Gutman, Aleksandar Hemon, Tim Judah, Dzevad Karahasan, Christopher Long, Anthony Loyd, Peter Maass, Semezdin Mehmedinović, Christopher Merrill, James Nachtwey, Michael Nicholson, Josip Novakovich, Elma Softić, and Tom Stoddart.

Readers interested in further exploration of the topic might find especially helpful *Blood and Honey: A Balkan War Journal,* by Ron Haviv with essays by Chuck Sudetic and David Rieff, afterword by Bernard Kouchner (Umbrage Editions: New York, 2000), *Sarajevo Self-portrait: The View from Inside,* edited by Leslie Fratkin (Umbrage Editions; New York, 2000), and *The Siege of Sarajevo: 1992–1996* (FAMA; Sarajevo, 2000).

—

Stephen Sellers Brings is a fiction, though his name belongs in part to that of my late father, S. B. McNally; there are certain places in the heart even the most ardent expressions of gratitude will fail to locate. Nonetheless, and to that end:

I am grateful to Heide Ziegler for the gift of the small polished stones she gave to my eldest son. I also wish to express my thanks to Regina Schmid and Tilman Weigele and my former students and colleagues at the Universität Stuttgart; to each of my early readers; to Martina Kohl for introductions abroad; to Ferida Duraković and Zvonimir Radeljković for their corrective and generous expertise. I am grateful to the members of the interreligious peace choir Pontanima for permitting me to visit during their marvelous rehearsals, and I am grateful to the many others who spoke to me candidly and always kindly.

To Amir (Lunjo!) Telibećirović and Šefko Rovčanin—*Hvala*!

I want to thank Rosemary Harris and Joe DeSalvo of the Faulkner Society in New Orleans. Susan Bless You Dodd. I am grateful to Chris Hebert for his friendship and conviction. I am grateful to Alexia Paul and to Joy Harris.

I am grateful to my wife, Sally Ball, for the gift of a lens.

—T. M. McN.